Steampunk FAQ

All That's Left to Know About the World of Goggles, Airships, and Time Travel

Mike Perschon

APPLAUSE
THEATRE & CINEMA BOOKS
An Imprint of Hal Leonard LLC

Published in 2018 by Applause Theatre & Cinema Books
An Imprint of Hal Leonard LLC
7777 West Bluemound Road
Milwaukee, WI 53213
Trade Book Division Editorial Offices
33 Plymouth St., Montclair, NJ 07042

The FAQ series was conceived by Robert Rodriguez and developed with Stuart Shea.

All images are from the authors collection unless noted otherwise.

Printed in the United States of America

Book design by Snow Creative

Library of Congress Cataloging-in-Publication Data
Names: Perschon, Mike, author.
Title: Steampunk FAQ : all that's left to know about the world of goggles, airships, and
    time travel / Mike Perschon.
Description: Milwaukee, WI : Applause Theatre & Cinema Books, 2018. | Includes
    bibliographical references and index.
Identifiers: LCCN 2018023163 | ISBN 9781617136641 (pbk.)
Subjects: LCSH: Steampunk fiction—History and criticism. | Steampunk culture.
Classification: LCC PN3448.S73 P48 2018 | DDC 700/.411—dc23
LC record available at https://lccn.loc.gov/2018023163

www.applausebooks.com

Steampunk FAQ

To Jenica, who dressed me up and sent me on my way in 2008,
who watched all those terrible movies with me,
and made sure the sky didn't fall while I was
shackled to the writing desk.

To Gunnar: the chapter on games is for you.

To Dacy: the chapter on music is for you.

Thanks to all three of you for putting up with me while I wrote this.

Thanks to Autumn, Diana, Erica, Kevin, Kristin, and Tofa
for putting up with all my questions.
You are my living, breathing bibliography.

And thanks to all the steampunks I met over the last ten years.
It's been a blast.

Contents

Introduction

Writing a FAQ book about steampunk is a uniquely challenging task, even for someone who's a so-called expert on the subject. It's not that I don't know a ton about steampunk. In terms of data, I've assessed the evidence—hundreds of items, if you count up all the novels, video games, comic books, movies, and television series that lay claim to the descriptor "steampunk," to say nothing of the seemingly endless supply of images of steampunk fashion and art. It's not a shortage of evidence that's the problem. It's the wealth and diversity of it. And it's that diversity that prompts most people to frequently ask one question above all others: What is steampunk?

In 2008, I had the same question. I'd uploaded concept art for a web comic about a kick-ass version of Cinderella to a forum, and someone commented that it "looked a little steampunk." Oddly, though the commenter could identify that the image looked steampunk, he was unable to tell me what that meant. So I did what any twenty-first-century person with an internet connection does when they have a question without an answer. I googled "steampunk." One of the first hits was a steampunked lightsaber, which looked exactly like a lightsaber from the *Star Wars* films, save that it had been created using brass embellishments. It had a slightly old-timey look to it. Then I came across an image of a steampunked computer. Again, it was immediately recognizable as a computer covered in brass made from wood. Its keys looked like they'd come off an antique typewriter. So near as I could tell, steampunk meant "old." Old as in "before-your-grandmother" old. But it was simultaneously about new technology. New like "your-grandmother-getting-on-social-media" new. It was contemporary or futuristic technology made to look like it was from the past—in some people's minds, a very particular past, in others' a more general sense of "old-timey."

Then I found a *Wired* article about Steam Powered, the "first ever" steampunk convention happening in California. I had been a geek my whole life, but aside from seeing *Star Wars* in theaters in 1977, I didn't have many instances where I could claim that I'd been there for any "first ever" moments. I clicked through to the event's website, which showed the Guests of Honor (including Jake von Slatt, the man who had built that steampunked computer!) wearing goggles, top hats, and corsets—they looked like they'd walked off the set of a Tim Burton or Terry Gilliam film. The design for the website echoed the blend of antiquated and futuristic technology I was already discovering was an essential part of steampunk. I figured if I was going to learn what steampunk was, a convention of steampunk fans would be a great place to start.

I was unprepared for what I experienced.

Firstly, *Wired* had described steampunk as a literary genre, so I figured there would be a lot of people sitting around talking about books. I didn't expect that in addition to the Guests of Honor, almost all the guests would be in costume, like the man who exited the convention hotel as I stepped from my taxi: he was dressed like he was ready to explore the darkest jungles of Africa, pith hat and faux British accent and all. It was all I could do not to make a Dr. Livingstone joke.

What I discovered over the course of that weekend is that steampunk is a lot more than a literary genre, though I continue (to this day) to see people describing it as such. At Steam Powered, I saw incredible costumes, attended a steampunk concert, held a steampunk ray gun, and met many "steampunks": people who used the word to describe their lifestyle. Consequently, I finally understood why that online forum commenter could identify my drawing as steampunk but could not define it.

When K. W. Jeter inadvertently coined the term "steampunk" in a letter to *Locus* magazine in 1987, he was ironically classifying the neo-Victorian stories he and fellow Californians James Blaylock and Tim Powers were writing. Despite such flippant beginnings, the word has demonstrated remarkable resilience, becoming the term for nearly every neo-Victorian work of speculative fiction since Jeter's second steampunk novel, *Infernal Devices* (1987). It has been used to retroactively include pre-Jeter fiction such as Michael Moorcock's *Nomad of the Time Streams* (1971–1981), the '60s television series *The Wild Wild West* (1965–1969), and films such as Disney's *20,000 Leagues Under the Sea* (1954). Even the scientific romances of H. G. Wells, Jules Verne, and their nineteenth-century contemporaries have been labeled steampunk. Online (and offline) debates have sought to define it, with answers ranging from narrowly restricting and exclusionary definitions—"it's only steampunk if it's set in London"—to uselessly inclusive indefinitions—"steampunk can be anything you want it to be." The ongoing popularity of steampunk books, film, games, fashion, and décor has only aggravated the problem, as steampunk has evolved from a literary subgenre of science fiction (SF) to a subculture of Goth fashion, do-it-yourself (DIY) arts, crafts, maker movements, and counterculture. Enter "steampunk" on *Pinterest* and it's going to want some clarification, a host of categories offered as possibilities: DIY, Fashion, Furniture, Jewelry, Girl, Weapons, or Artwork? You know it's getting diverse when you can steampunk a couch or a human being.

This book looks at the scope of current steampunk expression while engaging in an exploratory answer to the frequently asked question, "What is steampunk?" It seeks to answer this question with a more satisfactory and useful response than the catchy "Victorian science fiction," "yesterday's tomorrow today," or some other equally vague or limited definition. It goes beyond the prescriptive definitions of science fiction criticism, which have largely defined steampunk based on limited evidence—often the solitary steampunk novel of William Gibson and Bruce Sterling's *Difference Engine*, or equally prescriptive but far more subjective definitions from within the steampunk community, which are often based largely on what steampunk fans desire steampunk to be, not necessarily what an outsider can observe it to be. My approach to understanding steampunk is not prescriptive but rather descriptive of a surface style, or aesthetic, or mode for steampunk.

We'll begin our journey with a look at what I call steampunk's first wave. There are a number of theories about how to split up the periods of steampunk's growth, but I find it easiest to go with two: the first wave, when steampunk was a largely incoherent narrative genre, and the second wave, when steampunk went beyond its narrative roots to become a more unified aesthetic mode.

I date the first wave from the 1970s to the early 2000s. Our look at the first wave will begin with the genesis of steampunk in the novels and short stories of three Californians who hung out a lot with science fiction legend Philip K. Dick, before moving on to some of the oft-cited steampunk inspirations and antecedents. We'll start with the usual suspects of steampunk ancestry, Jules Verne and H. G. Wells, before moving on to the many films from the 1950s and '60s those writers inspired. Contrary to what many articles and books will tell you, steampunk's direct inspiration is arguably just as cinematic as it is literary, a probable reaction to the many Verne and Wells film adaptations, pastiches, and knockoffs. While Verne, Wells, and a host of other Victorian and Edwardian writers have definitely influenced steampunk fiction, films such as Disney's *20,000 Leagues Under the Sea* (1954) and George Pal's *Time Machine* (1960) show up more often as immediate influence. Returning to steampunk's roots, we'll see how steampunk developed as a bourgeoning narrative genre through print and the odd film throughout the 1990s before gaining widespread attention with a decade of steampunk cinema in the late '90s and early '00s.

From there, I'll have to abandon any pretense of chronological survey to look at the second wave of steampunk, which I date from around 2004 up until the present, through the variety of modes it became channeled through, moving from films to fashion, DIY maker culture, music, gaming, comic books, and more fiction. In every one of these instances, I will cover a mix of case studies, focusing on some of the most popular or notorious examples, digressing occasionally to treat you to a more esoteric example. In doing so, I am sure to miss a favorite book, artist, or fashionista. I hope you'll forgive the oversight; four hundred pages seem like too many when you start a project like this, and by the end, you find each chapter straining its corset lacing. But at the same time, I think I've sacrificed breadth in places for some depth of explanation and analysis, so that I don't make a drive-by reference to the first American steampunk novel without explaining its relevance and how it answers the question, "What is steampunk?"

The structure of this book is such that you can, to some degree, read any chapter as a sort of stand-alone essay, but you can also read it from start to finish as a mixture of survey of the history of steampunk and exploration of the term itself. By the end, this book demonstrates why it's so difficult to answer the question "what is steampunk?" with any-thing approaching concision. As I've already said, beyond its literary and cinematic beginnings, steampunk has been appropriated as a form of fashion, of DIY maker culture, of oppositional political stance. So when someone asks, "What is steampunk?" I have to clarify which expression they're referring to, and only then can I answer the question. As I will show, there's a world of difference between steampunk fiction in 1990 and steampunk fashion in 2010, or even more illuminating, between steam-punk anime in 1985 and steampunk anime in 2005.

To be clear, I'm very familiar with the many definitions of steampunk that have been suggested and widely employed; but they're usually too broad or too narrow to be of any use. Take, for instance, G. D. Falksen's definition of "Steampunk as Victorian Science Fiction," which is appar-ently the most quoted definition. To be fair, my guess is that Falksen built this definition out of a desire for a simplicity and succinctness rather than for intense critical accuracy. And he does a fine job of exploding his defi-nition at his website. But if it is the most quoted definition of steampunk, then it's being widely used without Falksen's further explanation, and is therefore misleading. Let me say it plainly: steampunk is *not* Victorian science fiction. Victorian science fiction (and I chafe at putting those three words together in a sentence, given that science fiction as a genre really coalesces in the 1930s in America—in the Victorian period, it would more likely have been called "scientific romance") is a nineteenth-century phenomenon, whereas steampunk is (largely) a twenty-first-century one. Victorian scientific romances looked forward to a fantastic future that might yet be, while steampunk (largely) gazes backward, looking at a fantastic past that never was. To define steampunk as Victorian science fiction is to efface the fact that it is a contemporary art form that plays in the past, not a past art form that plays in the future. We'll revisit the ques-tion of "is steampunk Victorian science fiction?" in chapter four.

Defining steampunk is further complicated by people using the term who want to make a great deal out of the words the term is comprised of. On the one hand, the steam: some definitions of steampunk limit "true steampunk" to works that involve steam technology, excluding any that involve combustion engines or magical or fictional forms of energy. The trouble with this approach is that there's a scant handful of steampunk that really employs steam technology. Never mind that the airship, easily one of steampunk's icons, is not a form of steam technology.

On the other hand of exclusionary and limiting definitions are those who demand there be some fidelity to the presence of punk. Be it a need for DIY ethos or an association with radical political positions (most often anarchist, in my experience), they define "real steampunk" with these radical ideologies in mind. Again, such an approach excludes not only a host of recent steampunk art and writing, but almost all of the original steampunk written in the 1980s, by the very writers whose work the term was coined to describe.

Rejecting these approaches, I suggest that steampunk isn't trying to reconstruct the past in literature, art, or fashion, but is instead building something new by choosing elements from the pre-digital past to create a style that evokes those periods but does not replicate them accurately. If steampunk is a mirror for earlier times, it's a distorted fun house mirror. After looking at over seventy novels, numerous films, attending steampunk conventions, listening to hours of steampunk music, getting lost in the time abyss of google images containing steampunk fashion, reading how-to books and articles on how to make steampunk objects, and engaging in copious online conversation, I've determined that the most useful description for steampunk is not as a genre but rather as a multimodal style or aesthetic: that is to say, a style that can be expressed in many different ways, as fiction genre (primarily under the larger umbrellas of science fiction and fantasy, but also frequently as romance and sometimes even horror), but also as often as maker objects, music, fashion, and even home décor.

Many publishers, bookstores, writers, and critics have defined steampunk as a genre, but I think that's a bit misguided: is there such a thing as genre in fashion or home décor? If we were only going to talk about steampunk fiction, then I suppose genre would be a useful designation. But if we call it a literary genre, then how do we talk about the fashion or home décor? Understanding steampunk as a style gives us the necessary flexibility to discuss its diverse expressions, from fashion to fiction, décor to DIY projects. Not everyone agrees with me. My naysayers worry when

I say steampunk is just a style, since we often think of style as empty. We say things like "it contains more style than substance," and this is largely true of steampunk as well. That isn't to say that steampunk is never about substance. As you'll see, steampunk can be used to make very important statements. However, the style we call steampunk is a design sensibility mixing retro-style and anachronistic and/or fantastic technology, and it can be applied for both silly and serious ends.

The three hallmarks of this style that I've seen repeated to varying degrees in most instances of steampunk will be explored in chapter one but are worth mentioning here briefly: hyper-vintage (evocative of the pre-digital but post-Renaissance past in broad and fanciful ways), techno-fantasy (looks like science but works like magic), and retrofuturism (how *we* imagine the past imagining the future).

I have to admit that I'm shocked to be writing a book about steampunk nearly a decade after I attended Steam Powered. You see, when I returned home from my first steampunk convention, I found the website Gizmodo proudly declaring that steampunk was dead. Given what I'd seen in California, this seemed ridiculous: in the years that followed, steampunk was alive and well across North America and the UK. Steam Powered was neither the last nor the largest steampunk convention I attended. Publishing saw a rapid rise in steampunk releases in 2009 and 2010. More steampunk bands and artists emerged. Nevertheless, someone declared steampunk dead on a nearly annual basis. Oddly, a few of these moments were due to evidence that steampunk was not only alive but thriving. When Disney steampunked its iconic mouse and friends in 2010, steampunk was dead. In 2011, when Justin Bieber used steampunk in his video for "Santa Claus Is Coming to Town," steampunk was dead. Even odder, it was usually steampunks who declared the death of steampunk whenever it got popular enough to end up at Hot Topic.

Not only is steampunk still alive, but it's being expressed in increasingly popular ways, in films like *Victor Frankenstein*, on television in *Penny Dreadful*, in video games like *Bioshock Infinite*, and in the unbroken line of *New York Times* best-selling novels from steampunk writer Gail Carriger. Steampunk is alive and kicking. So let me tell you about how a joke about 1980s science fiction and fantasy became a twenty-first-century buzzword. Given that steampunk has transcended its literary origins and become a collection of subcultures, I'm going to share some of my own stories, simply because steampunk isn't just read, or watched, or worn: it's participated in. Along the way, I'll tell you what's up with the goggles, why emancipated women are looking to wear the clothing of their repressed sisters of the past, and help you determine whether some show/book/jewelry/fashion/car is steampunk after all.

What Is Steampunk?

The Goggled Gaze

Imagine Jules Verne as an inventor instead of an author. Imagine Captain Nemo's *Nautilus*, a submarine capable of speeds rivaling modern Seawolf-class attack submarines, as a product of the nineteenth century instead of a prediction for the twenty-first. Imagine Frank Reade as real person instead of a character in dime novels; imagine his steam-powered robots of the American frontier as a fact instead of fiction. Envision a world where the speculative dreams of Victorian and Edwardian writers like Edgar Allan Poe, H. G. Wells, and Edgar Rice Burroughs were realities instead of fantasies, and you begin to see through steampunk lenses.

You want to know what steampunk is? Imagine a pair of brass aviator's goggles, with intricate filigree and extra lenses on levers that can slide over other lenses to adjust the view. You'll be needing these to understand where we're going. Will we be taking an airship? No. An airship is not guaranteed to fly you to a steampunk world. There are lots of airships in fiction, and not all of them are steampunk airships: think about that airship with the big screen on the side, flying above a smog-shrouded future Los Angeles in *Blade Runner,* the film versions of the historical tale of the *Hindenburg*, or the zeppelin Indiana Jones and his father board in *Indiana Jones and the Last Crusade*. None of these are steampunk vessels, per se. Will we be taking a vehicle that uses steam power instead? Possibly, but it's no guarantee either. While there are certainly such vehicles in steampunk, like the steam-powered bicycle in the 1999 film version of *Wild Wild West*, there are just as many that run on fictional substances like the Unobtanium of James Cameron's *Avatar*, or more often than you might think, pure magic.

Granted, those goggles I mentioned are not necessarily a greater assurance of the presence of steampunk than airships are. After all, as Radioactive Man said on *The Simpsons*, "The goggles do nothing!" I'm uninterested in the goggles themselves. It's the lenses that matter. Nevertheless, we have to admit that goggles are nearly everywhere in steampunk, available for purchase at every steampunk convention. Prominent steampunk maker and *Steampunk'd* judge Thomas Willeford conveyed this ubiquity when he said, "Whether you are a dashing airship pirate (or 'privateer' if you prefer to feign an air of legitimacy), skywayman (not to be confused with the more mundane 'highwayman'), or simply the maddest of scientists, nothing screams STEAMPUNK! quite as loudly as a good pair of genuine brass goggles." While there are those in steampunk who would love to see the goggles go (*Steampunk'd* contestant and steampunk designer Tayliss Forge sees no point in including goggles in her steampunk fashion), they remain arguably one of the most common motifs of steampunk fashion (Tayliss says people always ask "where are the goggles?" when she says she's dressed steampunk), and consequently act as style icons or *movement totems*, to borrow Bruce Sterling's term for the mirrorshades (sunglasses) of cyberpunk. But whereas cyberpunk's mirrorshades *hid* the eyes of the "crazed and possibly dangerous" sun-staring visionaries of cyberpunk, brass goggles might be said to *reveal* a different set of crazed and possibly dangerous worlds. So let's get to those revelations.

Again, imagine those aviator's goggles. Now imagine three extra lens attachments on the side that can be placed over top of the standard smoked lenses. Each of those lenses, once slid into place, will change the way you see things. We won't use all three lenses together just yet. In fact, we'll start without any lenses in place: look at the photograph of actor Will Smith. We see a handsome, smiling African American man wearing modern clothing. Now, slide the first lens into place (as represented in the second image of Will Smith on the poster for *Wild Wild West*), and you will note some significant differences about his attire: it has been replaced by clothes that say "Old West." His folded-down collar is folded up; his contemporary tie replaced with a cravat-styled tie; he's added a waistcoat, his wristwatch has been replaced by an ornate pocket watch, and he's wearing a Bailey Western Dillinger hat. This first lens has let you see the first feature of steampunk: hyper-vintage.

Lens 1: Hyper-Vintage

Now, when steampunk started out, we could have used the term "Victorian" instead of "vintage." Once upon a time, we could have said that the "hyper-Victorian" lens reveals that steampunk does not accurately imitate, but rather *evokes* and *exaggerates* the nineteenth century. In many alternate or secondary steampunk worlds, by fashion,

Actor Will Smith in modern attire, 1999.   *Alamy*

Will Smith and Kevin Kline in *Wild Wild West* (1999). Contrasting Smith's contemporary attire with his costume in the film, or considering the design of the mechanical spider can provide us with an idea of what steampunk is.   *Alamy*

architecture, or culture, steampunk style is only reminiscent of the Victorian era in the broadest sense of the terms. Most steampunk utilizes a look and feel *evocative* of the period between 1800 and 1914, unencumbered by adherence to rigorous historical accuracy. At its inception, steampunk was unarguably Victorian: early steampunk writers Tim Powers, James Blaylock, and K. W. Jeter set their seminal steampunk in London in the nineteenth century. Yet even those groundbreaking authors strained the term "Victorian": while Jeter and Blaylock set their tales in the late nineteenth century, the Victorian period proper, Tim Powers's *The Anubis Gates* takes place in Georgian England in 1801, and has consequently troubled the use of "Victorian" when describing steampunk ever since.

But Powers was not alone: steampunk continued to strain against the temporal boundary of Queen Victoria's reign. Both Scott Westerfeld's *Leviathan* trilogy and Paul Guinan and Anina Bennet's *Boilerplate* take place in the Edwardian period. Some steampunk happens in the future of the Victorian era: Michael Moorcock's *Warlord of the Air* is set in an alternate version of 1973; Abaddon Books' *Pax Britannia* series imagines an alternate history where the British Empire and Nazi Germany survive into the 1990s. Other steampunk is set in our own future: Clay and Susan Griffith's *Vampire Empire* series in 2020, Theodore Judson's *Fitzpatrick's War* in a postapocalyptic twenty-sixth century.

In addition to challenging the limitations of time periods, steampunk challenges geographic boundaries as well, rendering the term "Victorian" even more useless. While London is considered the quintessential steampunk locale, it is not always the London of history, but sometimes the fantastic London of an alternate world, as in Philip Pullman's *The Golden Compass*, with anbaric lights, compass-like alethiometers for divination, and animal-shaped demons all causing the reader to mutter, "I don't think we're in Cambridge anymore, Toto." This is not the London of history, but rather a popular, fantastic perception of London, mediated through the novels of Charles Dickens and a steady diet of BBC period dramas, shoved through the wardrobe door into Narnia, or some other fantasy realm. But this focus on London or alternative Londons should not mislead us: steampunk left London as early as Richard A. Lupoff's *Into the Aether* in 1974, and has since traveled across the globe. A sampling includes the

United States in the infamous remake of *Wild Wild West* as well as Cherie
Priest's *Boneshaker* novel and its sequels; Europe, North Africa, and India
in Gail Carriger's *Parasol Protectorate* and *Custard Protocol* series; Mexico
in Al Ewing's *El Sombra*; Canada in Lisa Smedman's *The Apparition Trail*;
Japan in Joe Lansdale's *Zeppelins West*; and the skies above Australia and
Antarctica in Kenneth Oppel's *Airborn* and *Skybreaker*. In the real world,
one can find steampunk on every continent on the planet. There's "Truth,"
a steampunk coffee shop in South Africa; the steampunk office space of
Three Rings Design in San Francisco; the Mysterious Island at Tokyo
Disney; *Le Machines* theme park in Nantes; the "steampunk town" of
Oamaru in New Zealand, which made it into the *Guinness Book of World
Records* for largest gathering of steampunks; the Steamcon gatherings
in Paranapiacaba, São Paulo, Brazil; and finally, Antarctica's Deception
Island, which is admittedly not intentionally steampunk, but is an inter-
esting instance where people looked at a rusty, industrial tableau and
labeled it "steampunk."

But steampunk hasn't just traveled to other places on *our* world: steampunk settings have also included fully secondary, fully fantasy worlds,
such as Chris Wooding's *Retribution Falls*, Stephen Hunt's *The Court of
the Air*, or Ekaterina Sedia's *The Alchemy of Stone*. Clearly steampunk is
no longer confined to Britain, or even Ruled Britannia. How can it be,
when the London of Philip Reeve's *Mortal Engines* is a seven-tiered, two-
thousand-foot-high city on massive caterpillar tracks, roaming a postapocalyptic Earth? If London itself is on the move, why can't steampunk
be as well?

While it must be admitted that many steampunk expressions are
inspired by the Victorian period, there are, increasingly, expressions
outside both that temporal and geographic limitation. Consequently, a
word that is more elastic is needed for the concept that "Victorian" used to
be shorthand for. I've struggled hard with this, since I started researching
steampunk in 2008.

Steampunk is vintage. In the plainest language possible, steampunk
is "old-timey." The term "vintage" can be used to mean *old* or *classic*.
When people say an object has "a vintage look," they generally seem to
mean before the atomic age but after the Renaissance. There are lots of
other terms people like to use for this feature of steampunk, but I choose

vintage because it is the most elastic term. Take "industrial," for example. It privileges steampunk that focuses on machines. And while some people think that you can't have steampunk without some form of industrial machine involved, I don't want to overemphasize the importance of the technology.

But the vintage feature of steampunk isn't your regular kind of vintage. It's hyper-vintage. It's vintage that's been messed with. While there are certainly historical recreationists who are attracted to steampunk, steampunk isn't about being genuinely vintage. As steampunk designer Diana Vick famously said, "Steampunk needs historical accuracy like a dirigible needs a goldfish." Steampunk plays with the past. Messes with it. Blends it with science fiction or fantasy or horror. Some people say it's only nineteenth-century vintage. But even most of those people want to take a ride in an airship that's based on zeppelin designs that are from WWII, not the Victorian period. We'll see in later chapters that this whole business of what period and style steampunk draws from is increasingly complicated. But trust me for now: it's hyper-vintage.

Lens 2: Technofantasy

This brings us to the second lens. Before you look through the lens that permits a mobile, city-eating London, try looking at a smartphone. You won't be able to see it, because the first lens won't permit you: hyper-vintage lenses can't see iPhones, since the technology is too advanced for the lenses to translate. Slide that second lens in and suddenly you're seeing an object resembling a *Star Trek* tricorder seemingly crafted by Nikola Tesla and Charles Babbage. You are looking through the second lens of steampunk: technofantasy. Going back to Will Smith in the poster for *Wild Wild West*, that technofantasy is illustrated by the giant steam-powered spider, which would be difficult to make a working version of today, let alone the nineteenth century.

Unlike the inscrutable inner workings of an iPod, you can see wires and coils, cogs and gears exposing a steampunk machine's inner workings. However, these machine parts are only exposure, not explanation: the brass punch cards of steampunk analytic engines are merely a design revelation, not a technological justification. Most steampunk gadgets and vehicles in film and books require some form of magical impulsion or cohesion to be rendered plausible. This merging of magic and technology permits the designs of da Vinci not only to be constructed, but to work; it permits safe airship travel at impossible speeds, using theoretical fuel sources such as aether or phlogiston; it permits self-actualized clockwork automatons in a world where positronic explanations are unthinkable.

While aether and phlogiston are windows into the history of science, steampunk's use of these elements varies in fidelity to their respective historical theories. Historically, the work of alchemy led to chemical discoveries that were considered as fantastic as the miraculous aether often employed as fictional fuel in steampunk. This progression is likely why alchemy is steampunk's preferred magical system, since many steampunk fans are remiss to admit steampunk's connection to fantasy magic. Alchemy shares the *appearance* of modern scientific method, appearing less frivolous than high fantasy's inherently ambient magic.

In Ian R. MacLeod's *The Light Ages*, the description of aether mined from the ground like petroleum is far afield from the historical theories of aether, shunning all physical rules and responding "to the will of the human spirit." With aether, England is able to accomplish miracles: "Boilers which would otherwise explode, pistons which would stutter, buildings and beams and bearings which would shatter and crumble, are born aloft from mere physics on the aether-fueled bubbles of guildsmen's spells." In the *Light Ages,* aether is necessary. Without it, steam engines halt, "wyreglowing" telegraphs fall silent, and architecture collapses.

Beyond alchemy, pure magic rears its head in steampunk as well: the scholarly "thaumaturgy" of China Miéville's *Perdido Street Station*; the clockwork magic Hethor Jacques taps into in Jay Lake's *Mainspring*, whereby aligning himself to the wheels that drive the world, he can perform miracles, transforming the frozen wasteland of the Antarctic into a blooming New England spring; steampunk automatons are rendered as kabbalistic golems in Ted Chiang's "Seventy-Two Letters" and Jay Lake's "The God-Clown Is Near." Stephen Hunt's steampunk fantasy *The Court of the Air* contains mechomancers, fey-folk, and world-singing sorcery. This is more than just Arthur C. Clarke stating in his famous third law that "any sufficiently advanced technology is indistinguishable from magic." This is an often blatant use of fantasy magic masquerading as technology.

In short, the technofantasy lens allows you to see steampunk technology that is dependent on the abandonment of real-world physics. Technofantasy permits real-world elements like steam to produce nuclear energy output, as in Katsuhiro Otomo's anime *Steamboy*. It is the wardrobe to Narnia, dressed up like Bill Ferrari's time machine or Harper Goff's *Nautilus*. It looks like science but works like magic.

So now you're seeing through a lens that evokes (not emulates) the past, and a lens that imagines impossible technology in that past. The third and final lens effectively combines these elements, but is more subtle than it appears. Shift the third lens into place. You'll see that the image of Will Smith on the *Wild Wild West* poster hasn't changed. But given that he is a person of color in the nineteenth century who works for the US government as a trusted spy, there is an unannounced but crucial change. That's the retrofuturist lens you're using now.

Lens 3: Retrofuturism

Steampunk retrofuturism is usually conflated with images of antiquated technology, of dirigibles and ornithopters, or steampunk maker Datamancer's brass-worked keyboards. Discussions concerning retrofuturism at conventions and online forums usually focus on technology. Yet steampunk retrofuturism is much more than just how the past imagined the future. Rather, it is the way *the present* imagines the past seeing the future. After all, it's rare that the steampunk aesthetic accurately conveys the social aspirations of the nineteenth-century. Steampunk technology's blend of past and future often ignores the ambitions of late Victorian progressives, less concerned with sky dreadnoughts and phlogiston-powered ray guns than with medical advancements and human rights. The nearly myopic focus of steampunk toward technology sometimes misses the opportunity to investigate social possibilities, not just technological ones. If the Industrial Era proved anything, it was that massive technological change results in massive social change.

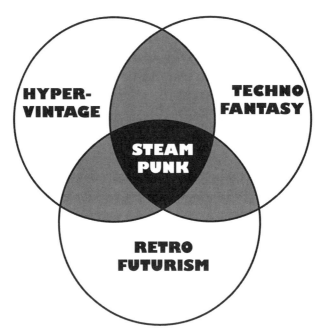

A Venn diagram of the three features of steampunk: a purist would say that only the perfect storm in the center of those three features is authentic steampunk, but as you'll see, I prefer to play in the grey areas: combinations of only two of the features are often identified as steampunk.

Thankfully, steampunk retrofuturism can be about more than techno-fantastic anachronisms, automatons, and airships. Even frivolous steampunk fiction engages in unintentional social retrofuturism when characters view the nineteenth century from a twenty-first-century perspective. SF critic Rob Latham has identified *nostalgia* and *regret* as typical retrofuturist emotions. These terms provide a continuum for understanding retrofuturism's range of commentary on the past. When the impulse of steampunk retrofuturism is only *nostalgia*, it produces conservative expressions of steampunk where Colonial perspectives are revived and potentially preserved. Nostalgic steampunk can become just the romantic desire for a reality without the complexity of globalization. If, however, the impulse of steampunk retrofuturism is *regret*, there is an opportunity to rewrite the past, not in the naïve hope it can be changed, but rather that retrofuturist speculations can affect the present and future.

But the idea of a continuum for understanding steampunk is not restricted to retrofuturism alone. Instead of asking if something is steampunk or not, the better question, inspired by a continuum view, answers the question, "how steampunk is it?" If you look at the side of those goggles you're wearing, you'll see a little dial attached to each lens's control—that's to govern intensity. With those dials, we can intensify each feature's presence in our goggle-gaze: if we turn down the technofantasy, turn up the retrofuturism, and crank the hyper-vintage, we will be seeing the world of Cherie Priest's *Dreadnought*, where the Civil War drags on in 1880. *Dreadnought* follows the adventures of Mercy Lynch, a nurse traveling cross-country on a monstrous steam train to see her dying father one last time. It's a steampunk *Planes, Trains, and Automobiles* with zombies, Texas rangers, and a helluva heroine. Turn the technofantasy *up* all the way to eleven, play down the retrofuturism, adjust the hyper-vintage a little, and you're looking at the world of S. M. Peters's *Whitechapel Gods*, where a huge containment wall around the Whitechapel district has created a steampunk Inferno, complete with dark deities.

Steampunk has been called a subgenre of science fiction, but is better understood as a style applied to the genres of science fiction and fantasy, and to many things beyond literature to which the word *genre* does not apply. We can view many types of stories through these three steampunk lenses, serious and whimsical alike. Consider the goggles as steampunk rose-colored glasses, which change the look of whatever we cast our gaze upon. Look at an adventure story and the goggles give you Scott Westerfeld's *Leviathan*; look at a romance and the goggles give you Kady Cross's *Girl in the Iron Corset*; look at space opera and you'll see Philip Reeve's *Larklight*; look at a Western and get Felix Gilman's *Half-made World*. Fantasy? *The Aeronaut's Windlass* by Jim Butcher. New Weird? *Perdido Street Station* by China Miéville. Superheroes? *The Falling Machine* by Andrew P. Mayer. Monstrous vampires? *Anno Dracula* by Kim Newman. Sparkly vampires? *Soulless* by Gail Carriger. Both? *Greyfriar* by Clay and Susan Griffith.

I could go on. And on. And on.

Allegra Hawksmoor, editor of *Steampunk Magazine*, once lamented the possibility that steampunk is an empty style. When the style of steampunk is symbolically understood as a lens, the possibility of emptiness is not a bad thing. A lens must be empty in order to be seen through; we need clear sight lines to see the steampunk horizon. The gaze is political in Moorcock, and whimsical in Blaylock. The definition of steampunk will remain contestable so long as the focus is on content rather than style. However, if we see steampunk as a stylistic gaze, then we retain the choice to turn that gaze upon political position, cosplay carnivale, or nostalgic narratives: these are not steampunk per se, but rather what become steampunked when the aesthetic gaze combining technofantasy and hyper-vintage retrofuturism is applied.

So slide the lenses in place and adjust your dials. I'll stoke up the boilers on the airship now. It's time to fly.

2

The California Trinity

Ask "When did steampunk begin?", and you'll get a host of different answers. So while it's a frequently asked question, it's also one that people needlessly complicate. I suspect many people do this to stand out from the herd: it's like people who do Shakespeare studies. In a sea of people talking about the Bard, the easiest way to get some attention is to say something no one else is saying. Suggest that the man never really wrote his plays. That gets everyone's attention.

Likewise, there are a number of ideas about how steampunk got started. There are those who say it gets started with Victorian scientific romances like Mary Shelley's *Frankenstein* in 1818, or Jules Verne with his *Fantastic Voyages* series in the 1860s, or H. G. Wells with *The Time Machine* in 1895. They're wrong, because none of those works are steampunk, but you'll have to wait a chapter to find out why. There are others who place the beginning of steampunk in the 1950s or '60s, with science fiction set in a world that evokes the Victorian, such as Keith Roberts's classic work of alternate history, *Pavane*, which imagines a Britain where electricity and diesel fuel are forbidden, or in the adventures of Oswald Bastable by Michael Moorcock. But these are problematic also. At best, we might call them antecedents, "before there was a term" works, which is an important designation to be aware of in steampunk, since there are a host of steampunk fans who are all too eager to trumpet that they were steampunk "before there was a term." It's like being into U2 before *The Joshua Tree*, or Metallica before the Black Album.

But if you ask me (and you are, because you're holding my book), you'll get the most basic and conservative of answers. Surprisingly, steampunk doesn't kick off in London—it kicks off in the one of the least Victorian of places, California in the 1980s, in the science fiction and fantasy writing of three friends under the mentorship of Philip K. Dick. And its genesis was largely a joke—a joke that caught on in ways these three writers never imagined. Contrary to popular belief, they were not as influenced by Jules Verne or H. G. Wells as much as they were by a book on the poor and destitute of London: *London Labour and the London Poor* by Henry Mayhew. This would later lead to the incorrect assumption that their works were politically motivated in ways they are not. The writing of James P. Blaylock, K. W. Jeter, and Tim Powers shares a penchant for witty humor and madcap adventures, but little in the way of socially conscious commentary.

Steampunk starts with a smart-ass response to the same question that provoked you to pick up this book. What do you call that science-fiction/fantasy stuff that mixes in Victorian elements? Granted, that's not *exactly* how the question was framed, but it's the same essential one everyone asks who gets a glimpse of steampunk and wants to know what it is.

This beginning of steampunk as I'm about to relate it is easily searchable on the internet, but since you're already holding this book, I'll save you the work. Besides, in the case of an apocalypse that knocks us back to the Victorian era (as in the first steampunk book I ever read, *Fitzpatrick's War* by Theodore Judson), it's best that we have it all down in a nondigital format for posterity (though I'm certainly not the first to record it on page).

In short, I'm going to begin with the American side of things, largely because that's where K. W. Jeter, the man who coined the term "steampunk" in April 1987, is from, but also because steampunk is all about messing with time. But rather than say, "That's absolutely the moment when steampunk began," I think it's better to consider April 1987 in the same way one might consider the historical Trinity, the first nuclear weapons test. Someone might say "that's when the Atomic Age began." And for concision and simplicity's sake, they'd be right. But read up on a history of the atomic bomb, and you find out that the blast radius of that event echoes backwards to 1933 when Leo Szilard theorized how a nuclear chain reaction could happen. So while 1987 might only be the naming, not the beginning, of steampunk, the California Trinity of Blaylock, Jeter, and Powers are certainly at the center of the blast radius that echoes back to earlier instances, and pushes forward to today, as steampunk continues to radiate.

Though the reference to the historical Trinity is a dark one, I like the term because of its additional (and better-known) religious connotations. I have seen the California Trinity invoked as justification for the serious, political nature of steampunk, an invocation I take exception with, as will be shown. Suffice it to say that there are steampunk fans who see these writers as foundational to steampunk, and are therefore held in high, though not necessarily religious, regard.

I also think there's something important about a few Americans who were hanging out with Philip K. Dick being the guys to get the steampunk party started. In his introduction to James Blaylock's *Homunculus*, Keith Roberts speaks with lighthearted chagrin at seeing London imagined through the eyes of an American who doesn't really know the city very well. And yet, it's this very inauthenticity that pervades steampunk. It isn't London we're dealing with, but rather an image of London, informed by *Classics Illustrated*, Disney films, and Masterpiece Theatre. And it's one of the ongoing frustrations for readers interested in alternate history who think that steampunk is offering the same rigorous historical speculation their beloved genre is. As we'll see in the next chapter, they're often greatly disappointed.

In the 1970s, Blaylock, Jeter, and Powers were struggling writers trying to make their way in the world of paperback science fiction and fantasy. In some strange turn of irony, it was Arthurian fantasy that got Jeter writing his "gonzo" Victorian fantasy *Morlock Night*, a fun sequel to H. G. Wells's *Time Machine*. British publisher Roger Elwood had imagined a series of books wherein King Arthur keeps reincarnating throughout various time periods: Jeter got the Victorian period, while his friend Tim Powers got the early 1800s.

But it wasn't King Arthur that would provide the steampunk link for the three friends. It was a book about the destitute of London: the prostitutes, the penniless, and the purveyors of all sorts of bizarre wares, from fish to fowl to flotsam. It was a version of Henry Mayhew's *London Labour and the London Poor*, a documentary work of several volumes itemizing in journalistic detail the lives of the London underworld, which all three writers used as source material for their first (and in Powers's case, arguably only) steampunk writing.

It's been suggested that the use of Mayhew's *London Labour* in the creation of Blaylock, Jeter, and Powers's steampunk writing makes these novels and short stories edgy, political, dark, or serious. While some writers could use Mayhew's *London Labour* as a means to shine light on the disparity between the wealthy and the poor in the Victorian period, and then turn that illumination on contemporary societies, using steampunk to create an analogy about the haves and have-nots, Blaylock, Jeter, and Powers were not those writers. Instead, the trio's inclusion of the lower-than-lower-classes of nineteenth-century London, while accurate due to the debt owed Mayhew, is almost uniformly plot-based. If the intention was to make a statement about modern poverty, then these men failed abysmally. What they succeeded at was creating entertaining stories filled with magic, adventure, and mad science that isn't terribly scientific.

But before we get started looking at the writing of these men in any depth, I have to make sure you understand something. While second-wave steampunk would champion them as the writers who started steampunk, their steampunk writing didn't make any of them particularly successful. You can't really understand steampunk without knowing about them, and yet at the same time, their influence on steampunk is marginal at best. While Blaylock has been called a steampunk legend, you won't find very many second-wave steampunk writers or creators who say that Blaylock really inspired or informed their creative choices. I've met many steampunk fans who've read something by Tim Powers, but it's not always *The Anubis Gates*, the closest thing to second-wave steampunk he ever wrote—it's more likely to be *On Stranger Tides,* the book that inspired the fourth *Pirates of the Caribbean* movie. And finding a copy of K. W. Jeter's steampunk books prior to their Angry Robot reissues in 2011 meant ordering used books off the internet. While nearly every history of steampunk will make much ado about these three men, the truth of the matter is that their impact on steampunk comes down to one, and only one, of them coining the term in the late 1980s.

But before a term was needed to describe these gonzo Victorian fantasies, as Jeter would refer to them, they needed to be written. And that takes us, appropriately, back in time to 1979.

K. W. Jeter: *Morlock Night* and *Infernal Devices*

Morlock Night

While James Blaylock's short story "The Ape Box Affair" has a strong claim as the first work of steampunk writing in the United States, the first steampunk novel by the California Trinity was K. W. Jeter's *Morlock Night*, which, unlike the steampunk of Powers and Blaylock, can be summed up relatively easily. Published in 1979, *Morlock Night* is a sequel to H. G. Wells's *The Time Machine*, though only in plot, and not in social commentary. In it, the Morlocks, beast-men from the future, have commandeered the time machine to travel back to nineteenth-century London, which they seek to overthrow. Their efforts are thwarted by Merlin (yes, *that* Merlin, the wizard) and the current reincarnation of King Arthur, Edwin Hocker, an utterly unremarkable Englishman. I was completely unaware of this when I first read *Morlock Night*, and was accordingly surprised when magic was used so overtly, since steampunk was supposedly Victorian science fiction. And yet here were King Arthur, Merlin, and Excalibur, a magic sword, in *the* seminal steampunk novel. Furthermore, the goal of the heroes was to save Christendom. I'd taken part in forum discussions where I was told steampunk was intrinsically political, and likely of an anarchic stripe, because that's the way original steampunk literature was. Yet there I was, reading original steampunk that shared greater affinities with Christian writer C. S. Lewis's *Cosmic Trilogy* than anything by anarchist writers like Michael Moorcock.

Fans of contemporary steampunk will likely have high expectations for *Morlock Night*. They might expect it to be derivative of cyberpunk, since steampunk has been associated with cyberpunk and admittedly, Jeter wrote a cyberpunk novel called *Dr. Adder*. But he is the only one of these early American steampunk writers to have any association with cyberpunk. Furthermore, *Dr. Adder* was published after *Morlock Night* in the 1980s, and bears little resemblance to the earlier book.

Readers of H. G. Wells's *The Time Machine* have further reason to raise the bar of expectation, since the original cover of *Morlock Night* boasted that the novel would explain "what happened when the Time Machine returned." Fans of Wells's serious social commentary will

The original DAW paperback cover to K. W. Jeter's *Morlock Night* with art by Josh Kirby. By second-wave standards, there's nothing about this cover that says "steampunk."

The Angry Robot reprint of *Morlock Night* with cover art by John Coulthart, which emulates nineteenth-century style with modern flourishes.

certainly be disappointed when they discover that Jeter's novel is pure page-turning fun. One of his characters self-reflexively warns the Wellsian faithful not to take things too seriously here: after all, it's only a story: "My good fellow, don't get so excited over a mere story! Divert yourself with whatever sequels you care to imagine, but save such passion for reality." The novel self-reflexively warns the reader that this isn't Wells's agenda anymore—Jeter is going in a new direction, and it's one with more fun and adventure than the original Time Traveler experienced, sharing greater similarity to George Pal's film adaptation than Wells's original.

However, some serious steampunks, undeterred by the lack of serious social commentary in *Morlock Night*, claim that it's really Jeter's second steampunk novel, *Infernal Devices*, wherein one finds the serious and gritty roots of steampunk.

Infernal Devices

There are three steampunk books with this name, and a few others with it for a subtitle. Do a web search for "Infernal Devices" without Jeter's name in the search, and you're more likely to get either Cassandra Clare's steampunk series or one of Philip Reeve's steampunk novels; both are targeted to young adult (YA) audiences and are far more popular than Jeter's original. I mention this only to once again underscore the obscurity of some of the so-called "classics" of steampunk fiction. This is not to say that they are terrible books. It is to demonstrate that Jeter's most lasting contribution to steampunk was the term itself, not the fiction he sought to describe.

Released in 1987, the same year that Jeter coined the term "steampunk," *Infernal Devices* tells the story of George Dower, a London clockmaker who becomes caught up in a series of madcap misadventures so bizarre, the connections between them strain a reader's suspension of disbelief. There are fish people who are the debased descendants of the mythological Selkies that feel like homages to horror legend H. P. Lovecraft's "Shadow Over Innsmouth," without any of the cosmic horror of that short story. There is a clockwork double who is a virtuoso at playing the violin and at playing upon the desires of upper-class London women. There is a comedic criminal duo who have gazed into the future through a device that sees through time and have come away from the experience with slang and social attitudes of that future: he is foul-mouthed and forthright, while she is a rapacious vamp who threatens George Dower's Victorian virginity until achieving both a literal and literary climax (the world is saved through orgasm at the end of the book).

Dower's adventures are picaresque to say the least: at times, I wonder if Jeter went into writing the book with a plan at all, or simply tied up loose ends as he went. As with *Morlock Night*, *Infernal Devices* has been mistakenly described as satirical commentary on the plight of the London poor. While the destitute of London make several appearances throughout the novel, it never seems to be in genuine service to considering the roots or solutions for poverty or class difference. Instead, the colorful lower-class citizens appear to ensure the reader believes in this fictional London, since it's so hard to believe in the mad coincidences Jeter invents for Dower and company. Consider the moment that a flying machine with the skins of recently slaughtered sheep stretched across its frame swoops down in the nick of time to save Dower, while one of its blood-spattered riders yells, "Eat shit, turkeys!" Dower's assailants, all religious fanatics, mistake the contraption for the Beast from the Book of Revelation as it bursts into flames from sparks generated by its metal frame. Deep commentary indeed.

Perhaps it is satire of the British upper class. Perhaps it is commentary on the plight of the London poor. What is beyond question is that it is the epitome of one of the words Jeter used when he coined steampunk: it's "gonzo." You don't hear that word much anymore, but it's only fair that a fabricated term like steampunk owe its meaning to another fabricated word. Gonzo was used by writer of the gonzo himself Hunter S. Thompson, who claimed it was Boston slang for the weird or bizarre. And that is as good a description for the steampunk fiction of Jeter as any other. But while the gonzo elements in Tim Powers's *Anubis Gates* signal its connection to steampunk, it has not proven enough to shield the book from the accusation that it's not actually steampunk.

Tim Powers: *The Anubis Gates*

Tim Powers's *The Anubis Gates* was published in 1983, which makes him the second of the California Trinity to publish a steampunk novel. However, prior to the resurgence of interest in these seminal novels during second-wave steampunk's quest for its roots, it was arguably the most famous of the California Trinity's steampunk offerings. The greater irony of this fame is that it's difficult to argue that *Anubis Gates* is steampunk at all, particularly by some of the limiting definitions of the second wave. Whenever Powers speaks about his connection to steampunk, it's with an air of bemusement. At Steamcon II in 2010, he jokingly asked his Guest of Honor audience what he was doing there. Powers is very sharp, and he knows enough about what steampunk has become to know that *The Anubis Gates* isn't it. It takes place *before* the Victorian period. While it has technofantasy, the emphasis is squarely on the fantasy, with no inclusion of brass-filigreed technology. And it could be considered retrofuturist, but only insofar as any time-travel story involves imagining how the past might interact with the future. As seen through the lens of second-wave steampunk, it requires a series of exceptions to bring Powers's novel into the steampunk corral. Nevertheless, steampunk fans continue to hail it as a favorite or a classic. So it requires our attention, if only to conclude that it is an anomaly.

Anubis Gates begins with a failed attempt to restore ancient Egyptian gods to their former presence and power in the world of the nineteenth century. While the ritual is partially successful, it fails to fully return the god Anubis to Earth in a human body. What it does instead is to tear holes in the fabric of space and time, inadvertently permitting time travel in the late twentieth century. Where *Anubis Gates* goes from there is as convoluted and madcap as Jeter's *Infernal Devices*, though with greater narrative cohesion.

The story follows the misadventures of Brendan Doyle, a literature scholar who specializes in Coleridge and an obscure poet named Ashbless (also the pseudonym Powers and Blaylock wrote poetry under in university). Doyle is recruited as a consultant in a trip back in time to 1810 to see Coleridge give a lecture at a London pub. Before he can return to the present (1983) along with his fellow time travelers, Doyle is waylaid and trapped in the past. In his attempts to get home, Doyle runs afoul of a beggar-king named Horrabin (a stilt-walking, clown-faced villain who gives Stephen King's Pennywise a run for his terrifying money), a gypsy conjurer who was involved in the ritual that ripped the holes in space and time, and Dog Face Joe, a body-swapping werewolf. He is aided against these varied enemies by a streetwise urchin named Jacky who turns out to be a young widow seeking vengeance against Dog Face Joe for the death of her husband (Jacky is the first incidence in steampunk of female-masquerading-as-male, a recurring motif in second-wave steampunk such as Scott Westerfeld's *Leviathan*, Gail Carriger's *Parasol Protectorate* series, and Lev AC Rosen's *All Men of Genius*, to name a few).

The Anubis Gates is exceedingly colorful and compelling, and though it is early in Powers's career, it remains one of the books he's best known for. I've read it three times, and never tire of the opportunity to read it again. It's a high point in my steampunk reading, and must be for many others, since it appears on many "best steampunk" or "important steampunk" lists.

However, the first time I ever met Powers and told him I was researching steampunk, he asked me if I thought *The Anubis Gates* should be considered such. Clearly, he knew the arguments against its inclusion, given what steampunk had become in the twenty years since Jeter coined the term. Those arguments for why *The Anubis Gates* isn't steampunk are as follows:

1. It does not contain any elements of technofantasy—the speculative elements are purely magical. This argument is based on the idea that steampunk is science fiction not fantasy and *must* involve some aspect of technological anachronism, preferably industrial-age in appearance.
2. It takes place in 1810, which is in the Georgian period, not the Victorian. This argument is based on the assumption that steampunk *must* be Victorian in some aspect.

I answered Powers by saying I thought *Anubis Gates* is steampunk, and I haven't changed my mind in the seven years since. To address the two arguments here at length is to get ahead of myself. I promise that the frequently asked questions of "Is Steampunk science fiction?" and "Is

Steampunk Victorian?" will be addressed in forthcoming chapters. But for now, I continue to argue for *The Anubis Gates* as steampunk because it challenges so many of the second-wave assumptions about what steampunk *is* or, more accurately, "should be." And this is going to keep coming up over and over throughout the book, so it's best we address it now, near the start.

Remember how I said my approach to defining and describing steampunk wasn't prescriptive but descriptive? That means that I don't make steampunk what I want it to be. Instead, I'm paying attention to what most people think steampunk is in a popular sense. And I don't just look at that popularity in a single moment, or even a year. The definitions of steampunk that would exclude Powers are moments in the history of steampunk; they are not the whole of that history. There are more voices that include Powers's *Anubis Gates* as part of the history of steampunk than those who do not. Which means two things: steampunk doesn't *have* to be Victorian, and it *can* be fantasy.

So long as steampunk fans want to include Powers as part of the steampunk canon (and I use that word intentionally, to invoke the sort of religious associations it implies), it means that steampunk can't be restricted to the exclusive parameters second-wave gatekeepers would be setting for it. Which is appropriate, given the air of mischief Powers exudes. He's got this grin that dares his fans to take him too seriously. On the two occasions I've seen him speak (one at a steampunk fan convention, the other at an academic conference that focused on Jules Verne, and by association, steampunk), he made this witty observation about Bram Stoker's *Dracula*: "People are always telling me *Dracula* is about the plight of women in the nineteenth century. And here I thought it was about a creature that stays alive by drinking the blood of humans."

It's that witty observation that is the other reason I want Powers around in the halls of hallowed steampunk: he's the second cog in the argument against the notion that steampunk is essentially political, is essentially counterculture. And while I'll discuss this at length in chapter ten, it's worth addressing briefly here: in no way do I want to discourage those who prefer their steampunk serious and political from creating steampunk that is serious and political. But I am equally opposed to those who would prescribe that steampunk *must* be serious and political.

And when I think about the tendency for some to dictate the parameters of steampunk thusly, I can't help but see Powers's smile, and imagine him saying, "People are always telling me steampunk is about resisting hegemony and uniformity. And here I thought it was about telling a good adventure story set in the nineteenth century."

James P. Blaylock

"The Ape-Box Affair"

Bob Dylan wrote "All Along the Watchtower," but most people know the song as a Jimi Hendrix tune. Jeter might have coined the term steampunk, but it was Blaylock who traveled the steam tracks farthest and most prolifically, even in those seminal ye ars. While Jeter's letter (and a copy of *Morlock Night*) sent to *Locus* was meant to settle the argument of who started writing steampunk first, Blaylock was unarguably the first of the three to do so: not with a novel, but with his madcap short story "The Ape-Box Affair" in 1978, and would have had a second had *Starwind* magazine not folded before publication of "The Hole in Space." Both of these early steampunk stories demonstrate beyond a shadow of a doubt that anyone who claims that early steampunk was more dystopian and edgy than later steampunk has never read Blaylock.

"The Ape-Box Affair" is about an orangutan landing a spherical flying ship in London, where he is mistaken for an alien. The hijinks that follow the crash landing are best imagined as a comedy shot as silent film. There are moments of physical slapstick of the Keystone Cop variety, but there are also many dry, ironic statements about how Victorian Londoners might react to an "alien invasion." Contrast the terror and dehumanization of the London refugees in H. G. Wells's *War of the Worlds*, with the Lord Mayor's response to Blaylock's "alien" in St. James' Park: "He rather fancied the idea of a smoke and a chat and perhaps a pint of bitter later in the day with these alien chaps and so organized a 'delegation,' as he called it, to ride out and welcome them."

Lines like these fly in the face of claims that early steampunk was saying something important and political that later steampunk fails to say. But Blaylock isn't looking into the past to say something profound about the present. Rather, he seems to be looking into the past because he thinks it would be a fun place to play for a while, a place where aliens arriving in London might be met with the hope for a smoke, a chat, and a pint of bitter, rather than the London of today, where an alien might be met by the military. In short, he's looking to be entertaining.

Homunculus

If all you ever read was steampunk commentary on Blaylock's writing instead of the writing itself, you would be unaware of his focus on fun-filled storytelling. Cynthia J. Miller and Julie Anne Taddeo made such an error concerning early steampunk in their introduction to *Steaming into a Victorian Future*, calling Blaylock's early steampunk "*darkly* atmospheric novels" in a "London *darker* and wilder than anything imagined by Dickens" [emphasis added]. Admittedly, there are many instances of nighttime dealings in *Homunculus*; but while the novel is filled with animated corpses, it still retains Blaylock's signature whimsy.

One need only look at the way in which such animated corpses are handled in chapter ten, "Trouble at Harrogate." It begins in the home of the novel's hero, Langdon St. Ives, where he has secreted two of the villainous Dr. Narbondo's zombies, in order to study them. The zombies expire (again) and are left in the pantry. Narbondo's henchman, Willis Pule, breaks into St. Ives's house, looking to make off with an essential diary, but is chased off by St. Ives's unflappable and remarkably capable servant, Hasbro. As St. Ives and Hasbro pursue Pule, one of crime boss Kelso Drake's henchmen takes the opportunity to search the property's silo, wherein St. Ives keeps his experimental spacecraft. The henchman inadvertently launches the craft, which bursts through the roof of the silo and crashes into a neighbor's barn, a neighbor who happens to be the secretary of the Royal Academy of Science. A local man named Binger witnesses the incident, and in an attempt to rescue his reputation as an inventor, St. Ives offers the man an inflated amount for a debt he owes, inviting him back to the house for an ale and a pie. He opens the door to the pantry to bring out the promised pie, only to reveal the two corpses, further adding to the muddle. St. Ives's attempts to buy Binger's silence only increase the comedy; the zombies are not meant to scare, but in this moment, provide a laugh.

In short, lighthearted whimsy rules in Blaylock's steampunk England. And it is apparent throughout one of his most famous steampunk novels, *Homunculus*. The plot is even more labyrinthine than Powers's *Anubis Gates*. One can only list off the various madcap elements: corpses animated by the power of Carp glands; a tiny man, an alien capable of performing miracles; the reluctant hero Langdon St. Ives, a scholar/inventor and his companions in the Trismegistus Club, a group of eccentric and somewhat bumbling erstwhile heroes, who meet in a smoke shop owned by former sailor Captain Powers (yes, it's a reference to *that* Powers— there are references like these in all of the California Trinity's steampunk books), who has a prosthetic leg made of ivory that one can use as a tobacco pipe while walking. See, that's how it happens. You start out trying to explain Blaylock's plots and end up saying something about one of his wonderfully colorful characters, which are the heart of all of Blaylock's books, steampunk or otherwise.

I've seen a number of references to Blaylock's works that focus on the plot, which involves the nefarious plans of Doctor Narbondo, a hunchbacked mad scientist who is the nemesis of St. Ives; Kelso Drake, a scheming millionaire; Shiloh, an aged, self-proclaimed messiah; and Narbondo's henchman Willis Pule, a bitter young man with a complexion so bad he's willing to try a compress comprised of carbon tetrachloride and anchovy paste. Opposing them are the Trismegistus club: the aforementioned St. Ives and Powers; Bill Kraken, a drunken derelict with a shady past and a heart of gold; William Keeble, a toymaker so brilliant he is capable of engineering a perpetual motion machine; and Jack Owlesby, ward of Keeble, whose late father's descent into madness precipitated the core events of the novel. Despite Ives and Keeble's brilliant scientific minds, the Trismegistus club is a band of everymen, save for Theophilus Godall, an aristocrat whose clandestine and investigative abilities render him a sort of Sherlock Holmes among bumblers. Yet even Godall is far from superhuman in his abilities. While Blaylock's steampunk novels are collectively titled *The Adventures of Langdon St. Ives* (literally the title of an anthology of short stories and two novels from Subterranean Press), St. Ives is not a lone wolf hero. He always needs the assistance of his companions. Community is the core of *Homunculus* and its sequels, even in the case of *Lord Kelvin's Machine*, where this theme is underscored through St. Ives's attempt to go it solo.

Lord Kelvin's Machine

In their *Steampunk* anthology, Ann and Jeff Vandermeer refer to the short version of "Lord Kelvin's Machine" as the "quintessential steampunk story, with its combination of darkness and diabolical invention and cosmic scope." While the novel version of *Lord Kelvin's Machine* has far less whimsy and is arguably darker than Blaylock's other early steampunk, both short story and novel retain Blaylock's brand of humor and hopefulness.

The novel is divided into three acts: The first part, "In the Days of the Comet," contains an expanded version of the text from the short story "Lord Kelvin's Machine," which originally appeared in *Asimov's SF* in December of 1985. A new prologue, "Murder in the Seven Dials," tells of the death of Langdon St. Ives's wife Alice at the hands of Ignacio Narbondo. The rest of "In the Days of the Comet" reads very much like the original short story, with St. Ives and members of the Trismegistus club racing to stop Narbondo from driving the Earth into the path of an oncoming comet using volcanic eruptions to thwart the British Royal Society's plan to shift the Earth's poles using Lord Kelvin's machine, save that in the novel, whimsy is abandoned; St. Ives is necessarily far more brooding, due to his wife's death.

The original "Lord Kelvin's Machine" reads like most other St. Ives's stories, with Blaylock jumping back and forth between adventure and absurdity. The absurdity of sabotaging Lord Kelvin's device with famished snakes and mice seeking grain stuffed into the machine remains in the novel, but loses much of its comic impact in the shadow of Alice's death. The first part of the novel ends much the same way as it did in the short story, with Narbondo seemingly drowned in a mountain lake, and Lord Kelvin's machine ruined by the offending snakes and mice.

In the second part, "The Downed Ships: Jack Owlesby's Account," Blaylock shifts to a first-person perspective via Jack Owlesby. Like the first part of the novel, "The Downed Ships" could easily stand alone as an independent short story. Through Owlesby's bumbling misadventures, we learn that Narbondo survived his plunge into the mountain lake.

The third part, "The Time Traveler," is what makes *Lord Kelvin's Machine* a steampunk classic. St. Ives uses the reconstituted core of Lord Kelvin's Machine to travel through time. His journeys share a kinship with the time-hopping in Powers's *Anubis Gates*, with Ives changing himself as he goes about changing the past. He believes that by altering the past, he can save his wife, but in the process ends up saving the young Ignacio Narbondo from death by meningitis. This act of compassion changes St. Ives as well, healing the bitter wound Alice's death left festering inside him. When he finally succeeds in changing the moment of the past when Alice was murdered, he has changed enough to realize that he cannot remain in that past; at this point, the book provides a powerful meditation on the nature of grief, and the need to move beyond it and live.

The passages where St. Ives visits the fitfully sleeping child Narbondo are beautifully heartbreaking, given how terrible the child will become in *Homunculus* and in recent St. Ives novels like *The Aylesford Skull*. Yet St. Ives cannot conflate that villain with this child. The moment when he traces the spine for a hump is particularly touching, since it echoes the sort of touch a parent visits upon his own child, checking for injuries. St. Ives changes the past by curing the child's ailment, but more importantly, he changes himself.

After the release of the novelized *Lord Kelvin's Machine* in 1992, Blaylock would give up on St. Ives and the Trismegistus club, writing chilling ghost stories throughout the '90s. Blaylock proved to be the only one of the California Trinity to return to writing steampunk in earnest (Powers wrote two books that might be considered steampunk, *Hide Me Among the Graves* in 2012, and *Nobody's Home* in 2014), but he wouldn't do so until 2009 with *The Ebb Tide*, the first in a new series of Langdon St. Ives books capitalizing on the rise of second-wave steampunk. But before anyone could identify a first or second wave of steampunk, someone needed to coin the word itself. And that someone was K. W. Jeter.

The Creation of Steampunk

Get a chance to be in a room with Blaylock, Jeter, or Powers, or some combination of the three, and you'll see how we ended up with the name steampunk. As I said earlier, Tim Powers almost always has a grin on his face like he knows a funny story and can't wait to tell it. When I saw him speak at Steamcon in 2009, he related a story about the time Jehovah's Witnesses came to his house: in the process of arguing with them (he's a Catholic), Powers had to resort to reading with a magnifying glass. And because it was a bright, sunny day, Powers accidentally set their Bible on fire while looking at it. It's a story that ended with the punchline, "Those Catholics just have to *touch* a Bible and it bursts into flames!"

James Blaylock has a warm, affable manner about him, but get *him* telling stories and he'll tell you how Jeter once said that he and Powers were so dense when it came to science that they'd plug a black hole with a Fitzall Sizes cork, to which Blaylock replied, "if you're not going to use that in a story, I will." Which he did. It was called "The Hole in Space," and it's easily one of my favorite pieces of steampunk fiction.

And finally, there's Jeter. His resting face looks serious, almost sad. But get him talking and there's a wry grin hiding in the wings. Listen to him speak and you can see where that cheeky moment, the moment the word steampunk was coined in *Locus* magazine, came from. It was Jeter's tongue-in-cheek response to the question of categorizing the "gonzo" Victorian fantasies he, Powers, and Blaylock were writing:

> Personally, I think Victorian fantasies are going to be the next big thing, as long as we can come up with a fitting collective term for Powers, Blaylock, and myself. Something based on the appropriate technology of that era; like "steampunks," perhaps.

Jeter has admitted he was playing on the popularity of cyberpunk and the pervasive use of punk as a suffix for any new form of science fiction that wanted to set itself apart from the popularity of *Star Wars*. He has also said repeatedly, both in person and print, that the word was never intended seriously. In his address at the Steamcon Airship Awards Banquet in 2011, Jeter said that he never imagined the term would grow to encompass the various artistic expressions represented by the current steampunk scene.

In agreement with Jeter, I wouldn't suggest for a moment that any of these men, these literary tricksters, would have intentionally created a word like steampunk simply as a joke. But one has to try very, very hard to imagine that Jeter meant it as the beginning of a movement, or the labeling of a manifesto. One couldn't even strenuously argue that they meant for steampunk to become associated with any of the things it would in its second-wave iterations. For example, Tim Powers has noted that not one of his steampunk books is really alternate history. Arguably, they are more like secret histories, with fantastic events happening within our own world, but beyond our knowledge. Take a look at Blaylock's and Jeter's steampunk and you'll find the same thing. So in the 1980s, we could have said with some confidence that steampunk was an American subgenre of both science fiction and fantasy that related madcap secret histories filled with adventure and whimsy. It wouldn't be until William Gibson and Bruce Sterling's *The Difference Engine* in 1991 that steampunk would become inextricably connected with alternate history and serious content. But before we go forward, let's go back a century or more to what many call the historical roots of steampunk, the nineteenth century, to answer the question "is steampunk alternate history?"

3

Is Steampunk Alternate History?

W hen someone says, "What is steampunk?" and the answer is "alternate history," I imagine there are a lot of people who must then ask (or feign understanding), "What is alternate history?" If you've never read a book or watched a film or played a game that was alternate history, you've likely created some yourself. Nearly everyone does it. But we don't necessarily consider it alternate history, because most of us don't consider our own lives "history." But if you have ever wondered what would have happened if you hadn't broken up with the "one who got away," or if you'd said yes to that career opportunity, or if you had or hadn't become a parent, then you've engaged in a bit of alternate history, or at the very least, counterfactual thinking.

A basic explanation of alternate history (a subgenre of science fiction sometimes called alternative history) is that it is an exploration of what might have happened if we (collectively or individually) had zigged when, in actuality, we zagged. The majority of alternate history contains a clearly established historical fracture point that breaks with established history, transforming a readily recognizable historical event and thereby setting off a chain of cause and effect resulting in a different version of history proceeding from that fracture point. One of the most famous instances of alternate history is Philip K. Dick's *The Man in the High Castle*, which has been made into a successful television series. It imagines an alternate history where the Allies lost World War II.

In every case of alternate history, there is an implicit question. David Kowalski's *The Company of the Dead* asks, "What if *The Titanic* hadn't sunk?"

What if those movers and shakers, people of power and influence who drowned that night in April 1912, had lived? How would it have changed world politics? These questions are not always about real-world events: Harry Turtledove's *Worldwar* series imagines an alien invasion in the middle of World War II. What would the Allies and Axis do in the face of a common enemy? The counterfactual question is still legitimately alternate history, but the fracture point that creates the divergence is more fantastic. Likewise, in Naomi Novik's *Temeraire* series, the question is utterly fantastic: what would the Napoleonic war have been like if both sides had dragons to ride on? In my experience, the majority of steampunk utilizes these fantastic fractures, where it is more than a matter of zigging or zagging, as opposed to mundane ones. It's zigging into space where there's atmosphere (Philip Reeve's *Larklight* and David D. Levine's *Arabella of Mars*) or zagging as human servants in a world where every other animal evolved as the dominant species (Bryan Talbot's *Grandville*). It's messing with history on a grander scale, often at the level of real-world physics, chemistry, or biology.

Alternate History and Anachronisms

Readers of alternate history who are interested in steampunk seem to prefer the fracture point as an investigation of historical potential, not just one that asks, "Wouldn't it be cool if the Victorians had computers?" In other words, they expect the writer of alternate history to generate a certain degree of real-world probability in their speculative rigor, or else the alternate history ostensibly ceases to be science fiction and enters the world of fantasy. Consequently, there are expectations of alternate history that demand authors demonstrate that they have thought through all the permutations of their story's fracture point. The more fantastic the cause of the divergence, it seems the less the die-hard fan of alternate history is interested.

The idea of steampunk as alternate history is often associated with the idea that steampunk is always about technology, specifically technology anachronistic to the industrial era. The speculative questions that might result from such a pairing are grounded in probable or existing technologies: What if the nineteenth century had computers? What if rigid-frame airships had been built fifty years earlier? What if steam technology could be made to work like nuclear energy? The problem with this combination of anachronism and probable or existing technology is that it only accounts for a very small percentage of existing steampunk narratives and creative works. Even if we were to just consider early steampunk, there is only one that is an alternate history with anachronistic technology as the fracture point, and that's William Gibson's *The Difference Engine*, which asks, "What would have happened if Charles Babbage's calculating machine could have been built and worked?"

The novel's answer in brief is that the industrial age becomes blended with an information age, resulting in a dizzying array of historical differences. And while anachronistic technology can be found in Blaylock and Jeter's early steampunk novels, neither their work nor the tech-free *Anubis Gates* of Tim Powers are alternate histories. They are better understood as secret histories. Even though Blaylock and Jeter's heroes construct fantastic, anachronistic machines, they do not bring any significant change to history. Large-scale events transpire as they did in real-world history.

It's difficult to say whether Kurt R. A. Giambastini's *The Year the Cloud Fell* is steampunk, but it's certainly alternate history. There are a few divergences in this alternate history of the post–Civil War American West, not the least of which is the inclusion of dinosaurs and other megafauna surviving on the American continent. Some alternate histories imagine a comet hitting the Earth and changing the course of history, such as in S. M. Stirling's *Peshawar Lancers*, where the Northern Hemisphere is thrust into an Ice Age from the debris from the meteor strike, forcing the British Empire to relocate to India. Instead, Giambastini imagines a North America where the Yucatan peninsula was never struck by the meteor that killed off the dinosaurs. So consequently, we get a book with Native Americans riding domesticated dinosaurs (and riding those dinosaurs up to the White House in the novel's climax!). While that's a bit crazy, it's not the same as having Native Americans riding around on dragons. Dinosaurs really lived on the planet at one time, so the idea of them surviving up to the nineteenth century, while highly improbable, isn't necessarily impossible.

But the larger corpus of steampunk fiction, film, and art demonstrates that steampunk's alternate history often plays in the sandbox of the impossible. Steampunk goes beyond speculations like "what if the Civil War didn't end in 1865?" That's a question about history based in the world as we know it, and one that writers of alternate histories love to play with. But steampunk like Cherie Priest's *Clockwork Century* series takes that question and adds another: "What if the Civil War ground on for decades *and* there was a highly addictive drug that turned people into flesh-eating zombies?"

Likewise, Mark Hodder's brilliant *Burton and Swinburne* kicks off with the question, "What if Queen Victoria had been assassinated?" and then makes her assassin Spring Heeled Jack, a spectral bogeyman of urban legend who supposedly haunted the streets of London in the nineteenth century. But Hodder doesn't stop there. He takes the question a step further and asks, "And what if Spring Heeled Jack was a time traveler?" thus accounting for the time gaps in reported Spring Heeled Jack sightings. And that's just the beginning; by the end of six books, Hodder created some of the most interesting alternative and parallel history writing I've ever come across. The initial trilogy, *The Strange Affair of Spring Heeled Jack*, *The Curious Case of the Clockwork Man*, and *Expedition to the Mountains of the Moon*, are the adventures of explorer/scholar Sir Richard Francis Burton and poet/dandy Algernon Charles Swinburne in the alternate London created by the historical fracture caused by the time-traveling Spring Heeled Jack. The second trilogy, *The Secret of Abdu El Yezdi*, *The Return of the Discontinued Man*, and *The Rise of the Automated Aristocrats*, might be said to be alternate histories of the alternate history of the first trilogy. Dizzying, I know. And it gets even more dizzying in *The Secret of Abdu El Yezdi*, in which these alternate histories intersect with fictional ones from Bram Stoker's *Dracula* and Sir Arthur Conan Doyle's *Sherlock Holmes*. As we'll see later in this chapter, this sort of alternate-history-of-literature is also common in steampunk.

And what does one do with Jay Lake's *Mainspring*? Unlike a historical fracture dealing with recorded history such as the French Revolution or World War I, Lake's alternate Earth has its fracture point before recorded history, at the moment of creation. When the God of *Mainspring* "hung Earth in the sky on the tracks of her orbit around the lamp of the sun," it

Cover to the hardback edition of the late Jay Lake's *Mainspring*, set in a fantasy version of Earth where the planet is bisected into north and south hemispheres by a massive clockwork wall.

was on a very real, not metaphorical track: *Mainspring*'s Earth is bisected by a massive clockwork gear, a colossal brass wall separating the world into a dystopic, industrialized Northern hemisphere, and a utopic, preindustrial Southern hemisphere. The inclusion of massive, physical proof of the existence of a clockmaker God permits Lake to have angels trouble the flights of his steampunk airships, and grant protagonist Hethor Jacques a type of clockwork magic to assist him on his quest; Hethor turns out to be a precision instrument himself, able to discern the music of the spheres, gears, and machinery that keep the Earth on its great brass track orbiting the sun. Connected to the clockwork mechanism running the world, Hethor can perform magic. And that troubles the idea of alternate history as science fiction. And science fiction doesn't involve magic. And steampunk is supposedly alternate history and therefore science fiction (not fantasy). You see how this gets messy? One might argue that the world of *Mainspring* is clearly our world with anachronistic elements. And admittedly, there's London, but it's a London where you can look out your window and see that great big clockwork gear in the sky. There's South America, but it's South America inhabited by little furry creatures somewhere between an Ewok and a sexy hobbit (you know, like the ones in the Peter Jackson films). So sure, there's London, but it's not our London, and there's a South America, but it's not our South America. Consequently, the historical fracture being theological in nature (God creates the world in a radically different way) doesn't generate alternate history so much as it does an alternate, or secondary world.

Steampunk Secondary Worlds

Some steampunk does more than propose a break in history: it constructs a whole new world with its own history: a secondary world. Fantasy writer J. R. R. Tolkien coined the term "secondary world" in an essay called "On Fairy Stories." And Tolkien's fantasy world of Middle-earth is easily the most famous of all secondary worlds. A secondary world is, simply put, not our own. And a number of steampunk books take place in a secondary world, in realms as fantastic as Middle-earth. There are still telltale cues of the steampunk aesthetic, from the ubiquitous airships and goggles, to the style of attire and architecture, the inclusion of Dickensian figures that are reminiscent of the orphaned Oliver Twist or the villainous leaders of workhouses or criminal gangs: sometimes there's even the use of steam technology.

Stephen Hunt's *The Courtyard of the Air* takes place in a fantasy world that bears similarities to nineteenth-century Europe. While the Kingdom of Jackals feels like Dickensian England, the presence of technology-bending "worldsinger sorcery" tells the reader we're nowhere near Kansas, let alone London. China Miéville's imagination runs even further beyond our world in his steampunk *Bas-Lag* series. In the second book, *The Scar*, a floating city called Armada, populated by Cactus-people, vampires, and steampunk cyborgs, is towed by a Godzilla-sized creature called an avanc while staving off attacks from Grindylow, fish-men from English folklore, and seeking out the island of the blood-sucking Mosquito People. Neither Hunt nor Miéville do what Lake does in *Mainspring*: in their secondary steampunk worlds, airships and automata, giant monsters and magic swords are the way things are. The steampunk elements are not historical fractures in these worlds; they are just history.

And consequently, Hunt and Miéville's steampunk fictions are not alternate histories; so the airships and clockwork automata in their pages are not anachronisms. Yet a number of definitions for steampunk continue to state that steampunk must contain anachronistic technology. However, an anachronism involves mixing elements from different time periods. When William Gibson and Bruce Sterling posit a nineteenth century with a viable computer in it, that computer is anachronistic. They have taken the real-world Babbage Engine and made it work in a time period when it didn't. This is very different from positing that the world turns on a giant mainspring, or that debunked scientific theories such as aether or phlogiston actually work, or that fictional substances exist which make the impossible possible. Those are instances of fantasy, not anachronism. And steampunk abounds with them.

Hunt and Miéville are only two writers among many who have chosen to set their steampunk in a secondary world, not some alternate history or version of our own. There are other examples of this in all media: in other fiction such as Ekaterina Sedia's beautiful novel *The Alchemy of Stone*, where, as the title indicates, alchemy works and stone gargoyles live; in comics like Giovanni Gualdoni and Gabriele Clima's *The Ring of the Seven Worlds*, where multidimensional gates link seven planets together, save one, which is meant to keep an ancient enemy at bay; in video games such as *Final Fantasy VI* that traded in the popular franchise's medieval setting for a steampunk one; in many of the films of Hayao Miyazaki, especially *Howl's Moving Castle*; and even in steampunk fashion and cosplay, where I've seen elf ears next to those gears.

Steampunk Futures

But those pointy ears could just as easily be a Vulcan's from the fictional future of *Star Trek*, couldn't they? And steampunk has also been set in the future. When you consider that Michael Moorcock's *Warlord of the Air* was published in 1971 but is set in 1973, it is an early instance of futuristic steampunk. S. M. Stirling's aforementioned alternate history *The Peshawar Lancers* takes place in an alternate British Empire in the twenty-first century. Theodore Judson's *Fitzpatrick's War* is set in the twenty-sixth century after a global apocalypse, when humanity rebuilds society on the blueprint of the British Empire. More recent instances of futuristic steampunk include Clay and Susan Griffith's *Vampire Empire* and *Riftwalker* series, which take place in a postapocalyptic future where humans are at war with vampires. Most of these steampunk futures are postapocalyptic, with the Victorian or Industrial European vintage elements the result of a technological setback or sociological throwback. These future steampunk societies are not uniform in their attitude toward their fictional reifications of Victoriana or European imperialism. In some cases as with *The Peshawar Lancers*, it is seen positively. In others, such as *Fitzpatrick's War*, it is decidedly dystopian.

Given how often it takes place in alternate worlds and speculative futures, steampunk cannot simply be called alternate history. While steampunk is certainly concerned with history, not every instance of steampunk is alternate history. Perhaps it would be better to say that steampunk is playing with history. Sometimes changing it, sometimes borrowing from it, sometimes messing it up nearly beyond recognition. So how can we recognize steampunk? How do we distinguish it from other science fiction and fantasy that play with history? After all, high fantasy plays with ancient, medieval, and Renaissance history. What period of history does steampunk play with?

Is Steampunk Only Victorian?

In chapter one, I identified two of the three features of steampunk as hyper-vintage and retrofuturism. Both terms imply a sense of the past, but what past, particularly? And how does that past contribute to the steampunk aesthetic?

To begin this exploration of what history steampunk draws upon, we need to address the frequently asked question, "Does steampunk have to be Victorian?" There are many versions of this question, but they all boil down to an attempt to set fast and easy boundary lines. More broadly, the question would be, "What time period is steampunk set in?" The most common answer is the Victorian period. A steampunk writer told me that her publisher was adamant that steampunk *must* be Victorian. Go on any steampunk forum or message board and you'll discover there are many steampunk fans and creators who agree. A number of steampunk celebrities from the former Seattle Steamcon organizer Diana Vick to *Steampunk'd* contestant and steampunk cosplayer and designer Tayliss Forge have used this boundary, intending to create what I believe is simply shorthand. When someone asks "what is steampunk?" at a party, you're hoping to give them an answer brief enough that they don't start looking for a way to head back to the bar, and "steampunk is Victorian science fiction" is a pretty decent way to explain it, when you're short on time and, potentially, listener interest.

But stating that steampunk is limited only to the Victorian era is fraught with problems. A closer look quickly reveals that the temporal boundaries of steampunk are rather imprecise, and not always as Victorian as a first glance might indicate. Admittedly, there are many steampunk works that are either set within a somewhat accurate or at other times entirely alternate Victorian period. The alternate future of 1973 in which Michael Moorcock's Captain Bastable finds himself in *Warlord of the Air* is, at the very least, evocative of the Victorian period and its culture, though its technologies span the 1920s to 1940s. Moorcock's sequel is set in a postapocalyptic 1904, in the aftermath of a devastating world war. Neither of these can claim to be entirely Victorian since neither is set in the Victorian period. Similarly, Tim Powers's *Anubis Gates* is set just before the Victorian period, in what we call either the Regency or Romantic period.

Every rigid airship pictured in steampunk draws from the Edwardian period if not later, and more precisely from the Wilhemian or Weimar period, since those rigid airship designs are almost always based on German zeppelins, not British dirigibles. Talking about time periods across Europe demonstrates how "Victorian" is problematic not only from a temporal standpoint, but from a geopolitical one as well: requiring that steampunk be Victorian privileges stories or art set in Britain or within the British Empire. German steampunk might best be called Wilhemian speculative fiction, while Swedish steampunks use the term "Oskarian." And what of nineteenth-century spaces without a monarch? Or France, where the government wavered between monarchy and republic? You can see how using the term "Victorian" for the historical period steampunk draws from gets pretty messy very quickly.

So it's not just the historical period "Victorian" evokes that is a problem. It's the geography of history that challenges the limits a solely Victorian steampunk would impose. If steampunk is only Victorian, people assume it can only take place in London (another limitation a publisher set for a writer friend), which excludes one of the biggest inspirations for steampunk, and one its most famous examples, *The Wild Wild West*, both as original 1960s television series and as 1990s film adaptation.

Steampunk Westerns

And *The Wild Wild West* is hardly the only instance of steampunk that evokes nineteenth-century America. From an extended Civil War in Cherie Priest's award-winning novel *Boneshaker* (2009) to the City-Beautiful Movement evidenced in the floating city of Columbia in the video game *Bioshock Infinite* (2011), the American nineteenth century is a favorite steampunk setting.

Steampunk set in the Wild (or Weird) West is very common—nearly as common as steampunk set in London, though I've never done a side-by-side comparison. From the proto-steampunk television series of *Wild Wild West* to the film of the same name, Western Steampunk abounds. It's odd to me that people often make a distinction by calling steampunk set in the American West "Western" Steampunk or Steampunk Westerns but make no such distinction for steampunk set in London, for example, Imperial Steampunk or some such.

Of the deviations from Victorian steampunk, Steampunk set in the Wild West is arguably the least contested to be steampunk proper. But even with Steampunk Westerns, the debates about what can be considered steampunk or not persist. For example, the film version of *Wild Wild West* is indisputably steampunk, while the anime *Trigun* and US television series *Firefly* are contestable. Yet I often have people ask me if either *Trigun* or *Firefly* could be considered steampunk, which leads me to ask the question, "What are they seeing that reminds them of what they think steampunk is?"

Trigun follows the adventures of Vash the Stampede, a gunslinger with a notorious reputation for devastating property damage (which is usually caused by the bounty hunters trying to kill him). While the story line is in many ways that of the classic Western wanderer made famous by TV shows like *Have Gun, Will Travel*, the action takes place on another planet, and is therefore considered a blend of science fiction and Western. Discussions about whether *Trigun* is steampunk will often concede that it has "steampunk elements" but that it is ultimately not steampunk. However, I have to wonder if this isn't simply the same dismissal many works of first-wave steampunk face from the second wave's quest for a more unified aesthetic. Like some of Miyazaki's steampunk, *Trigun* was created in the 1990s, before there was a unified vision for what steampunk should look like.

Somedays, I'm tempted to say Joss Whedon's *Firefly* is steampunk just to watch the fur fly. While the show's aesthetic doesn't perfectly match second-wave steampunk, the basic premise is very similar to *Trigun*—Western in space. Admittedly, the relationship between Westerns and space opera is already a close one, but *Firefly* signaled its relationship to the Western in far more overt ways, from characters' accents to costume and prop design. In the broadest application of the term, *Firefly* is steampunk, science fiction messing with the nineteenth century.

Other steampunk explorations of the Wild West include Joe Lansdale's short fiction "The Steam Man of the Prairie and the Dark Rider Get Down: A Dime Novel," which was made into *The Steam Man*, a graphic novel by Dark Horse Comics. Lansdale's earliest steampunk novel, *Zeppelins West*, has a host of heroes from the Old West such as Annie Oakley, Sitting Bull, Wild Bill Hickok, all traveling in Buffalo Bill Cody's Wild West Show to Japan by airship. Buffalo Bill isn't half the man he was in history, he's perhaps one eighth: he's been reduced to a head in a Mason jar filled with pig urine, which is sometimes affixed to the body of a steam man, designed by Edisonade hero Frank Reade, who often invents in steampunk what he only wrote about in real life (see Paul Guinan and Anina Bennett's *Boilerplate*, another great instance of steampunk in America, for another example of this). But this only scratches the surface of Lansdale's anachronistic deviations and deviances. Lansdale's steampunk is not for the faint nor prudish of heart. It is bawdy, violent, and uproariously funny in the same way that a session of *Cards Against Humanity* can often be. Though sadly out of print (the original editions from Subterranean Press are lovely hardbacks with original art), *Zeppelins West* and its sequel, *Flaming London*, have been collected into an omnibus edition titled *Flaming Zeppelins: The Adventures of Ned the Seal* from Tachyon Books.

And America is only the start of steampunk's journey around the world: to Canada, in Lisa Smedman's novel *The Apparition Trail,* and editor Domonik Parisien's anthology *Clockwork Canada*; to France in both the comic and film of Jacques Tardi's *The Extraordinary Adventures of Adèle Blanc-Sec*; to Japan in the anime *Sakura Wars* and *Kabaneri of the Iron Fortress*; to India in Gail Carriger's *Prudence* and Alan Moore and Kevin O'Neill's comic *The League of Extraordinary Gentlemen*; to Norway in the film and novel of Philip Pullman's *The Golden Compass*; to Tibet in *The Geomancer* by Clay and Susan Griffith; and then, from Germany to Switzerland to Turkey to Russia and back to America in Scott Westerfeld's high-flying *Leviathan* series. After all, when you have an airship, how can you be expected to stay in one place? I could go on, but you see my point.

Steampunk left London a long time ago, and it's been flying around the globe (and beyond, into space!) ever since.

Give me fuel, give me fire, give me steam for my aether flyer!

Some people try to untether steampunk from "Victorian" by saying it takes place in the "industrial era," but this is a really problematic term as well. Do we mean the Industrial Revolution in Britain, which began in the eighteenth century? Do we only include the first one, or the second Industrial Revolution as well? And whose Industrial Revolution are we talking about? When we talk about the Industrial Revolution in the West, we're often talking about a series of events in Great Britain, again limiting the idea of steampunk to a particular place in a particular period. Industrial revolutions occurred elsewhere, coming to the European mainland and Sweden later than England, and the early or mid-nineteenth century and late nineteenth century to Japan. Japan's industrial era lasted well into the early twentieth century, exceeding the Victorian era by decades. So simply saying "industrial era" has the opposite problem that using the term "Victorian" does. Victorian is too precise. Industrial may be too imprecise. Industrial is also troublesome in that it limits the types of technology employed in steampunk, which leads to yet another troubled approach to determining what history steampunk plays with.

Tayliss Forge believes that, in addition to being Victorian science fiction, steampunk should have something to do with the era of steam technology. Again, she's certainly not alone in this sort of restrictive categorizing, which has resulted in the creation of yet another term for works where anachronistic technology is powered by combustion engines instead of steam: "dieselpunk," which is said to draw from the aesthetics of the period between the World Wars and up to the beginning of the atomic age. Game designer Lewis Pollak coined the term "dieselpunk" in 2001 to describe his now-defunct role-playing game, *Children of the Sun*. The term was later championed by Nik Ottens, editor of *The Gatehouse Gazette*, a steampunk/dieselpunk ezine. Ottens emphasized Pollak's idea of dieselpunk as a darker and grittier alternative to steampunk.

The thinking seems to be that once we started using combustion engines, we stopped using steam and began using diesel fuels. The trouble with making the distinctions for steampunk and some other retrofuturistic work of speculative fiction is that steampunk hardly ever uses steam. Steampunk engines are more likely to run on a fictional substance than coal and steam. And what do you do with Cherie Priest's *Dreadnought*, where giant automata run on steam, unless they're from Texas, where they appropriately run their giant robots using diesel. Is it steampunk? Is it dieselpunk? Is it both? Beyond dieselpunk, one finds more terms such as "decopunk" and many others as attempts to further define (or potentially confuse) the landscape of retro-speculative fiction that doesn't fit into the neat and tidy categories of fantasy and science fiction.

Determining taxonomies based on fuel? That way lies madness. Teslapunk (which was originally the name of a video game) has been said to signify narratives that focus on electricity as the primary mode of power. But between Teslapunk and dieselpunk, Scott Westerfeld's *Leviathan* trilogy is all over the map, sometimes within the same book. It's steampunk because it takes place in the Edwardian period? But it's dieselpunk because the war machines of the Clanker nations run by combustion engines? Then it's Teslapunk in the last book because . . . Tesla's in it? Or is it not Teslapunk because Tesla's electrical device is a sham? And from the start, the series is even arguably a bit of biopunk, due to the weaving of DNA strands (called "life threads") to create the biological technology of the Darwinists. There are as many instances of electrical and diesel-powered machines in steampunk as there are ones powered by steam, or as I noted back at the beginning of this book, a litany of fictional substances. We ought to have aetherpunk and magic-crystal-punk then as well.

Raygun Gothic and Atompunk

Raygun Gothic and atompunk are both terms meant to speak to retrofuturistic visions that draw from the architecture and art movements of the 1930s to 1950s. The term "Raygun Gothic" was coined by

William Gibson in his short story "The Gernsback Continuum," which originally appeared in the cyberpunk anthology *Mirrorshades*, but was also anthologized in Ann and Jeff Vandermeer's *Steampunk II*. In the story, the concept associated with Raygun Gothic is "The Tomorrow That Never Was," which sounds antithetical to steampunk, which has been described as the "past that never was." However, Gibson's short story *and* Raygun Gothic and atompunk are all retrofuturistic. They are, as I said earlier, how the past imagined the future.

Steampunk is mostly set in times when there are still frontiers—still borderlands beyond which lies mystery or monsters. And in steampunk times, the greatest frontier of space is yet to be explored at all. Even more fun, that final frontier doesn't have to resemble the one that the Space Race launched us into. While we might know there's no life on Mars, steampunk stories can play off the theories of Giovanni Shiaperelli, which makes writing in such fiction worlds a lot of fun. Not all steampunk that takes place in space could be called Raygun Gothic or atompunk, necessarily. Philip Reeve's children's series *Larklight* has a decidedly industrial feel to its aesthetic, but something about it remains related to film SF like *Flash Gordon* and *Buck Rogers*.

Greg Broadmore's Rayguns series of artworks and books are a mix of industrial design, Art Deco, and the propaganda posters of the two World Wars. The "hero" of the series is Lord Cockswain, the epitome of British imperialist hypermasculinity, who goes to other planets to hunt alien species as trophies in the tradition of the Great White Hunter. I met Greg at Steam Powered, where he was unveiling and selling his Raygun creations.

The retrofuturist stylings of Raygun Gothic and atompunk are all over works that have been described as steampunk. Nemo's Nautilus car from the film *League of Extraordinary Gentlemen* is based on 1930s automobile designs, its sleek lines evocative of the streamline moderne style that is associated with Raygun Gothic. The design of the Rocketeer's helmet and rocket pack have the same sort of design, the influence of which can be seen in steampunk from Greg Broadmore's *Rayguns* series to Marshal Pomeroy's costume in Warren Ellis's comic *Ignition City*. One begins to see the confusion of such subgeneric divisions, since websites like Steampunk Wikia state that Disney's *The Rocketeer* movie is clearly dieselpunk, while I can make a solid argument for it being Raygun

Greg Broadmore's *Victory*, one of several satirical books in the Dr. Grordbort's Infallible Aether Oscillators universe: "Where Science Meets Violence!" The books were companion volumes to the line of incredible hand painted and hand assembled ray gun replicas designed by Broadmore.

Gothic, with Dave Stevens's designs for the Rocketeer's costume being an obvious homage to late '40s and early '50s Republic Studios serials *The King of the Rocketman* and *Commander Cody*. At the very least, it must be admitted that steampunk borrows from these toolboxes as much as it does from any other. And perhaps more importantly, people regularly mistake Raygun Gothic and atompunk for steampunk—and the more they mistake it for steampunk, the more the word steampunk will change to mean those things.

A Messy Hybrid

Steampunk is a messy hybrid, and accordingly, it's tough to define sharp distinctions for when one crosses some arbitrarily imposed line from steampunk to dieselpunk. Furthermore, in some sort of specfic Darwinism, the term dieselpunk hasn't really caught on, whereas steampunk is increasingly used to designate any pre-atomic retrofuturistic work involving speculative elements. Consequently, a movie that some hard-core aficionado might call dieselpunk, like *Sky Captain and the World of Tomorrow*, ends up on a list of great steampunk movies.

So for now, trust me when I say that steampunk's historical toolbox ranges from the early nineteenth century to the middle of the twentieth. Recurring historical figures in steampunk include nineteenth-century fixtures like Charles Babbage and Ada Lovelace (designers of the difference engine, a mechanical-computer that didn't work in real life but always does in steampunk), and Isembard Kingdom Brunel (designer of just about everything else of importance in the British Empire), but also twentieth-century ones like Nikola Tesla (who is often considered a hero), Thomas Edison (often considered a villain because of how he treated Tesla). In addition to historical figures, steampunk plays with technologies from this historical range, anachronistically imagining the early or advanced development of airships, introducing futuristic weaponry such as ray guns, or expanding the capabilities of steam technology beyond its historical application. While steampunk occasionally seeks to be historically accurate, history is more often used as a fictional playground than a foundation for serious historical speculation. We can say with certainty that, alternate history or alternate world, steampunk is *playing with history*. And it evokes but does not necessarily replicate a very particular range in world history, going from the start of the Industrial Revolution to the beginning of the atomic or, in some cases, the digital era.

A useful way of considering this might be the idea of the blast radius from the last chapter on Early Steampunk. Except instead of the naming of steampunk in 1987, one might think of the nineteenth century or industrial revolution, be it under the reign of Victoria, Bismarck, Oskar, or Meiji, as the nucleus of the blast. Steampunk draws most heavily upon styles from this period. But it also draws upon other styles predating and postdating that period. Prior, steampunk seems to have drawn in elements from as far back as the early eighteenth century, perhaps earlier, as evidenced by the *Doctor Who* episode "The Girl in the Fireplace," which takes place in Versailles, France, and involves Madame de Pompadour, a real-world member of the French court and mistress of Louis XV from 1745 to 1751. The episode involves clockwork automatons that do not seem drastically out of place. Post-nineteenth century, the label "steampunk" gets applied regularly to fantastic narratives up to either the end of World War I or the beginning of World War II. I have observed people wondering if speculative fiction set in the 1950s is steampunk.

The desire to limit the period and place that steampunk is set in or draws from is born out of a positive impulse, a desire to have a clear idea what a thing is. While there are fancy goggles and an airship in Ridley Scott's retrofuturistic *Blade Runner*, I think it would be difficult to shoehorn that film into the steampunk family. For a while, any work that showed someone in goggles or flying in an airship was labeled steampunk, and the response to this wild inclusivity was to try and draw up the boundaries for what steampunk is and isn't.

Apparently, someone coined the term "stitchpunk" for Shane Acker's technofantasy film 9, and like the very sock-puppet heroes of the film, the term gained a life of its own. But to categorize stories by an element as arbitrary as animated stitch-dolls results in a genre that conflates the Sackboy characters of the *Little Big Planet* video game franchise with the nightmarish world of Acker's dieselpunk-postapocalypse. This would get immediately messier, given the presence of clockwork and Victorian elements in *Little Big Planet 3*, to say nothing of an automaton resembling

Elvis Presley before he got his leisure suit in Vegas. So what is *Little Big Planet 3*? Steampunk? Dieselpunk? Sockpunk? Presleypunk?

I have to admit, I understand the impulse to come up with a new term. It's a way of putting your "steampunk that isn't your grandma's steampunk" on the map. Jeff Vandermeer lampooned this propensity when he jokingly coined the term "squidpunk." Much to my chagrin, I ran into steampunk fans who were gushing about squidpunk a year later. I can't really complain, though. After all, wasn't that what Jeter was doing decades ago?

But I'm not rejecting dieselpunk or atompunk or any of these terms out of snobbery or some attempt to argue "my _____punk is better!" No, I'm rejecting them because the English language seems to be rejecting them. They're esoteric terms for specialists. I've introduced you to them because they are the close relatives of steampunk and you ought to know they're out there. But when someone picks up a book like Warren Ellis's *Ignition City* in a comic shop, I rarely hear them say, "Is this dieselpunk?" That's not the frequently asked question. The frequently asked question is, "Is this steampunk?"

And while the pedant, the specialist, the gatekeeper, and every other exclusivist know-it-all would like me to tell you all it's not, I'm not sure I can do that in good conscience. You see, language becomes how it's used. As an English teacher, I might not like that the word "random" is used as a designation for social media photo albums that might be more precisely termed "miscellaneous." There's nothing particularly random about choosing to take a photo, then choosing to upload said photo to a social media platform, perhaps going so far as to clearly identify the people appearing in the photo or to come up with a clever caption for it. That is actually the opposite of random. For one to truly have a random photo album on social media, you'd have to take photos at irregular intervals without being aware you were doing it.

And yet the word changes, whether I want it to or not. Is there anything more random than a term like "steampunk" gaining enough cultural currency to last forty years? Steampunk may not have much steam, but the term itself has lots of it, and it only seems to be building steam. So now you know the difference between dieselpunk and atompunk, or maybe you don't at all, and to be honest, neither do I. Because, to

While the fantastic worlds of Zakk Snyder's *Sucker Punch* (2011) ranged from medieval fantasy to science fiction futures, one sequence took place in a vague vintage warzone with trenches, undead soldiers in goggled gas masks, zeppelins, and World War I fighting planes, causing many to ask if the film was steampunk.   *Alamy*

appropriate Billy Joel's lyrics, "dieselpunk, ribofunk, even if it's stitch-punk, it's still steampunk to me." And increasingly, to many others.

In the course of writing this book, I've become more convinced than ever that steampunk, insofar as the term is popularly used, refers to any "old-timey-looking" speculative fiction that takes place after the rise of the Enlightenment and before the splitting of the atom. I'm sure this won't stop anyone from inventing yet another "punk" term as a way of putting themselves on the speculative fiction map, but the proliferation of those terms has not gained the same cultural currency that steampunk has. As a result, steampunk gets used as the descriptor for the design style of moments like the World War I scene in *Suckerpunch* and entire films like *Sky Captain and the World of Tomorrow*. It's similar to how most of us call almost any music from before the twentieth century "classical," while a professor of music history might tell you it's from the baroque or romantic period. Specialists know specialized terms. And now you know some of those. And now you can choose whether you want to use them. Purists will balk at my ostensible "caving" on the boundaries of definition, but since I'm not the King of Steampunk, I'm pretty sure I don't get to make the rules about what people think about it.

Which is why I settled on hyper-vintage for that time-placement feature of steampunk. While it may be too broad a term, I think it fits the range from the English Romantic period to the start of the Atomic Age in America: when we see cars or clothing from this range in history, we might choose to use the term "vintage." And there's an end to the use of that term to describe old objects. We don't call swords "vintage." We're more likely to use words like "ancient" or "medieval." But even once we locate the historical period steampunk plays with, our understanding of it is further complicated in that it messes with not only real-world history, but fictional history as well.

Historical Fiction or Fictional Histories?

I've heard steampunk defined the following way numerous times: "Steampunk is how the nineteenth century would have been if Jules Verne and H. G. Wells's stories were historical accounts, not fiction." On the surface, that description seems to suggest the idea of alternate history, one based in the ideas of technological anachronism. But there's another idea lurking under the surface there: that Verne and Wells's characters could likewise be historical anachronisms. Historically, there is no person like Verne's Captain Nemo. But I can (and have) constructed a sort of fictional biography of Nemo. Others, like American science-fiction writer Philip José Farmer, appropriated Nemo and a number of other Vernian characters to tell their own story in *The Other Log of Phileas Fogg*. Farmer is arguably one of the masters of taking fictional characters and giving them a "history," complete with family trees and anecdotal details. In *Tarzan Alive* and *Doc Savage: His Apocalyptic Life*, Farmer charted the history and genealogy of the Lord of the Jungle and the Man of Bronze. In doing so, Farmer breathed new life into old bones, bringing sophistication and complexity to characters who arguably lacked either. In both these biographies, Farmer justified the exceptional nature of these heroes by way of a meteor striking the Earth near Wold Newton, Yorkshire, England, in 1773. This meteor produced genetic mutation in passersby, thus explaining the exceptional intelligence and strength of characters like Tarzan and Doc Savage, as well as Sherlock Holmes and his nemesis Moriarty.

Maurice Grunbaum takes steampunk outside the confines of Victoriana with his steampunk samurai cosplay.   *Renaud Mentrel*

Farmer's treatment of these characters is called the Wold Newton Family, which exist in the Wold Newton Universe.

The Wold Newton Family and Universe has had a profound influence on steampunk, particularly in works that, instead of simply being about a break in history, treat fictional characters as historical entities. Kim Newman's *Anno Dracula* is certainly a type of alternate history, but instead of asking "what might have happened if Queen Victoria had been assassinated?" it asks, "What might have happened if, instead of being driven back to Transylvania, Count Dracula had succeeded in his invasion of England, going so far as to marry Queen Victoria, thereby becoming the King of England?" Newman's novel is a who's who, not only of historical persona, but also fictional ones. Jack the Ripper is there, but his real identity is a fictional character, not a historical one (and one that I find delightfully convincing, though I don't want to give any spoilers).

This type of fiction is called crossover fiction or recursive fantasy: once again, we see that steampunk is a hybrid, a blending of disparate sources. There are numerous crossover fictions under the steampunk parasol: from the already discussed Jeter novel *Morlock Night* (a mash-up of King Arthur with H. G. Wells's *The Time Machine*) to one of the most famous steampunk comics, Alan Moore and Kevin O'Neill's *The League of Extraordinary Gentlemen* (which combines too many fictional characters and worlds to list here comprehensively, though it can be said in brief to draw from *Dracula*, *20,000 Leagues Under the Sea*, *The Invisible Man*, *King Solomon's Mines*, and *Dr. Jekyll and Mr. Hyde*. See chapter sixteen for an extended exploration).

As you can see, many of the so-called alternate histories of steampunk aren't asking questions about real-world history. They're asking questions about fictional histories, or fictional histories blurred with real-world ones. "What if Verne had met Nemo?" is the question explored in Kevin J. Anderson's *Captain Nemo: The History of a Dark Genius*. "What if a young Arthur Conan Doyle had gone on adventures with a man who formed the inspiration for Sherlock Holmes?" is answered by Mark Frost's *The List of 7* and *6 Messiahs*. Sir Richard Burton is a version of Burroughs's John Carter in Philip Reeve's *Larklight*. The list goes on and on.

So yes, steampunk *is* alternate history. But steampunk can also be an alternate world, one that is completely secondary to our own, primary world. Or steampunk can be about alternate histories of the secondary worlds of stories that are so well known they feel like history, repeatedly blurring the lines between fiction as history, and history as fiction. But not all nineteenth-century fictions are given equal play in the worlds of steampunk, as we'll see in the next chapter.

4

Are Jules Verne and H. G. Wells Steampunk?

Steampunk is occasionally alternate history, but just as often, if not more often, it's fictional history: the alternate history of fictional worlds. As we saw in the last chapter, it's less often about the historical London than it is some fictional version of it. The other toolbox steampunk frequently draws from is literary, looking to nineteenth-century writers as inspirations for content frequently, and style occasionally. In addition to using the historical foundation of Henry Mayhew's *London Labour and the London Poor*, James Blaylock lists other Victorian-era writers as inspirations for his steampunk writing, such as Robert Louis Stevenson, Jules Verne, and H. G. Wells. An understanding of who these writers were and what their fiction was about helps us understand steampunk better.

It's not every author of the nineteenth century, nor is it even the most respected that steampunk writers draw their inspiration from. Instead, it is the predecessors who laid the groundwork for the genres we now call horror, science fiction, and fantasy. In the nineteenth century, such terms were not used to describe these genres. Instead, authors wrote Gothic fiction, scientific romances, and fairy tales. It is from these writers that steampunk most frequently finds its inspiration.

But in a conversation about the relationship between steampunk and nineteenth-century literature, there are two names that surface quicker than any others: French writer Jules Verne and British writer H. G. Wells. There are those who would like to name these giants the grandfathers of steampunk, and a number of lists of steampunk authors and works include them, but that's ridiculous. If they are the grandfathers of any modern genre, it is science fiction, and insofar as steampunk is science fiction, these two writers are certainly part of its pedigree. But to call their works steampunk is terribly misleading. Once again, we find ourselves facing the question of whether steampunk is Victorian science fiction, but with another set of answers related to the lives and books of the writers from that period.

Is Steampunk Victorian Science Fiction?

To begin somewhat pedantically, the term "science fiction" wasn't in popular use in the Victorian period. It had been coined but wasn't in mainstream use until the early twentieth century. Even early pulp science-fiction magazines like *Amazing Stories* used other compound words or portmanteaus like "scientifiction" to describe this new and growing genre. Still, it's also fair to argue that science fiction existed before there was a word to categorize it. H. G. Wells's *The Time Machine* and *The War of the Worlds* are unarguably science fiction, but were not called that at the time. There was no genre to define Mary Shelley's *Frankenstein* upon its release, while the works of Verne were called Extraordinary Voyages, while both his and Wells's works are also often called scientific romances.

But even if we accept certain stories of the nineteenth century as "science fiction before there was a term for it," steampunk still shouldn't be considered Victorian science fiction for a very important reason. It's the same reason that would stop me from calling James Whale's famous cinematic version of *Frankenstein* starring Boris Karloff a work of Victorian (or more precisely, Georgian) science fiction. Whale's film is a product of the 1930s. Shelley's novel was about parenthood and abandonment more than it was about mad science. Today, use of "Frankenstein" most popularly indicates that science has gone horribly wrong. Genetically modified foods are called "frankenfoods." But when Mary Shelley wrote the original novel in 1818, the scientific method hadn't existed long enough for anything scientific to go horribly wrong. The nineteenth century was dominated by a fairly uniform positivity toward scientific progress. World War I would be one of the first great blows to this rose-colored view of progress, and the detonation of the world's first nuclear weapons would be the nail in the coffin. After Hiroshima, we could say without question that science could go, and had gone, horribly wrong.

Consequently, the time in which a work is written impacts the attitudes of that work. Even when Verne or Wells is being progressive, they're still progressive for their time, not necessarily ours. They are concerned with the matters of the day before them. Even when Verne was anticipating future technologies, he was still writing about current affairs. Some of these narrative themes take on an air of timelessness: the issues of Empire that Wells was addressing in *War of the Worlds* still have resonance today, as evidenced by the way in which Steven Spielberg applied them to twenty-first-century America in his cinematic version in 2004. But clearly, the Empire being invaded by a force vastly superior in technology has changed: for Wells, it was Britain. For Spielberg, it is the United States. That isn't simply a cosmetic change because Wells was British and Spielberg is American; it's one with thematic resonance. I'd never consider calling Spielberg's *War of the Worlds* "Victorian science fiction" simply because it's based on a work of science fiction from the Victorian period.

Likewise, consider steampunk works related to Wells's *War of the Worlds*. In the second volume of *The League of Extraordinary Gentlemen*, writer Alan Moore and artist Kevin O'Neill create a faithful retelling of Wells's seminal alien invasion story, but diverge from it in ways that, though based in literature and facts about the nineteenth century, make the story fresh for twenty-first-century readers. In Wells's novel, the Martian invaders are killed when they fall ill to earthly bacteria, a way for Wells to critique British complacency resulting from overconfidence in the might of their global empire. Whereas later versions of the alien invasion story, especially American ones, would see humans triumph over the invaders, it was evolution that was the hero of Wells's novel. While humans also triumph over the invaders in *League Vol. II*, the destruction of the Martians is bought with massive collateral damage of impoverished South Londoners. *League*'s bacteria conquer not as evolutionary agents, but as chemical warfare perpetrated by the British government's secret service. In both works, British powers are being criticized, but in ways relevant to the time of publication.

Outside the socially conscious work of H. G. Wells (Verne has his moments of social commentary but is not as consistent in this as Wells was) lurks a more compelling reason to avoid characterizing steampunk as Victorian science fiction. The Victorian and Edwardian periods predate a number of human rights movements, and the social advances made in the wake of those movements. To conflate steampunk with Victorian science fiction alone is to associate an often progressive and socially conscious movement with works like the Edisonades, which are unabashedly (and at times even proudly) racist and misogynist. In the nineteenth century, women could not yet vote, were trapped in social roles and norms that cosseted them either as the "angel in the house" or the "whore in the streets," and were generally thought of as inferior to men. Despite being legally freed from slavery, African Americans would not begin to see the benefits of the Emancipation Proclamation of 1863 for a century, until after the 1960s and the civil rights movement in the United States. Chinese and Japanese immigrants were seen as the "Yellow Peril," while European outsiders were demonized metaphorically in works such as Bram Stoker's *Dracula*. Female characters are in short supply in both Verne and Wells's entire oeuvre. In short, while the Victorian and Edwardian periods were filled with technological advances, when it came to issues of race and gender, we still had a long way to go.

Nevertheless, given the frequency with which Verne and Wells's names are invoked as inspirations for or examples of steampunk, a brief look at each writer and their most influential works on steampunk is in order.

Jules Verne and the *Voyages Extraordinaires*

Jules Verne was a nineteenth-century French writer, which is yet another reason to avoid calling steampunk "Victorian." Verne would have bristled at the idea of being called a Victorian writer. He was the son of a successful naval lawyer whose failure to follow in his father's footsteps led to his grand success as one of France's most celebrated writers. While Verne aspired to be like Alexandre Dumas, author of *The Three Musketeers* and *The Man in the Iron Mask*, his brilliance was revealed and honed in the genre he effectively created by combining science fact with exciting fiction: *voyages extraordinaires,* the extraordinary voyage tale. Verne grew to great celebrity in France writing these science adventures for French publisher Pierre-Jules Hetzel, who wanted fiction that would entertain readers while teaching them about science. The conservative French school system in the mid-nineteenth century was not teaching science, and Hetzel wanted to fill the gap in a way that would attract young readers. Jules Verne proved to be his solution, starting with his first novel, *Five Weeks in a Balloon* in 1863.

However, Verne's work was never just for children. Adults also enjoyed the *Voyages Extraordinaires,* although in the English-speaking world, Verne's reputation remains largely as a writer of mere boy's adventure stories. This reputation owes much to the inadequacy of Verne's early translators, who were poorly paid and required to change or omit entire sections that reflected badly on the British Empire. Consequently, Verne is thought of as being unconcerned with complex social issues. This is far from the truth.

In the original French text of *20,000 Leagues Under the Sea*, antihero Captain Nemo, the enigmatic inventor of an advanced submarine called the *Nautilus*, gives an impassioned speech about the injustice of the Indian pearl-diving industry in the British Raj, a section that demonstrates an interest in social justice to rival Wells's criticism of British colonialism in *The War of the Worlds* or Dickens's criticism of child labor in *Oliver Twist*. These passages were entirely excised from the earliest English translation of *20,000 Leagues Under the Sea*. The same problem exists for many of Verne's most popular works. They are repeatedly released in often visually stunning editions with lush illustrations such as the 2015 Sterling Press edition illustrated in steampunk style by William O'Connor. The French text of *The Mysterious Island*, sequel to *20,000 Leagues Under the Sea*, reveals Captain Nemo to be an Indian Prince who helped lead the Sepoy Mutiny, a historical uprising of Indian nationals against the British colonialists. In the English version, one is given the impression that Nemo got involved because of peer pressure, but that he really didn't want to be a revolutionary, while in the French original he is revealed as the "heart and soul of the uprising." It is only in recent years that Verne's reputation is slowly being rescued by excellent translations. Sadly, these are rarely the ones employed in prestige format editions, to say nothing of free e-books of the *Voyages Extraordinaires;* as a result, the majority of English readers continue to experience a lesser version of Verne.

The Sterling Children's Books edition of Jules Verne's *20,000 Leagues Under the Sea*, which contains one of the early translations of Verne's novel, but is filled with amazing steampunk illustrations by William O'Connor.

It is therefore most likely that those flawed translations have exercised the greatest and most widespread influence on steampunk, since it is only since the 1960s that better translations began to be produced, and only in the last two decades in any earnest. Nevertheless, those flawed translations were still good enough to convey the heart of the Vernian imagination.

Through the broad conceptual framework of the *Voyages Extraordinaires*, Verne's influence is more diffuse than specific, and as we'll discover in the following chapter, more about the cinematic perception of his works than the works themselves. Presenting on Verne at steampunk conventions has taught me that, while people may know *of* Jules Verne and have some concept of the sort of writing he did, few have actually read any of his books; if they have read any, they have read a poor translation or some children's abridgement. More likely, they've seen one or more film adaptations of Verne's work. Consequently, I've learned to never assume people know exactly what I'm talking about when I mention even his most famous works: *Journey to the Center of the Earth, 20,000 Leagues Under the Sea,* or *Around the World in 80 Days.* They are likely to be thinking of the film versions rather than the books.

Yet it is the broad concept of the *Voyages Extraordinaires* that makes the greatest impression on steampunk, making Verne's name synonymous with the idea of adventure and exploration in marvelous machines. A famous adage of the nineteenth century was that inventions like the steam train and the telegraph "eliminated space and time." Verne's fantastic machines allow his adventurers not only to travel at optimal speeds, thus eliminating space and time, but to do so in style: Verne's marvelous machines are the nineteenth-century equivalent of a private jet or tour bus capable of traveling many times beyond even the current top speed for said vehicle, and doing so with maximum efficiency—the plane or bus would run on electricity generated by water, but run faster than petroleum-burning vehicles of the same type. Verne's marvelous machines included such comforts as a twelve-thousand-volume library, a pipe organ, a smoking room, and/or some form of fully enclosed or perfectly safe viewing window or platform that allowed the adventurer and Verne's readers to observe the unexplored wilds of the world removed from all potential harm (unless it helps the plot to remove this safety).

In *20,000 Leagues Under the Sea*, it's a submarine (one whose speed remained unbeaten by real-world Seawolf-class submarines until only recently); in *From the Earth to the Moon*, it's a projectile launched from a cannon (an endeavor that would actually result in all the astronauts being flattened into human pancakes), and in *Robur the Conqueror* it's a giant flying machine (which can maneuver better than a Harrier Jet).

The influence of these extraordinary vehicles on steampunk cannot be overstated. The reality of airships is far less romantic than steampunk idealizes. The airships in Gail Carriger's steampunk novels provide perfect examples of how steampunk heroes and heroines ride in decadent comfort compared to their real-world equivalents. They contain tea rooms and comfortable cabins, only crash when narratively necessary, and in her *Finishing School* series, comprise an entire floating school, a sort of Hogwarts of the air for young ladies training to be assassins. Carriger has never read Verne, but is clearly influenced by the diffuse idea of the fantastic vehicle of comfort.

There is an exception to Verne's broad influence on steampunk, and that is his novel *20,000 Leagues Under the Sea*. Steampunk creators reference *Leagues* more than any other of Verne's works. As I argue in the next chapter, I think that's largely due to the popularity of the Disney film, but here are a few examples that focus on either the plot of *Leagues* or Verne's most famous character, Captain Nemo: Kevin J. Anderson's *Captain Nemo: The Fantastic History of a Dark Genius* is a crossover fiction of many of Verne's works, but it focuses primarily on a wonderful recursive fantasy that asks, "What if Jules Verne had been good friends with Nemo?" Nemo's *Nautilus* makes an appearance in the anime film *Empire of Corpses* and the television series *Nadia: The Secret of Blue Water*. Nemo is one of *The League of Extraordinary Gentlemen*. The majority of Arthur Slade's second Modo book, *The Dark Deeps*, is a fast-paced retelling of *Leagues*. It was the theme for Steamcon III.

H. G. Wells: Martians, Time Machines, and Beast Men

Unlike Verne, Wells's influence is more specific than general: steampunk writers and artists tend to revisit events, creatures, and machines of

Wells's most famous works while leaving behind the bigger themes, from the earliest steampunk of K. W. Jeter's *Morlock Night* acting as sequel to *The Time Machine* to Dynamite Comics' *Legenderry* series use of *The Island of Doctor Moreau*. Unlike Verne's broad themes of exploration and adventure, however, Wells's governing attitude of cynicism toward the human race as one step away from plunging into the abyss of bestial behaviors is

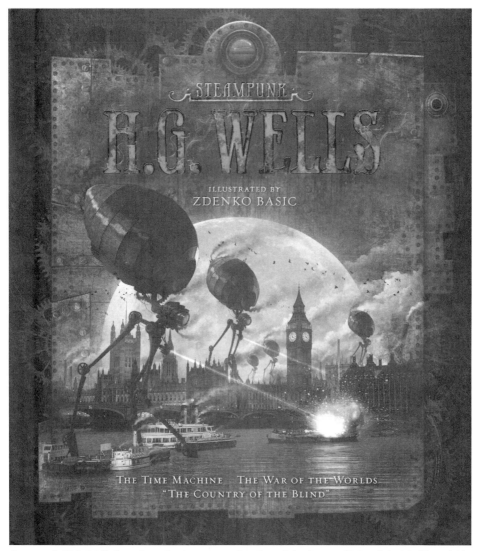

Steampunk H.G. Wells from Running Press contains the original text of *War of the Worlds* and *The Time Machine* and "The Country of the Blind" with illustrations by steampunk artist Zdenko Basic.

overlooked by these pastiches. Instead, steampunk writers see opportunities to have steampunk machines fight Martian tripods from *The War of the Worlds*, endanger heroes through fistfights with the subterranean bestial Morlocks from *The Time Machine*, or see heroines menaced by Doctor Moreau's beast men.

This isn't to say that steampunk never borrows from Wells's social and political themes, but rather that the social and political borrowing could as easily be from non-Wellsian sources. Many steampunk books play with the stratified upper and lower divisions of society outlined in *The Time Machine*. S. M. Stirling's novel *Whitechapel Gods* places a section of London behind a containment wall, forcing its people to build upward; Cliffhanger/DC Comics' *Steampunk* series imagines a London with a dark labyrinthine underground and an upper level of aristocrats and light; Jim Butcher's *The Aeronaut's Windlass* features Albion, an enclosed fantasy layer cake of a city. All, somewhat predictably, have the haves on the top and the have-nots beneath. But having the hardy workers below and the soft upper class above could owe as much to Fritz Lang's silent classic *Metropolis* as it does *The Time Machine*. The idea of the rich on top of a hierarchical pyramid is hardly Wells's alone.

It's an irony that one of steampunk's most politically minded progenitors is rarely utilized effectively to put the "punk in steampunk." A notable exception to this reduction of Wells's themes in favor of props and creatures is Alan Moore's madcap take on *War of the Worlds* in *The League of Extraordinary Gentlemen*. The earliest example of this emphasis on Wells's plot points at the expense of his politics is also the first American steampunk novel, *Morlock Night* by K. W. Jeter. As noted in chapter two, Jeter is less concerned with the symbolic class divisions of Morlocks and Eloi than he is with a reincarnated King Arthur getting medieval on the Morlocks with Excalibur. This is even odder when one considers Jeter's use of Henry Mayhew's *London Labour* as a source for *Morlock Night*. *The Time Machine*'s symbolic stratification of London society in the Morlocks and the Eloi could have easily echoed the subterranean denizens of the London sewers and the wealthy above them. Yet this was not Jeter's agenda.

Nor does this trend end with Jeter. Recently Bill Willingham—best known for his comic series *Fables*, which imagined fairy-tale characters in the modern world (a definite precursor to *Grimm* and *Once Upon a Time*, television series that share the same premise)—placed the heroes of Dynamite Comics into a steampunk world called *Legenderry*. Characters as disparate as the sword-wielding Red Sonja (originally of Marvel Comics *Conan the Barbarian* fame) and the 1970s television action hero the Six Million Dollar Man (rendered the Six Thousand Dollar Man, apparently adjusted for reverse inflation) team up to solve a globe-spanning mystery. At one point, they are beset by Doctor Moreau's beast men. But instead of having anything to do with Wells's big idea that humans are just one step away from being beasts, these beast men are simply monstrous challenges for the able-bodied (or in the case of the Six Thousand Dollar Man, clockwork-bodied).

This is not a critique of steampunk, mind you—it is simply an observation. It demonstrates that more often than not, steampunk is mostly about the open-ended question, "Wouldn't it be cool if . . . ?" than it is about more challenging questions. Steampunk creators are far more likely to use Wells's stories like a toy box filled with action figures and vehicles than they are to go rooting around for thematic inspiration.

Jane Austen, Bram Stoker, and Charles Dickens Walk into a Bar . . .

There are many Victorian writers that steampunk draws inspiration from, but an exploration as deep as the one I've just done with Verne and Wells is both beyond this book's scope and would misrepresent the frequency with which those other writers are utilized as inspiration. While first-wave steampunk is largely Wellsian when it announces direct association with an earlier author, second-wave steampunk went mining the past for any writer it could slap goggles onto. Consequently, there are a few notable writers who have been used repeatedly in steampunk.

Jane Austen: As with Verne, it's the widespread idea that Austen's works are lighthearted and romantic, and both these concepts proved hugely successful for steampunk. Every one of Gail Carriger's steampunk books and novellas evoke a sense of Austen's comedy of manners, and many writers and creators, seeking to emulate Carriger's style or success (or both), have employed lighthearted love stories to attract readers or viewers. The impact of steampunk's popularity can be seen in the stylized cinematic adaptation of *Pride and Prejudice and Zombies*. Most recently, Austen's impact can be seen on the Norton-Award-winning steampunk-in-space adventure *Arabella of Mars*.

Bram Stoker: I've already mentioned *Dracula* as an example of a nineteenth-century cultural artifact, but it's also a favorite of steampunk creators, such as Kim Newman's amazing crossover fiction *Anno Dracula*, which imagines the alternate fictional history of what England would have become had Dracula not been stopped by Van Helsing and his brave cohorts. NBC's short-lived *Dracula* series asked the same question, but with the change that Dracula is a hero, not a monster.

Charles Dickens: Once again, it's not any particular work that steampunks emulate, but an amalgam of Dickensian features. Save for the complete absence of any steampunk technology or alchemical magic, *Dickensian*, BBC's crossover fiction of Dickens's wider storyworld, demonstrates how certain character types from *Bleak House*, *A Christmas Carol*, and others need no introduction: the streetwise orphan, the doomed prostitute, the corrupt businessman, the noble thief. There are exceptions to this general use of Dickens's archetypes: Cory Doctorow's short story "Clockwork Fagin" announces its literary debt to *Oliver Twist*. But while the characters of Dickens's original work and their legion film and stage adaptations pale in comparison to steampunk's use of Dickensian London, a dark and menacing labyrinthine city of threatening alleyways and narrow streets filled with refuse and vice.

Sir Arthur Conan Doyle: Doyle's use in steampunk is less about the writer than his most famous characters, Sherlock Holmes and his side-kick, Doctor Watson. Mark Frost's *The List of Seven* plays yet another "author meets character" game with Doyle as Watson meeting the inspiration for Holmes. Watson is the protagonist of *Empire of Corpses*. Homages to the detective and the doctor are found in Warren Ellis's comic book *Aetheric Mechanics*.

While I could mention many other writers from before the 1930s such as Edgar Allan Poe, H. P. Lovecraft, E. Nesbit, Oscar Wilde, Hans Christian Andersen, and the Brothers Grimm, each instance of those authors' impact on steampunk is less widespread, though becoming more frequent as new steampunk writers seek new directions for steampunk that *aren't* directly inspired by these better-known and oft-used writers.

Boy Inventors, Girl Geniuses

A frequently mentioned predecessor to steampunk is the Edisonade, a term coined by John Clute for dime novels that featured young American boy inventors who use their superior intellects to overcome dangerous situations. The name Edisonade refers to the hero of these stories, a young Thomas Alva Edison. Edisonades combine exploration adventure, wherein the hero takes a journey into dangerous, uncharted country, with xenophobic colonization fantasy, wherein the hero defeats enemies from other countries or other worlds. While this might sound like typical fodder for steampunk stories, and has certainly filled pages of books about steampunk, the fanciful tales of a fictional Thomas Alva Edison or Frank Reade Jr. are not necessarily the clear-cut steampunk inspiration they appear to be.

Like the idea that Verne and Wells had a direct influence on steampunk, it's questionable whether the Edisonade has had any real impact on the writers responsible for steampunk. Did you know about Edisonades before you read this chapter or any book on steampunk? Likely not. But you may have known about Jules Verne and H. G. Wells. That's because their works survived, while the Edisonade disappeared into obscurity, only to be rescued from the forgotten corners of literary history by librarian extraordinaire (and I use that term genuinely, without a hint of sarcasm) Jess Nevins, who spoke of them in the introduction to the Tachyon anthology *Steampunk*, the first of its kind. The influence of Nevins's introduction trickled down into a good deal of steampunk writing about the roots of the genre. Steampunk fans trying to legitimize what they were doing sought early instances of steampunk writing. The problem with assuming that the Edisonade is a precursor to steampunk is simple: one of the hallmarks of the Edisonade is the boy inventor, and I can't think of *one* steampunk story with a young boy inventor. This isn't to say there isn't one. I just haven't read it, I suppose. Nevertheless, for the space books on steampunk give to the Edisonade, you'd think we'd see more instances of this key feature of the boy inventor.

While steampunk may not have many, science fiction in general abounds with examples of boy inventors, like Tom Swift, the Hardy Boy of space travel. The abundance of Tom Swift books for young readers is where we see the survival of the boy inventor. What we can say about the Edisonade is that it inspired books like *Tom Swift*, and *Tom Swift* in turn helped build American science fiction in the twentieth century. Since the first book was published in 1910, there have been five series, the most recent in 2006–2007. The early series were an influence on science-fiction giants such as Isaac Asimov and Robert Heinlein.

But there are few boy inventors in steampunk. Where we have young men in YA series like Kenneth Oppel's *Airborne* or Arthur Slade's *Hunchback Assignments*, they are all men (or boys) of action, not intellect. While they are clever, they are not brilliant savants creating clockwork automatons in their basements. There are more examples of boy inventors in Japanese steampunk, with Jean in *Nadia: Secret of Blue Water* and Ray Steam in *Steamboy*. While this may be indicative of a troubling stereotyping of young males as physically capable but intellectually inept, that's a problem for another book, since that trend extends beyond steampunk to the construction of that famous trio of children in the *Harry Potter* series, to name but one non-steampunk example. But Hermione Granger, the brightest witch of her age, is certainly indicative of the steampunk's trend in terms of youthful inventors.

What we find in steampunk is not boy inventors but girl geniuses. Phil and Kaja Foglio have been regular attendees at steampunk conventions around North America since Steam Powered in 2008. I knew of Phil's work from his comic adaptation of Robert Aspirin's *Myth Adventures* in the 1980s and was excited to see he had a steampunk book out called *Girl Genius*, a collection of a web comic he and wife Kaja had been working on since 2001. But *Girl Genius* bears little resemblance to the Edisonades or Tom Swift books. It takes place in a fully secondary world that has elements of nineteenth-century Europe, where a young woman has the spark that makes her a brilliant inventor.

Steampunk is filled with girl geniuses. Gail Carriger's *Finishing School* series features a ten-year-old girl whose abilities with technology far exceed those of boys much older than her. However, she is not the focus of the narrative, whereas Cora, an inventor's assistant (who does all the work for him) from Adrienne Kress's *The Friday Society*, is one-third of the narrative focus. Think steampunk *Charlie's Angels* with an inventor, a magician's assistant, and a ninja, and you have the gist of it. Sometimes, the girl genius isn't a real girl; like the robot boy from *Rust*, the clockwork woman in Ekaterina Sedia's *Alchemy of Stone* is a brilliant alchemist, the fantasy equivalent of scientific invention (insofar as alchemy was a historical precursor to the advent of the scientific method).

Now, someone might say girl geniuses are just gender-bent Edisonades. And while that might be true on the surface, we have to consider how great a change that gender shift is. But traditionally, girls don't get to play in the lab. If they do, they're the assistant who isn't smarter than the inventor. Steampunk regularly imagines women doing things they weren't supposed to be doing in the nineteenth century, as we will see repeatedly throughout this book. While many people will tell you that the key features of steampunk are clockwork, airships, and corsets, one of the recurring features of steampunk is giving women opportunities that the nineteenth century either didn't afford or would have been difficult for them to find. In this respect alone, neither Jules Verne nor H. G. Wells were forward thinking.

I came across the girl genius trope most recently in David D. Levine's *Arabella of Mars* (2016), the first in *The Adventures of Arabella Ashby* series. The series' eponymous heroine is adept at repairing automatons, though she has no formal training and only sporadic opportunities to practice her art, since it's considered unladylike to tinker with clockwork robots. But Arabella, born on Mars, is most unladylike in a number of ways, thwarting her chances at a good marriage, and by extension, her sisters' potential for the same. Consequently, the cover blurbs praising *Arabella of Mars* compare the book to the work of Jane Austen, and rightly so. There is certainly an air of the comedy of manners in the opening chapters, before Arabella's scheming cousin sets off to Mars to murder her brother and gain the family inheritance; Arabella sets off in pursuit, and her expertise with automatons gains her passage on board a spacefaring sailing vessel that rides the cosmic winds between planets. Arabella must masquerade as a boy as she learns the ropes, and her life and adventures as part of the crew of the *Diana* are what garners the book many comparisons to Patrick O'Brien's Aubrey-Maturin series, which was adapted into the film *Master and Commander*. Both of these comparisons are accurate ones: what mystified me was that so many of them said that the book was also like the work of Jules Verne—and these comparisons were made by science-fiction writers! It seems like using Jules Verne's name is a way of saying "this is steampunk" without saying "this is steampunk."

Granted, there's the legend that Verne himself stowed away on a sailing vessel as a cabin boy at the age of eleven. And many of his books are concerned with fantastic voyages on sailing vessels. And a few are about journeys into space. But none of them are about sailing vessels that travel into space utilizing the cosmic winds to travel at speeds in excess of 7,000 knots, or 12,964 km/hour. The provenance of such a sailing vessel is more likely found at the movie theater, in films like *Treasure Planet* and the 2012 version of *The Three Musketeers*. So how did Verne become a synonym for nearly every retrofuturistic design? I suspect that, contrary to the regular appeals to steampunk's literary roots, film adaptations and pastiches of Verne and Wells's scientific romances are as much, if not more, to blame for the inception and continued interest in steampunk. With seven decades of twentieth-century cinema based on and inspired by the scientific romances of the nineteenth century, it's hard to argue steampunk was inspired by Verne and Wells's writing alone. From Disney's classic *20,000 Leagues Under the Sea* to the B-movie matinee pastiche of *Warlords of Atlantis*, steampunk is as much a child of the screen as the page.

5

In the Grand Fantasy Tradition of Jules Verne and H. G. Wells

While nineteenth-century literature cannot be ignored as steampunk's literary ancestor, I can't help but wonder at the impact the proliferation of cinematic adaptations of Victorian scientific romances from the 1950s to 1970s had on the impulse to create steampunk in the 1970s and '80s. Even if this cinematic niche did not have an impact on the writers who began steampunk, it certainly had an impact on steampunk fans, who regularly cite the hugely successful Disney adaptations of *20,000 Leagues Under the Sea* and *Around the World in 80 Days*, MGM's *The Time Machine*, or the family fantasy-musical *Chitty Chitty Bang Bang* as their love of "steampunk before they knew what it was."

At the root of many fans' love of steampunk is a nostalgic longing for Saturday matinee filmgoing experiences between 1951 and 1971, when an average of at least one new Verne film was released annually, along with numerous adaptations of the works of H. G. Wells, Edgar Rice Burroughs, Edgar Allan Poe, and Sir Arthur Conan Doyle, to say nothing of films that were not direct adaptations of a particular work, but were instead made in the science-fiction, fantasy, or adventure tradition of these authors.

One of the earliest and most famous films of all time (you might not know the film, but you know that image of the pie-faced Man in the Moon with a rocket in his eye), George Méliès's *A Trip to the Moon* is a perfect place to begin charting the way cinema links the nineteenth century to the twentieth, since the 1902 silent film is an amalgam of elements from Verne's

From the Earth to the Moon and *Around the Moon* in the first half, and H. G. Wells's *The First Men in the Moon* in the second. It's unsurprising that both Verne and Wells were used as inspiration and source material, since both writers were still immensely popular at the dawn of the silent film era. This blending of Verne and Wells is also a perfect way to begin charting the relationship between twentieth-century film and steampunk, since both Méliès as filmmaker and *A Trip to the Moon* as film are featured prominently in Brian Selznick's *The Invention of Hugo Cabret* and its film adaptation by Martin Scorsese, *Hugo*. Both book and film are beloved by steampunks for their stunning visuals, evocative of a vintage past.

There were other direct adaptations of both writers' works, as well as other silent films that were inspired by the spirit of the scientific romances and adventure stories. But besides *A Trip to the Moon*, few are relevant enough to the discussion of steampunk to include here.

There is one exception: one of the most notable Vernian silent films is the 1916 production *Twenty Thousand Leagues Under the Sea*, which combines scenes and characters from *20,000 Leagues* and *The Mysterious Island*. Despite being the first film to include underwater photography, and garnering major box-office success, it is little known today, and accordingly, cannot be said with certainty to have impacted steampunk, though the exceedingly steampunk set of Mezco Toys' "Cabin Control Nemo," which bears more than a passing resemblance to Allen Holubar as Nemo standing on the deck of the *Nautilus*, indicates otherwise. Nevertheless, the film is noteworthy for Holubar's portrayal of Captain Nemo as Indian Prince Daaker (the film's misspelling of Dakkar). This would be the last time Nemo would be portrayed as Indian until Naseruddin Shah played the Captain in the film adaptation of the comic series *The League of Extraordinary Gentlemen* in 2003. In both cases, the press would be misled to assume that Nemo's ethnicity was not Verne's idea but an egalitarian innovation. The 1916 film is also important in considering later adaptations that follow in its footsteps by replacing the ever-loyal manservant Conseil with Arronax's daughter and then including Nemo's daughter. In later iterations, these female Conseils either fall in love with Ned Land, as in the 1997 Hallmark telefilm of *20,000 Leagues*, or Nemo, as in the 1997 ABC miniseries of *20,000 Leagues Under the Sea*, where it is Nemo who has the daughter who falls in love with the youngest Arronax in Verne cinema's history by Patrick "McDreamy" Dempsey of *Gray's Anatomy* fame. As we'll see in the chapter on steampunk anime, both Nemo's daughter and Nemo's love interest are utilized in *Nadia: Secret of the Blue Water*, while Alan Moore's *League of Extraordinary Gentlemen* spin-off focuses on Nemo's daughter's rise to power. In every one of these instances, the inclusion of a woman or women aboard the *Nautilus* is an adaptive response to Verne's underwater androtopia.

There was a stream of films that sought to capitalize on the success of silent Verne adaptations from the late 1920s through to the 1950s, with limited success. In the meantime, radio adaptations along with reprints in pulp magazines kept interest in Verne's work alive. But it would be cinema that would restore Verne's popularity during the Cold War era and launch the stream of films based on his and Wells's scientific romances.

Disney's *20,000 Leagues Under the Sea* (1954)

Disney's 1954 film version of *20,000 Leagues Under the Sea* was a major box-office hit and remains one of the company's most successful live-action films. It is unarguably the elephant in the room when discussing cinematic scientific romances, Verne, Wells, or otherwise. Because of the massive success of *20,000 Leagues Under the Sea*, when most people think of the *Nautilus* or Captain Nemo, they think of the Disney film. It's the same thing with MGM's *Wizard of Oz*. Very few people have read L. Frank Baum's *The Wonderful Wizard of Oz*. But even if they haven't *seen* the musical classic, most people are aware of an iconic moment, like Judy Garland singing "Somewhere over the Rainbow." Likewise, when I have spoken on Verne's underwater adventure epic, there's a sort of glazed look on many attendees' faces until I say something about the Disney film, at which point the room lights up. This is less the case among millennial fans of steampunk, but steampunk boomers are likely to remember seeing the film when it was first released or in a rerelease matinee, while Gen-Xers who grew up in the 1970s might recall seeing it as the major network event it was when it premiered on television in October 1976 as part of the *Walt Disney's Wonderful World of Color* series. Others may have first or further experienced the story (as I did) in the proliferation of movie tie-in books, records, and View-Master slides.

The first half of the film follows Verne's story line fairly faithfully, with only a few minor changes. But the shift in focus from Verne's first-person narrator Professor Arronax (who, despite remaining the narrator of the film, is not the focus of dramatic action) to the robust Canadian harpooner Ned Land is a significant one. Paul Lukas was sixty-three years old when he played Arronax, and was already suffering memory loss, which may have contributed to his flat performance and upstaging by the thirty-eight-year-old Kirk Douglas in the lightly comic role of Ned Land. Douglas's casting as Ned Land would have created an expectation in viewers who knew the rising star as a tough, rugged individualist:

Harper Goff's brilliant design for Captain Nemo's remarkable submarine, *The Nautilus*, has proven to be an iconic influence on steampunk.   *Alamy*

Douglas's Land is a solidly American hero, in contrast to the active foil he provides to the passive Conseil in Verne's novel.

In the Disney film, Arronax's sympathies with Nemo are vastly over-shadowed by Land's need for freedom, so that the second half of the film becomes a prison break narrative, pitting Land as an American man of action against Nemo as the man of science. This break in fidelity from the novel is not necessarily detrimental to the film's narrative: the final act on Nemo's secret island base created a template for many Cold War films, from other Verne adaptations such as *The Fabulous World of Jules Verne* (1958), to James Bond films like *Dr. No* and *You Only Live Twice* and parodies of the same in the "Dr. Sinister" episode of *The Flintstones*, the *Austin Powers* films, and in Pixar's *The Incredibles*. In a way, James Mason's Nemo is like a Bond villain in a world without Bond, the precursor to the popular idea of the quintessential steampunk mad scientist. Arthur Slade would place his mad scientist on such an island in the final book of the *Hunchback Assignments* series, *Island of Doom*.

One of the film's greatest strengths was its advances in underwater photography, which echo Verne's lengthy didactic passages on sea life. Like those moments of marine-life exposition, the underwater scenes in *20,000 Leagues* likely drag on for modern viewers, but when one con-siders that the scuba gear used by cameramen was still in its infancy, the images take on a greater significance. Public access to such diving gear in the 1950s was unheard of (recreational use of scuba gear was not widespread until after the end of the Cold War), and Kirk Douglas found it a wonderful opportunity to learn how to use the equipment. In 1954, Disney was one of the best champions of nature cinema, long before the ubiquity of wildlife documentaries or the opportunity to google underwa-ter species and locate a corresponding image or video. Despite not being the first instance of underwater photography, the underwater scenes in *20,000 Leagues* are magnificent, especially compared to other contem-porary instances. Disney's underwater photography sparkles and shines with well-lit underwater environments, a clarity the underwater scenes in 1954's *Gojira* do not even begin to approach. In 1954, *20,000 Leagues* provided one of the greatest special effects of all: moving Technicolor imagery of a world beneath the waves.

Of course, the actual special effects in 20,000 *Leagues* were its other area of critical praise; the film won the Academy Award for Best Special Effects that year. Again, while modern audiences might find the movie's iconic battle with the giant squid a bit clunky, it was cutting-edge in 1954. The scene had originally been shot under brighter lighting, which revealed the puppeteers' wires for the animatronic squid's tentacles. The scene was reshot with night lighting and falling water to replicate a storm, making it far more frantic and exciting. It is unarguably the most memorable scene in the film: a survey of the film's marketing and paraphernalia show the squid attacking the *Nautilus* more often than any other moment. The association between this monster and Verne would be further entrenched in future film adaptations, even when the source material called for no tentacled monsters.

Harper Goff's *Nautilus*

But just as iconic as the squid is the submarine vessel it attacks. Fiction author Greg Bear suggested that steampunk began with Harper Goff's design for the *Nautilus* in the Disney film. Goff's *Nautilus* design is a far cry from the cylindrical metal vessel from Verne's book, or in the illustrations of Edouard Riou and Alphonse de Neuville. Goff's design looks like a sea monster, with its porthole eyes and vicious ridges meant for tearing out the bottom of a boat. As with any film that takes place in an oceangoing vessel, it is the setting within a setting. To use the *Nautilus*'s motto from Verne's original novel, it is *Mobilis in Mobilis,* or "mobile within the mobile element," which may be understood as "free in a free world." The miraculous *Nautilus* empowers Nemo to be free beyond the restraints of imperial civilization.

Yet this masterfully mobile vessel is likely the most iconic of all cinematic renderings because it was made to stand still, to become an exhibition at Disney parks in three locations. The *Nautilus* was not only a cinematic creation but an exhibit at Disneyland from 1955 to 1966, allowing visitors to walk through *Nautilus* sets from the film, decorated with authentic props, experiencing the cinematic world for themselves. Then again from 1971 to 1994 as a hugely successful underwater submarine ride through a massive lagoon filled with locations from the film at Disney World; while Tokyo Disneyland has featured the film and ship as inspiration for one of its attractions since 2001, creating over sixty years of nearly unbroken opportunities to have a firsthand experience of the *Nautilus*.

Attending my first steampunk convention, I was struck not only by how many *Nautilus* items were for sale in the vendor's hall, but how all of them were based on Goff's design. At Steamcon 2011, the theme was "20,000 Leagues Under the Sea," and the convention art gallery contained the work of the Vulcania Volunteers, a group of artists and craftsmen devoted to creating art based on Goff's design of *The Nautilus*. I was lucky enough to meet Mikel Suave, model maker for the VV, and he showed me the VV's gorgeously accurate blueprint art of Goff's *Nautilus*.

Consequently, it is not only Goff's *Nautilus*, but a long line of copies and homages to his design that have kept that distinct silhouette in the popular imagination, from the submarine's subsequent cinematic appearances in sequels and pastiches (which gained a second life in regular repeats on television) like *The Mysterious Island* (1961) and *Captain Nemo and the Underwater City* (1969), to steampunk art like Myke Amend's "The Rescue" to many of the ships in "A Catalogue of *Nautilus* Designs" at *Vernianera.com*, to every movie tie-in product from posters to scale-model kits. Steampunks love Goff's *Nautilus*, and many get a glassy, nostalgic look in their eye when I show a presentation slide of the famous submarine, which rivals the generic zeppelin for supremacy as the ultimate steampunk vehicle.

As to one of the reasons steampunks love going up in the air in their flying machines, we must turn to the next massive success of Vernian cinema, which is most famous for a mode of flight Verne wasn't nearly as enthusiastic about as many would believe him to have been.

Disney's *Around the World in 80 Days* (1956)

The success of *20,000 Leagues Under the Sea* led Disney to seek other possible hits in Verne's repertoire, hoping to have lightning strike twice. As it turned out, Disney's next Vernian adaptation, *Around the World in*

The cover of the DVD release of Disney's *Around the World in 80 Days* (1956), featuring the iconic balloon from the film which was never in Verne's original novel.

80 Days, exceeded the success of its predecessor, winning critical and popular praise, as well as five Academy Awards, including best picture.

Around the World in 80 Days, both as novel and cinema, is a picaresque adventure tale that follows the journey of the punctual and pragmatic epitome of British gentleman Phileas Fogg and his French valet Passepartout as they race to win a bet by circumnavigating the globe in eighty days. This is probably the Verne story most people could summarize in brief, since its title says it all; what most people can't recall are all the modes of transportation Fogg and Passepartout employ to win their race against time. While the odd elephant—and in the Disney film, ostrich—are employed, steam trains and steamships are Fogg's transportation of choice, with Verne creating a fictional argument for the oft-stated claim that steam technology along with the telegraph had annihilated time and space. Readers of Verne's original novel are often surprised to discover that there is no travel by hot-air balloon.

As with Dorothy's ruby slippers, the hot-air balloon pictured on almost all the marketing for Disney's version of *Around the World in 80 Days* demonstrates how much the Disney films eclipsed Verne's novels, despite tie-in versions being published with each film's release. The dissonance between the perception that steampunk is Verne-based/inspired and the reality of Verne's work is seen in the proliferation of the balloon image in association with the film: it was Verne's belief that heavier-than-air flight would win the day for air travel, not lighter-than-air. Nevertheless, the proliferation of the image of Fogg and Passepartout in the balloon alongside Verne's name on posters and tie-in media for *Around the World in 80 Days* ensured that Verne would forever be associated with travel by balloon. The wondrous airship in the 1961 film *Master of the World* starring Vincent Price would further extend that association to airships, securing the conflation of Verne with steampunk airships.

The reason for the inclusion of the balloon in the film is readily apparent. Once Fogg and Passepartout take to the air, 1956 audiences were treated to aerial views of the French countryside: in both cases, these were spectacles few filmgoers had the opportunity to experience firsthand. While the 1950s are considered the beginning of the golden age of air travel, as evidenced by a discarded frame narrative for the film that featured the cast on board a modern airliner, the cost of a transoceanic flight was too expensive for most travelers. Modern viewers of the film find it tedious, but that's to be expected given the nature of modern CGI spectacles and the ability to see the entire world through a Google image search. Not so the original audiences: just as *20,000 Leagues Under the Sea* captured underwater vistas in a time before scuba lessons, *Around the World in 80 Days* provided an opportunity to see the world from vantage points few filmgoers had access to. For all these reasons, the balloon scene achieved producer Michael Todd's hope that it would be the visual motif most associated with the film.

Around the World in 80 Days also repeated Disney's other great cinematic contribution to steampunk: the studio's consistent refusal to contemporize Verne's work, as was done with *From the Earth to the Moon* in 1958 and with recent Verne adaptations in the 3D films *Journey to the Center of the Earth* and *Journey to the Mysterious Island*. A contemporary adaptation can be very successful in its own right, as evidenced by both George Pal and Steven Spielberg's versions of Wells's *War of the Worlds*. But in these early and hugely successful adaptations, Disney created a technicolor Vernian utopia. They are unapologetic period films, albeit ones that romanticized that period, making it brighter and more cheerful: the cinematic nineteenth century of *Around the World in 80 Days* is arguably the one many steampunks want to live in, not the one Dickens described, with coal smoke falling from the sky like snow, or the one Mayhew documented with its abject poverty. Disney's Vernotopia is filled with color, and while there is danger, it is never truly life-threatening. But Disney was not the only filmmaker creating a storyworld out of Verne's novels. Across the ocean and behind the Iron Curtain, a Czech filmmaker whose reputation was also in animation had turned to live action to adapt Verne's adventures for the screen.

The Fabulous World of Jules Verne (1958)

In addition to Mayhew, Verne, and Robert Louis Stevenson, early steampunk writer James Blaylock credits his interest in Victorian fantasies to *The Fabulous World of Jules Verne,* an award-winning movie by Czech film legend Karel Zeman. Zeman began his career in film just as Disney had, by making animated shorts. Like Disney had with *Snow White*, Zeman demonstrated an aptitude for longer animated narratives before branching into cinema that combined both animation and live action in 1955 with *Journey to the Beginning of Time*, which contained several nods to Verne's *Journey to the Center of the Earth*.

But it was *The Fabulous World of Jules Verne* that was Zeman's greatest contribution to steampunk: released in seventy countries, it was shown in ninety-six theaters in New York alone, while in Japan, it was screened in one of Toho's largest theaters, exposing audiences around the world to Zeman's wondrous cinematic storytelling. The film's English title is a testament to how bankable Verne's name was in the 1950s; Joseph Levine, one of the men responsible for the successful American edit and release of the Japanese *Gojira* as *Godzilla King of the Monsters* in 1956 was the entrepreneur who brought Zeman's Vernian vision to North America in 1961. It was his idea to retitle the film rather than translate its Czech title as *The Deadly Invention*. Levine arguably hoped that Verne's name would draw audiences.

But Zeman's highly stylized cinematic vision clashed with what American audiences expected of science-fiction films, and *The Fabulous World of Jules Verne* was not a box-office success in the United States. Instead, it gained a cult following among cinema and SF aficionados who saw the genius of Zeman's approach, such as filmmakers Terry Gilliam and Tim Burton, whose films in turn provided inspiration for second-wave steampunk. Many of Gilliam and Burton's films bear the inspirational stamp of Zeman's stylish approach. *The Fabulous World of Jules Verne* has been praised as one of the greatest Verne adaptations ever made. And while Zeman's film is certainly faithful to *Facing the Flag*, the Verne novel it is based on, it is also peppered with plot and visual references to *20,000 Leagues Under the Sea* and *Robur the Conqueror*. It has airships, balloons, submarines, and even a monstrous octopus attack. But it wasn't just Verne's stories Zeman sought to adapt. As with all of his live-action films, Zeman utilized a stylistic continuity in *The Fabulous World of Jules Verne*. In *Journey to the Beginning of Time*, it had been Czech artist Zdeněk Burian's paintings of the prehistoric world. In *The Fabulous World of Jules Verne,* it was French artists Léon Benett, Édouard Riou, and

Alphonse-Marie-Adolphe de Neuville, whose engravings illustrated the original editions of Verne's works.

The production design of *The Fabulous World of Jules Verne* emulates those engravings, so that every set, many of the costumes, the matte paintings, props, stop-motion puppets, and miniature models are decorated with the wavy lines common to engravings. Only the actors are spared this treatment. The effect is visually stunning, and is indicative of Zeman's approach to special effects that showcase their contrivance and make no attempt to appear photorealistic, in opposition to the increasingly realistic direction North American films were going and would continue to go. *The Fabulous World of Jules Verne* feels like a silent film at many points, engaging in the same cinematic art that silent classics like *Metropolis*, *Faust*, and *The Cabinet of Dr. Caligari* had achieved.

Like Disney's *20,000 Leagues Under the Sea*, *The Fabulous World of Jules Verne* is clearly a Cold War film, a warning about the proliferation of nuclear weapons. Both films share the volcanic hideaway and the character of the mad scientist (in Zeman's film embodied by two characters), both true to Verne's *Facing the Flag*, which might be argued as the seminal instance of both mad scientist and secret lair.

In America, Verne would receive one more period treatment before Wells would join him in Hollywood's cinematic past, establishing another Verne-association in the popular imagination, that of the lost world story, whereby explorers discover a world out of time or place. While some consider H. Rider Haggard's *King Solomon's Mines* the first lost world story, Verne's *Journey to the Center of the Earth* beat Haggard by thirty years. *Journey to the Center of the Earth* added dinosaurs to Goff's *Nautilus* and Todd's balloon to images Verne's name would bring to mind. Perhaps it was the success of a film featuring giant lizards that would inspire Columbia Pictures, the makers of the 1961 *Mysterious Island*, to secure the talents of stop-motion legend Ray Harryhausen to populate Captain Nemo's island with fantastic creatures such as a monstrous crab and giant bees. Whatever the case, both *Journey to the Center of the Earth* and *The Mysterious Island* were further cogs in a machine that was making Verne's name popularly associated not only with adventure but fantastic adventures. At the same time, that machine was about to incorporate H. G. Wells into that association.

George Pal's *The Time Machine* (1960)

MGM's *The Time Machine* was the second of George Pal's adaptations of H. G. Wells's novels. As mentioned earlier, the first was *The War of the Worlds* in 1953. *War of the Worlds* was a huge critical and financial success, and like *20,000 Leagues Under the Sea,* won the Academy Award for special effects. But *The Time Machine* differed from *War of the Worlds* in that Pal stuck far closer to Wells's novel, making minor changes while keeping the period setting. By contrast, *War of the Worlds* received two changes of setting—location was changed from England to America, and the time from late Victorian period to contemporary Cold War.

While the initial setting of *The Time Machine* is the late Victorian period, the film is purely a Cold War product. Whereas Wells's Time Traveler skips from the nineteenth century directly to A.D. 802701, George, played by Australian actor Rod Taylor, makes several stops between New Year's Eve of 1899 and the far future. George feels a stranger in his own time, when his country is embroiled in the Boer War: "It seems people aren't dying fast enough," he states, and observes that science seems dedicated only to inventing "new, more efficient weapons to depopulate the earth."

George expresses a desire to live in the future when war is no more. Consequently, against his best friend's advice, he enters his time machine and leaves the nineteenth century, arriving in 1916 to find one of his friends has died in World War I. The next hop takes him to 1940, where he witnesses the Blitz of London during World War II. And finally, he witnesses the destruction of the planet by nuclear apocalypse in 1966, a scene that, despite dated special effects, is chilling when you consider 1960s audiences witnessing a near and present danger of atomic warfare. This entire section is the creation of screenwriter David Duncan, but it is consistent with themes in Pal's films, which despite being spectacular examples of the imagination of disaster, are filled with images that call for the rejection, not valorization, of violence. Even the design of the time machine follows this: rather than make its motive power nuclear, Pal encouraged designer Bill Ferrari to choose a different fuel source: consequently, unscientific as it may be (and therefore all the better to stand as an antecedent to steampunk), a pure crystal powers the time machine.

For Pal, nuclear energy was a symbol of destruction, not hope. The use of atomic weapons in *War of the Worlds* only shows humanity's impotence in the face of the alien invasion. Likewise, nuclear power is uniformly negative in *The Time Machine*, bringing an end to twentieth-century civilization across the globe.

This film is therefore another example of why it's misleading to call steampunk "Victorian science fiction" or to suggest that cinematic adaptations like *The Time Machine* are early instances of steampunk. Pal's *Time Machine* is a product of the Cold War, with Cold War concerns. In first-wave steampunk in England and the US, only Michael Moorcock echoes

Rod Taylor as George Wells sitting in Bill Ferrari's iconic time machine in George Pal's 1960 adaptation.   *Alamy*

some of these concerns. Japanese steampunk is very concerned with the problems of nuclear energy, but that is endemic of all Japanese science fiction. Of course, the threat of nuclear destruction looms large in the minds of the only nation on Earth to have been attacked with nuclear weapons.

Pal's *Time Machine* further shows its provenance in 1960 by its optimistic and therefore un-Wellsian ending. Despairing that the human race will ever achieve peace, George rockets into the far future, where he finds London replaced by a verdant landscape unmarred by violence. As in Wells's novella, George discovers the Eloi, meets Weena (the film replaces the platonic relationship of the novella with a romantic one that would be far more appealing to 1960s moviegoers), and is forced to battle the Morlocks to retrieve his stolen time machine and return to his own time.

However, two small changes result in a far different conclusion: first, George never travels to the point in the future where the sun is dying and Earth is a virtually uninhabited wasteland. Secondly, Weena does not die. Both of these changes provide the film with a positive ending, echoing the sentiments of postwar America: while war was in the past, there may be hope and love in the future. Where Wells ends with uncertainty about the Time Traveler's fate, it is clear that Pal's Time Traveler returns to the future for romantic reasons: both the romance with Weena and the romantic notion that the future can be changed for the better. The ending subtly asks the audience to consider such changes, as George's friend and his housekeeper puzzle over the library's three missing books, clearly taken by George back to the future. George's friend asks the housekeeper, "What three books would you have taken?" And we ask ourselves the same question.

Ferrari's Time Machine

But the legacy of *The Time Machine* has not been that implied question, but rather the question of what time one might travel to if given the chance to ride Bill Ferrari's brilliantly designed time machine. As with Goff's *Nautilus* and Todd's balloon, Ferrari's design for the scale prop of the time machine has been a vintage cinematic icon, arguably as memorable as the film itself. The first half of the 1993 TV documentary *Time Machine: The Journey Back* chronicles the prop's colorful history, from creation to loss to thrift store recovery and journey into further notoriety. Now owned by Bob Burns, the prop has appeared on a number of programs, most notably in a promotional short for *Back to the Future*, where Michael J. Fox sat in the machine to segue to talking about Marty McFly's time-traveling Delorean the character traveled in.

Interest in creating scale models of Ferrari's time machine began almost immediately after the film was made, with one of the most famous renderings created the same year as the film's release by the then twenty-year-old Michael Minor, who would go on to work as an art director for the original *Star Trek* series and the first two *Star Trek* motion pictures, as well as help to restore the time machine prop after Bob Burns acquired it. A google search for "time machine models" reveals that people are still purchasing model kits or custom-building their own. Like the *Nautilus*, North Americans have had repeated exposure to Ferrari's time machine. And like the *Nautilus*, it's clear that Ferrari's design influenced the look of second-wave steampunk. The combination of brass rails, the great brass disc with its rococo arabesques and rivets (365 in total, to mirror the days of the year), the hybrid of antique Victorian chair with an old-fashioned barber's chair created yet another proto-steampunk icon: beneath the water, one travels in Goff's *Nautilus*. Above, you travel by Vernian airship or balloon. And to travel to the future, you take Ferrari's time machine.

The massive success of these films, along with other Verne and Wells adaptations set in both the nineteenth and the then-contemporary twentieth century resulted in the belief that the mere presence of Verne or Wells's name on the marketing would ensure box-office success. In the 1960s, not a year passed without the release of a Vernian or Wellsian film adaptation. One last notable instance of these adaptations was the 1964 production of Wells's *First Men in the Moon*, which featured the original novel's fictional Cavorite, an antigravity substance that permits the journey to the moon, and has been borrowed by steampunk art and fiction, most notably in Alan Moore and Kevin O'Neil's first volume of *The League of Extraordinary Gentlemen*. Like Columbia's *Mysterious Island*, *First Men in the Moon* had employed the "Dynamation" of Ray Harryhausen for special effects such as the "moon cow," a giant red-eyed caterpillar-monster that menaces the explorers (and might well be an inspiration for the Ohm in Miyazaki's *Nausicaä of the Valley of the Wind*). Furthermore, the film's spacesuit design recalls the bell-helmeted diving suits of Disney's *20,000 Leagues Under the Sea*. That bell-helmeted suit is another fixture of steampunk iconography, anticipating the diving-suit-clad cyborg Big Daddies of the *Bioshock* video game franchise

In this way, *First Men in the Moon* is a stylish blend of Wellsian narrative and Vernian cinema, mirroring the conflation of these two science-fiction giants as box-office tickets to a wondrous and exciting yesteryear. So much so that by the 1970s, it was no longer necessary to directly adapt Verne and Wells. One could simply create an entirely original film in the tradition of those writers, or more accurately, the tradition of over fifty years of Vernian and Wellsian cinema.

Hi! I'm Doug McClure! You May Remember Me from Such Films as . . .

In addition to the host of direct adaptations of Verne and Wells (however tenuous the connection between adaptation and original proved to be in terms of fidelity), there were a number made "in the grand fantasy tradition of Jules Verne and H. G. Wells," as the description for *Island at the Top of the World* reads on iTunes. While not all films made in the spirit of Verne and Wells cinema admitted the inspiration as explicitly, they all convey what the names of Verne and Wells evoked in audience expectations by the 1970s: giant monsters (preferably a squid or a dinosaur, or in the case of *Warlords of Atlantis*, both), volcanoes (or at the very least, subterranean lairs with lava lakes), submarine vessels (from other *Nautilus*-like supersubs to bathyspheres), and infernal devices (the zanier the better).

It's clear that many 1970s filmmakers perceived the Victorian and Edwardian period as a time of adventure and exploration, but among the most memorable was the team of English director Kevin Connor and American actor Doug McClure. Connor had only directed one film for British horror production house Amicus, a company attempting to compete with the giants of 1960s horror films Hammer Film Productions, when he was asked to direct *The Land That Time Forgot*. Doug McClure was better known in America than Britain, and as a country singer, beer ad celebrity, and for a recurring role on *The Virginian*, a TV Western; but McClure was about to become known for a different sort of nineteenth-century adventure. His name would become synonymous with the Amicus films, if the DVD packages of the trilogy are any indication: it is McClure's name, rather than Amicus or Kevin Connor's direction, that are used to market them.

Connor and McClure took their maiden voyage with Amicus in 1975 with *The Land That Time Forgot,* the first in a trilogy of films based on Edgar Rice Burroughs's *Caprona* books. It was not the first time Burroughs's work had been adapted for cinema; however, for nearly sixty years, those film adaptations had been dominated by his most famous creation, Tarzan. *The Land That Time Forgot* was the first time one of the *Caprona* books was adapted for screen. While not particularly retrofuturistic or hyper-vintage, *The Land That Time Forgot* was still set in a past that was becoming romantically distant: the Great War. The plot is simple: a group of survivors from a torpedoed British merchant vessel commandeer the German U-boat responsible for their plight. Both groups inadvertently travel to the island of Caprona, inhabited by both dinosaurs and cavemen. Like Verne's *Journey to the Center of the Earth*, it is a lost world tale, and both Burroughs's original novel and the film owe an inspirational debt to that heritage.

Some noteworthy trivia, perhaps only apparent when looking at the pedigree of steampunk, is that science-fiction and fantasy legend Michael Moorcock is credited along with James Cawthorn for the screenplay of *The Land That Time Forgot*. It had been only four years since the release of Moorcock's proto-steampunk novel *The Warlord of the Air*, and only one since the release of its sequel, *The Land Leviathan*. But it wasn't Moorcock's interest in scientific romances that prompted his work on *Land That Time Forgot*; it was anxiety over an unfaithful adaptation of one of his own novels. The film proved to be Moorcock's first and final foray into screenwriting: frustrated with the film's laughably lackluster special effects and studio interference, he and Cawthorn both declined to work on the sequel to *The Land That Time Forgot*.

Despite the screenwriters' misgivings, *The Land That Time Forgot* was a major, if not blockbuster, success, prompting Amicus to try Burroughs's material again: rather than working on the immediate sequel to *The Land*

That Time Forgot, the producers turned to *At the Earth's Core,* the first book of Burroughs's *Pellucidar* series, to produce an equally popular, if not even worse film. The low-budget B-movie quality of the Amicus films is evident from the inclusion of both *The Land That Time Forgot* and *At the Earth's Core* in the Netflix reboot of *Mystery Science Theater 3000*, a comedy series that mocks terrible films. The episode with *At the Earth's Core* contained a number of steampunk jokes, such as "engines at maximum steampunk" and "gluing some gears to an old hat turns low self-esteem into high self-esteem . . . punk."

As with *The Land That Time Forgot*, *At the Earth's Core* involves a journey to a lost world, this time beneath the Earth. While the opening moments contain promising special effects, most of the film is slow moving, cheaply made, and poorly performed. But its popularity cannot be denied, coming in as the eighteenth most popular film in Britain in 1976. The film's legacy, as well as the tendency to closely associate Verne and Burroughs's hollow earth stories, is evidenced by how much the 1993 version of *Journey to the Center of the Earth* borrows from *At the Earth's Core* rather than Verne's original novel.

The People That Time Forgot is a direct sequel to *The Land That Time Forgot*, once again turning to Burroughs's Caprona books for source material. The film concerns an expedition (led by Ben McBride as played by Patrick Wayne, John Wayne's son) to find the missing adventurers from *The Land That Time Forgot*. Released in 1977, the film would have the stiff competition of George Lucas's *Star Wars* to contend with at the SF box office (as well as sharing the side-bun hairstyle sported by both Carrie Fisher as Princess Leia and Sarah Douglas as Lady Charlotte, a reporter documenting the expedition. But Princess Leia and Lady Charlotte shared more than just a hairstyle: both were early attempts to create women who weren't just damsels in distress, and steampunk is filled with female leads who are the fruition of that feminist vision). As is common knowledge, *Star Wars* dominated the 1977 box office, becoming the highest-grossing movie in history, a feat it would retain until the release of *E.T. the Extra Terrestrial* in 1982. But *Star Wars* was more than just a financial success: George Lucas's film series would forever change the perception of B-movie science fiction as low-budget, lowbrow kiddie fare, and along with the rise of home video entertainment, consign films like *The People That Time Forgot* to the cinematic purgatory of direct-to-video markets.

It may seem like a digression to be taking a look at the influence of *Star Wars* on popular culture in a book on steampunk, but that influence informs one of the impulses behind second-wave steampunk, which this chapter is meant to demonstrate. While films like Disney's *20,000 Leagues Under the Sea* and *Around the World in 80 Days,* and George Pal's *The Time Machine,* are well crafted works that earned both popular and critical praise, the Amicus films did not. They are products of a largely bygone era in filmmaking, save for contemporary studios like *The Asylum,* which thrive by making films "so bad, they're good."

But given my own nostalgia for these low-budget adventure films, I can't help but wonder how many steampunk creators felt much the same and decided to play with "the tradition of Verne and Wells" themselves. But crafting fantastic adventures in the post-*Star Wars* world is very different from crafting them before audiences traveled to that galaxy far, far away. Contemporary audiences and readers are far more willing to consume fantasy and science fiction. As with the growth of any genre, an increase in demand leads to an increase in competition.

Today, a sequel like *The People That Time Forgot* would receive a budget grandiose in comparison to the one Kevin Connor was working with in '77. Consider *Jurassic Park III,* a sort of lost world tale, which, despite receiving middling to low critical reviews, was spectacle enough to be a box-office success. One might decry the acting and story of modern sequels, but they're positively brilliant when compared to the slipshod writing of the Amicus films. In short, *Star Wars* raised the bar for science fiction and fantasy. Creators looking to emulate the stories of childhood favorites like *The People That Time Forgot* would have to take the raw materials of the story but leave behind the hackneyed writing and wooden, stereotyped characters.

The People That Time Forgot was both the conclusion of this loose trilogy of Burroughs films, but also the swan song for Amicus productions. However, it was not the end for Connor and McClure, who would go on to collaborate on one last proto-steampunk production that would mash up all the elements that go into "the grand fantasy tradition of

Jules Verne and H. G. Wells (and Edgar Rice Burroughs)." Rather than being a direct adaptation of any one of these writers' works, *Warlords of Atlantis* (also billed as *Warlords of the Deep*) is like a greatest hits album of what cinematic scientific romances had come to be known for: it features the mandatory monsters of the genre, the iconic giant octopus (which over time had eclipsed the squid of *20,000 Leagues Under the Sea*) and an indeterminate species of dinosaur. It has scientists and explorers, sunken treasure, and a secret world with an ancient race of aliens beneath the ocean.

Warlords was written by Brian Hayles, a television writer who had worked on *Doctor Who*, and the time-travel hybridity of that series is evident in *Warlords*. While *Warlords* does not draw particularly from Verne, Wells, or Burroughs, it is certainly evocative of what audiences had come to think of when they thought of these writers. As a kid growing up in the '70s, seeing *Warlords* on the screen didn't make me think of Verne, Wells, or Burroughs in particular. It made me think of them all as a sort of hybrid collective.

And I don't think I am alone in this experience. As an adult who studies the writing of Verne and Wells, I know full well the differences between them, differences that are even sharper when brought into contrast with the writing of Edgar Rice Burroughs. But I am also aware of what marketing is trying to do when it includes that "in the tradition of" line. It is synthesizing the audience's expectation of what it means to see a film based on or inspired by Verne, Wells, and Burroughs. And that is precisely what many people interested in steampunk are looking for: a twenty-first-century approach to "the tradition of Verne, Wells, and Burroughs." But many popular articles on steampunk seem to trace that tradition directly from the nineteenth-century literature straight to the pens, keyboards, sewing machines, and lathes of steampunk writers and artists. Where books on steampunk *do* mention these films, it's more as a quick footnote before rushing on to the main event of steampunk proper.

What all the films in this chapter have in common is a sense of spectacle. A very particular niche of spectacle. It's not the sleek, high-tech spectacle of most science-fiction films in this period, with ultramodern rocket ships, shiny spacesuits, and clean white surfaces. It's a neo-Victorian spectacle: airships, baroque-looking submarines and spacesuits, menac-ing monsters of the deep or the deep past. It's a spectacle of yesteryear, made with contemporary glitz and whimsy. And to ignore two and a half decades of solid, neo-Victorian spectacle as a factor in the growth of steampunk is foolish. So perhaps when someone says steampunk is inspired by Verne and Wells, they really mean the cinematic tradition they inspired.

6

The Underground Resistance

Steampunk in the 1990s

In 1977, two crucial works were introduced to fantasy and science fiction. One was *Star Wars*, a cinematic space opera. The other was *The Sword of Shannara*, an epic fantasy novel. Both were hugely successful. Both utilized the talents of the Hildebrandt Brothers, who were best known at the time for their Tolkien calendars, with their trademark hypersaturated, light-filled style. This connection is not insignificant. Both *Star Wars* (arguably more science-fantasy than science fiction) and *Sword of Shannara* arguably traded on the popularity of *The Lord of the Rings* in the public consciousness of the 1970s. *Star Wars* had its wizard, its sword fights, and its Dark Lord. The first *Shannara* book is, at best, an homage to Tolkien's trilogy, and at worst, a blatant rip-off. It was the first of many such 1980s novels to fill a gap, not for more original fantasy, but for more fantasy that in one way or another replicated the experience of reading *The Lord of the Rings*.

It has been said that there is no science-fiction equivalent to Tolkien's influence on fantasy. Instead, there are multiple voices that are lauded as the giants of science fiction: Isaac Asimov, Arthur C. Clarke, Robert Heinlein, Ursula K. Le Guin, Ray Bradbury, Philip K. Dick. But unlike single authors, *Star Wars* would become to science fiction what Tolkien is to fantasy, at least insofar as the popular perception of science fiction outside dedicated fandom goes.

Michael Drout credits the rise of cyberpunk to the refusal to produce science fiction like *Star Wars*. I credit the rise of steampunk to a refusal to be either *Star Wars* or *Shannara*.

One of the most basic ways of differentiating science fiction and fantasy is that science fiction imagines fantastic possibilities rooted in the physical sciences, while fantasy imagines fantastic impossibilities rooted in magic. In other words, the basic idea is that the fantastic elements in science fiction such as robots or interstellar travel *could* potentially happen, whereas the ideas in fantasy such as magic swords and flying on a broomstick never will. Steampunk incorporates elements from both genres: it is often technocentric like science fiction, but rarely provides a probable explanation for its fantastic technology. Instead, it almost always imagines either a fictional substance like Wells's Cavorite or *Star Trek*'s dilithium crystals or rigorous magical ritual with a name like alchemy or thaumaturgy to account for why steampunk's idealized past has better technology than we do today. In this way, it is fantasy. Remember, steampunk technology looks like science fiction, but most often works like magic.

There is another way in which steampunk overlaps these genres: basic definitions of science fiction and fantasy also say that science fiction is about the future, while fantasy is about the past. At one time, the imagined futures of science fiction were mostly the far future. With the coming of cyberpunk in the 1990s, it became more common for that future to be just around the corner. Similarly in fantasy, Tolkien's influence often resulted in imaginary far pasts that were always a romanticized version of the medieval or Renaissance period. But unlike science fiction, imagining a more recent past was less commonplace until the 1980s. Steampunk provided an opportunity for science-fiction and fantasy writers to reject both temporal choices. It is neither the medieval past nor the immediate or far future. Instead, it was a setting that had been widely underutilized in post-Tolkien fantasy, and almost entirely overlooked by science fiction (after all, it *was* the past).

So why is it, if steampunk blends both science fiction *and* fantasy, that it is widely understood to be a subgenre of science fiction? And why have so many people said that steampunk arose from cyberpunk, when none of the early writers were cyberpunk writers? I believe the culprit is the book that lifted steampunk out of relative obscurity and put it on the map like no book by Blaylock, Jeter, or Powers had.

The Difference Engine (1990)

In 1990, William Gibson was one of the hottest names in science fiction, with the critical and financial success of his cyberpunk *Sprawl* trilogy behind him. The first of that series, *Neuromancer* (1985), made cyberpunk and Gibson's name famous in science-fiction fandom. If you trusted many of the steampunk book lists on the internet, you'd think Gibson had done the same for steampunk. There's no arguing that Gibson's next book, a collaboration with Bruce Sterling called *The Difference Engine*, was a success: it was nominated for several science-fiction awards and has been in print since its publication.

Like other Gibson novels, *The Difference Engine* tells three characters' stories that are linked, unbeknownst to those characters. These three characters are Sybil Gerard (from the nineteenth-century novel *Sybil* by Benjamin Disraeli), a courtesan with a score to settle; Edward "Leviathan" Mallory, a robust paleontologist-explorer who is the focus of much of the novel's action; and Laurence Oliphant, a Royal spy. Their stories converge around a mysterious set of innovative computer punch cards and the various factions seeking to acquire them.

But *The Difference Engine* owed much of its success to William Gibson's name, not its narrative: the success of the *Sprawl* trilogy had ensured that any book with Gibson's name on the cover would be picked up by science-fiction fans with high expectations. So it's not surprising that many people who have never heard of James Blaylock or K. W. Jeter know about *The Difference Engine*. But what I've discovered in my conversations with steampunk readers is that while many of them credit *The Difference Engine* with popularizing steampunk in the early '90s, fewer actually own the book, and of the brave few who started reading it, even fewer ever finished it. Attempting to ape the style of nineteenth-century writing, *The Difference Engine* is a bit tedious, and unlike *Neuromancer* and its cyberpunk sequels, *The Difference Engine* features very little fast-paced, gritty adventure. It does a wonderful job of exploring the counterfactual question, "What if Charles Babbage had succeeded in making a working mechanical computer in the nineteenth century?" It explores the social, economic, and technological ramifications of such a break in history. And as such, it's a great example of alternate history.

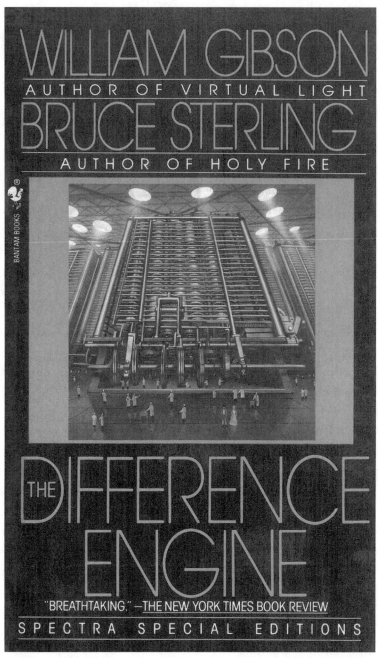

The cover of *The Difference Engine* (1990), one of the most famous works of steampunk fiction.

But it's debatable whether or not it exerted any significant influence on later iterations of steampunk. The shadow cast by *The Difference Engine* is a large one, but it's also given rise to a number of misconceptions. First, that steampunk is alternate history. As was shown in chapter three, it's clear that steampunk fiction and alternate history are not synonymous. But because *The Difference Engine* is alternate history and is also one of the most famous steampunk books ever published, people assume steampunk is likewise alternate history.

The other oddity of *The Difference Engine*'s large shadow is the idea that steampunk emerged from cyberpunk. As was shown in chapter two, none of the writers associated with early steampunk writing were cyberpunk writers. Philip K. Dick's mentoring influence on the California Trinity is not the same influence that Dick had on cyberpunk writers like William Gibson. One can draw a fairly neat line between a number of Philip K. Dick's ideas and cyberpunk narratives. The same cannot be said for steampunk. Moorcock was part of the New Wave in science fiction, which preceded cyberpunk. In short, the *only* early steampunk writers associated with cyberpunk were Gibson and Sterling.

But that influence seems to be more a realization of what Gibson's fans were *hoping The Difference Engine* would be, as opposed to being inspired by what it actually is. In theory, *The Difference Engine* made the word steampunk famous. In practice, if it inspires at all, it's most often used as a starting point for any number of departures to more exciting avenues of creativity.

Nevertheless, there's no ignoring its place in the development of steampunk. Outside fiction, steampunk maker Jake von Slatt spoke of its influence on his steampunk creations, citing specifically the descriptions Gibson and Sterling use for how the analytic engines of their steampunk world work: "They describe computer displays like the European train boards with the flipping, clacking letters" (Wired.com). And perhaps that's true for von Slatt. But my guess is that more steampunk makers were inspired by his realization of Gibson and Sterling's vision than by that vision itself.

Following the release of *The Difference Engine*, the 1990s produced a handful of steampunk books, most of which bear little to no resemblance to each other. In addition to Blaylock's novelized version of *Lord Kelvin's*

Machine in 1993, the decade also saw the publication of Kim Newman's brilliant *Anno Dracula* in 1992 and Paul Di Filippo's oddball literary triptych *The Steampunk Trilogy,* a collection of three novellas that tell the tale of a mad scientist and his creation of an amphibious and amorous version of Queen Victoria, an ironically brilliant response to H. P. Lovecraft's racism via a racist naturalist's adventures with monsters and magic, and an intertextual and interplanar love story between nineteenth-century poets Walt Whitman and Emily Dickinson. Given how challenging and bizarre *The Steampunk Trilogy* is, I credit its second life and reprinting to the popularity of second-wave steampunk and the presence of "steampunk" in the title. Doing a search for "Steampunk" on Amazon would inevitably turn up Di Filippo's *Steampunk Trilogy.* At least, before there were a host of other steampunk books to fill the search results.

The Iron Dragon's Daughter (1993)

One of the most interesting examples of the lack of consistency in 1990s steampunk can be found in Michael Swanwick's *The Iron Dragon's Daughter.* Swanwick himself said that *Iron Dragon's Daughter* was an homage to Tolkien, but an homage borne out of a frustration with the Tolkien wannabes, not Tolkien himself. By the publication of *Iron Dragon's Daughter* in 1993, fantasy was in need of new direction, and Swanwick provided it. As we will see again with Michael Moorcock's *Warlord of the Air* in chapter ten, the original cover of *Iron Dragon's Daughter* does not adhere to standard second-wave steampunk visions. But just as Moorcock's *Warlord* and its sequels have been repackaged to appeal to second-wave steampunk aesthetics, so too Swanwick's *Iron Dragon* has been given a new cover to help it sell to an ever-increasing steampunk fandom. The sleek, *Terminator 2* chrome finish of the original paperback has been replaced with dirty, iron plating with rivets for the *Fantasy Masterworks* edition. Sadly, the most recent example only amounts to the complete replacement of the dragon with an array of cogs and gears.

This is not entirely misleading, since Swanwick's novel begins in a dragon factory—an industrial workspace manned by orphaned child labor. One of these children, a changeling girl named Jane Alderbery, is entering puberty, and her transition from child to woman involves opening her mind to one of the dragons in the factory. The dragon promises to free her from her servitude to the abusive and oppressive control of the factory's troll-like overseer. But while Jane's first adventures in the factory are a strong mix of Dungeons and Dickens, once she is free, the steampunk gives way to an even more bizarre mix. Jane enters high school in something more like *Sixteen Candles* and Sorcery, or Fast Times at Ren-Faire High, with shopping malls where time moves at a different speed than the rest of the world, coke-snorting elves in business suits, and prom queens destined to be burnt as sacrifice. Nevertheless, it forms an important link in the progression of steampunk from alternate history in *The Difference Engine* to the gonzo genre-splicing in China Miéville's *Perdido Street Station*.

Then, in 1995, two different stories about lost children yanked steampunk out of obscurity, or could have, if either had been marketed as such. It's only in hindsight that Philip Pullman's *His Dark Materials* series and Jean-Pierre Jeunet and Marc Caro's surreal and beautiful *The City of Lost Children* are recognized for their contributions to the further development of steampunk.

His Dark Materials (1995–2000)

Philip Pullman published *Northern Lights*, the first book in the *His Dark Materials* trilogy, which was released in North America as *The Golden Compass* in 1995. The first in a trilogy for young adult readers, it told the many harrowing adventures of twelve-year-old orphan Lyra Belacqua along her journey to rescue a friend abducted by a mysterious organization intent on experimenting on kidnapped children. The society's scientific inquiry is into the nature of elementary particles called Dust. *The Golden Compass* takes place in an alternate version of Earth that differs from ours primarily through several fantasy elements.

The first is that a part of a person's self or soul exists outside the body in the form of talking animal companions called daemons. Prior to adolescence, these daemons shapeshift to match a person's moods: upon maturity, the shape of the daemon becomes fixed forever. It's one of the most brilliant ideas in children's fiction, tapping into our youthful desire for a constant companion, and a youthful love of animals. That love of animals is further exploited through the introduction of Iorek Byrnison, the king of a race of talking polar bears who craft their own battle armor. The final difference between our world and Lyra's is her ability to use a clockwork device called an alethiometer for divination. That device is the most obviously "steampunk-looking" object in the book, though *The Golden Compass* is clearly set in a world that matches the early twentieth century: there are airships and steamships, and one of Lyra's allies, Lee Scoresby, is a Texan aeronaut, a cowboy balloonist.

There were two sequels to *The Golden Compass*: *The Subtle Knife* and *The Amber Spyglass*, along with several spin-off books. The later books varied in their use of steampunk elements, since the second book was set largely in another parallel world as well as our own reality. The series was both a popular and critical success. While J. K. Rowling's *Harry Potter* series dominated 1990s' children's fantasy, Pullman's trilogy, particularly the first book, is recognized as one of the most influential works of children's literature. It placed third in the BBC's Big Read poll, behind *The Lord of the Rings* and *Pride and Prejudice*.

Unlike the supposedly influential *Difference Engine,* Pullman's trilogy has also been adapted many times: as two stage plays, an ill-fated film adaptation and tie-in video game, a riveting full-cast audiobook (with Pullman himself as narrator), and a BBC radio drama. As of 2017, the BBC has commissioned a television series of the trilogy. While it's rare to find someone who has read *The Difference Engine*, it's relatively easy to find people who have read or experienced Pullman's fantasy in some way.

So why is *The Difference Engine* a steampunk classic, while Pullman's fantasy is rarely included in steampunk book lists? It's likely the prevalence of fantasy elements in *His Dark Materials*: though the series is concerned with physics through the study of Dust, the entire trilogy's focus on strong theological elements (a quest to kill God), the aforementioned armored polar bears, daemons, and divinatory alethiometer code the books heavily as fantasy. And initially, second-wave steampunk wasn't interested in being associated with fantasy. After all, steampunk was supposedly science fiction.

Yet to discount the potential impact of Pullman's fantasy on second-wave steampunk is to overlook one of the most popular works of speculative fiction from the 1990s. Unlike other steampunk writing of the '90s, *His Dark Materials* was widely read by both children and adults. And by 2004, when second-wave steampunk really started to emerge, that widespread experience likely became widespread influence. However, even if we can't draw a line of influence between the second wave and *His Dark Materials*, there are certainly affinities between Pullman's trilogy and steampunk. The orphaned protagonist is common: Stephen Hunt's *Court of the Air*, Phil and Kaja Foglio's *Girl Genius* comic, and Philip Reeve's *Larklight* trilogy are just a few examples. The use of fabulous animal companions is common as well, as seen in Scott Westerfeld's *Leviathan* series and Jim Butcher's *Aeronaut's Windlass*. But any of these could be discounted as common to many other subgenres in young adult fiction. And perhaps that is also what kept *His Dark Materials* out of the steampunk limelight.

While I find young adult steampunk to be some of the best steampunk fiction written, it doesn't appear on "essential" reading lists as often as I think it deserves. Perhaps, as with the repackaging of the *Harry Potter* series with "serious" adult covers, young adult steampunk suffered the dismissal of readers who refused to "stoop" to what they believed to be inferior writing or simpler story lines. *His Dark Materials* certainly puts the lie to those assumptions, and young adult steampunk such as Arthur Slade's *Modo/Hunchback Assignments* and Cassandra Clare's *Infernal Devices* series follow in its wake.

The general dismissal of *His Dark Materials* as steampunk is all the more mystifying when you consider that Jean-Pierre Jeunet and Marc Caro's film *The City of Lost Children* is never disputed to be steampunk but contains just as many fantasy elements as Pullman's trilogy.

The City of Lost Children (1995)

In 1995, smack dab in the middle of this decade of obscurity comes one of the finest steampunk films ever made, Jean-Pierre Jeunet and Marc Caro's surreal and beautiful *The City of Lost Children*. The film features a cult of Cyclops, men who have literally "plucked out their eye" and had it replaced with an ornate mechanical one, who are abducting very young children from the streets of the unnamed city the film takes place in. One of these abductees is Denree, the younger "brother" of One, a simple harpoonist-turned-strongman played by Ron Perlman. One is joined in his search for Denree by Miette, an orphan who is part of a criminal gang run by Siamese twins who call themselves the Octopus. The gang of orphans presenting their stolen wares to the Octopus feels reminiscent of the popular perception of the Dickensian orphan typified by Oliver Twist and the Artful Dodger.

Through many mishaps and misadventures, One and Miette finally prevail, locating Denree and the other stolen children aboard an offshore oil rig inhabited by an ersatz family of engineered humans: a matronly dwarf; six clones (brilliantly played for frequent comic relief by Jeunet regular Dominique Pinon); their "Uncle Irwin," a brain-in-vat connected to a hyper-vintage speaking and listening apparatus; and Krank, a man whose vast intelligence is marred by his inability to dream. Krank has been connecting himself to the stolen children to experience their

The steampunk dream device, Krank the dreamer, and his idiot brothers from *The City of Lost Children* (1995).   *Rex*

dreams, but has experienced only nightmares, since the children are terrified of him. Only Denree, fixated as he is on consuming food, is unafraid of Krank. One and Miette arrive just in time to rescue Denree and the other children; at the same time, the lost creator of the misfits returns to the rig to destroy it.

Don't be disappointed by that spoiler-filled summary: *The City of Lost Children* is a film that is just as compelling for its style as it is for its story: the action hangs together on fairy-tale logic and demonstrates that cinema can be so much more than plot and dialogue. *The City of Lost Children* is cinema you watch for its *mise en scène*, a French film term that refers to production, set, and costume design. While the film's performances are engaging, the sets the actors move through are equally captivating. *The City of Lost Children* is filled with rich steampunk imagery, from the fantastic machine that connects Krank to the lost children to the ornate eyepieces of the Cyclops.

However, it would be remiss to only comment on the hyper-vintage technology without noting the film's costume design, which was done by another unsung hero of steampunk: costuming for *The City of Lost Children* was the work of famed fashion designer Jean-Paul Gaultier (who, incidentally, designed the retro fashion of Marilyn Manson's *Grotesk Burlesk* tour, and has included steampunk elements in his couture occasionally): the costumes for the film, like the sets, are clearly vintage, but determining a clear time period for their provenance is difficult. About all one can say with certainty is "early twentieth century." But not Victorian. Just "old-timey." As will be shown in chapter twelve, Gaultier is one of the most likely suspects for helping to develop the steampunk aesthetic, yet he is rarely mentioned, even in steampunk discussions that include *The City of Lost Children*.

I have yet to find someone who refuses *The City of Lost Children* a place in steampunk, and yet the film is decidedly science fantasy, not science fiction, drawing from more than just the Victorian period for its aesthetic creation. It is a prime example of technofantasy, where the magical is rendered technological but never explained. The next significant entry in the development of '90s steampunk takes the concept of technofantasy even further by combining industrial mechanics and early science with ritual magic.

Perdido Street Station (2000)

At the tail end of this decade, a book was published that would prove to be both a popular and a contentious read for steampunk's second wave: China Miéville's *Perdido Street Station*.

I still see discussion over the question, "Is *Perdido Street Station* steampunk?" Steven Poole of *The Guardian* said it was in his review of *The Scar*, Miéville's ersatz sequel to *Perdido*. Those who have firmly tethered steampunk to the Victorian era and by extension England will say no. And while divergences from the locality of London and the period of the Industrial Revolution were still the exception in steampunk in 1999, the decade following the release of *Perdido* would strain those confines.

Others would say it's not steampunk because it includes magic and steampunk is science fiction, not fantasy. And while Tim Powers was still largely the odd man out in using magic in steampunk, we have to remember that Jeter had used it in his seminal steampunk *Morlock Night*. Furthermore, I'd be hard pressed to find anything particularly reminiscent of science fiction in Paul Di Filipo's *Steampunk Trilogy* (1995). The 1990s were a steampunk tug-of-war, pulling the still-developing genre back and forth between science fiction and fantasy.

Perhaps this is why some voices abide by Miéville's self-determined category of "Weird" or "New Weird" fiction, a genre designation even more maddeningly vague than steampunk has been at points. The short version is that Weird fiction is science fiction, fantasy, and horror that crosses genre boundaries (which is also what steampunk had been doing throughout the '90s, if we allow Kim Newman's *Anno Dracula* as part of steampunk's development). But that elastic definition sounds suspiciously like speculative fiction, so to clarify, I'll add that Weird writers tend to subvert traditional fantasy and science-fiction elements, refusing the "consolation" Tolkien's happy endings offered, and instead looking to disturb or provoke the reader. Yet even if we accept the idea of the New Weird as a genre, the very definition proposed by its proponents must allow that New Weird could be both Weird *and* steampunk, since that would be a blurring and blending of genres and subgenres.

I call *Perdido Street Station* steampunk first and foremost because the book's setting of New Crobuzon, a sprawling, filthy city, is clearly a fantasy iteration of industrial London; a London filled with fantasy races such as the khepri, whose males are fully insect and females are insect-headed with fully human bodies; the Cactus People, the water-controlling, froglike Vodyanai; the gargoyle-like wyrmen; and finally, the birdmen Garuda. While it may be filled with fantasy creatures straight out a Dungeons and Dragons *Monster Manual,* the streets, buildings, and especially rail lines of New Crobuzon evoke London or some other European city. But even without the affinities with nineteenth-century London, New Crobuzon is obviously a fantasy city that has grown beyond the settings of high fantasy that echo or ape J. R. R. Tolkien's Middle-earth.

Miéville is very outspoken about the detriment he believes Tolkien's influence has exerted on fantasy writing. One can see that *Perdido Street Station* is an attempt to reject Tolkien's influence while simultaneously exerting a new and alternative influence, one that replaces the feudal, pastoral setting of Middle-earth with the industrial, urban setting of New Crobuzon. New Crobuzon is the fantasy city after the coming of the factories.

Perdido Street Station's success is another node in the perception that steampunk is closely associated with cyberpunk, via the character of the Construct Council, a powerful calculating engine that has become self-aware and constructed itself both a body out of industrial garbage such as "girders and steam engines from ancient locomotives," and an avatar from a brainless human puppet. The Construct Council has gathered other constructs to it, ordering them through an extensive hive mind, while having become a god to humanoid citizens of New Crobuzon. The Construct Council is an amalgam of the sorts of artificial intelligence seen in Gibson's Wintermute computer in *Neuromancer* or the Puppet Master from anime cyberpunk classic *The Ghost in the Shell.* But it is also an expansion on the possible future of Gibson and Sterling's self-aware difference engine, with Miéville picking up in New Crobuzon where *The Difference Engine* left off in London.

But this connection to cyberpunk should not lead you to think that *Perdido Street Station's* blend of steampunk is science fiction. Though the trappings of science and technology are widespread, *Perdido* is most certainly fantasy, albeit a fantasy with a technological bent. There are two scenes that illustrate this, involving communication across distance: one geographical, the other planar. In both cases, what would have been a magical ritual or ability has been rendered technological, scientific.

In one instance, a woman wishes to speak with an incarcerated friend. She goes to a "communicatrix," who is a steampunk medium. In straight fantasy or occult-based horror, the communicatrix would need no technological assistance to perform her telepathy. In *Perdido*, the communicatrix amplifies her psychic ability with the assistance of a wood and leather box filled with "a tight interlocking tangle of valves and tubes" connected to a "ridiculous-looking brass helmet, with a kind of trumpet attachment jutting from the front." Miéville fastidiously describes these devices, and goes so far as to justify how they work within the physical laws of the secondary world of Bas Lag. The helmet permits communication across distance and through physical barriers, such as a phone or walkie-talkie would, but does so through magical means rendered in a technological aesthetic: technofantasy.

The other instance involves conversation from Bas Lag into an infernal dimension, the facilitator of the conversation is referred to as a "karcist," a reference to *The Grand Grimoire*, a book of magic mentioned in A. E. Waite's *Book of Ceremonial Magic*. The *Grimoire* uses the word karcist to refer to the person who performs the sacrifice and rituals to bind a demon to one's will. In *Perdido*, karcist Vansetty produces a conversation with a demon, but without the bother of a "live offering," adding, "Science is a wonderful thing."

But no matter how scientific such explanations appear within the world of Bas Lag, they are never science. There is a scientific and rational rigor to Miéville's world building, but that doesn't make *Perdido Street Station* science fiction. It remains fantasy, though fantasy of a very different stripe than *Lord of the Rings* and its countless imitators. We could use terms like technofantasy or urban fantasy to classify *Perdido*, but many have also slapped the steampunk label on it. Others argue that it isn't steampunk, in what appears to be an attempt to keep their favorite writer at some distance from a genre too silly or subpar for Miéville's fan base.

But to deny that *Perdido* is steampunk, or is filled with steampunk elements, is asinine. Aside from those who wish to distance Miéville from steampunk, there are those who see steampunk as the sole property of science fiction: magic does not belong in steampunk. There is currently no better example of how technofantasy is clearly part of steampunk than *Perdido Street Station*. That technofantasy permits Miéville to not only distance himself from Tolkien's fantasy, but thumb his nose at the type of secondary world Tolkien's Middle-earth represents. Miéville's dislike of Tolkien's massive influence over fantasy is most clearly expressed in his statement that Tolkien is "the wen on the arse of fantasy literature." While Miéville concedes Tolkien's influence, he rightly thinks it's impossible to avoid it. "The best you can do," he states, "is to consciously lance the boil."

In creating the magic system of *Perdido*, Miéville has certainly done that. Tolkien disliked fantasy magic that was too ritualistic, going so far as to use the word "machinery" for the sort of magic his villains use. Benevolent magic in Middle-earth was inherent—it was part of the land and the creatures who lived in it. But Miéville's magic is thoroughly ritualistic and mechanistic. Machinery is precisely the right word for the magic of the world of Bas-Lag. Miéville goes beyond ritual magic by referring to the power of magic as "thaumaturgic" and the study of magic as "thaumaturgy." In *Perdido*'s sequel, *The Scar*, magic is called "puissance." Both words are fancy ways of saying magic without saying magic. In the secondary world of Bas Lag, magic is as viable a source of energy as electricity is in ours. It can be channeled through wires, stored in batteries, and calculated by mathematics. Miéville's thaumaturgy may well be one of the most unabashed examples of technofantasy in steampunk writing.

The idea of harnessing magic as an energy source is both derivative of and distancing from Tolkien. Tolkien imagined magic as being an inherent part of the natural world of Middle-earth. Miéville's thaumaturgy doesn't contradict this, but the use of magic as power source shares affinities with Sauron's desire for power in the use of the One Ring. In Tolkien's imagination, magic should not be controlled per se. Gandalf refers to himself as a channel for the magic he uses, whereas Sauron seeks to control it, to wield it for his own purposes. While none of the characters who harness thaumaturgy are rendered *evil* by Miéville (the moral landscape of *Perdido Street Station* is nowhere near as black and white as the one found in *The Lord of the Rings*), I can certainly imagine Tolkien rejecting the idea.

As we'll see in chapter eight on steampunk anime, this distancing from Tolkien may be one of the reasons for the popularity of steampunk. For now, I'll let it suffice to say that the oversaturation of traditional high fantasy may have created a desire in fantasy readers for something new, something off the beaten path from the Shire to Mount Doom. And they found it in writers like Miéville. I say "distancing" rather than "rejection," though rejection is definitely what Miéville is doing, because not all steampunk is the result of an aversion to Tolkien's high fantasy. In the case of Hayao Miyazaki, Tolkien provides a source of inspiration that doesn't result in slavish imitation. But whether by hatred or homage, Tolkien's vast shadow in fantasy is still present in steampunk, even in overt rejections like Miéville's.

Science fiction or fantasy, steampunk was still chugging along like the Little Engine Who Could, though in such diverse ways as to belie the development of anything resembling a coordinated effort. Unlike the second wave of steampunk with the internet to help disseminate a standard idea of what steampunk should be, the 1990s were a time of steampunk variety. I've seen some histories of the genre that call this decade the second wave of steampunk. My problem with that designation is apparent in my title for this chapter—steampunk had been coined, but it was underground, far from being in the public consciousness. As popular as *The Difference Engine* was in terms of sales, it only popularized the term steampunk in science-fiction and fantasy reader circles. In short, if steampunk was anything in the '90s, it was an underwater current, not a wave, moving into the twenty-first century; but not with any significant force until the very end of the decade, when a summer film with block-buster potential would bring steampunk to very public attention.

7

A Decade of Steampunk Cinema

The Good, the Bad, and the Disney

When presenting at fan conventions, I've often been asked the question, "Are there any good steampunk movies?" The question implies either a very limited range of what is meant by a steampunk movie, or a limited awareness of steampunk cinema, since there are many steampunk films. And while admittedly, some of the most well-known examples are also some of the worst, there are also several instances of genuinely good filmmaking ranging from family-friendly animation to serious live-action drama. The decade from 1999 and the release of the summer blockbuster-bomb of *Wild Wild West* to 2009 and Guy Ritchie's irreverent revision of *Sherlock Holmes* is filled with cinema that was simultaneously influencing what steampunk would become, as well as being influenced by steampunk visions of the past. Remakes of old films and television series that predated steampunk, adaptations of comic books, children's books, and novels that contributed to steampunk history, as well as entirely new stories, made 1999–2009 a noteworthy decade of steampunk film.

Wild Wild West (1999)

Though few people knew what to call it, steampunk was in the mainstream at the start of the '90s with *Back to the Future Part III,* and after a decade of relative obscurity, was back in the mainstream in 1999 with the release of another film set in a steampunk Old West. Banking on the popularity of Will Smith, who was at the height of his career, Warner Bros. released *Wild Wild West*, a remake of the 1960s television series of the same name.

The original television series is often cited by fans of steampunk who "loved steampunk before it had a name." Like many of the examples of proto-steampunk, the television series *The Wild Wild West* bears little to no resemblance to second-wave steampunk. The impetus for *The Wild Wild West* in 1965 was arguably a way to cash in on the ongoing popularity of the television and cinematic Western and the rising popularity of spy films and TV series, particularly the newly minted *James Bond* franchise. The initial concept for the show, according to series creator Michael Garrison, was "James Bond on horseback," a motivation demonstrated through execution: like the James Bond films, *The Wild Wild West* featured a debonair leading man as well as megalomaniacal villains bent on world domination, which, if you believe what I said about Disney's Captain Nemo and his secret base in a volcanic island, is less a borrowing from the spy film than a return to proto-steampunk's roots.

The film largely follows the plot of the television series, with '90s action-film superstar Will Smith as a sexy, roguish James West whose approach to spy work is aptly described by the president as "shoot first, shoot later, shoot some more, and then when everybody's dead try to ask a question or two." Kevin Kline, whose career was not soaring like Smith's, but solid and furthermore, largely dramatic, was an odd casting as Artemus Gordon, West's gadget-building partner in frontier-America spywork (think a younger version of James Bond's Q in the field). Kline never seems to land a joke in this film, though that might be blamed on the writing, not the performance, as both Smith and Kline appear to be doing their able best to elevate the material. Both pale in their enthusiasm next to Kenneth Branagh as the film's villain, the steam-wheelchair-bound Dr. Arliss Loveless; as Loveless, Branagh steals any scene he's in, though his efforts are in vain as well. The film simply isn't funny or entertaining. The jokes are mostly in bad taste: they're either racist, sexist, or ableist.

Salma Hayek's scrappy Rita Escobar has enough agency to go in search of her kidnapped scientist father but is relegated to simpering damsel in distress as soon as she's paired with West and Gordon. One moment, she's facing off against West, fuming that she had "to do something" to save her father, and the next, she's baring her backside through the flap of full-body long johns. Most of Hayek's performance is relegated to gasping breathily every time West does something heroic. Hayek's treatment echoed that of the television series' inspiration, James Bond: that summer saw the release of *The World Is Not Enough*, the nineteenth film in the Bond franchise, in which Denise Richards played a nuclear physicist named Christmas Jones. The character was nothing more than a cursory nod to making a Bond girl more than pretty and in need of rescue. She was still pretty, still in need of rescue, and not one bit convincing as a nuclear physicist. Likewise Rita, who, despite lip service dialogue indicating a strong will and clever wiles, never rises above sex object and damsel in distress. Unlike the steampunk it would inspire, *Wild Wild West* was more than content to reify outdated representations of women in film.

Smith as West is another wasted opportunity. While *Wild Wild West* is admittedly a comedy, a film that casts an African American as a secret service agent in nineteenth-century America has to do more than just rehash racist slurs and stereotypes as a way of acknowledging the difficulties such an undertaking would entail. While most of those racial slurs and stereotypes are voiced by the villains in the film, they are nonetheless voiced. Furthermore, there's a subtle undermining of the audience's perception of West: he is primarily a man of action, and not a particularly bright one. Following one of West's life-threatening blunders, Artemus Gordon shouts that West is "the master of the *stupid stuff!*" It's certainly a common approach to a buddy movie to make one smart and the other a bit dull, but West's stupidity is linked to his fists. He believes violence can solve any problem. And the idea of the African American hero as man of violence was already a tired stereotype in 1999.

Despite these serious shortcomings, the film was a financial success, earning $222 million worldwide on a budget of $170 million. But it's no secret that the film bombed critically, and you'd be hard pressed to find many who would include it as a favorite. Even in steampunk circles, I get little to no push-back when I make jokes about how bad this film is. Nevertheless, its impact on second-wave steampunk is undeniable. While the film's dialogue and direction are atrocious, the production design is fantastic. I can remember thinking I wanted a suit like James West's. Given many outfits I've seen at steampunk conventions, clearly many women looked at what Salma Hayek or Branagh's henchwomen were wearing and thought the same thing.

While it was critically panned, it remains one of the highest-profile expressions of steampunk before or since 1999. Ten years later, when steampunk fans were speculating on when the genre would go mainstream, I was thinking that it already had, though admittedly not in the way the fans would have chosen. In many ways, *Wild Wild West* is like that relative no one wants to admit they have, but who did something crazy enough to have achieved notoriety. Personally, though I'm loathe to do so, I often resort to simply saying "Did you ever see *Wild Wild West* with Will Smith?" when looking for an example of steampunk many people will be familiar with.

Sleepy Hollow (1999)

That same year, Tim Burton's *Sleepy Hollow* was also released. Tim Burton is a name often mentioned in discussions of steampunk roots and influences. He seems to act as a de facto synonym for bizarre neo-Victoriana, for hybridity of an indeterminate past mixed with the fantastic. For example, in an article in *Locus* magazine, Cherie Priest said, "I've always been really interested in Victoriana. I love me some Tim Burton." But she does not go on to explain how those two statements are connected, nor what Tim Burton's name in association with steampunk means. I've been told often that many of Tim Burton's films are not steampunk. But many of the artists and authors who create steampunk cite him as a huge influence. Given the timeline of the rise of second-wave steampunk, how could they not?

By 1999, Burton had become a household name as both director and producer, with a solid string of hit movies in the late 1980s and early 1990s: *Beetlejuice* (1988), *Batman* (1989), *Edward Scissorhands* (1990), and *The Nightmare Before Christmas* (1993). These films firmly established him as a director who could reliably attract audiences. Furthermore, all these films displayed Burton's consistent retro-sensibility with a touch of the Gothic. The sensibility is found in *Beetlejuice* through the use of special effects meant to evoke a sense of B-movies of the past; in *Batman*, it was displayed in the Gothic design of Anton Furst's Gotham, where 1980s beat boxes blared out Prince while 1940s automobiles and fashions lined the streets under gargoyle-festooned towers; in *Edward Scissorhands*, it was the contrast of a pastel 1980s suburbia in the shadow of a Gothic castle; and finally, in *The Nightmare Before Christmas*, Burton employed stop-motion animation at a time when CGI was increasingly popular, and designed Halloween town in a style of German Expressionism reminiscent of the silent classic *The Cabinet of Dr. Caligari*. Repeatedly, Tim Burton's films were filled with a past that never was, a mélange of fashion trends and architectural and technological design that defied precise identification.

Following *The Nightmare Before Christmas*, Burton released films whose reception was varied, veering from critical failure with *Cabin Boy* to critical success with *Ed Wood*, along with the failure to relaunch the Superman franchise. In 1998, he was approached to direct an adaptation of Washington Irving's classic short story "The Legend of Sleepy Hollow."

While some would debate whether Tim Burton's *Sleepy Hollow* (1999) is a steampunk film, there's no denying Burton's influence on steampunk art and fashion.   *Alamy*

From the vision of a night-and-coal-stained 1799 New York that evokes shades of Victorian London to detective Ichabod Crane equipped with steampunk-style forensic accoutrements, *Sleepy Hollow* is filled with visuals to delight a fan of steampunk.

Crane as detective is, in itself, a moment of technological advancement that most purists seemed to miss when dismissing the film's place in steampunk. A New York constable at the avant garde of forensic science, Crane's use of "up-to-date scientific techniques" to solve crimes has earned him the dubious assignment of investigating a series of grisly beheadings in the upstate town of Sleepy Hollow. But despite these rational beginnings, Crane's journey takes the story, as per the movie's source material, into the realms of horror.

One of Burton's goals with *Sleepy Hollow* was to pay homage to British Hammer horror films; Hammer horror is popularly associated with their Gothic horror films, many of which were about Dracula and the Frankenstein monster, and consequently set in the nineteenth century, or in the case of Hammer's mummy films, the early twentieth century. So despite the film's setting being pre-Victorian and American, it was inspired by one of the most prolific producers of Gothic horror in the history of film. The climactic scene in the windmill is a clear nod to James Whale's *Frankenstein* (1931), which Burton referred to as "classic horror movie imagery," once again demonstrating how important twentieth-century cinema is in understanding steampunk's roots. As with the Verne and Wells adaptations and pastiches, Hammer was responsible for the dissemination of a cinematic vision of a Gothic and Victorian past. Once again, it is arguably this vision of the past that has inspired steampunk more than has real-world history, or potentially even the literary sources of Shelley and Stoker that inspired both Universal and Hammer.

Crane discovers that the beheadings are the work of the Headless Horseman, a reanimated corpse of a Hessian mercenary who fought in the American Revolutionary War. While he is initially skeptical, an encounter with a witch who reveals the Horseman's origin and a journey to the macabre tree that is the site of the Horseman's grave begins to change his mind. At this point, the film increasingly highlights supernatural horror, which is both further homage to Hammer horror as well as another instance of horror in steampunk. While steampunk fans focus on

Crane's hyper-vintage forensic tools as the steampunk in *Sleepy Hollow*, I would argue that it is the use of horror in association with those tools that makes *Sleepy Hollow* part of the steampunk family.

Disney's *Atlantis: The Lost Empire* (2001)

The year 2000 had no steampunk films, but 2001 was filled with neo-Victorian delights, from the dynamic but largely unfaithful film version of Alan Moore's *From Hell* to the French monster-hunt-meets-martial-arts adventure film *Brotherhood of the Wolf*. But the most conspicuous steampunk offering of 2001 was Disney's venture into steampunk waters with *Atlantis: The Lost Empire*. *Atlantis* was one of several departures from the Broadway musical approach that Disney had taken since the late 1980s beginning with *The Little Mermaid* and culminating with *The Hunchback of Notre Dame*. These departures left behind the musical numbers, cute animal sidekicks, and fairy tales in favor of stories of classic adventure.

Atlantis is set in 1914, at a time the directors and producer said was modern enough to have a form of advanced technology, but still far enough in the past to have a once-upon-a-time feel. It's the story of a journey to find the lost city of Atlantis, which focuses on Milo Thatch, a linguist and cartographer who guides the expedition on their adventure.

Though the production team stated that *Atlantis* was inspired by the adventure stories of Jules Verne, H. G. Wells, and Edgar Rice Burroughs, it's another example of a film made "in the tradition of" those writers, with as many cinematic homages as literary ones. The *Ulysses*, the submarine that was featured in much of the promotional material for the film, has clear design references to Harper Goff's *Nautilus*; the drill-nosed digging machine driven by a character with the nickname "Mole" is reminiscent of the Iron Mole from the Amicus version of *At the Earth's Core*. The motley team of scientists, explorers, and soldiers reminded me of a twenty-first-century update of Doc Savage and his cohorts with greater racial and gender diversity.

But in addition to the usual steampunk suspects, *Atlantis* has a number of visual references borrowed from the Japanese steampunk that will be discussed in the next chapter: the blue crystal technology of the

Atlanteans is clearly inspired by two anime: the film *Laputa: Castle in the Sky* and the TV series *Nadia: The Secret of Blue Water*. Milo Thatch bears more than a passing resemblance to the boy inventor Jean from *Nadia*, while the Atlantean woman Kida shares affinities with Nadia herself. The military's desire to weaponize the crystal technology is similar to the ending of *Laputa*.

This is not to say that *Atlantis* rips these ideas off from either the lost world adventure stories of Burroughs, Verne, and Haggard, or the steampunk anime of *Laputa* and *Nadia*, but rather than it exists as an intersection between these traditions, contrasting the rusty-sheet-metal-and-rivets aesthetic of the one with the magic crystal technology of the other, combining the streams of science fiction and fantasy in steampunk yet again.

Treasure Planet (2002)

Disney's second foray into steampunk was *Treasure Planet*, a science-fiction retelling of Robert Louis-Stevenson's 1833 adventure novel. As with *Atlantis*, Disney not only was trying to forge new paths for its animated storytelling, but was revisiting another live-action classic, the 1950 *Treasure Island*.

The design rule for *Treasure Planet* was called the "70/30" rule, which meant the production design was 70 percent traditional European eighteenth and seventeenth century, and 30 percent science fiction, which is as good an explanation of most steampunk design as I've ever seen. The film's art director, Andy Gaskill, said that this was to avoid creating another period remake of *Treasure Island*, but also to sidestep making a contemporary-looking science-fiction world reminiscent of *Star Wars*. As with the writers of cyberpunk, artists and writers were looking for a way to do science fiction in a different world, a world inspired by baroque sensibilities.

In this film of hybrids, even outer space is a hybrid: ships travel through a colorful, cosmic ocean called the Etherium, outer space with atmosphere instead of vacuum. The moon-shaped Crescentia is a space port or harbor, not a space station. Though the sailing ships have

The RMS *Legacy* from *Treasure Planet* (2002), one of steampunk's many flying vessels, resembles a masted sailing ship.   *Alamy*

thrusters, their sails are not affectations, but harness solar energy to drive the engines. The provenance of these ships is not only in eighteenth-century rigged sailing ships, but in a constellation of fantasy and science-fiction works. The earliest antecedent of these ships can be found in the planetary romance of Edgar Rice Burroughs's John Carter/Barsoom books, the first of which was *A Princess of Mars*. The fliers of the Red Martians are based on earthbound naval vessels with open decks, but with turrets and propellers instead of sails. *Spelljammer*, a campaign setting for the *Dungeons and Dragons* role-playing game, joined various high-fantasy worlds together through space travel in sailing ships.

Flying galleons and schooners abound in retrospec fiction, and steampunk has appropriated their use from time to time: in Philip Reeve's *Larklight* series, David D. Levine's *Arabella of Mars*, and Jim Butcher's *The Aeronaut's Windlass*. Influence or coincidence, the design of the ships in these series share a number of strong affinities with those in *Treasure Planet*, particularly the starboard and portside sails (pointless in water but helpful in the air or in space). Despite the repetition of such craft in steampunk, it's difficult to ascertain how influential *Treasure Planet* has been on steampunk style; in an unfortunate inversion of the reception of *Wild Wild West* and *Atlantis*, *Treasure Planet* received critical praise, but was a box-office failure. Sadly, one of the best examples of what steampunk has to offer in Western cinema has been relegated to the space of cult classic, while the next film, the visually brilliant but narratively disastrous *The League of Extraordinary Gentlemen* is far better known.

The League of Extraordinary Gentlemen (2003)

The year before steampunk anime gained worldwide attention through Disney's distribution deal with Studio Ghibli, thereby introducing North America to numerous critically acclaimed steampunk films, saw the release of yet another steampunk disappointment, *The League of Extraordinary Gentlemen* or *LXG*, the big-screen adaptation of Alan Moore and Kevin O'Neill's superb comic series. Like big-budget predecessor *Wild Wild West*, it would also prove to be a moderate financial success but a massive critical flop. Once again, brilliant steampunk design work and costuming was undermined by a terrible script and flawed direction.

Let me clarify that I love adaptations, and I also love adaptations that depart significantly from their source work. I do not see fidelity to the original source as the be-all and end-all of criteria for whether a cinematic adaptation of a book, comic book, or video game is a success. As will be seen later in this chapter, the changes made to the cinematic version of Christopher Priest's *The Prestige* created a different story than its literary source, but a potentially superior one. That said, I believe one of the reasons *LXG* failed critically was its departures from Moore and O'Neill's comic.

The film's general departure from the League in the comic is understandable. The comic-book versions of the characters are too much the antiheroes; despite the box-office success of the R-rated *From Hell*, another cinematic adaptation of Moore's work in 2001, a film about a

Victorian super-team arguably needed as wide an audience as possible. Consequently, almost all of the League were softened for younger filmgoers. Alan Quatermain went from opium addict to grieving father; Captain Nemo went from oceangoing terrorist to mysterious sage; Mr. Hyde's relish for bloodshed was corralled to a sort of Hulk-like ferocity; and the Invisible Man's introduction as mystery rapist and later betrayal of his teammates were excised entirely. But the last of the original team underwent a transformation from ostensible weakness to power, in a way that ultimately undermined the character of Mina Murray/Harker.

LXG commits the same sin as *Wild Wild West* in its treatment of the League's sole female member, Mina. In *LXG*, Mina is sidelined in numerous ways: unlike in the comic, she has not taken back her maiden name, but remains Mina Harker, wife of a man too weak to protect her. As in the comic, she has been the victim of Dracula's vampiric attack but, likely in an attempt to make her equal to the physical prowess of the men of the League, possesses vampiric powers: she can drink blood, fly, has extraordinary strength, and can control bats. This could be seen as an exciting improvement on Moore and O'Neill's Mina Murray, who has no extraordinary powers save one: leadership. Moore and O'Neill's Mina Murray is a perfectly normal woman in every way, save that she is clearly the leader of the League of Extraordinary Gentlemen. Mina Harker, for all her vampiric powers, is not.

This is likely the result of casting Sean Connery as Alan Quatermain; in the comic, Quatermain is not only happy to follow Mina Murray, but eventually becomes her lover. In the film, Quatermain tries to sideline Mina Harker. Admittedly, the typical Victorian male would not have seen women as likely candidates for membership in a covert team out to save the world; but Moore and O'Neill achieve Mina Murray's position as team leader while still acknowledging such difficulties, largely because she has no super powers. When *LXG* gives Mina Harker vampiric powers but removes her as team leader, it undercuts her place in the League: only men like Sean Connery, whose on-screen persona will always recall his performance as the virile, clever, and physically capable James Bond, can be "normal." In both film and comic, Quatermain has no supernatural or technological superiority—he's simply an outstanding hunter, and a geriatric one at that. As far as *LXG* is concerned, old men can be adventurers, but normal women cannot.

I'm in no way suggesting that this blunder was necessarily intentional. I don't think scriptwriter James Dale Robinson thought, in any of the twenty rumored revisions the screenplay received, "I'm going to undermine the female role in this film." But given how enthusiastically steampunk would be received and supported by women, and how women would figure significantly as authors and heroines for the fiction, it was a crucial blunder nonetheless. Mina Harker is quite possibly the worst of the lost opportunities of *LXG*, especially considering the casting of Peta Wilson, whose on-screen persona would have recalled her recent success playing the female assassin lead in the television series *La Femme Nikita* for five seasons.

The film further blunders by bloating out the comic's five-person League to seven, then focusing on the two additions more than the original team, with the exception of Connery as Quatermain. The original team is very well cast and contain two of the best performances of the film: Wilson as Mina Harker and Naseerudin Shah as Captain Nemo. The script overlooks the potential richness of these characters in favor of the immortal Dorian Gray and American secret service agent Tom Sawyer. In both these cases, significant departures were taken from those characters' original story lines. Admittedly, Oscar Wilde's Dorian Gray does not age, and shows no signs of the ultra-hedonistic lifestyle he engages in. However, the reader is never given the sense that Wilde's Gray is indestructible; *LXG's* Gray survives point-blank automatic rifle-fire with only a ruined coat and shirt as evidence the violence occurred. And even someone with only a cursory awareness of Mark Twain's Tom Sawyer would know that the character never handles a gun, let alone becomes part of any American secret service. I can't help thinking that it would have been terribly entertaining for Will Smith to step onto the screen instead of Tom Sawyer to reprise his role as James West, since that would have made more sense than the idea of Twain's boy-hero as a gun-toting secret service agent. One might argue that the film needed Dorian Gray to be the turncoat double agent. But Moore and O'Neill's Invisible Man is already aptly suited to such a role, given that he does that very thing in the comic's second volume. A large cast of diverse characters requires a very deft hand and a tightly woven script. *LXG* had neither.

What *LXG* had was a few well-designed steampunk vehicles, and lovely costuming. Captain Nemo's *Nautilus* was an inspired design, despite keeping a great deal of distance from both Harper Goff's famous rendering and Kevin O'Neill's brilliant combination of *Nautilus* with iconic squid elements. *LXG*'s *Nautilus* looks like a massive blade (Nemo refers to it as the "sword of the ocean"), literally cutting through the water with its sleek design. While the size of the submarine strains even comic-book-hero credulity, especially when emerging vertically from the Thames or cruising through the canals of Venice, one can't help but think it looks cool. Ornate embellishments decorate both the massive submarine and Nemo's automobile, a twenty-four-foot, six-wheeled convertible based on a Cadillac limousine with the head of Hindu elephant-god Ganesha done steampunk style above the headlamps.

The car gets its due diligence in a high-speed race through the streets of Venice to outrun the city's destruction—it's one of the film's high points, ending with the vehicle's destruction. The *Nautilus*, on the other hand, is nothing more than a glorified conveyance. While the exterior is gorgeous and pleasing to the eye, the interior of the submarine looks like the interior of a 1970s spaceship, with white walls, floors, and beams, but little in the way of effective or interesting design, save for the odd Art Deco embellishment.

LXG is notorious in steampunk circles—one of the two most mainstream, big-budget steampunk films ever made, which steampunk fans would, for the most part, prefer to forget. As with *Wild Wild West*, there are few people ready to come to *LXG*'s defense, save as guilty pleasure or eye candy. But that's all most steampunks care to take away from these films—the eye candy is grist for the maker and fashion mill. Costume ideas and design concepts are all the reason a steampunk fan might need for watching a movie as bad as *LXG*. For the rest of moviegoers, it looked like steampunk cinema was a lost cause, though the following year would prove them both right and wrong, when five North American films with retrofuturist and hyper-vintage production design were released to varying degrees of success.

2004: A Series of Fortunate Films (and One Unfortunate One)

Whereas each of the other films in this chapter tends to dominate its release year as the solitary or most influential example of steampunk cinema, 2004 had multiple contenders for this distinction: in March, Guillermo Del Toro's stylish and exciting film adaptation of *Hellboy*; May, *Van Helsing*, Stephen Sommers's homage to the classic Universal monsters of Dracula, the Frankenstein monster, and the Wolfman; June, Disney's remake of Verne's *Around the World in 80 Days*, which was a massive box-office failure; September, *Sky Captain and the World of Tomorrow,* a film that not only employed a retrofuturistic story but film style as well; and in December, *Lemony Snicket's Series of Unfortunate Events*, based on a series of children's books by the same name starring Jim Carrey.

Hellboy

The first of these films is an adaptation of the *Hellboy* comics by Mike Mignola, who was the concept artist for Disney's *Atlantis*. The inclusion of *Hellboy* on steampunk lists is both widespread and a little confusing. I've seen it in print books on steampunk and on many web lists. I have to wonder if its inclusion isn't simply unknowing perpetuation. Admittedly, there are retrofuturistic elements, like the design of Hellboy's "Samaritan" pistol, a revolver in a world of high-tech gadgets that shoots custom ammunition filled with white oak, holy water, garlic, silver shavings, and clove leaves, as a sort of catch-all bullet for killing monsters. The obvious contender for steampunk in *Hellboy* is the design and backstory of Kroenen, a Nazi assassin whose clockwork heart makes him almost impossible to kill. The designs of Kroenen's masks, along with the clockwork mainspring that he winds himself up with share design affinities with second-wave steampunk. However, the rest of *Hellboy* is a dark fantasy with Lovecraftian monsters. Although the film begins with a brief origin story for Hellboy in World War II, the rest of the film takes place in a contemporary, albeit fantastic, version of our world. A better contender for steampunk film from Mignola would have been the cartoon pilot for

The Amazing Screw-on Head. So why bother taking the time to address it at all? Why not simply omit its inclusion in this book?

Because *Hellboy* was not the last film to be labeled steampunk when only a few props or costume items made it so. The film's sequel, *Hellboy II: The Golden Army*, replaced the single clockwork threat of Kroenen with a magical clockwork army. Similarly, there are films and TV shows that are not steampunk but include steampunk devices. The interior of the TARDIS, Doctor Who's time machine, was clearly inspired by steampunk for several seasons. The horror film *Cabin in the Woods* featured a steampunk-looking doomsday device that captured the blood of human sacrifices. Captain Nemo's *Nautilus* in *Journey 2: The Mysterious Island*, a modern adventure comedy, had steampunk design. Rather than play a "steampunk or not" game, I prefer to consider why the aesthetic is being used: what does it convey? In every instance I've listed here, it's meant to convey a sense of technological antiquity. This amazing device is old, but it's not just magic, it is also machine. *Hellboy* and films like it demonstrate the way steampunk signifies the features of hyper-vintage and technofantasy by contrasting those features with contemporary or futuristic ones.

Van Helsing

In 1999, director Stephen Sommers and producer Bob Ducsay had successfully taken audiences to a vintage past with the remake of the classic horror film *The Mummy*. Following a sequel in 2001 called *The Mummy Returns*, the screenwriting duo turned their attention not to one but *all* of the rest of the classic Universal monsters from the 1930s and '40s. *Van Helsing* brought Dracula, the Frankenstein monster, and werewolves together under one cinematic umbrella for the first time in decades. And although you'll see *Van Helsing* described as an homage to the classic Universal monsters with steampunk influences, I'd say skip the influences: this film is steampunk.

While *The Mummy* is set in a 1930s world of pulp-serial-action, *Van Helsing* is set smack dab in steampunk central, in 1888. It messes with its nineteenth-century sources, moving the Frankenstein story forward seventy years, giving Dracula aspirations of mad science by appropriating Frankenstein's lab (complete with goggle-masked minions amid Jacob's

Van Helsing (2004) is both steampunk adventure and homage to the classic Universal monster-mashups of yesteryear.   *Alamy*

ladders arcing electricity), making Van Helsing a much younger man played by Hugh Jackman in his physical prime, and then making him part of an ecumenical religious order devoted to monster hunting. Van Helsing hunts these classic monsters, including Mr. Hyde in a rooftop battle on Notre Dame (killing two monsters with one grappling hook) with steampunk gadgets like a repeating crossbow and rotating saw-blade weapon.

Sommers filmed *Van Helsing* with a number of stylistic techniques based on those Universal monster films, from the spectacular opening black-and-white sequence to the use of rain, snow, and fog to create atmosphere. In some ways, *Van Helsing* anticipates *Victor Frankenstein* (2015), another steampunk homage to Universal horror, though centered on the titular creator and monster, along with a revisionist Igor played by Daniel Radcliffe of *Harry Potter* fame.

Although the film was critically panned, I'm an outlier in agreement with the late Roger Ebert, who thought it contained great visuals and an ambitious plot. I'd go so far as to say it succeeds where *LXG* failed in creating a crossover-fiction steampunk spectacular audiences would flock to at the box office—*Van Helsing* came in at #16 in the 2004 box office, while *LXG* only climbed to #44 in 2003. It also outsold every other steampunk film released in 2004.

Around the World in 80 Days

Disney's remake of *Around the World in 80 Days* attempted to be an updated steampunked tribute to Michael Todd's 1956 adaptation and a vehicle for Jackie Chan's blend of comedy and martial-arts choreography. These goals are not necessarily at odds, but the script that tried to synthesize these disparate elements failed to do justice to either. In both Verne and Todd's versions, the Bank of England is robbed early in the story, and Detective Fix doggedly pursues Phileas Fogg, believing him to be the thief. In the 2004 version, Jackie Chan is that thief, Lau Xing, whose noble theft of a Jade Buddha is part of his quest to return it to his village as guardian talisman. To evade Scotland Yard, Lau Xing masquerades as Passepartout as a half-Chinese, half-French valet—he foists his services on Phileas Fogg, who is no longer simply a wealthy gentleman with an obsession for punctuality, but an inventor of various steampunk contraptions. The challenge to circumnavigate the world is wagered by Lord Kelvin, the British Minister of Science: if Fogg loses, he must stop inventing. If he wins, he takes Kelvin's job.

The film is a terrible mess, rarely blending Verne's story effectively with Lau Xing's martial-arts/quest story. The film's attempt at including cameos in the style of Todd's film is also poorly executed, with the lowest point likely resulting from the highest-paid actor, in a scene where Arnold Schwarzenegger plays a Turkish prince. His portrayal is largely emblematic of the film's representation of world culture outside England, which at times feels less accurate or respectful than Todd's casting of Shirley MacLaine as the Indian Princess Aouda in 1956. When Fogg says that he has visited and experienced other cultures at the conclusion, it's simultaneously the easiest laugh and worst joke of the film.

Sky Captain and the World of Tomorrow

Sky Captain and the World of Tomorrow is a contentious inclusion in steampunk film lists. Purists call it dieselpunk or decopunk, but whatever one calls it, it's easy to see why fans of steampunk might enjoy it: it's a cinematic love letter to the adventure serials of the 1930s, but a love letter written on yellowed pulp-quality paper, a spectacularly stylish movie that *looks* like it could have been filmed in the 1930s. I'm not about to argue strenuously against it being included in the lineage of steampunk cinema, simply because I can see how it belongs there; perhaps not as steampunk per se, but like *The Rocketeer*, *The Shadow*, and *The Phantom*, pulp-era superhero films of the 1990s, it has that hyper-vintage element that steampunk artists draw inspiration from, as evidenced by steampunk cosplay and couture that resembles Jude Law's costume.

Lemony Snicket's A Series of Unfortunate Events

The last steampunk offering of 2004 came during the holiday season, with the promise of film adaptations of popular children's books trying to cash in on the popularity of the *Harry Potter* franchise. *A Series of Unfortunate Events* seemed a likely candidate to attract fans of *Harry*

Potter, given how the Hogwarts film universe was often drawing from a neo-Victorian costume and set design shared by Brett Helquist's art in the *Unfortunate Events* books. But production designer Richard Heinrichs, who had worked on a number of Tim Burton films including *Sleepy Hollow*, emphasized the steampunk embellishments in the film's *mise-en-scène*, making it a popular repository of costuming ideas for Goth, Goth Lolita, and steampunk styles in the years to come.

The story of *A Series of Unfortunate Events* was well suited to a steampunk retrofitting: three orphaned children (one of whom is a girl genius!), adopted by a villain with a penchant for melodramatic performance (and not just because he was played by over-actor of over-actors, Jim Carrey), evade his clutches through ingenuity and invention. Though the film failed to produce a sequel, the series was adapted for television by Netflix in 2017, combining contemporary styles with vague vintage production design reminiscent in some ways of Terry Gilliam's madcap cinema.

The Brothers Grimm (2005)

Like Tim Burton, the cinematic influence of Monty Python alumnus Terry Gilliam on steampunk cannot be overstated. From the retrofuturistic visions of *Brazil* to the gonzo *Adventures of Baron Munchausen,* Gilliam's work is often mentioned as inspiration for steampunk creativity. This is likely less about any one particular film or visual motif of Gilliam's than it is his overall oeuvre, which has always contained a sense of hybridity and pastiche. But if you do a search for steampunk films, you're likely to find one of Gilliam's less celebrated works, *The Brothers Grimm*.

As with *Hellboy*, we might wonder what *The Brothers Grimm* is doing on any list of steampunk films, given that it's mostly a mash-up of the Grimm Brothers' fairy tales, lightly peppered with steampunk gadgets (all of which are shams—part of the Gilliam-Grimms' con-artistry—the brothers perpetrate supernatural hoaxes and then offer their services as steampunk ghostbusters).

But Gilliam's vision of Napoleonic Germany shares a number of affinities with Tim Burton's *Sleepy Hollow,* despite being far more colorful; the production design, digital color-correction, and CGI enhancements contribute to a stylized, heightened sense of reality that seeks to evoke but not recreate the past. Increasingly, this stylized past would become associated with steampunk, whether or not there is an overt focus on technology. Additionally, it is possible that the general influence of Gilliam's retro-style on steampunk has created a sort of feedback loop, whereby steampunk fans mistakenly assumed Gilliam was being influenced by steampunk, when it was arguably the other way around.

Sadly, *The Brothers Grimm* was not a critical success, and so it was that steampunk fans were still waiting for a serious critical hit when Christopher Nolan finally gave them one by adapting a book that is sometimes considered a classic of first-wave steampunk, *The Prestige*.

The Prestige (2006)

The Prestige is one of the most critically praised steampunk films ever made, though on first glance its steampunk features might not be obvious. Where *Wild Wild West* and *LXG* have steampunk elements running riot all over the screen, *The Prestige* does not appear to contain any speculative elements in it until far past the halfway mark. One might argue that it achieves this distinction by showing restraint in its use of steampunk elements.

Directed by Christopher Nolan before he attained the status of one of the most successful filmmakers of the twenty-first century, *The Prestige* is based on Christopher Priest's 1995 novel of the same name. The novel won the World Fantasy award in 1996, and is one of Priest's most critically acclaimed works. Both print and cinematic versions tell the story of rival magicians in the late nineteenth century, whose obsession with upstaging each other eventually leads to tragedy.

While steampunk fans and neo-Victorian enthusiasts are aware of Priest's novel, the film has largely achieved that moment when "the book isn't always better than the movie" (an adage I don't subscribe to, but that is wildly prevalent in North America), and then goes the step further by eclipsing the memory of the book, as the MGM film *The Wizard of Oz* did to *The Wonderful Wizard of Oz*.

I'm going to warn you to skip ahead to the next section in this chapter if you haven't seen *The Prestige*. Like a number of other Christopher Nolan films, it features a trick ending, and I don't want to spoil the fun for you.

But I can't talk about the steampunk elements of the film if I don't summarize the ending and its surprise.

The intense competition between two stage magicians leads one to seek the assistance of Nikolai Tesla, who successfully builds a device that can duplicate any object placed inside it. The device is the only overtly steampunk element of the film. Everything else about the movie is meticulously designed to evoke period accuracy. Because the film employs crosscutting between a frame narrative and flashbacks, the Tesla device is effectively present throughout the story, if only indirectly as audiences wonder what really happened in the opening scene when one of the magicians, Robert Angier, drowns in a locked tank, and his rival, Alfred Borden, is accused of Angier's murder. The audience learns that Angier, attempting to duplicate one of Borden's acts, used Tesla's device to duplicate himself, drowning one of his selves in the process. I won't spoil how Borden did the same thing, nor how the film ends, to save at least a few of *The Prestige*'s surprises.

The Prestige is that rarest of birds in steampunk film: it received both high critical and popular acclaim. It is well acted, well directed, beautifully filmed, and most importantly, impressively edited. The film's puzzle box of a plot relies heavily on the editor's use of crosscutting throughout. It joins *The City of Lost Children* and the animated films of Hayao Miyazaki as among the few works of steampunk cinema that are unreservedly works of film art.

Stardust (2007)

I'm sure I'll be given the steampunk cane for including this film on this list. I remember talking to a steampunk author in 2008 who was incensed that people thought anything by Neil Gaiman was steampunk. At the time I wondered what he was talking about, as I hadn't yet seen *Stardust*. And when I saw it, I had to admit that, while Neil Gaiman's books aren't steampunk, the film adaptation of *Stardust* might very well be.

If nothing else, the cinematic design of lightning-pirate Captain Shakespeare's sky vessel is more steampunk than its literary counterpart, with a dirigible-gondola lashed to an open-deck sailing vessel; in the book, Gaiman describes it only as a "sky-ship" with "sails billowing." Since the movie is about a falling star that manifests as a young woman being chased by witches who want to eat her heart to gain immortality, one wonders why a flying sailing ship would have strained the film's sense of verisimilitude. Nevertheless, the change from flying masted ship to a hybrid of open-deck vessel and airship is an indication of how in 2007, steampunk continued to prove an enticing design approach.

Yet even without the remarkable sky-ship, the film's design aesthetic is firmly nineteenth century, as Gaiman set the book when "Queen Victoria was on the throne of England" and "Mr. Charles Dickens was serializing his novel *Oliver Twist*." It's a far brighter neo-Victorian fantasy world than many steampunks were imagining at the time, but it's yet another instance of fantasy film messing with the nineteenth century. Once again, though steampunk purists argued steampunk was science fiction, films like *Stardust* continued to strain that designation.

Sherlock Holmes (2009)

This decade of steampunk film closed with Guy Ritchie's iconoclastic take on Victorian icon Sherlock Holmes. Holmes and Dracula are said to be the most filmed fictional characters in existence, with most of the Great Detective's appearances featuring an upper-class Englishman in a deerstalker hat on head with a curved pipe in hand. Basil Rathbone's hawk-like features became synonymous with Holmes, while Nigel Bruce's portly figure became the norm for Watson. Consequently, the casting of American Robert Downey Jr. in the role of Holmes sans deerstalker and a prosthetic nose (well, he does wear one, but only in disguise!) and the virile Jude Law as Watson (he was nicknamed "Hotson" on the set) came as a surprise for diehard Sherlock Holmes purists.

While Ritchie and crew went to some pains to justify their casting choices in terms of fidelity to Sir Arthur Conan Doyle's original Sherlock Holmes stories and novels, faithfulness is beside the point when considering Ritchie's *Sherlock Holmes* as steampunk cinema. And therein lies another consideration.

Like Ritchie and crew, I've gone to great lengths at points in this chapter to argue for a film's inclusion in some canonical steampunk list, when I don't really care if there's such a list or not. Perhaps it is most fruitful not to ask whether something *is* steampunk or not, but to ask "what happens when we consider it as steampunk?" I can only hope that this becomes a frequently asked question, using this film as a case study.

Recall those features of steampunk as a hybrid of hyper-vintage, retrofuturistic technofantasies.

Let's start with the technofantasy, because that's the easy part. Most of the arguments for considering *Sherlock Holmes* as a steampunk film were based in the doomsday device that the villain uses in an attempt to wipe out Parliament in the film's last act. With its tubes, coils, and wires, there wasn't a steampunk maker in the audience who wasn't thinking about how they could build one (perhaps minus the cyanide cylinders) when they got home after the credits rolled. While the device looks like something that could have been built in the 1890s, its abilities are far advanced (and never fully explained). In this sense, we might consider it retrofuturistic as well, since it has the appearance of the past, but the capabilities of the future.

But how is *Sherlock Holmes* hyper-vintage? It is clearly set in 1890, and the film was shot on location in London. It looks authentic from start to finish. There's hardly anything that feels like an exaggeration of the Victorian era, aside from some of the costume design. The audience is not meant to consider the setting a heightened reality like Tim Burton's *Sleepy Hollow* nor as the alternate history of *LXG*. But when we consider the characters of Holmes and Watson, we find that they are potentially hyper-vintage instances. Recall that I said that "hyper-vintage" encompasses a messing about with the past—in this case the heroes of the past. It is not nineteenth-century London that has been exaggerated, but the residents of 221B Baker Street. One of the reasons *Sherlock Holmes* was a hit at the box office is that Ritchie had updated the seminal buddy-cop duo of Holmes and Watson for modern audiences. As with any widely adapted work, new versions seek innovation as a way to refresh the content or be at risk for creating another clone.

So in place of the dapper, emotionally distant, intellectual Holmes of the past, we get a fashionably bohemian, eccentrically quick-witted martial-artist cum forensic scientist in Robert Downey Jr.'s performance. This is not your grandfather's Holmes. Watson's place as ineffective sidekick was replaced with Jude Law's militarily capable veteran field surgeon with a penchant for women and gambling (which is apparently closer to Doyle's vision than Nigel Bruce's famous portrayal, which had largely eclipsed the original). This is revisionist Holmes. It is steampunk Holmes.

And so it is that steampunk cinema starts with a whimper and ends with a bang, though *Sherlock Holmes* was hardly the end of steampunk in film. Elements of steampunk were seen in Zack Snyder's 2011 flop *Suckerpunch,* as well as one of that year's critical successes, Martin Scorsese's *Hugo.* There was steampunk aplenty in Paul McGuinan's *Victor Frankenstein,* which seemed to be an attempt to repeat Ritchie's approach with the original mad scientist as played with relish by James McAvoy and his assistant Igor, made less monstrous by Daniel Radcliffe's sympathetic performance. However, the film was a box-office bomb, perhaps adding further weight to the perception that there aren't any really good steampunk films. And while it's true that steampunk cinema is hit and miss in the English-speaking market, the perception that steampunk films are all terrible would be difficult to substantiate in Japan, where the genius of animation legend Hayao Miyazaki produced a whole string of steampunk classics, and others followed in his wake.

8

Steampunk Anime

While many of the films from last chapter are visually captivating, many of them were either critical or box-office flops. Consequently, it should come as little surprise that I was once asked at a comic and pop culture expo, "Are there any *good* steampunk movies?" The answer is yes, absolutely. But the majority of them are animated and were made in Japan. This next chapter looks at a host of very successful steampunk films and television series, and how Japan's early steampunk works contributed to the aesthetic vision of the second wave.

Several of the films and television series in this chapter (*Nausicaä of the Valley of the Wind, Laputa: Castle in the Sky,* and *Nadia: The Secret of Blue Water*) were all made before the majority of steampunk films outlined in the previous chapter. Although fashion blogger lacarmina stated that "The concept of Steampunk is only beginning to gain recognition in Japan" in 2013, her comment can only be applied to steampunk fashion or culture (and even then, as we will see in chapter eleven on fashion, it's a questionable claim), since these films represent a significant inspirational force in the rise of second-wave steampunk. As will be shown, they comprise a rise of first-wave steampunk in Japan contemporaneous with the rise of steampunk in America. It might be remiss to say that just as the California Trinity were creating steampunk in the United States, and Moorcock and Priest were creating it in Britain, Hayao Miyazaki was arguably creating first-wave steampunk in Japan with Studio Ghibli's *Tenkuu no Shiro Laputa* (*Castle in the Sky*) in 1986. But again, there is a blast pattern, with many different creators generating works with no classification other than fantasy or science fiction, which have been clearly instrumental in the development of second-wave steampunk.

However, Japanese influence on North American steampunk was admittedly not widespread until after the international success of Hayao Miyazaki's *Spirited Away* in 2001. Consequently, while *Nausicaä*, *Laputa*, and *Nadia* were instrumental as steampunk antecedents in Japan, their international influence was largely delayed until the mid-'00s. Hence their inclusion at this point in our survey of steampunk, since it is only in the early '00s that they are released domestically in North America. Furthermore, it is easier to chart the influence of these films on Japan's steampunk cinema and television by looking at them in a single chapter, since there is so much borrowing and homage going on.

While some have stated that steampunk in Japan begins as early as 1948 with Osamu Tezuka's *Lost World* manga, it is more accurate to say that Tezuka's manga, including *Metropolis* (1949) and *Next World* (1949), forms part of the same sort of chain of cinematic inspiration followed by a blast radius pattern that happened in the US and the UK.

Given the nineteenth-century history of Japanese industrialization in the reign of Emperor Meiji (1868–1912) and Emperor Taisho (1912–26), I have to wonder if it's Japan we have to thank for the strong propensity steampunk art has toward drawing in technology and styles that antedate the Victorian era. The late end of industrialization arguably contributed to a love for modern scientific romances, which contribute to the look and feel of second-wave steampunk. This is arguably why people are uncomfortable with the conflation of steampunk with the Victorian era and prefer the term industrialized era. As identified earlier, the problem with using a word like "industrialized" is that it puts the focus on a particular facet of technology again, when, as we've seen, steampunk is often concerned with other technologies, or only uses technology as a backdrop for other issues.

At any rate, this late end to Japanese industrialization informs an associated Japanese interest with premodern, post-medieval Europe, forming one of the uniting features of Japanese steampunk: anime scholar Helen McCarthy wrote about the Japanese fascination with the "never-never land that is the Japanese dream of Europe," a view that echoes Tim Powers's comments about London as a completely fictional city in early steampunk. McCarthy was referring especially Hayao Miyazaki's first film, *The Castle of Cagliostro*, but the concept is found in many facets of Japanese culture. The Japanese use the phrase *akogare no Paris* to describe this fascination, which McCarthy translates as "the Paris of our dreams," though it is by no means limited to Paris any more than it is to Miyazaki. First-wave steampunk anime is frequently set in this "Paris of our dreams," which is often a hodgepodge of picturesque nineteenth-century European locations ranging from Italy to Stockholm. Since 1995, anime such as *Sakura Wars* and *Kabaneri of the Iron Fortress* have set steampunk outside this idealized Europe, in a fictionalized Japan. But at the beginning of steampunk anime, it was still about the Paris of our dreams: Hayao Miyazaki modeled the setting for his third film and steampunk classic *Castle in the Sky* on South Wales, going so far as to take his animators there for reference work, and it is there where we begin.

Laputa: Castle in the Sky (1986)

Though it is predated by *Nausicaä of the Valley of the Wind*, I am going to begin with *Laputa: Castle in the Sky*, since *Nausicaä*'s contribution to steampunk is more questionable. There is little debate about *Laputa*'s inclusion in the steampunk canon. This is perhaps due to *Laputa* wasting no time kicking off with a scene in all the high-flying action glory many people expect from a film that is quintessentially steampunk. *Laputa* opens with a group of sky pirates descending on an airship where Sheeta, a young girl in possession of a mysterious crystal, is imprisoned. Sheeta falls from the airship in an attempt to escape both her captors and the pirates, but her fall is slowed by the power of her crystal. The film's credit sequence, which plays during Sheeta's descent, alludes to the prehistory of *Laputa*, displaying scenes of giant windmills, gears, cogs, and digging machines; factories reminiscent of William Blake's "dark Satanic mills" of the Industrial Revolution, spewing coal smoke into the sky; armadas of fabulous airships and archipelagos of floating islands covered in marvelous, utopian cities. These credits have an antique look to them that anticipates the rust-and-dust look of most second-wave steampunk.

After the credits, the film introduces Pazu, a young man who works on the machinery above a silver mine. He spies Sheeta's feather-fall and rescues her: as with many of the steampunk anime works to follow *Laputa*, they are orphans. While orphaned characters are hardly novel nor unique to steampunk, the trope of the Dickensian orphan remains a favorite in steampunk fiction. And the quest for the lost parent, even more so, from *Laputa* to China Miéville's *Railsea*.

The air pirates, led by their formidable matron Captain Dola, find the pair, and a series of fantastic chases, escapes, and adventures ensue. The air pirates are not the only group interested in the mysterious crystal; Sheeta's original captor, Colonel Muska, a secret agent working for an unseen government, also maintains pursuit. Sheeta and Pazu learn that the crystal is from the floating island-city of Laputa. In the Japanese version of the film from 1986, the crystal is made from volucite. In the 1998 English dub, the substance is called Aetherium. In either case, it shares qualities with H. G. Wells's Cavorite, but is also an early instance of the magical substances so often used in steampunk to power the miraculous machines. Given that it is effectively contemporaneous to the start of steampunk in the United States, it is yet another nail in the coffin of the contention that steampunk involves science, not magic.

Colonel Muska is eventually successful in capturing Sheeta and Pazu; he reveals his desire for the power of the crystal, but claims he needs Sheeta to operate it. He coerces Sheeta into telling Pazu to leave her; crestfallen, he does, but returns home to find it occupied by Captain Dola and her bumbling pirate progeny. Pazu and Dola create an alliance of convenience, and set out to rescue Sheeta: Pazu, out of concern; Dola, for greed (though this will be increasingly tempered by a growing affection for the two children). Their arrival at Muska's fortress coincides with Sheeta's remembrance of a spell her mother taught her, a magical cry for help that awakens a broken Laputan robot soldier that Muska revealed to Sheeta only hours earlier. The robot soldier breaks free of its dungeon and implacably seeks out Sheeta to protect her. In its single-minded execution of Sheeta's plea for help, the robot lays waste to Muska's fortress. Sheeta is horrified and tries to stop the destruction; her struggles with the robot soldier result in the loss of her Laputan crystal. Dola and Pazu swoop down in the nick of time to rescue Sheeta even as Muska's military forces destroy the robot. Pazu and Sheeta sign on as crew aboard Dola's pirate vessel, now headed east, toward where the crystal revealed the location of Laputa.

Muska, now in possession of the crystal, follows on board the massive airship *Goliath*. The vessels discover Laputa within moments of each other, while Pazu and Sheeta are separated from Dola's pirates by the storm surrounding the floating city. The orphans discover an upper city, comprised of awesome stone architecture, underwater districts, and vast indoor greenhouses containing forests and rampant gardens. Their crash landing is greeted by a benevolent brother to the robot soldier from Muska's fortress, which moves their crashed vessel to rescue a bird's nest. Where the robot soldier was clearly designed for war, this one appears to be designed to tend the garden spaces of the upper city.

Meanwhile, in the lower city, Muska's military forces have captured Dola and her crew, and are busy plundering the riches of Laputa, while Muska and his flunkies descend into the heart of the lower city. They cross paths with Pazu and Sheeta, who are trying to rescue the pirates, and Sheeta is taken captive by Muska. They continue into the depths of Laputa, where Muska commandeers a weapon of mass destruction, turning Laputa into a cross between *Star Wars'* Cloud City and the Death Star. Muska obliterates his own military in a display of the weapon's power. Pazu frees the pirates, then returns to rescue Sheeta: together, hand in hand, they use the power of her crystal to destroy the lower city. Muska is lost in the ruin, but Sheeta and Pazu are protected by the roots of the massive tree that shelters the upper city. As Laputa, unencumbered by the ancient weapon, rises higher into the skies, Sheeta and Pazu rejoin the air pirates, and literally sail (on a hang glider) into the sunset.

Several thematic concepts from *Laputa* are repeated in subsequent steampunk anime: most closely in *Nadia* (and Disney's *Atlantis*), but also diffusely in *Steamboy* and *Howl's Moving Castle*. Yet the retrofuturistic designs of the sky pirates' insect-like ornithopters, the military airships, and the flying castle's robots are also an undeniable influence on second-wave steampunk, given their antiquated and utterly fantastic aspect. These are the impossible machines of Albert Robida's artwork, but more importantly, as will be noted in the section on *Howl's Moving Castle*, they are rejection of real-world physics: it is a whimsy of design rather than words, but it echoes Blaylock's early whimsy in America, and anticipates where second-wave steampunk will find its greatest success.

While the whimsical design of *Laputa* is not repeated by the next work of steampunk anime, the lighthearted sense of adventure that permeates the adventures of Sheeta and Pazu certainly is. And this is no coincidence. *Laputa* and *Nadia: The Secret of Blue Water* share a common genesis, in the early drafts of a series Miyazaki was developing based on Jules Verne's *20,000 Leagues Under the Sea* and *Around the World in 80 Days*. Miyazaki abandoned that project, but formed those ideas into *Laputa*, while the television production companies went on to complete the project as *Nadia: The Secret of the Blue Water* in 1989.

Nadia: The Secret of Blue Water (1989)

Nadia: The Secret of Blue Water is yet another instance of the influence of Jules Verne on steampunk, and once again, the particular work of *20,000 Leagues Under the Sea*. The opening moments of the first episode echo the opening pages of *Leagues*, telling of ships sunk by a mysterious sea monster. But instead of a professor, his valet, and a harpooner ending up on Captain Nemo's remarkable submarine, the cast of *Nadia* are two fourteen-year-old orphans (see? Again with the orphans!), the jewel thieves who chase them, and Nemo and the submarine crew who, more often than not, rescue them from the clutches of a villainous overlord and his military forces. The orphans are Nadia, an acrobatic circus performer who can speak to her pet baby lion king and possesses a mysterious blue jewel; and Jean, a young inventor who builds fantastic machines with limited utility. They are capable of getting Jean and Nadia away from trouble, but that's about as far as they will travel. Throughout the series, Nadia vacillates between calling him a true genius and complaining that his machines never work, since Jean's flying machines largely serve as devices to get the pair out of one situation and promptly into another.

And that's largely the plot for the first episodes: the Grandis Gang, a group of bumbling jewel thieves, want Nadia's mysterious jewel, the series' titular Blue Water. If the plot of *Nadia* sounds suspiciously similar to *Laputa*, you wouldn't be alone in thinking so. The story line for *Nadia* was developed by Miyazaki before he left Gainax, taking the ideas that birthed *Nadia* and forming *Laputa* from them. Nor was this the last time that a steampunk story would involve a mysterious blue crystal, a lost ancient civilization, and competing agencies vying for new sources of military technology.

As in *Laputa*, where the pirates are not truly villainous, Madame Grandis and her idiotic thugs demonstrate sympathy and cooperate with Jean and Nadia. The real threat is the secret society of Neo-Atlan, or New Atlantis, a fascist military force lead by Gargoyle: it is Gargoyle and the New Atlanteans who own the submarine mistaken for a sea monster sinking ships at the start of the series. In this way, *Nadia* splits Verne's Captain Nemo into two entities: Gargoyle represents the Nemo who sinks ships in *20,000 Leagues Under the Sea*. *Nadia*'s Nemo shares greater kinship with the Nemo from *The Mysterious Island*. *Nadia* pits these two sides of Nemo against each other, with the "real" Nemo and *Nautilus* representing good, and Gargoyle and his submarine, *The Garfish*, representing evil.

Gargoyle's connection to Verne's Nemo is also seen in the form of his secret base, hidden in the center of a dormant volcano, evoking Nemo's base in Disney's *20,000 Leagues Under the Sea*. Gargoyle's base is full circle from the Disney film, incorporating the elements of many James Bond villains' secret bases, in their turn inspired by the cinematic Nemo's.

The series not only contains the character and ship of Nemo, but also loosely follows the events in *20,000 Leagues Under the Sea:* in episode 3, "The Beast," Nadia and Jean find themselves aboard the *USS Abraham*, clearly a reference to Verne's *Abraham Lincoln*, the ship that pursued and fired upon Nemo's *Nautilus*. During the *Abraham*'s altercation with the sea monster (which deviates from Verne by being Gargoyle's *Garfish*, not Nemo's *Nautilus*), Jean, Nadia, and King fall into the ocean. In episode 4, "Nautilus: The Fantastic Submarine," they are rescued by the crew of the *Nautilus*. Nemo's reveal is a close adaptation of Verne, emerging from shadow and remaining a figure of shadow and mystery for most of the series. Jean occupies the character position of Professor Arronax, admiring Nemo and his invention until he discovers fully the man's violent nature and the ship's true purpose. Jean is likewise in awe of Nemo's technological achievement, an admiration he shares with one of the Grandis gang, Hanson, the engineer who built *The Gratan*. Hanson's partner in crime, Sanson, is the analogue for Ned Land: he complains about having to incessantly subsist on a seafood diet, and is certainly the man of action that Kirk Douglas portrayed in the Disney film.

But *Nadia* is not simply a retelling of *20,000 Leagues*. It uses Verne's tale as a foundation to build a new story, one that involves Nemo and his nemesis Gargoyle as the last members of the race of Atlantis. The fantastic anachronistic technology of the *Nautilus* and Neo Atlantis is all the result of the ancient Atlantis's superior engineering.

The engineering provides several instances of anachronism in steampunk that would have been rejected as examples of steampunk by second-wave gatekeepers. The list of anachronisms in *Nadia* is extensive. The story takes place in 1889, but includes combustion engines, electricity, and nuclear power. None of these are rendered in a baroque fashion, as Harper Goff's *Nautilus* was. Instead, all advanced technology in *Nadia* looks either contemporary or advanced for the years the show was produced. Amusingly, the galley of the *Nautilus* contains an electric mixer, dishwasher, and blender that look no different than the ones in use in 1989–1991. The *Nautilus* itself has an ultramodern design, as sleek and jet-like as the airships on the 1971 paperback cover of Moorcock's *The Warlord of the Air*, or of the hugely popular spaceships of 1980s *Star Wars* fervor. While second-wave steampunk has a somewhat unified baroque antique look to its anachronistic or fantastic technologies, first-wave steampunk does not.

Yet this lack of aesthetic influence doesn't mean *Nadia*'s place in the pedigree of both Japanese and American steampunk should be ignored. It was a huge success in Japan, as attested to by the somewhat infamous anecdote that episodes 23–34 were farmed out to other studios, providing Studio Gainax the necessary time to complete the series. The popularity of Studio Gainax's other anime hit, *Neon Genesis Evangelion*, further assured the popularity of anything they produced, especially given the thematic overlap in both series. *Nadia* is considered an anime classic, but this is not the reason for including it in this book. Instead, the marks it left on two key animated works in Japan and America demonstrate its influence on steampunk. The first, Walt Disney's *Atlantis: The Lost Empire*, discussed in the previous chapter, would complete the chain of influence begun with *Laputa*. The second, Katsuhiro Otomo's *Steamboy*, forms one of several links between first- and second-wave steampunk in Japan.

Katsuhiro Otomo's *Steamboy* (2004)

Katsuihiro Otomo is an anime legend. This is the man arguably responsible for bringing anime from Japan to the United States with his 1988 film *Akira*. There had been a few anime programs that made it onto Canadian TV when I was a kid, and some really terrible dubs of great anime that ended up on video shelves in the 1980s, but *Akira* was the movie that legitimized what was then called "Japanimation" by science-fiction and fantasy fans in North America. *Akira* had been a monster hit in Japan, and it made a big enough impact in the States that anticipation and expectation for Otomo's next big project was high.

Reviews of *Steamboy* spoke around its steampunk look without ever using the word "steampunk," demonstrating that the word hadn't gained widespread use in 2004. Consequently, Roger Ebert described it as "H. G. Wells and Jules Verne meet *Akira*." The problem was, *Steamboy* wasn't much like *Akira* at all. Because Otomo had admitted that cyberpunk writer William Gibson was an influence on *Akira*, J. Hoberman of *The Village Voice* assumed that Otomo's decision to use steampunk for his next big project was due to Gibson's collaborative effort with Bruce Sterling on *The Difference Engine*. But there are few (if any) direct correspondences between *Steamboy* and *The Difference Engine,* and a survey of the films in this chapter reveal likelier influences in Japan's own steampunk tradition.

Steamboy begins with a prologue involving the experiments and explorations of Doctor Lloyd Steam and his son Edward, who are seeking a highly stable liquid of extreme purity to enable steam to produce greater quantities of energy. When a test goes awry, Edward is wounded, though a metal sphere lies unhurt in the middle of the aftermath. Cut to Manchester 1866, three years later, where Ray Steam, son of Edward, is a budding inventor, not unlike Jean Roque Raltique of *Nadia*. The comparison is not simply the relationship of a boy genius. Ray is working on a powered monowheel like the one Jean and Nadia use to escape the

This monowheel chase scene from Katsuhiro Otomo's *Steamboy* (2004) has strong parallels with a scene in Hideaki Anno's *Nadia: The Secret of Blue Water* (1990–91).   *Alamy*

Grandis Gang in the first episode of *Nadia*. Rather than riffing off Gibson, it seems far likelier—especially when one considers the images of both chases on the opposite page—that Otomo was paying homage to *Nadia* (as opposed to ripping it off, as some anime fans claim).

Another influence to be noted in this chase sequence is *Laputa: Castle in the Sky*. When Sheeta and Pazu are first pursued by the air pirates, the orphans flee to Pazu's boss's home. The boss's wife hides the children, and then ushers them out the back door. This might seem like a standard trope of action films, to come in one door and leave by another, unless you consider the nature of the chase scene that follows. In *Castle* (and *Nadia*), there are two competing groups seeking a mysterious crystal. In *Steamboy,* while it is not immediately apparent, there are two competing groups bent on retrieving the steamball, the metal sphere from the prologue: the O'Hara Foundation and Robert Stephenson (a reference to the rail engineer, not the writer).

The finale of the film once again references *Laputa* in the structure of the steam castle, which, like the floating island of Laputa, has two functions: one military and one benign. Doctor Lloyd Steam's original plan for the steam castle was a flying fairground, but it has been appropriated as a weapon of mass destruction. Otomo shares Miyazaki's pacifist inclinations, as evidenced by Ray's horror at violence perpetrated by both his father and those in Stephenson's camp. Here too, Otomo and Miyazaki share philosophical visions: there is no one government that can be called evil in *Steamboy*. All the nations of the world are represented by the emissaries who come to the Exhibition to see the demonstration of the steam castle.

As with my earlier comparison of the covers for K. W. Jeter's *Morlock Night,* a comparison of these chase scenes reveals a great deal about how much steampunk owes to antecedents such as *Nadia*, while also revealing how much the steampunk style changed with the arrival of the second wave. The color palette of *Nadia* is bright and saturated, while that of *Steamboy* is earth tone and muted. Jess Nevins has been widely quoted (though not always credited) as saying that "steampunk is what happened when Goths discovered brown." But watching early steampunk anime and contrasting it with later works, it would also be accurate to say that "twenty-first-century steampunk is what happened when twentieth-century steampunk discovered brown." This contrast extends beyond the color palette, though: *Nadia*'s characters have the exaggerated expressions typical of anime, while the figures of Ray Steam and his pursuers are more realistic. If we were to go back through every instance of steampunk prior to 2000, we'd find more of the same. There was no self-aware, self-regulating fandom with its gatekeepers and style makers dictating "real steampunk" vs. "false steampunk."

Though it's difficult to chart lines of influence, it's safe to say that, while Otomo's *Steamboy* was a disappointment for anime fans hoping for a second *Akira*, this sepia-toned vision of a fantastic nineteenth century proved highly influential on the look of second-wave steampunk, mirroring the shift to a more desaturated approach in steampunk anime, as evidenced by the TV series *Last Exile*.

Last Exile (2003)

Last Exile is the story of a pilot, Claus Valca, and an engineer, Lavie Head, who find themselves embroiled in politics and intrigue in the middle of a massive war when they take on a commission that involves the protection and delivery of a mysterious girl.

Given that *Last Exile* was released in 2003, the year before *Steamboy*, it's difficult to avoid comparing the two, speculating on secret luncheons to ensure adherence to the desaturated, earthy tones for both productions' color scheme. Like *Steamboy,* the design work for *Last Exile* sits at the liminal point between first- and second-wave steampunk. Technological advances in digital coloring permitted the costume design of the lead characters to contain subtle shades of earth tones, anticipating second-wave steampunk fashion.

Like so much first-wave steampunk, *Last Exile* is not set exclusively in the Victorian period nor England but draws on a host of retrofuturistic inspirations from the Napoleonic Wars in France to the 1920s in America. However, due to advances in 3D animation, the designs of *Last Exile's* retrofuturistic technology were rendered in a photorealistic manner, paralleling the industrial obsession of second-wave steampunk.

The production design of *Last Exile* pays keen attention to ensuring the various airships are heavily industrial in design: both the sky dreadnoughts of the Anatoray navy and the sleek vanship that Claus and Lavie travel in are aerodynamically impossible flying vehicles. The Anatoray dreadnought looks like a massive naval destroyer as improbable as the ones in the comics *The Adventures of Luther Arkwright* by Brian Talbot and *Aetheric Mechanics* by Warren Ellis, while the two-passenger vanships are a mash-up of World War II fighter planes and 1920 and 1930s streamliner-shaped racing cars such as the famous Stutz Blackhawk Streamliner, which set a land speed record at Daytona Beach in 1928.

Range Murata, one of the concept artists for *Last Exile*, credits the look of the vanships to his fascination with the period of industrialization in Europe along with a preference for automobile over airplane design. From there, it's not a great leap to imagine Murata needing to have a design for a fast flying ship and choosing the design aesthetic of the fastest car of the early twentieth century. It's a design choice based in story and "what looks cool" preference, rather than adherence to a prescribed set of features.

Design mash-ups abound in *Last Exile*: the weapons and costumes of the Anatoray musketeer squad are evocative of eighteenth-century military. The rifles resemble black powder technology but are driven by advanced steam power, augmented by the magical Claudia. The design of those rifles has strong affinities with the steam rifles in the 2016 anime *Kabaneri of the Iron Fortress*.

This approach to hybridity is a notable one, because it demonstrates once again how steampunk is often neither historically accurate nor confined to the Victorian period. *Last Exile*'s vanships have an early-twentieth-century design to them but run on steam, albeit steam created from a fictional and somewhat magical substance called Claudia. Claudia is fluorescent blue, reminiscent of the magic stone in *Laputa* and *Nadia* and the magical technology of Disney's *Atlantis*. But *Last Exile*'s magical fuel is easier to argue into the steampunk fold than some other magic, such as the alchemy of *Fullmetal Alchemist*, along with its abundance of colorful costume and lack of brass and leather. Yet *Fullmetal Alchemist* is certainly steampunk.

Fullmetal Alchemist (2001–2011)

In the midst of the deluge of brass and leather typical of second-wave steampunk, it was tough to see the bright red jacket and chrome cyborg prosthetics of Edward Elric, the eponymous protagonist of the very popular *Fullmetal Alchemist*, a manga and anime franchise, as steampunk. The original manga of *Fullmetal Alchemist* debuted in Square Enix's *Monthly Shōnen Gangan* magazine in August 2001, with the first anime adaptation in 2003 (which differs from the manga in a number of ways) and a second, very faithful adaptation of the manga titled *Fullmetal Alchemist: Brotherhood* in 2009. Both anime series were followed by film sequels: the first series by *Fullmetal Alchemist the Movie: Conqueror of Shamballa* in 2005, and the second series by *Fullmetal Alchemist: The Sacred Star of Milos* in 2011. With new content spanning the decade that saw the rise of steampunk as popular culture in North America, the franchise is one of several works occupying the liminal space between the first and second waves, before attempts to unify the steampunk aesthetic.

While the series has a number of subplots and a broad cast of heroes, allies, and villains, the heart of *Fullmetal Alchemist* is the bond between two brothers, Edward and Alphonse Elric, who are questing to restore their original bodies, lost in a taboo alchemical experiment gone disastrously wrong. As a result of this disaster, Edward has lost his right arm and the lower half of his left leg, both of which have been replaced by cyborg prosthetics, while Alphonse is a disembodied soul bound to a suit of armor.

Online discussion of *Fullmetal Alchemist*'s place in steampunk is divided; those who argue for its exclusion seem wrapped up in the idea that steampunk must involve industrial technology. Oddly, many of those who argue for its inclusion say the same thing, limiting the 2005 film *Conqueror of Shamballa* as the only *Fullmetal Alchemist* feature that can properly be considered steampunk because of the film's World War I technology. Then there are the brave few who argue that the entire series is, and has always been, steampunk because of Edward's arm.

In "Road of Hope," the fourth episode of *Brotherhood*, the brothers return home to have Edward's arm repaired by childhood friend Winry Rockbell and her grandmother, Pinako, who is a surgeon and weaponsmith. Pinako served as caretaker of the Elric brothers after they were orphaned, and the Rockbell women built Edward's prosthetic arm and leg, which are called *automail* in the series. Automail was a form of motorized battle armor that the Rockbells used to repair Edward in the aftermath of the brothers' alchemical accident.

Edward's automail is a silver-grey color and resembles a combination of plate armor and advanced robotics. It is not brass. It has no exteriorized cogs or gears. When Edward gives the damaged pieces of his arm to Winry, those pieces are decidedly modern, not industrial in appearance, and are in some opinions cause to say "it's not steampunk." However, to reduce steampunk to the appearance of its advanced technology is to limit artistic expression, and reduce steampunk design to "cumbersome, rusty, industrial-looking." Consider the cyborg prosthetic of Cole Blaquesmith in the comic book series *Steampunk*: like Edward's, Cole's arm (and blast-furnace chest) was built with a combination of alchemy and engineering. In one artistic vision, that advanced technology is sleek and made of chrome; in the other, it is brass and bulky, like someone built an arm out of steam locomotive parts. To say one is "more" steampunk than the other is somewhat arbitrary, especially given that the

While *Full Metal Alchemist* takes place in a technofantasy version of early twentieth-century Europe, fans of second wave steampunk might fail to see Edward Elric's automailarm as an example of steampunk technology.

advances in *Steampunk* are the result of traveling through time to the 1950s; arguably, there should be more chrome and deco streamlining in Blaquesmith's arm.

I could argue that deco streamlining was the possible reason for the design of Edward Elric's arm. Instead, I'll remind you that the manga and first anime of *Fullmetal Alchemist* predate the cog-corset-leather-and-brass uniformity of second-wave steampunk. Like *Nadia* and *Laputa*, it is Japanese steampunk before the influence of the second wave in North America and Europe. It should also be noted that the design of *Fullmetal Alchemist* is on the cusp of animation innovations that permitted shows like *Last Exile* and films like *Steamboy* to render machine parts with exact precision using 3D technology. Edward's arm is like Jean's monowheel in *Nadia*, designed for ease of hand-drawn animation; the later anime and films retain that design because of fidelity to a now-iconic design that immediately signals "Edward Elric" to knowing fans. To change the design to something "more steampunk" would signify a betrayal to fans, a largely unnecessary betrayal. Edward's arm is like the cyborg prosthetics in *Trigun*: steampunk designs before second-wave and CGI advances. And Ed is not the only character in *Fullmetal Alchemist* with automail; had *Fullmetal Alchemist* used a more second-wave design, there would be no question about its contribution to steampunk, given the number of major characters who have automail prosthetics in the series.

Regardless of aesthetic design, Edward's automail arm is also the engineering invention of a girl genius, tinkering at her worktable with wrenches and screwdrivers. While automail sometimes resembles the cyborg components of cyberpunk narratives, there is nary a computer in sight. Edward calls Winry a "crazy gearhead" after she waxes eloquent on the wondrous beauty of automail: "The smell of the oil, the hum of the bearings, the rugged, yet beautiful form. . . ." Like Agatha Heterodyne, Winry is a girl genius in a pre-digital world based on the European Industrial Revolution, brilliant enough to repair "first-rate automail" in three days. The combination of the girl genius character type with the industrial setting is enough to claim *Fullmetal Alchemist*. Industrial mechanical design cannot be held up as the sole signifier of steampunk; the anachronism of a girl genius, a female inventor in a period when women were fighting for the vote in real-world history, is equally if not more important. As we've seen repeatedly throughout this book, the gear-head girl is a common figure in steampunk.

Or I could argue that *Fullmetal Alchemist* deserves a place in steampunk because of its use of alchemy, which is often used in fantasy to indicate the shift from the sort of pure magic we find in Tolkienesque high fantasy to the first moments of science. Alchemy is the place where magic and science come together. In *Fullmetal Alchemist*, alchemy is regularly referred to as science. In history, alchemy was the gateway to modern chemistry. But in fiction, it is still magical. Yet it appears over and over again in steampunk: in Ekaterina Sedia's brilliant novel, *The Alchemy of Stone*, the tale of a clockwork woman who wishes she were real; in Edward Poulton's Steampunk Death Star, which was built with alchemy; in the propulsion system of spaceships in Philip Reeve's *Larklight* series. Steampunk may look like science, but very often, it works like magic. And there is no better example in anime of such technofantasy than Miyazaki's *Howl's Moving Castle*.

Howl's Moving Castle (2004)

Howl's Moving Castle is the story of Sophie, a young hatmaker who is transformed into an old woman when she is cursed by the wicked Witch of the Waste. Sophie wanders into the fog-shrouded Waste in search of a way to end her curse. There, she meets an animated scarecrow she names Turniphead, who leads her to the utterly fantastic contraption-conveyance of the film's name, the moving castle of the wizard Howl. Howl is reputed to steal pretty girls away to take their hearts, but also claims to be heartless himself. If you're already thinking, "this sounds an awful lot like *The Wizard of Oz*," you're not far wrong. While *Howl's Moving Castle* is a loose adaptation of Diana Wynne Jones's fantasy novel, it also borrows liberally from L. Frank Baum's well-known quest story. There's no yellow-brick road, since Sophie doesn't need to journey to meet "the Wizard." Sophie encounters Howl early in the film, a meeting that precipitates and initiates the witch's curse. Howl is not only the ostensible wizard, but is also an amalgam of the Tin Man, for he is literally missing his heart, and the

Cowardly Lion, because he has a reputation for running away from his problems.

Once aboard the moving castle, "Grandma Sophie" sets herself up as Howl's cleaning lady, having made a bargain with the castle's motive power source, Calcifer the Fire Demon. The bargain is simple: if Sophie can end the curse that keeps Calcifer in service to Howl, Calcifer promises to end the curse that keeps Sophie an old woman. Themes of transformation permeate the film, from Sophie's curse, to Calcifer's constantly changing fire form, to the witch's jelly-like body, to Howl's hair color or ability to transform into a fanged, black-winged creature, to the moving castle, which, in addition to its initial haphazard construction, also undergoes four shuddering variations before the credits roll.

Surrounding Sophie's personal journey of transformation is the backdrop of an "idiotic war" that Howl is violently opposed to and opposes with violence in a one-wizard crusade against both sides of the conflict. The audience is never privy to a reason for this war, perhaps underscoring

Hayao Miyazaki's *Howl's Moving Castle* (2004) featured the perfect hybrid of industrial design and magical impulsion, a common combination in steampunk fiction and film.   *Alamy*

its ridiculous nature, a hallmark of Miyazaki's films: war is always monstrous, and the retrofuturistic air-dreadnoughts serve to underscore this. The machines are rendered as monsters, like great metal flying beasts that drop more monsters, both conventional bombs and flocks of wizards-turned-monsters, with wings like wasps and bodies like black toads. All of these monsters, technological and magical, are designed to convey size and threat; the designs are too improbable to imagine them actually flying, despite possessing wings and metal cilia-like propulsion.

As with Miyazaki's *Laputa*, it's certainly the design of these air-dreadnoughts and their lighter, ornithopter-styled counterparts that earn the film the question, "Is *Howl's Moving Castle* steampunk?" But more so than any flying vessel, it is the moving castle itself that inspires that question. It is an utterly implausible clockwork hodgepodge powered by Calcifer's magic; Pete Docter, director of the English translation of the film, said that the moving castle struck him as reminiscent of Terry Gilliam, whose work as steampunk inspiration was discussed in the last chapter. It certainly has the whimsical cut-and-paste look of the work of Gilliam or Karel Zeman.

The moving castle signals the shift in steampunk anime from the clean lines of the airships and ornithopters of *Laputa* to the rust and ruin of second-wave steampunk. *Howl's Moving Castle* was released to North American theaters in 2005 and to DVD in 2006, the year before steampunk would become somewhat mainstream with its appropriation by DIY maker culture. As we will see in the discussion of another of Miyazaki's films, *Nausicaä of the Valley of the Wind*, the timing of this release exerts considerable influence on the look of second-wave steampunk.

It's also one of the strongest arguments for rejecting the limited definition of steampunk as science fiction, since the castle is not run on steam proper. While it certainly belches clouds of steam and must possess the boiler that provides Howl with hot-water baths throughout (to clean off the aftermath of his violent interactions with the warring armies), it is ultimately Calcifer the Fire Demon who not only provides the fuel to make the castle move, but is the very force that runs its gears, and ultimately holds together the eccentric patchwork of scrap iron, turrets, tiny houses, smokestacks, cranes, apparently vestigial bat wings, and walking talons. This is not science fiction. To look at the moving castle is to behold a rejection of real-world physics. It is not held together by engineering, but elemental force. When Calcifer is removed from the castle, it falls into disarray. When Calcifer is wounded (in another moment screamingly reminiscent of *The Wizard of Oz* where the witch is defeated with a bucket of water), the castle goes to pieces until all that remains is a wooden platform and the walking talons. Don't be fooled by the wheels and pulleys. This is mechanized magic, not industrial verisimilitude.

It answers the question "is steampunk science fiction?" by pointing at the rickety ensemble of haphazard parts and says, "Sometimes, but not here. Here, it's fantasy."

Nausicaä of the Valley of the Wind (1984)

Nausicaä of the Valley of the Wind is considered one of the greatest animated movies of all time, with good reason. Set in a postapocalyptic future one thousand years after the Seven Days of Fire, a devastating event that nearly wiped out humanity and created the sprawling Toxic Jungle, a no-man's land filled with poisonous spores and deadly megafauna insects. The film begins with Nausicaä, a young woman wearing a gas mask flying a glider over a densely forested landscape: she enters this forest, the Toxic Jungle, and collects some of its deadly toxic spores. She discovers the carcass of an Ohm, a massive, beetle-like creature; her explorations are interrupted by the sound of concussions in the distance. Nausicaä discovers that a living Ohm is on a rampaging pursuit and rescues Lord Yupa, the greatest living swordsman, by calming the Ohm and sending it back to the forest. Lord Yupa is in awe of Nausicaä's ability to calm the colossal insect.

Nausicaä lives in the Valley of the Winds, an idealized pastoral landscape under the benevolent feudal rule of King Jihl, her father. The idyllic tranquility of the valley is shattered when a great airship from the military state of Tolmekia is attacked by insects and crashes. The crash kills everyone on board, but Nausicaä is able to hear the dying wish of Lastelle, princess of Pejite, the ostensible enemy of the Tolmekians. Lastelle encourages Nausicaä to burn the cargo of the Tolmekian airship, which turns out to be the egg of a God Warrior, the very creatures responsible for the apocalyptic Seven Days of Fire. As one might expect, the villainous Tolmekians, under the command of the heavily armored Princess Kushana, arrive to retrieve their unhatched God Warrior, killing Nausicaä's father and imprisoning the valley denizens.

It turns out that the Tolmekians stole the God Warrior embryo from Pejite, along with their princess. Kushana departs with Nausicaä and four other valley dwellers on a diplomatic mission to Pejite. Though their transports bristle with firepower, the Tolmekian ships are brought down en route to Tolmekia by a lone pilot, whose ship is destroyed in the fire-fight. Nausicaä, Kushana, and the hostage valley dwellers escape the ruin of the Tolmekian ships, but Nausicaä is separated from the rest of the group when she goes to save the Pejite pilot from the insect denizens of the Toxic Jungle.

Nausicaä and Mito, the Pejite pilot, discover an underground forest with an abundance of clean water, a hopeful validation of Nausicaä's experiments to grow untainted plants using spores planted in untainted soil nurtured by pure water drawn from deep in the earth. The pair travel to Pejite, to find the city ruined by insects. The Pejites reveal they lured the insects to the city to destroy the Tolmekians and have incited a herd of Ohm to stampede the Valley of the Wind, wiping out the remaining Tolmekians. Nausicaä, aided by Pejite women and Mito, escapes from the Pejites and races home. She finds a baby Ohm being used as bait to lure the adult stampede. Kushana, having returned to the Valley of the Wind, unleashes the half-grown God Warrior in an attempt to stop the stampede. The effort of expending its catastrophic energy ray—which does not stop the advancing Ohm horde—kills the God Warrior.

Just as all seems lost, Nausicaä sets the Ohm baby free, and in a moment of utter sacrifice, places herself in the path of the oncoming wave of adult Ohm to return their child to them. For a moment, it seems as though her sacrifice is in vain, until the Ohm restore her to life. The film ends on a hopeful note, with end-credit images revealing that peace and prosperity lie ahead for these embattled nations and Nausicaä's people.

If you're like my son, you say at the end, "That was a great movie . . . but it didn't seem very steampunk." Sure, there's retrofuturistic airships and Nausicaä's cool glider, but in the first case, the design is more evocative of World War II than the Victorian period, and in the second, that glider has French artist Moebius written all over it. Yeah, there are goggles, but goggles protect your eyes when you're flying or driving fast. The gyro-copter pilot in *The Road Warrior* had goggles: but few people have been working hard to get the early *Mad Max* movies into the steampunk fold.

But if you google "steampunk anime," you'll often see *Nausicaä of the Valley of the Wind* included among the best. Admittedly, *Nausicaä*'s inclusion on such lists might be explained by an uninformed but tacit association of Hayao Miyazaki's works with steampunk. Remember the question that this entire book is devoted to answering, the one I hear more often than any other: What is steampunk? If I don't have an answer, but I google "steampunk" and see images of *Howl's Moving Castle*, follow that link and find myself in Miyazaki-land, I might associate steampunk with Miyazaki's work in general. And to be fair, that machine-era retro-futurism appears in many of his films. But I don't think that's all that's going on when *Nausicaä* ends up on a list of steampunk anime.

The astute fan of anime may have been wondering why I saved one of Miyazaki's earliest (and some might argue, myself among them, the best) films for last. It's because it's an indication of the elasticity of how people perceive the word "steampunk." If steampunk fans regularly place *Nausicaä* under their steampunk umbrella, then *what* about *Nausicaä* informs steampunk?

Once again, we might say that the bourgeoning concept we have labeled steampunk was different in 1984. There was no term for it. There were no prescriptivists drawing lines in the sand and saying, "cross this, and you're no longer in the steampunk camp." And we cannot deny that Miyazaki is a major contributor to modern steampunk.

Nor can we deny the massive impact the sequential home video release of *Castle in the Sky* in 2003 and *Nausicaä* in 2005 had on the grow-ing number of North American fans of Studio Ghibli films, following the North American theatrical run and DVD release of *Princess Mononoke* in 1999 and 2000, respectively. Add to this the huge success of *Howl's Moving Castle*, whose steampunk elements are more pronounced and in line with second-wave steampunk. In his seminal interview with *Wired* magazine, steampunk maker Jake von Slatt listed *Howl's Moving Castle* as one of the visual inspirations for his steampunk creations. In short, the growth of steampunk into a subculture is contemporaneous with the release of these films in North America. Even if *Nausicaä* has no direct aesthetic impact on steampunk in a clearly identifiable way, Miyazaki's broad retrofuturist vision is clearly felt.

What *Nausicaä* is certainly indicative of is the way in which steampunk as fantasy may have been a reaction to the slavish cloning of Tolkien's high-fantasy epic *The Lord of the Rings* in the 1980s. Miyazaki has openly admitted that Tolkien's fantasy is among the influences for his work, particularly for *Nausicaä*. Unlike much fantasy in the 1980s that expressed a debt of inspiration to Tolkien, Miyazaki has other influences like Ursula K. Le Guin. Le Guin's *Wizard of Earthsea*, while inspired by Tolkien, is not a carbon copy of *The Hobbit* or *The Lord of the Rings*. When writers like China Miéville react to Tolkien negatively and seek to write fiction that doesn't just repeat, they effectively end up doing the same thing writers like Miyazaki who love Tolkien but include disparate influences in their own work do: create fantasy that forges new ground. Consider how Miyazaki accomplishes something very similar to what Miéville does with New Crobuzon, which is to create a fantasy secondary world where industrialization has, effectively, come to Middle-earth. If one looks at the fairy-tale landscapes of the Miyazaki films covered in this chapter, you see pastoral landscapes that echo Tolkien's Shire and Hobbiton: verdant fields and forests, cozy cottages, and happy communities. But like New Crobuzon, industrialization is here too, and the impact of industry, especially its effect on military technology, is one of Miyazaki's recurring themes. Consider the quaint seaside town Sophie is from in *Howl's Moving Castle*. Viewers experience it as a tranquil, halcyon location before seeing it ruined by an air raid by steampunk flying machines. So Miyazaki, like Miéville, is creating fantasies in worlds that were Tolkien's nightmare: they are filled with steam-powered machines. For Miéville, it's rejection. For Miyazaki, it's revision.

Considering *Nausicaä* as steampunk usually provokes the conclusion that it's about the steampunk airships or the goggles or Princess Kushana's brass-armor prosthetic legs and arm that justify the film's inclusion on steampunk anime lists. But what if it's because the idea of steampunk is, in the popular imagination (or at least in the imagination of people who put *Nausicaä* on lists of steampunk anime), about more than those individual elements? What if steampunk has become a wide-ranging signifier for fantasy that isn't based in an idealized pre-Enlightenment past? One that isn't just swords and sorcery, or wizards and warriors, dungeons and dragons? What if steampunk is the nostalgia for a past, but not one so distant as the medieval period or Renaissance? And what if that wide-ranging signifier also indicates science fiction that isn't based in the future? Science fiction that won't concern itself with technology beyond the machine era? Because a steampunk definition that included that kind of breadth would explain the presence of people riding around in the belly of a flying whale, a walled Seattle infested with zombies, or a romance between a werewolf and a woman with no soul, which is where steampunk ends up going in its second wave.

9

Writing the Second Wave

2009

The rise of the steampunk community announced that there was a market for steampunk fiction, and in 2009, three novels were released that were critically praised and financially successful: Cherie Priest's *Boneshaker*, which tells the story of a mother who pursues her prodigal son into nineteenth-century Seattle, which is walled off to contain a plague of zombies; Gail Carriger's *Soulless*, which proved to be the most successful of all these series, despite being derided as "not steampunk enough," because it was primarily a paranormal romance between the head of a werewolf pack and a preternatural woman, someone who negates supernatural abilities due to a lack of soul. It parodied Jane Austen's comedy of manners but was viable on its own story line, producing Manga adaptations, four sequels, and two spin-off series. And finally, Scott Westerfeld's *Leviathan,* the first in a Young Adult trilogy set in a steampunked version of World War I, waged between the Darwinists, who use biological weapons in the form of fabricated animals such as airships that are living whales that can fly, and the Clankers, who use steam-driven iron machines.

Up until 2008, few books overtly claimed to be steampunk. Review blurbs would sometimes identify them as such, and many have been retroactively welcomed under the steampunk parasol. In other cases, the books did not make a long-lasting impact on steampunk. In 2008, Tachyon books released *Steampunk*, an anthology that contained short stories and excerpts dating back to Michael Moorcock in the 1970s and James Blaylock in the 1980s, with "Reflected Light" by Rachel E. Pollack bringing the collection up to 2007. In the UK, Solaris books released *Extraordinary Engines*, an anthology of brand-new stories (every story shares the copyright date of 2008) from a host of hot science-fiction and fantasy writers. The anthologies shared a few names, like Ian MacLeod, who had written a steampunk duology a few years earlier; Jay Lake, whose *Mainspring* trilogy had kicked off the year before; and Jeff Vandermeer, who would share editing duties with his wife Ann on two more *Steampunk* anthologies for Tachyon before releasing *The Steampunk Bible*, a coffee-table book. While both anthologies are filled with great stories and, in the case of the Tachyon anthology, act as a sort of survey of steampunk writing from first-wave inception to second-wave innovation, neither was hugely influential on second-wave steampunk. Popular reviews of the Tachyon anthology in particular express a sense of disappointment, a lack of cohesion between what steampunk *seemed* to be when one looked at images of steampunked *Star Wars*. Looking back now, those anthologies seem like a warning shot across the airship bow, portending the wave that was about to come.

The year 2009 was a watershed for steampunk fiction, and in particular the fall of that year, with three writers publishing the first in their series in a tight succession. The first two writers out of the gate were to become closely linked to each other in the steampunk scene: Cherie Priest's *Boneshaker*, the start of her *Clockwork Century* series, was first on September 29. On October 1, hot on Priest's heels, Gail Carriger published *Soulless,* the first volume of her *Parasol Protectorate* books. And finally on October 6, Scott Westerfeld released *Leviathan,* the first book in what would become a trilogy by the same title. Only weeks before, on September 5, *Goodreads* "popular steampunk" list had *Perdido Street Station, The Different Engine*, and the Tachyon *Steampunk* anthology in the top three spots. Using the Wayback Machine, an online se rvice that collects snapshots of websites, I was able to see that by November 6, *Leviathan* had ousted *Steampunk*, and by January 23, 2010, *Soulless* and *Boneshaker* joined Westerfeld's novel in the top three spots, where they remained for the next two years (at the time of writing, *Boneshaker* was in fourth place behind Carriger's second steampunk novel, *Changeless*).

Every one of these series have books that are among my favorite steampunk reads. To understand how they contributed to the growth of steampunk and are indicative of the second wave of steampunk, I'll need to provide summaries for the books, along with some commentary. I will do my best to avoid climactic spoilers but will be unable to stay away from some major ones that are crucial to the growth of this new wave of steampunk writing.

Cherie Priest: *Boneshaker* and the Clockwork Century

Cherie Priest's *Boneshaker* was a "first" for second-wave steampunk in several ways.

Boneshaker was arguably the first really popular steampunk novel to address the dissonance that readers expressed about the Tachyon *Steampunk* anthology: steampunk fans wanted goggles, airships, and ass-kicking adventure, and Priest provided all three. She was the first to invert the direction of steampunk fiction's inspiration by incorporating narrative elements from steampunk fashion/cosplay community. In 2009, there was already a sense of the pervasiveness of steampunk goggles. They were, along with cogs, one of those things that immediately signaled that what you were looking at might be steampunk. Priest's *Boneshaker* was the first novel to unabashedly embrace the goggles, putting them front and center on her cover. But it wasn't just a marketing ploy: Priest had come up with a reason for her heroine to be wearing those goggles, and for why the world they looked at was sepia-toned, as many steampunk photos were, in emulation of early photographs.

Boneshaker is largely set inside an imprisoned, late-nineteenth-century Seattle surrounded by a containment wall. The wall has been built to contain a dangerous gas called the Blight, which effectively turns people into zombies (it's more complicated and involved than that, but for simplicity's sake, they are zombies), whom the locals refer to as Rotters. The Blight also has a corrosive effect on the buildings and landscape: "The Blight eats up paint and fixings," says one denizen of the enclosed city, "and makes everything go yellow-brown." The Blight gas is invisible, save through polarized lenses. Hence, the goggles. They both protect the eyes from the taint of the Blight, but also allow someone to see the gas and thereby take evasive precautions.

The book contains other hallmarks of steampunk fiction, like airships run by smugglers, mercenaries, and pirates, but like the goggles

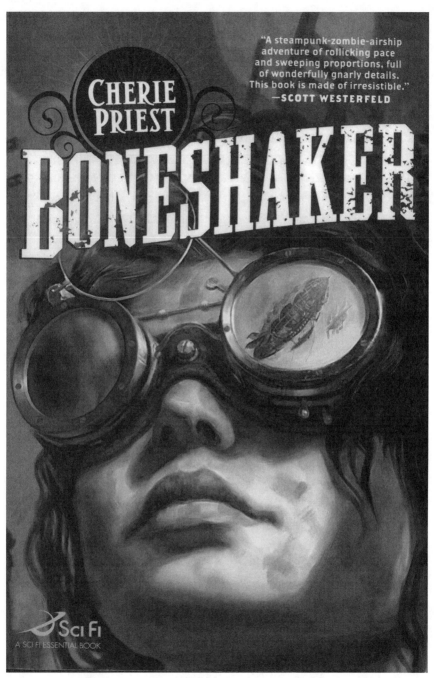

Cherie Priest's *Boneshaker* was one of the first steampunk novels to feature the iconic brass goggles so prominently on the cover.

and the sepia tone, Priest has good narrative reasons for including what were already fast becoming steampunk clichés. Plotwise, *Boneshaker* is a mash-up of John Carpenter's *Escape from New York* and Hans Christian Andersen's "Story of a Mother." Consequently, where *Escape from New York* has the President of the United States in need of rescue, *Boneshaker* has a fifteen-year-old boy. And instead of Snake Plissken, a cynical anti-hero on his way to prison, *Boneshaker* has Briar Wilkes, a factory-working, frontier-toughened mother.

Priest's second *Clockwork Century* book, *Dreadnought*, disappointed some readers by not only leaving the embattled, walled city of Seattle, but for abandoning the Wilkeses as protagonists. Yet to tell the story of Mercy Lynch, a widowed Civil War nurse on her way to see her estranged father on his death bed, Priest arguably had to abandon Briar and Zeke, or risk straining credibility far beyond that which zombies or airships would do. It's the Jack Bauer syndrome—there's only so many times an audience will buy that only one man (or woman) is capable of saving the day. And despite the presence of the Rotter zombies, Priest's series strives for a realistic tone.

This realism comes out best in Priest's use of steampunk's ubiquitous airships. In most second-wave steampunk, airships are made to operate like fighter jets, or spaceships like the *Millennium Falcon* or *Serenity* of *Firefly* fame. As discussed in the chapter on steampunk and alternate history, airships often use fictional elements to enable them to fly the way they do: a lifting gas superior to hydrogen, a magic crystal, alchemy, or some combination of these. In Priest's Clockwork Century, airships are anachronisms, but ones that fly and crash the way real-world physics demand of them.

Early on in *Dreadnought*, Mercy Lynch's airship crash-lands near the front lines of a Civil War that still hasn't ended by 1880, drawn out, as Priest's website states, "by English interference, a different transportation infrastructure, and a powerful Republic of Texas that discovered oil at Spindletop some fifty years sooner than real life allowed." The airship is crippled, unable to get back in the air; Mercy is forced to finish her journey by train, the book's *Dreadnought*.

In the third *Clockwork Century* release, *Clementine* (which is the second book by the series' chronology), airships rise and fall with the same struggle their real-world counterparts do. They are incapable of carrying the huge libraries, drawing rooms, and ballrooms of the airships (and airschools) in Gail Carriger's steampunk world. Priest's airships are sometimes armored, as the stolen vessels of *Clementine* are, but the armor requires those ships carry less cargo: the heavier the ship, the more difficult the lift. *Clementine* picks up where *Boneshaker* left off, but still not with the story of the Wilkeses. Instead, it's the tale of Captain Croggon Beauregard Hainey, an ex-slave, ex-convict-turned-airship-pirate in pursuit of his stolen ship, the *Free Crow*. Now dubbed the *Clementine*, the stolen airship contains cargo crucial to the development of what turns out to be the steampunk equivalent of a laser cannon. Enter Maria Isabella Boyd, a Confederate-spy-turned-Pinkerton-agent who's been sent to ensure that cargo arrives at its destination.

The *Clockwork Century* series ran for five novels, two novellas, and a few short stories before Priest brought it to a close in 2015 with the novella *Jacaranda*. Most steampunk book lists include *Boneshaker* as a crucial work of steampunk fiction, while the sequels fall somewhat into obscurity, save with diehard Cherie Priest fans. Priest's *Clockwork Century* represents the trend of realistic and gritty steampunk fiction. In an article for *Locus* magazine, Priest claimed that Seattle was the perfect setting for a steampunk novel, because it's a "dark, wet place," a testament to her vision of violence and horror for her steampunk. Her approach is also the path least taken in steampunk writing, even when writers share her vision of darkness and brutality. When writers adopt an approach similar to Priest's, it is realistic only insofar as that secondary world permits, such as in the *Vampire Empire* series by Clay and Sue Griffith, which shares the brutality and seriousness of Priest's series but incorporates magic, monsters, and fantastic transportation in a way that identifies it with fantasy. With the exception of the novella *Jacaranda*, none of Priest's steampunk books could properly be called fantasy.

Nevertheless, her realistic approach is arguably the least successful approach in steampunk writing; fans of the genre tend to enjoy things a bit more on the side of the marvelous, which likely attests to the massive success of Gail Carriger's *Parasol Protectorate* series, and its associated prequel and sequel series, *The Finishing School* and *The Custard Protocol*.

Gail Carriger: *The Parasol Protectorate, The Finishing School, The Custard Protocol*

Gail Carriger is a steampunk Cinderella story. While it took until her second book to make the *New York Times* Bestsellers list (an honor she has garnered with nearly every release since), her first book, *Soulless*, was a success in its own right, and one that exceeded its publisher's expectations. Carriger once told me that they expected it do to reasonably well and were caught off guard by *Soulless*'s wide success and critical praise. It won several awards, and within a year was being developed into a manga version for Yen Press that was released in 2011. The *Parasol Protectorate* series is easily one of the (if not *the*) most successful steampunk series ever published. Carriger dominates steampunk lists on *Goodreads*, which is ironic given that early criticism Carriger received had determined that her books weren't "steampunk enough" due to the lack of focus on technology. Looking at steampunk lists today, it seems that the whimsical paranormal steampunk adventure Carriger pioneered is where the genre thrives best.

But in 2009, there was nothing like *Soulless*. Describing it was difficult.

"It's like *Underworld*," I'd say, because it involves a world where vampires, werewolves, and ghosts have their own societies.

"Oh, I don't like horror," would be the reply.

"It's not horror," I'd say, "It's paranormal romance."

"I don't like *Twilight*."

"It's not like *Twilight*. It's funny."

"It has vampires, werewolves, and ghosts and it's funny?"

"Yes. It's funny because they're part of proper Victorian society. So the vampires have to ask permission to drink people's blood. It's bad manners to bite without consent."

I could say the books are like Jane Austen's comedies of manners meets *Dracula*, but that almost always resulted in people saying, "I'm reading something like that right now. It's called *Pride and Prejudice and Zombies*." Which *Soulless* does not resemble, save perhaps in irreverent reverence for Austen's work. Where Seth Grahame-Smith took Austen's plot (and entire swathes of text) and inserted zombies, Carriger is only writing in the spirit of Austen. Or to be more precise, the spirit of Austen via British cinema and comedy.

Soulless is the story of Alexia Tarabotti, a spinster (in her late twenties, a reminder of how different the world was in the Victorian era—a woman was almost a write-off for marriage prospects at that age) who is too well read, smart, and opinionated to find a good match. Alexia is a preternatural, a woman with no soul, living in a world filled with beings who while living had too much soul: vampires, werewolves, and ghosts. Due to her utter lack of soul, Alexia is able to cancel out the abilities of the supernatural creatures through a mere touch, skin to skin. The book begins with a vampire attacking Alexia at a dinner party; she inadvertently stakes her assailant with a wooden hairpin. Consequently, she is questioned by Lord Conall Maccon, a werewolf who wears his alpha male emotions on his sleeve and is the head of the BUR, the Bureau of Unnatural Registry, which monitors the actions of supernaturals. It's clear that Conall and Alexia have a history (involving hedgehogs), and that in an opposites-attract fashion, are reluctantly attracted to each other.

The vampire attack leads both Alexia and Conall to investigate what would have driven the vampire to attack Alexia (instead of asking politely for a drink). What they discover is a secret society of scientists, intent on eradicating supernaturals. In the process, Alexia and Conall find themselves in each other's presence; with close proximity to the full moon, Conall is unable to hide his attraction for Alexia, and kisses her after rescuing her from a wax-faced automaton/golem. In conventional romantic form, it can never be that easy: werewolf pack dynamics dictate that Alexia make the first move, and so Conall avoids her at a social gathering the next evening. It finally takes the intervention of Conall's right-hand man, Professor Lyall, to set the lovestruck pair on a proper collision course, while the story barrels toward its own set of collisions with mad science and fear of the Other.

While Carriger writes exciting adventure and engaging romance in terms of plot, the real attraction of the *Parasol Protectorate* is not so much the plots Carriger constructs, but the world she has built and the characters who inhabit that world.

Take Lord Akeldama, a vampire so flamboyant he makes Liberace look restrained, whose foppish ways are a mask for his political

Gail Carriger's Parasol Protectorate series has proven to be the most successful steampunk fiction series to date, spawning prequels, sequels, and a Manga adaptation from Yen Press.

machinations. Or the ever-obtuse Ivy Hisselpenny, Alexia's best friend, with a taste for gaudy hats and a propensity to fear more for Alexia's social standing than her safety. In both characters, Carriger exercises a focus on fashion that echoes the steampunk community's interest in clothing. This is so much a staple of Carriger's books that it has formed one of the pillars of her identity on social media: a cursory look at Carriger's blog, Facebook, or Twitter account reveals endless photos of shoes, updates on good fashion (as well as faux pas).

Carriger's fascination with fashion might be one of the reasons for her success: go to any steampunk convention to see the bevy of booths devoted to steampunk fashion, especially for women, to say nothing of the endless parade of ladies dressed in steampunk finery. Beyond the work of cosplay and fashion, fans of steampunk are often fans of fashion. And Carriger feeds the fire of that fandom in her commitment to detailed descriptions of her characters' attire. This is never rendered in a clunky way, as some steampunk writers are wont to do. Whereas many writers are forced to include such descriptions as expository info-dumps about bowler hats and waistcoats, Carriger has constructed a steampunk world where, just as in the real world, characters care about what they wear. And not just care. The cast of Carriger's prequel series, *The Finishing School* series, are educated in the esoterica of formal dress. The foppish Lord Akeldama is known for being a fashionista, setting the trends of London society.

Carriger is clearly writing steampunk, despite allegations to the contrary. As stated earlier, Carriger shared with me that she has her fair share of naysayers who try to argue that *Soulless* isn't "real steampunk." They cite her lack of focus on technology, which is a very restrictive way of understanding steampunk. Carriger's world is clearly steampunk, even if her immediate focus isn't on the technology that is part of the setting.

What's especially interesting about the naysayers claiming Carriger doesn't write steampunk is how *The Parasol Protectorate* is easily among the most successful steampunk series in print, if not among the top three, along with Phillip Pullman's *His Dark Materials*. While Pullman's *His Dark Materials* is considered a classic of children's fantasy, Carriger now has three best-selling series to her name, all within the *Parasol Protectorate* universe. *The Parasol Protectorate* was followed by

The Finishing School series, set decades before *Soulless*, which follows the adventures of Sophonia, a young woman sent to learn to be a proper lady at a school where "finishing" isn't just about manners, it's about learning the art of espionage and assassination. Even before *The Finishing School*'s final volume was released, Carriger returned to the Maccon family with the *Custard Protocol* series, in which Alexia's daughter Prudence is the protagonist. Both these prequel and sequel series feature younger heroines than her first series but continue to appeal to fans of Carriger's earlier work. Add to this the very successful manga adaptation of the first two books in the *Parasol Protectorate* series and translation into over a dozen languages.

From a popular perspective, Carriger's brand of steampunk has won the day. Again, look at the top steampunk Goodreads and you'll see a plethora of covers mimicking the approach Carriger's marketing teams use for all her series. Second-wave gatekeepers may have wanted steampunk to be serious and gritty, but the popular consensus has clearly demanded whimsical and brassy. One might say that Blaylock's approach won out over Moorcock's in the end. When I asked Carriger for her thoughts on why her books have become so popular, her concise answer said everything: "People like to laugh, and they like to love. My books are filled with laughter and love."

Consequently, steampunk isn't just filled with fictional women with agency like Alexia, Sophronia, and Prudence who forge their own way in a man's world. Steampunk is *created* by women with agency, who likewise are forging their way in a man's world. The clamor of those who declared Carriger's "not steampunk enough" has been drowned out by the landslide of fans who have declared with their hard-earned dollars not only that is it steampunk enough, but that it's the dark and gritty works that may have to earn their place inside this ever-changing space called steampunk.

The two-to-one ratio of male to female authors of this chapter has been supplanted since 2009, with that Goodreads "popular steampunk" list populated predominantly by women in the top ten titles: Carriger, Priest, with Scott Westerfeld as the token male. But as we'll see, even Westerfeld was contributing to the larger, unified story this new steampunk trinity was telling.

Scott Westerfeld: *Leviathan*

Scott Westerfeld's *Leviathan* series is clearly aimed at a young adult audience; while it contains the seeds of romance, it has none of the naughty bits in *The Parasol Protectorate*, and is less dark and brutal than Priest's *Clockwork Century*.

The first book begins in the bedroom of Aleksandr, the fictional son of Archduke Franz Ferdinand, as he plays with toy soldiers representing the two factions in the European politics of Westerfeld's steampunk Great War. On the one side, the industrial Clanker nations, of which Austria is one, with their "diesel powered walking machines"; on the other, the Darwinists, with their biologically manipulated creatures. It's a brilliant start to the series, since it tells the reader about the geopolitical landscape *and* conveys the fictional novum of the series without any sense of heavy exposition.

Aleksandr is spirited away in the dead of night by his father's close aides: Alek's fencing teacher, the ever-scheming, ever-brooding Count Volger; his father's master of mechanics, the optimistic and affable Otto Klopp. Chased by German forces who seek to eliminate Alek from the political field, they escape Austria-Hungary in the family's Stormwalker, which Klopp is teaching Alek to drive. Meanwhile, in England, a young woman named Deryn Sharp makes a dangerous break with convention by joining the British Air Service under the gender-bending guise of Dylan Sharp. After airman midshipman's exam goes awry (a sudden storm blows Deryn far off course, strapped to a Darwinist airbeast, a modified hydrogen-breathing jellyfish hybrid called a Huxley ascender), Deryn finds herself serving aboard the *Leviathan*, a massive airbeast contrived from the life threads of a whale, but containing within itself an entire ecosystem contrived to keep it aloft and flying. It is, without a doubt, one of the coolest airship novums in all of steampunk.

Westerfeld explains that the ship creates its own hydrogen by housing bees, which build honeycombs in the *Leviathan*'s gastric region. The ship's "microscopic hydrogen-farting bacteria" consumes the honey, and then excretes the necessary gas to create lift, thereby "extracting fuel from nature." In addition to its stingerless bees, the airship is home to double-snouted, six-legged dogs called hydrogen sniffers, responsible for ensuring there are no leaks in the *Leviathan*'s membrane. There are strafing hawks and flechette bats (the hawks carry huge nets to entangle Clanker aircraft, while the bats consume figs with spikes in them, which they then dump—literally—onto enemy ships), glowworms in the hull to keep it lit enough to walk on at night, but not be seen by enemies, and messenger lizards that crawl all over the ship, inside and out, capable of mimicking the precise commands of officers, right down to the way they sound.

One of my favorite aspects of *Leviathan* is how Westerfeld weaves the life threads of his setting, this wonderful steampunk world of flying whales and steampunk walkers, along with his plot of an Austrian prince on the run and a girl masquerading as a boy to join the British air service. Alek and his guardians reach a safe haven, a ruined castle in the Swiss alps, ready to wait out the war. Meanwhile, *The Leviathan* engages in air combat with German forces and crashes onto a glacier in the Alps, conveniently located near the castle Alek is hiding at. Against the suspicious Count Volger's wishes, Alek secretly goes to the aid of the downed *Leviathan*'s crew. Westerfeld brings his plotlines together like life threads when Alek serendipitously finds Deryn unconscious on the glacier and revives her. Despite his gifts of medicine and food, Alek is made captive by the *Leviathan*'s crew, which brings Volger, Klopp, and company to the rescue in their Stormwalker. In an instance of "the enemy of my enemy is my friend," the *Leviathan* crew and the disenfranchised Austrians drive off a German attack, but not before the Stormwalker is irreparably damaged. Once again, Westerfeld's idea of blending life threads comes to the fore. With another German onslaught imminent, both sides contribute from their ruined vehicles to create something new: the *Leviathan* gains new Clanker engines, cobbled together from the abandoned Stormwalker. This fusion of technologies is more than simply an escape; it is an emblem of cooperation between these warring factions.

The second book, *Behemoth*, begins over the Mediterranean Sea, with the *Leviathan* en route to Constantinople, as the ship's crew calls it, highlighting another of the series' recurring themes, which is the perception of difference. In addition to how the Clankers see the Darwinists' fabricated beasts as "Godless," a subtle inclusion of European Roman Catholicism (again, steampunk often jettisons religion without explanation or vilifies

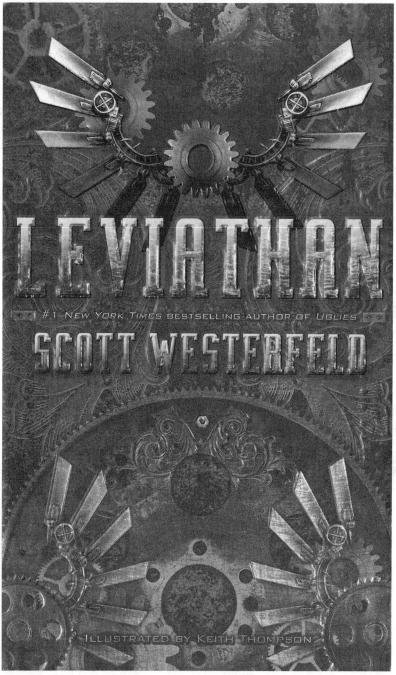

The original cover for Scott Westerfeld's *Leviathan*, prominently displaying the steampunked Hapsburg crest. Subsequent editions would feature the series' young protagonists.

it cartoonishly), and the Darwinists see the Clankers' industrial technology as noisy and backward, we are also shown how the West imposes its perceptions on the East (and vice versa). Doctor Nora Barlowe, the granddaughter of Charles Darwin and a scientist and diplomat, was introduced in the first book, but her mission to bring Darwinist technology to the Ottomans is at the forefront of *Behemoth*. Doctor Barlowe corrects her companions, telling them that the residents of "Constantinople" call the city Istanbul, and have for hundreds of years. "Maybe it's time to fix our barking maps," Deryn comments, underscoring the theme of difference for Westerfeld's YA reader.

Behemoth's story centers on the race between the Germans and the British to win favor with the Ottoman Empire. The British face an added challenge created by Winston Churchill, current Lord of the Admiralty, who absconded with a brand-new airship meant for the Ottomans. Doctor Barlowe's journey aboard the *Leviathan* is a mission of diplomacy, meant to make right Churchill's grave error. This diplomacy is thwarted at every turn, despite Deryn and Alek's best, and oftentimes unintentional, efforts. Alek becomes the recipient of one of the creatures Doctor Barlowe brought aboard the *Leviathan* as a gift for the Turks.

The weaving theme continues in this book with the *Leviathan* becoming something new because of the merging of Clanker and Darwinist technology. Near the end of the first book, Deryn observes that the ship had "developed an independent streak, a tendency to choose its own way among the thermals and the updrafts." She credits this to the *Leviathan*'s new Clanker engines, for "Who wouldn't feel feisty with all that power?" The ship exhibits further independence when it turns from the danger of a Tesla cannon at the beginning of *Behemoth*. The airship continues to be a metaphor for the war: what could these great nations accomplish if, instead of fighting, they chose to put aside differences and strive together?

The design of the Ottoman machines expands this theme, demonstrating how Istanbul and its people are trapped between these warring giants. The Ottomans use Clanker technology such as walking machines and airships, but the designs are always clearly inspired by Darwinist designs. The walking machines resemble elephants or scorpions, while the gondola on an airship is shaped to look like a falcon. Even the *Orient*

Express exhibits this mix, being a steam train with an engine shaped like a dragon's head.

One of the most steampunk novums that Westerfeld employs is the Spottiswoode rebreather, an underwater apparatus created from fabricated creatures: "The suit had been woven from salamander skin and tortoise shell. The rebreather itself was practically a living creature, a set of fabricated gills that had to be kept wet even in storage." The rebreather is an echo of Verne's *20,000 Leagues Under the Sea*, and then the underwater photography of Disney's version, but rendered by H. R. Giger or David Cronenberg. Westerfeld described the way the rebreather's tendrils creep into Deryn's mouth "seeking a source of carbon dioxide" as "uncanny and a bit horrid." But it's as steampunk as a diving apparatus that doesn't require a long tube connected to a ship: the nineteenth century wasn't just about industrial revolution. Westerfeld's inclusion of Darwinist technologies is a reminder of how revolutionary Darwin's *Origin of Species* was. The use of biological technology in steampunk doesn't necessitate the creation of yet another subgenre such as biopunk, since steampunk's evocation of the nineteenth century demands a look at biological technology. Alongside those great machines that changed everything about how we do everything were changes in chemistry and medicine. It wasn't just steam, clockwork, and electricity. It was also anesthesia, birth control, germ theory, and of course, vaccines for cholera, anthrax, rabies, typhoid fever, and *plague*. I love that last one. We live in a world beyond these diseases, and far too often, steampunk forgets that the Victorian world was, by comparison to our own sterile, vaccinated life, a filthy, plague-infested one. While Westerfeld only makes a passing reference to innovations in medicine, anachronistically moving the discovery of penicillin back by a decade or so. Nevertheless, the use of biological technology in the *Leviathan* pays attention to one of the other sides of the technological revolutions of the nineteenth century, in a way that is as much technofantasy as Gibson and Stirling's Babbage Engine was in *The Difference Engine*.

And *Behemoth* highlights one other technology that underwent revolutionary change in the nineteenth century: print technology. The print revolution of the nineteenth century permitted the production and distribution of massive amounts of printed works that were now more affordable and accessible. This in turn led to the spread of those printed ideas and an increase in adult literacy. To understand the leap forward in print technology, consider that the first iron printing press built by Charles Stanhope in 1800 could print between two hundred and four hundred sheets per hour, but was still hand-cranked. Within less than twenty years, the innovation of the steam press had increased that to one thousand per hour. By the middle of the century, the rotary press could make millions of copies a day. This proliferation of material led to an increase in not only demand for *more* books, but books to match a demand for diverse material, which led to the rise of the genre. More than any other technological innovation of the nineteenth century, steampunk owes its existence to print technology: no increase in print, no diversification of readership, no genres, no subgenres, no steampunk.

Westerfeld's printing press in *Behemoth* is called the Spider and belongs to a revolutionary group called the Committee. Dylan comments that it resembles a spideresque, a fabricated beast that weaves parachutes. Zaven, a member of the Committee, agrees that the Spider is for weaving, but for weaving "the threads that hold our revolution together." It is the source of radical ideas, like women being given the vote, and the speed and volume of production means that it is, as Zaven declares, "far mightier than any sword!"

The final book, *Goliath*, follows Deryn and Alek's travels after their exploits with the revolution in Istanbul. To the surprise of Alek, who returned to the *Leviathan* expecting to be imprisoned and taken to Britain for detainment, the mighty airbeast heads east first to Russia, where the ship rescues Nikolai Tesla and a group of stranded Russian airmen, then on to Japan, and finally America. It is Tesla who drives the extended detour, claiming to have created a device responsible for the Tunguska event, a historical explosion that occurred in Siberia in June 1908 that flattened trees (two thousand square kilometers) and shattered windows hundreds of miles away from the epicenter of the explosion. While the explosion is generally held to have been the result of a meteor, an air of mystery still surrounds the event, and since it occurs within the temporal blast radius of steampunk "history," writers like Westerfeld have used it. Thomas Pynchon also includes the Tunguska event in his epic novel *Against the Day*, which has a steampunk adventure as one of its story lines. Like Westerfeld, Pynchon also references Tesla as a possible cause for the Tunguska event, as does the *Assassin's Creed* comic book set in this period, *Assassin's Creed: The Fall*.

Tesla claims responsibility for the Tunguska event, and announces that the device that caused it, named Goliath, will be able to end the war. Alek, feeling useless since leaving Istanbul, recognizes an opportunity to become instrumental in Tesla's mission. He convinces the captain of the *Leviathan* to assist Tesla by getting him to New York with all available speed.

While I don't want to give away the ending of *Goliath*, I can reveal that Westerfeld brings his theme of interdependence full circle, demonstrating that we do better to realize we need each other; on the large scale, Clankers and Darwinists can achieve more when they work together, demonstrated on a smaller scale by cooperation between Count Volger and Doctor Barlowe, and more consistently, between Deryn and Alek.

The Common Thread: Steampunk's Come a Long Way, Baby

It's interesting to look back on the confluence of these three successful steampunk series and recognize a common thread that runs through them all. You might think it would be romance, but that's not a feature of the majority of Priest's stories. You might say it is "high-flying adventure," but that's something common to almost all steampunk. All of these books are concerned with the position of women in the Victorian and Edwardian periods. You might think this would be a default position for twenty-first-century writers looking at a nineteenth-century past, but as a rule, much of steampunk was more concerned with male heroes prior to 2009. In many ways, the success of these books would set the course for what literary steampunk would become after 2009.

Westerfeld's Deryn Sharpe is an exploration of the way in which society once thought of females as incapable of doing the same things men could; she regularly has to swallow her pride when her companions and crewmates comment on how a girl couldn't be doing the same things they are. She's also a mild queering, since her cross-dressing subterfuge results in a girl falling in love with Deryn in *Behemoth*, culminating in a kiss from the girl, who finally reveals that she *knew* Deryn was a girl the whole time. Deryn, rather than engaging in a standard heterosexual response of comedic revulsion, sides with Katy Perry in being a little surprised that she liked it. Furthermore, once Alek becomes aware of Deryn's deception, one has to admit that his sudden attraction to her cannot simply be the result of a shift in gender perception. Since the beginning of their relationship, Alek has admitted that Deryn is the boy he wishes he could have been had he not been born a prince. While this is obviously admiration, there is also a sense of latent attraction, which cannot be ignored. There are other gender reversals that are notable. Although both characters rescue each other repeatedly, Deryn's rescues of Alek and other crew are always of the Douglas Fairbanks derring-do variety, a position normally reserved for, well, Douglas Fairbanks, not his leading lady. Repeatedly, Deryn Sharpe pushes at the boundaries of what it means to be female.

Gail Carriger's Alexia occupies a series of traditional female roles from the nineteenth century (spinster, wife, and mother) that get overturned or transformed in some way. She is not a typical Victorian spinster in that she is not actively pursuing her romantic interests, but instead chases after new scientific and technological knowledge. She is more interested in being useful than being used. When she becomes romantically involved with Lord Maccon, it is on her own terms, not as some fallen woman who needs to be married because her honor has been besmirched. Whereas Victorian women were expected to be sexually passive, Alexia is sexually active, telling Maccon she is about to seduce him, mirroring the sexual agency of twenty-first-century women. When they become married, she continues to lead an active life of adventure and espionage, gaining a secret government position that has her doing far more than choosing wallpaper. When she becomes pregnant, she continues these activities, right up to the moment she goes into labor. When told by one of her servants that she ought not to go into a battle zone because she is about to give birth, Alexia replies, "Oh that's not important. That can wait."

Cherie Priest's *Clockwork Century* series contains a succession of strong, capable women living in a world that doesn't recognize them for their potential contribution. When Briar Wilkes of *Boneshaker* hires an airship to take her over the Seattle Blight's containment wall, one of the crew protests, shocked that his captain has agreed to take a woman into the walled city. Wilkes replies "there's no need to hold my funeral yet," but her confidence in no way diminishes the struggles she faces as a woman in the nineteenth century, even a steampunked one. Likewise Mercy Lynch, the heroine of *Boneshaker*'s sequel *Dreadnought*, is capable in ways her male companions are not in this steampunk *Planes, Trains, and Automobiles* (fraught with more peril, and with Sam Elliott as a companion instead of John Candy), but Priest never makes this easy. There are numerous examples of second-wave steampunk that, seeking to emulate Priest and Carriger, would imagine emancipated and empowered female protagonists. However, that emancipation and empowerment came with no cost, no price, thereby erasing the very real struggle almost all women faced in the nineteenth century, and the one that many women still face today.

Priest said that one of the things she was trying to do with the *Clockwork Century* series was to give voice to the historically voiceless. She dedicated *Ganymede* "to everyone who didn't make it into the history books . . . but should have." Priest gives voice to women and minorities who, as characters, never existed, and by doing so, gives voice to those who still do. But historical fiction by women is a way of rewriting history from a female perspective, thereby recovering the lives of women who were excluded or marginalized by those who write the history books. Some might argue that the exaggerated worlds of steampunk are too whimsical a vehicle for such lofty social activism. Clearly, people like Carriger, Priest, and Westerfeld disagree, choosing to embed their social commentary in worlds filled with airships and automatons. These three seem to be saying, if there are steampunk adventure stories being written, then let's write steampunk adventure stories that imagine a better world, not ones that repeat and support ideas that oppress others. And as we'll see in the next chapter, that impulse toward social reform wasn't just in steampunk fiction.

10

Putting the Punk
in Steampunk

In 2008, pulp historian Jess Nevins's introduction to Jeff and Ann Vandermeer's *Steampunk* anthology laments that "most second generation steampunk is not true steampunk—there is little to nothing 'punk' about it." Nevins never provides any particular works of second-generation steampunk as examples of the omission of punk; he speaks of authors and not filmmakers, or I'd have thought he was leveling his critical sights on some of the films from chapter seven. Nevertheless, Nevins was not alone in the impression that in 2008, there was no punk in steampunk. That statement was a popular chestnut of second-wave discussions even before the publication of the *Steampunk* anthology; the year before, *Steampunk Magazine* launched its first issue with the subtitle "Putting the punk back in steampunk." The idea that there was once punk in steampunk and it needs to be restored continues to be part of the broad rhetoric of steampunk, appearing as recently as May 2017 in a subtle paraphrase in Ashley Rogers's blog post "More Punk Than Steam: The Journey of Bringing a 'Non-Steampunk' Show to a Steampunk Con" at the Airship Ambassador website.

Nevins's introduction provided oft-quoted ideas about the relationship of steampunk and punk ideology, such as the idea that rebellion is an essential facet of steampunk expression: "Steampunk, like all good punk, rebels against the system it portrays (Victorian Longon or something quite like it), critiquing its treatment of the underclass, its validation of the privileged at the cost of everyone else, its lack of mercy, its cutthroat capitalism." The implication that early steampunk had contained this rebellion led me to believe I'd find such antiestablishment themes in the writing of the

California Trinity. This expectation was bolstered by Blaylock, Jeter, and Powers's use of Henry Mayhew's book on the London poor. Imagine my surprise when I'd finished all their books and found little to no such commentary. Where was the first-wave steampunk Nevins was talking about? I wouldn't have my answer until I read Michael Moorcock's *Nomad of the Time Streams*.

Michael Moorcock: The Punk Before Steampunk

There are some who argue that steampunk begins with Michael Moorcock's *Nomad of the Time Streams* trilogy in the early 1970s to '80s and may well wonder why I would place a chapter about Blaylock, Jeter, and Powers earlier in the book. After all, it's a chronological fact that *Warlord of the Air* was published in 1971, beating Blaylock's "Ape-Box Affair" by seven years. It's because, while Blaylock, Jeter, and Powers are closely connected to the coinage of the term steampunk, it's Moorcock who provides the precedent for giving steampunk rebels a cause.

Besides, outside steampunk, Moorcock is best known for his response to high fantasy, not to British imperialism. Like many fantasy fans in the 1980s, I had my dalliance with Moorcock's fantasy. I was one of those kids who read *The Lord of the Rings* while in grade school, before moving onto any fantasy I could lay my hands on, from Terry Brooks's *Shannara* series to *Conan* paperbacks and beyond. I would stand in front of the science-fiction/fantasy section and stare at the covers, looking for a new series, and better yet, authors with more than one series. Reading was to me what athletic achievement was to others. Where others were bragging about how much weight they could bench press or how quickly they could run fixed distances, I was bragging about how fast I could tear through a book. Reading a series of books was like committing to a marathon, and Moorcock had several series on the SF/Fantasy shelf of my modest Coles Bookstore in Medicine Hat, Alberta. I include those personal details because, like an Outer Rim planet in *Star Wars*, Medicine Hat still only has that one small chain bookstore thirty-five years later. I love my hometown, but a literary hub it is not and never was, despite being immortalized in a famous quote by Rudyard Kipling. Because our bookstore was

The White Wolf omnibus of *A Nomad of the Time Streams*, which included *Warlord of the Air*. Again we see the fleet of the world's allied nations, but here artist Chris Moeller has painted the airships to resemble stylized rigid frame zeppelins, as per Moorcock's description in the book. Once again, as with K. W. Jeter's *Morlock Night*, we see the changing style of steampunk.

so small, Medicine Hat got the popular books, the books *everyone* was reading. And of Moorcock's books, the ones that had the greatest popularity in the 1980s were unarguably his *Elric of Melniboné* series, with a distant second to the *Corum* series.

I've described Elric as the "emo Conan," but others have said the anti-Conan. He's a tragic figure, a sickly albino who holds the throne of a dying empire. Sustained by drugs and magic, he's no Arthur or Aragorn. In many ways, Elric is a Dark Lord as protagonist. He's an antihero verging on villain, and as such, was the perfect angst-ridden figure for teenagers looking for fantasy that was edgy. It was cool to like Elric. And when I was done reading all the Elric books, I moved on to Corum, another tragic (though not nearly as decadent nor corrupt) fantasy hero. I would have likely picked up Moorcock's Count Brass books as well, but by then I'd rediscovered comic books, and found Elric there as well. Google Moorcock and you get Elric.

Or New Wave. That's the other thing Moorcock is known for. As the editor of *New Worlds* in the 1960s, Moorcock has been said to be at the forefront of a major shift in science fiction. While it's true that he championed a new way of imagining science fiction, and by extension, fantasy, it's only true insofar as his reach extended within the editorial reach of *New Worlds*. Without getting too far into the details of the New Wave of science fiction, it will suffice to say that it was an antiauthoritarian, rebellious response to the golden age of science fiction. In the 1960s, Moorcock was the literary punk who wasn't going to write your dad's science fiction or fantasy or publish it in the magazine he was editor of.

But if you read a history of steampunk, it's likely to include Moorcock's *Warlord of the Air* and its sequels as part of the story. And I'd be the last person to say it isn't. But I don't think Moorcock is as influential in the development of the style of steampunk as those histories would have you believe. He is perhaps as influential as any other seminal steampunk, which I've already stated had little significant impact on second-wave steampunk. It is debatable how soon Moorcock's *Warlord of the Air* would have gained widespread recognition as part of steampunk history if the Vandermeers hadn't used an excerpt from the novel to kick off that *Steampunk* anthology in 2008. And even then, it took Titan Books until 2013 to release new editions of Moorcock's *Nomad of the Time Streams* series; until then, one had to track down original used paperbacks, or the lovely omnibus from White Wolf publishing. How popular or influential can we really say Moorcock's steampunk was when it was out of print at the height of second-wave popularity?

This isn't to say that Moorcock isn't an important part of the history of steampunk. But he's arguably a far less influential one than we've been led to believe, and it's high time that was admitted. This is similar in many ways to the idea that the Edisonades influenced modern steampunk prior to Jess Nevins suggesting they did. Instead, what appears to have been the case is that well-read steampunk activists like Margaret Killjoy, looking to legitimize the punk in steampunk, went looking for an origin story, one that would cohere better with punk ideas, and found what they were seeking in Michael Moorcock's *Nomad of the Time Streams*. As with *The Difference Engine,* I've come across far more people who crow about Moorcock's contributions to steampunk than those who have actually read those contributions.

Nevertheless, Moorcock deserves attention simply *because* steampunks have adopted him as one of the early contributors to the aesthetic. And I have to concede that Moorcock's *Nomad* series fits inside that blast pattern around the California Trinity, as works leading up to the moment of critical mass, or the tipping point, or whatever we want to call it. Admittedly, he wasn't the only British writer in the '70s and '80s writing fantasies about the Victorian era: but he is the best known, and largely because of that association with the "punk" in steampunk.

Warlord of the Air (1971)

Warlord of the Air is a time-travel story, a sort of steampunk Rip Van Winkle. While seeking to quell a rebellion in northeast India, a British officer named Oswald Bastable is transported through time after becoming lost in a mysterious Himalayan temple. He travels from 1902 to an alternate version of 1973 where the British Empire remains one of the great world powers. The mode of transportation is as mysterious and magical as John Carter's out-of-body traveling to Mars in Edgar Rice Burroughs's *A Princess of Mars.* While there are technological advancements in Bastable's future, the world is not the world of the reader's when

The original paperback cover for Michael Moorcock's *Warlord of the Air* depicting the novel's airship battle: note how artist David Meltzer painted the airships to resemble chrome rocket ships, demonstrating marketing approaches in 1971.

it was published in 1971. Advanced airships that use hulls made of a plastic stronger and lighter than steel are the way to fly, not heavier-than-air craft (I find Moorcock's use of plastic in his airships interesting, given how second-wave steampunk strenuously avoided any appearance of plastic in the construction of steampunk objects; the plastic NERF gun is modded by spraying it with a flat black primer before giving it a faux-finish appearance of aged metals and/or wood).

Bastable, now a stranger in a strange time, sets about making himself useful, initially serving as a lieutenant of His Majesty's Special Air Police on board a passenger airship. He believes this future Britannia to be a utopia and cannot imagine anyone fighting to ruin it. His first impression of London is that poverty and disease have been ended. It is this point of view that Moorcock uses to convey his criticism of capitalist imperialism, since Bastable is a loyal British patriot. Since the book is told in first-person perspective, the reader is subjected to Bastable's initially conservative narrow-mindedness about women, other cultures, and the superiority of the British worldview and the British people. Over the course of the book, Bastable goes from being a staunch supporter of his countrymen's domination of other nations to hoping that the Warlord of the Air, a half-Chinese insurgent, succeeds in repelling an attack by the great nations of the world: Japan, France, Russia, Germany, and America.

He comes to this change of heart after being dismissed from the Special Air Police for brutally beating an obstinate and offensive racist American scoutmaster (who may be based on Ronald Reagan; it is also one of the first indications that Bastable is not as narrow minded as he initially seems, since the beating is ostensibly in defense of Indian civil servants whom the passenger repeatedly calls "niggers"). Bastable then finds work aboard a freight airship, which is later hijacked by General O. T. Shaw, the Warlord of the Air. Shaw is a militant idealist who has built his own utopia near Wuchang, the site of a real-world Chinese rebellion, the Wuchang Uprising in 1911, which led to the Chinese revolution. Like the insurgents of that rebellion, Shaw is a communist, but unlike those insurgents, possesses a weapon that could help him rule the world, not just China.

But before he reveals his weapon, Shaw reveals to Bastable the peace and tranquility of his own vision, and as contrast, the corruption and brutality of the world powers, causing the unswervingly loyal British officer to, finally, swerve and instead to serve Shaw and his Dawn City. Shaw assigns Bastable to captain his own airship, which he has reserved for "the most important assignment of them all," which turns out to be the dropping of his new weapon on a Japanese city: Hiroshima. Outcast scientists have flocked to Shaw's utopian city and developed for him an atomic bomb. Bastable successfully delivers the bomb to Hiroshima, and the events of August 6, 1945, happen in this alternate future. The shock of the bomb arguably casts Bastable back in time to 1903, where he has been telling his story to Moorcock's "grandfather" as a frame narrative for the main adventure.

When Ann and Jeff Vandermeer included an excerpt from *Warlord of the Air* in their *Steampunk* anthology, they admitted that they couldn't "help but think Moorcock's work must have been in the minds of many of those formally labeled 'steampunks' in the 1980s." I see no such lines of influence or even awareness in the writing of Jeter, Powers, or Blaylock. Moorcock's steampunk is utterly lacking in those writers' whimsy (unless one counts the inclusion of a young Mick Jagger as a junior army officer who travels with Bastable from India to England), while theirs lacks his political subtext. *Warlord of the Air* is clearly an indictment of Western imperialism, and its bleak ending suggests the inevitability or perhaps ubiquity of inhumane warfare, no matter how good the intentions. Neither empire nor freedom fighters are valorized by Moorcock's book. As Joseph Weakland and Shaun Duke have argued in their article in *Like Clockwork*, "While Moorcock critiques the world as it is through the variant worlds that might have been," *Warlord of the Air* never offers an alternative to these competing utopias. This lack of a solution agrees with Jess Nevins's ideas about the punk in steampunk: "Like the punks, steampunk rarely offers a solution to the problems it decries—for steampunk, there is no solution—but for both punk and steampunk the criticism must be made before the change can come." And so the first novel ends ambiguously with Bastable disappearing from the atomic blast of 1973 into the past of 1903, only to disappear from there as well. Moorcock would locate his troubled hero again for a sequel, *The Land Leviathan* in 1974. Yet again, criticisms would be identified, but no solution offered.

The Land Leviathan (1974)

The Land Leviathan, like *Warlord of the Air,* uses the technique of a frame narrative to get the reader into Bastable's adventures. *The Land Leviathan's* frame narrative takes up one-quarter of its length, whereas the frame narrative of its predecessor doesn't even run 10 percent of *Warlord.* Most of *Land Leviathan's* frame narrative is about Moorcock's fictional grandfather's search for the Valley of the Morning, hoping to find Bastable, but it is filled with ruminations and conversations about the impact of real-world European colonialism on China in 1910. It's clear that the lengthier frame narrative is a vehicle for some of Moorcock's political ideas, since the search for Bastable is largely a red herring: instead of finding Bastable, he meets Una Persson. This confounds him, since she had been killed in Bastable's tale of the future. Persson mysteriously disappears without explaining this mystery, but leaves behind another of Bastable's manuscripts, which the elder Moorcock (and we) begins to read.

Bastable's second tale tells of his apparent return to his own time. After departing from Moorcock's grandfather at the end of *Warlord of the Air*, Bastable returns to Teku Benga hoping to be transported, in the same mysterious fashion he had before, to his own time stream. While he is successful in making such a journey, he fails insofar as his intended destination. He lands instead in an alternate, apocalyptic version of 1904, where the technological innovations of a thirteen-year-old boy genius have resulted in a devastating World War. Europe, Britain, and America have been reduced to wastelands, but the war is largely over, due to a fuel shortage. Nevertheless, privateers of the warring nations still ply the waters of the world's oceans, and Bastable finds himself aboard a *Nautilus*-like submarine captained by Joseph Korzeniowski, another person who had supposedly died in *Warlord's* steampunk future of 1973.

Korzeniowski transports Bastable to Britain, which has been transformed by chemical weapons into a wasteland worthy of the *Mad Max* films. Upon arriving, Bastable rescues Una Persson (though not necessarily the *same* Una Persson from the frame narrative) from savage Britons. Bastable returns to Korzeniowski's submarine; the privateer vessel then enlists in the service of Bantustan (a South Africa that will never see the rise of apartheid), which is governed by the benevolent and pacifist

President Gandhi. Gandhi invites General Cicerco Hood, aka "The Black Attila," a warlord who is purportedly bent on world domination and the destruction of white races, to Bantustan for a state visit and dinner. During that visit, Bastable, as necessarily dense as Moorcock needs him to be, blurts out his contempt for Hood's agenda. Rather than being offended, Hood is impressed by Bastable's nerve, and invites him to New Kumasi, Hood's version of the utopic New Dawn City of *Warlord*. Under some duress, Bastable agrees, believing it might provide him with an opportunity to assassinate Hood.

Bastable's journey with Hood takes him to the shores of America, where Hood launches a brutal military assault on New York, bringing the once great city to its knees. Hood then launches his land army, unveiling the eponymous technological terror the Land Leviathan, a massive pyramid-shaped war machine. Bastable, horrified by what promises to be the obliteration of American whites, sneaks away from Hood's army and joins up with a group of Americans. However, his horror at the American military's treatment of black slaves (they are placed on Washington City's barricades as a deterrent to Hood battering the city to dust with the Land Leviathan's cannons) causes Bastable to rethink his abdication from Hood. With the help of black slaves, Bastable mounts an uprising, allowing Hood to attack Washington City with impunity. After a series of further campaigns, Hood is finally successful in his overthrow of the United States.

Beyond Bastable's thrilling adventures, *The Land Leviathan* is as filled with commentary as its frame narrative promised, from debates between Gandhi and Hood on the nature of war, to Hood's disruption of Bastable's prejudices about black men, to manifestos of equality for oppressed peoples. A cursory read might lead some readers to conclude that it is an alternate history that asks the question, "What if black slaves could have overthrown the United States," a sort of power fantasy for African Americans.

But Moorcock provides no easy answers to these problems. In the wake of the final conflict, Hood's war machines are put to use in farming and transportation of food and goods, the proverbial swords to plough-shares. However, Hood's emancipation of his own people is only a turning of the tables, as whites become the enslaved underclass. As with *Warlord*, it is as though Moorcock only presents us with the overthrow of one tyrant to install another, albeit a potentially more benevolent one. Once again, Bastable's adventure ends on an ambivalent note.

Moorcock wrote one other Bastable book, *The Steel Tsar* (1981), which takes place in yet another alternate historical timeline where World War II and the Russian Revolution never happened. Because the events of the book take place in 1941, it is often dismissed as not being steampunk. Interestingly, Moorcock had another trilogy that was in conversation with the nineteenth century; unlike *Nomad of the Time Streams*, *Dancers at the End of Time* is virtually unknown in steampunk circles.

Dancers at the End of Time (1972–1976)

Much is made of Moorcock's *Nomad* trilogy, and very little of his other hyper-Victorian fantasy, *Dancers at the End of Time*. And this is too bad, at least in terms of looking for the punk in steampunk, because the *Dancers* trilogy could have provided a sort of prescient satirical commentary on what steampunk would become in the twenty-first century.

The initial setting of *Dancers* is the End of Time, an era in which the supposed heat death of the universe or point of maximum entropy has been reached. The End of Time is populated by decadent beings who share ancestry with humans, the ostensible "Dancers" of the series' title. Through the use of marvelous power rings, the Dancers are able to manipulate reality to suit their amusements, such as perfect facsimiles of the entire solar system as backdrop for actually playing out every war in history with actual beings. They are effectively immortal and capable of changing the nature of their own being, switching genders and appearances at will. These abilities have made the Dancers so complacent that the revelation that the End of Time is approaching and that "All life will, effectively, die," is met with a mix of boredom or feckless delight.

In the first book, *An Alien Heat,* one of these godlike decadents, Jherek Carnelian, is fascinated by the concept of virtue, an idea alien to his people, as well as nineteenth-century England. Although time travel is available to Jherek, he chooses to forgo it in favor of indulging in imaginative re-creations of the period using robots in hilariously inaccurate period costume consisting of "a derby, an ulster, chaps, and stout brogues" and carrying "several meerschaum pipes in its steel teeth." Like most of the Dancers, "he found that real places were rather disappointing."

Mrs. Amelia Underwood, a conservative Victorian woman kidnapped from her own time, fulfills a possibility for truly understanding both the virtue and the nineteenth century. However, the Dancers' understanding of the past is so poorly informed that, for example, they believe that Billy the Kid was a legendary astronaut and socialite. Consequently, Jherek makes a series of hilarious mistakes, the first of which is to replicate Mrs. Underwood's feminine fashion for his own with the intention of making himself more relatable to her. As a proper Victorian woman, she is horrified by what looks to her a male in a woman's clothing. When Jherek asks her to teach him about virtue, Mrs. Underwood is more than happy to oblige: the contrast between Jherek, Moorcock's immortal decadent who has never known restriction, pain, or unhappiness, and Mrs. Underwood, who as a child of the nineteenth century knows much of all three things, is both funny and insightful.

When Mrs. Underwood returns to her own time, a love-smitten Jherek follows her, only to be exposed to the underbelly of Victorian London, where he becomes entangled with a small-time criminal, is captured by the police, and placed on trial. During the trial, Mrs. Underwood embodies virtue by jeopardizing her good reputation when she speaks in Jherek's defense before he is whisked back to the End of Time. The ongoing contrast of Jherek's obtuse ignorance of the period in history he is most fascinated with, and the gritty and grimy realities he experiences, frequently feels like an uncanny predictive criticism of some second-wave steampunk expressions.

In *The Hollow Lands,* the second *Dancers* book, Jherek meets a robot Nanny who has specialized in time manipulation and is able to send him back to the nineteenth century to further pursue virtue and the love of Mrs. Underwood. Their conversations about how the denizens of the future view the past seem like further commentary on second-wave steampunk: Nanny has worked with Pecking Pa the Eight, whose amusements are in realist re-creations of past events such as King Herod's massacre of first-born children at the birth of Christ (Nanny has secreted a group of children to keep them from their dire fates). When she sees

Jherek dressed to travel into the nineteenth century, she compares his clothing to something she saw in one of Pecking Pa's amusements, a "remake of the classic *David Copperfield Meets the Wolf Man.*" She calls it "fanciful" but admits that "Pecking Pa always ran to *emotional* authenticity rather than period exactitude."

Jherek's combined fascination and ignorance about the nineteenth century would have provided a far better punk foundation than Bastable's adventures, but it's unsurprising that *Nomad* has received so much attention while *Dancers* is the more esoteric of Moorcock's Victorianesque fictions. Inasmuch as *Nomad of the Time Streams* contains some great political and social commentary, it must be admitted that the *Bastable* trilogy is, at points, some great steampunk adventure. While *The Land Leviathan* might not match *Warlord of the Air* for commentary, it outpaces it by far for imagining what is arguably the first postapocalyptic steampunk world. Many second-wave steampunk works would follow in *Leviathan's* footsteps (or wheel tracks?), from the very obscure *Fitzpatrick's War* by Theodore Judson to the more popular *Vampire Empire* series by Clay and Susan Griffiths. But I still rate Moorcock's seminal approach as among the best steampunk adventures, with parallel visions of both utopic and postapocalyptic Britain and war-torn and gangster-filled New York.

Reviews of *The Land Leviathan* on Goodreads complain of how the political subtext is more heavy-handed than in *Warlord of the Air.* Yet even the most subtle of the political commentary in Moorcock's steampunk remains heavy-handed compared to any of the California Trinity's books, even combined. Moorcock's characters don't just engage in dialogue; they discuss politics. Bastable's inner musings are often political. Political commentary is woven into the very fabric of the *Nomad of the Time Streams* books. Inasmuch as not *all* early steampunk is political or serious, it's impossible to say that *none* of it was.

Moorcock's political intentions are indisputable. In Blaylock's *Homunculus*, when Willis Pule thinks about his dislike of organized religion, it's a character moment, with no greater thematic import. Shiloh's religious fanaticism lends him an air of yesteryear quackery that is distinct from Narbondo's mad science. But *Homunculus* is not, at its core, a rejection of organized religion. Likewise in *Infernal Devices*, Jeter's farcical scene of fishing tackle and anglers' periodicals in an English church is less a mockery of the institution than another opportunity to heighten the gonzo nature of George Dower's adventures. Yet when Bastable speaks about his dislike of organized religion, it is an extension of the greater theme in *Warlord of the Air* of antiauthoritarianism. It is linked to Bastable's ever-growing cynicism about Empire.

It's apparent in the historical figures Moorcock chooses to include in Bastable's adventures: there's clearly a sense of whimsy in the inclusion of Mick Jagger in *Warlord of the Air*. But including a very aged Lenin—whose revolution never succeeded—as one of General O. T. Shaw's mentors in Dawn City allows not only a political conversation, but a very particular political conversation. In *The Land Leviathan*, this approach allows Moorcock to bring Mahatma Gandhi into that extended fictional conversation. Joseph Conrad, the author of *Heart of Darkness*, a classic work of English literature that interrogates racism and British imperialism, appears as Joseph Korzeniowski, his real name, in the first two books. These are not arbitrary, fan-boy choices. They are not simply "wouldn't it be fun if?" choices. They are choices that allow Moorcock to engage in counterfactual political conversations with great political minds from the nineteenth and twentieth centuries. And when we consider how he renders the then-governor-of-California Ronald Reagan as a bumbling scout troop leader, we can see the direction of that conversation.

Ultimately, it is Moorcock's politics not plots that won him a secure spot in the history of steampunk, which is why I lament the relative obscurity of *Dancers at the End of Time*, as it forms a sharper criticism of second-wave steampunk. Nevertheless, when politically minded second-wave steampunks began asking what, particularly, was "punk" about steampunk, they found their answer in Moorcock's *Bastable* books. And we know this because we have an artifact to prove it: *Steampunk Magazine*.

Steampunk Magazine: Putting the Punk Back in Steampunk

In March 2007, the front cover of the first issue of *Steampunk Magazine* boasted the subtitle "Putting the punk back in steampunk." It also promised a contribution from Michael Moorcock. None of the subsequent issues would ever feature interviews with the California Trinity, which is a telling omission. To put the punk back into steampunk, you must construct a steampunk timeline that demonstrates it was there in the first place. And to do that, you certainly have to go back to Moorcock.

Steampunk Magazine was the brainchild of anarchist writer and editor Margaret Killjoy (who also goes by Magpie) and photographer and writer Libby Bulloff. At the time, both were prominent voices in the steampunk scene, online and at steampunk gatherings, but of the two, Killjoy was the more visible. The answer to the frequently asked question, "Where's the punk in steampunk?" was at one time unarguably Margaret Killjoy. Killjoy is first and foremost an anarchist and anything else, including steampunk, second: she lived and traveled in her van for seven years, is a vegan, a trans-woman, and insofar as any anarchist living in the United States ever can, has lived with the courage of her countercultural convictions.

And in 2007, Killjoy publicly appropriated the literary and cinematic world of steampunk as the vehicle for her countercultural voice. When I look back on the decade since the release of that first issue of *Steampunk Magazine*, no other name comes as readily to mind when I think of the punk in steampunk as Killjoy's does. Under the pseudonym Margaret P. Ratt in that first issue, she wrote that steampunk was more than an online or print phenomenon: Killjoy championed the idea of steampunk as a way of life. While it's impossible to say if she was the first to express this point of view, it's certainly one that steampunks took up with relish in the years to come.

The ethos of punk in steampunk was a grab-bag of activism: steampunk was eco-friendly because it was about repurposing junk, it was counter-capitalist because it adopted the do-it-yourself (DIY) attitude of the original punk movement. It was not meant to romanticize Empire and colonialism, but to satirize and criticize them.

But not everyone wanted steampunk to be about these ideas. In the years that followed, the contention that steampunk was a way of life was a point of friction in the wider steampunk community as well. Some of those who had previously enjoyed it as literature and cinema were angered at the implication that their love of steampunk solely as fiction

was somehow less than those who went beyond experiencing to embody-
ing steampunk culture. The conversation took on a nearly religious
dimension in online forums, where steampunks who didn't adhere to the
DIY punk philosophy that steampunk was becoming increasingly associated with felt, or were sometimes flatly told, they weren't "real" or "true"
steampunks. The situation was divisive, and sometimes alienated people
interested in getting into steampunk as a culture.

None of this contention can be laid solely at Killjoy's feet, though
there's a propensity in her writing to assume her readers were squarely on
the same page she was. In issue eight of *Steampunk Magazine,* returning
from a hiatus as editor, Killjoy lamented how "Sometimes—and haven't
we all felt this way?—steampunk was just some gears hot-glued onto
the boring mainstream culture I'd long ago rejected." Here especially,
Moorcock's prescient criticism in the *Dancers* trilogy seems relevant, with
Jherek Carnelian as hyperbolized North American of privilege, thinking
he understands the past while living out his decadent amusements in the
future. Yet many of her readers were potentially members of that mainstream culture, looking to understand what steampunk was. The depth
of Killjoy's conviction about steampunk as a way of life was difficult for
many new steampunk fans to live up to.

I see an analogy to this situation in Killjoy's blog post "Home Sweet
Not-A-Van," where she speaks of how people both romanticized and
criticized her lifestyle while living with no fixed address. "I think both
these positions derived from the same impulse. By existing, and seeming
to thrive, I called into question people's own decisions to be sedentary
and people were either excited to live vicariously through me or they
were defensive about the compromises they'd made in life." Years before,
the same thing had happened in steampunk: Killjoy's convictions about
steampunk as radical political movement called into question people's
decisions to either appropriate Killjoy's stance and romanticize the idea
of steampunk as political position, or unreflectively take part in the
consumer side of steampunk culture represented by the proliferation of
kitschy steampunk trinkets on Etsy.

I met a lot of steampunks who could parrot Killjoy's steampunk
stance, but few who really lived it. Those who flew the steampunk-

Jaymee Goh, an outspoken activist for issues of race and gender in steampunk, hosting a discussion at The Canadian National Steampunk Exhibition, 2011.

as-lifestyle banner with greatest integrity were fewer than those who adopted it as steampunk slacktivism, but those few were vocal and visible. This list is hardly comprehensive, but I hope it is demonstrative: people like maker Jake von Slatt, blogger and editor Diana Pho, academic Jaymee Gho, activist Miriam Roček, whose persona was a steampunk Emma Goldman, a political anarchist and writer from the nineteenth century.

Steampunk Magazine published its ninth and ostensibly last issue in 2013: the website promised a tenth and definitely final issue, but as of the writing of this chapter, that has yet to be released. Killjoy has said in interviews that she's moved away from steampunk. When I contacted Libby about this book, she declined to comment, saying simply that she couldn't speak to steampunk anymore. So what's the answer to the question now? Where do we find the punk in steampunk now?

PASS/FAIL

According to Diana Pho, it's become more localized and consequently, quieter. But that doesn't mean it's gone away. It's still there, in events like Vandalia Con, which is dedicated to raising money for cancer research; it's still there, in makers like Bruce and Melodie Rosenbaum of ModVic, who specialize in creating disability assistance devices in a steampunk aesthetic, and researching how steampunk design helps people on the autism spectrum; it's still there in local clubs like Airship Ashanti, who use their steampunk cosplay to raise awareness about charity organizations; it's still there in individuals like Ashley Rogers, who performed her one-woman show PASS/FAIL at the International Steampunk Symposium in Cincinnati and the Steampunk World's Fair in 2017.

PASS/FAIL is a moving mix of comedy and confessional that chronicles Rogers's own struggles with failure and the challenges she's faced as a transgender person in America. It's not steampunk at all. Rogers does not dress steampunk when she presents this show. She has presented it at many non-steampunk venues. So why would I include it in this chapter on the "punk" in steampunk? Is it because it was requested for these steampunk events? Because K. W. Jeter endorsed it publicly at the Steampunk World's Fair? Because best-selling steampunk writer Gail Carriger praised it at her blog? No.

It's because, as Rogers herself has said, the word "Punk is about resistance and the upheaval of oppressive social constructions." In some ways, it echoes the sentiments of Magpie Killjoy, who said that if steampunks didn't want punks coming to their party, they should have chosen a different term for their fandom. But it also goes beyond Nevins's idea that punk only criticizes and doesn't offer a solution, for Rogers's PASS/FAIL is definitely interested in finding solutions to the problems it identifies.

But I've also chosen to end this chapter on Rogers's story because it struck me as the perfect example of how the punk in steampunk works. There's nothing inherently punk about steampunk. Steampunk is often expressed and enjoyed by people with no political agenda. Its roots, at least in the writing of Powers, Blaylock, and Jeter, are whimsical entertainments. But on the other side of the Atlantic, those roots were radically political. But that's not because steampunk is radically political. It's because Moorcock is radically political, and his writing is an expression of those politics. But Moorcock or not, Killjoy didn't need to put the punk back in steampunk, because even if steampunk had never been political, Killjoy was about to make it so. *Steampunk Magazine* made the discussion of radical and oppositional politics part of steampunk. Just as there was once no word to describe gonzo Victorian fantasies, there was also a time when few steampunk fans worried much about whether their fandom was punk in the sense of radical or oppositional politics. Margaret Killjoy, Libby Bulloff, Combustion Books (the publisher of *Steampunk Magazine*), and everyone who took up the idea that there needed to be punk in steampunk changed that.

But take away those people, and the punk goes with them. So the answer to the question, "Where's the punk in steampunk?" could be Michael Moorcock, and it could be Margaret Killjoy, but I think it's currently more accurate to say it's in people like Ashley Rogers. On its own, steampunk is a style. It can be whimsical and wonderful, but it can also be thought-provoking and transformative.

I once said steampunk is like an empty teacup. And that bothered some of the people who worried steampunk wasn't serious enough. If steampunk was just an empty aesthetic, what did that bode for its ability to communicate challenging ideas? But an empty teacup can have anything put inside. And ultimately, it's people who put the punk in it. And really, what could be more DIY than that?

11

The Maker Invasion

U p until 2007, steampunk had largely been a matter of fiction, of fans of books, comic books, films, or television. That year, steampunk went from fiction to fact in the workshop of Jake von Slatt, who became the face of steampunk almost overnight through an interview in *Wired* magazine. Von Slatt became a staple of the steampunk community both online and at conventions, sharing his approaches to "steampunking" computer keyboards and building retrofuturistic contraptions. Online and less in the public eye, the late Richard Nagy, aka Datamancer, was producing amazing works of functional steampunk art. However, while their work was responsible for increasing steampunk's popularity, the introduction of maker culture to steampunk fandom also proved divisive, splitting the community as to the necessity of a "punk" aspect to steampunk art and creativity.

As with the spread of steampunk as a lifestyle, steampunk as maker project was given a massive signal boost through the rapid growth of internet forums, blogs, and webzines either devoted to or capitalizing on its growing popularity. Within two months of going live in February 2007, the Steampunk Forum, the online forum for steampunk weblog *Brass Goggles*, saw the number of forum users grow to six hundred, which was tremendous growth for a niche forum. Those six hundred users were a varied lot, with interests ranging from neo-Victorian fiction to neo-Victorian fashion, from DIY tailoring to DIY tinkering. It was that last group that were about to change the face of steampunk and usher in the second wave of steampunk.

Wired, Boing Boing, and the Steampunk Workshop

In June of that same year, *Wired* magazine published an interview with Jake von Slatt, who was then virtually unknown but was referred to as "Mr. Steampunk" in the interview. In the interview, von Slatt openly admitted to co-opting steampunk for his own agenda. He wanted to make steampunk about DIY making, which he admitted "wasn't part of the definition of steampunk . . . but I wanted it to be." Within a scant few years, von Slatt would become one of the most prominent faces and voices of steampunk, and that DIY component would be unquestionably associated with steampunk. Like Jeter's own coining of the term in 1987, it's doubtful that von Slatt imagined his statement would gain as much cultural currency as it did.

Within a year of that *Wired* interview, articles related to steampunk focused almost exclusively on the use of technology in the aesthetic, and attempts to define what steampunk was looked backwards in time and found earlier instances lacking by this new rubric. Online discussion boards debated whether Tim Powers's *The Anubis Gates* should ever have been considered steampunk because of the utter lack of technofantasy in the novel.

But by design or accident, von Slatt had shifted the course of steampunk decisively. While industrial technofantasy had been a facet of much steampunk, it now moved to the forefront, and stayed there. And with the speed of information and breadth of dissemination made possible by the internet, maker culture quickly outshone the narrative conversation about steampunk. As steampunk pioneer Bruce Sterling quipped, "Steampunk certainly received a boost from the vivid Web 2.0 hackerspace culture promoted by *Make* magazine." After all, it's easier to say "this is steampunk" by showing someone Jake von Slatt's modded computer than it is to explain the plot of *The Difference Engine,* and it's cooler to show someone a steampunk motorcycle than it is to admit that what you're into draws its stylistic inspiration from either really bad popular movies or really great foreign (and consequently, often unknown) films.

But it's also important to note the connection between von Slatt and Mark Frauenfelder, editor in chief of *Make* magazine and co-founder of Boing Boing, who were engaged in a project of digital making that would reuse, recycle, and repurpose steampunk as more than just narrative expression. The *Wired* interview with von Slatt openly stated that Frauenfelder shared the idea that an element of DIY needed to be central to steampunk. Between *Make* magazine's debut in 2005 and 2013 (years that correspond with second-wave steampunk's sharp rise in popularity), steampunk was mentioned or focused on in twenty-four of the thirty-four issues. In some cases, those mentions were brief: in others, they were tutorials for DIY projects. Admittedly, a current search at the *Make* website shows 546 hits for steampunk, which seems like a lot, until you check one of the other popular topics, like robotics, which gets 1,609 hits, or robots, which results in 6,030.

Nevertheless, at the height of second-wave steampunk's popularity, *Make* magazine was one of the voices of steampunk. *The Economist* called *Make* magazine a "central organ of the Maker movement," showing how important the publication is to the identity and ideology of makers. So it's unsurprising that steampunk became relatively synonymous with steampunk in this period.

But now add the connection between *Make* and the Boing Boing website, which calls itself "a directory of wonderful things." Among the things Boing Boing finds wonderful, steampunk is certainly one. And one of the strongest voices of steampunk wonder is Cory Doctorow, author and co-founder of Boing Boing. I could unreservedly add Doctorow's name to the voices I listed that put the punk in steampunk in the previous chapter. From digital rights management to intellectual property, Doctorow is an outspoken activist who has a serious love of steampunk: he regularly reviews new steampunk fiction at Boing Boing, owns a steampunk keyboard by Datamancer keyboards and one of Greg Broadmore's rayguns, and has his own steampunk togs for public appearances. He's even written some steampunk fiction.

Now, before anyone accuses me of crafting a conspiracy theory about how von Slatt, Frauenfelder, and Doctorow conspired to appropriate steampunk, I want to say that I've met two out of three of these men, and von Slatt and Doctorow are a treat to be around. Von Slatt's quiet and laidback and was terribly encouraging to me every time I saw him at a convention. Doctorow is smart as hell and just as funny to boot. And while I don't have a beef with the maker takeover of steampunk in 2007 and

2008, there were a good number of old-guard steampunks who were. Just as the introduction of the punks was a problem for first-wave steampunk fans, so too was the influx of makers. And sadly, every group made it their business to advocate for some form of real or authentic steampunk. Some argued steampunk fiction and film was the real thing, because it came first. Others argued steampunk maker art was obviously the real thing because you could hold it in your hand, you could drive it, fire it, light your den with it. And still others argued that only steampunk that advocated for social change was authentic, because everything else was just buying into some ideological lie. And so it went.

What is certain is that the tripartite voice of Jake von Slatt at *Steampunk Workshop*, Mark Frauenfelder at *Make Magazine*, and Cory Doctorow at Boing Boing loved steampunk, and shared a similar vision for what that could look like. As we'll see in the following chapter on steampunk fashion, the idea that steampunk emerged from Goth fashion and DIY maker culture sometimes eclipsed what had gone before, save for cursory inspirational nods to Jules Verne and H. G. Wells, Disney's *20,000 Leagues Under the Sea*, *The Difference Engine*, and with some hesitation, *Wild Wild West* and *League of Extraordinary Gentlemen*. Few second-wave steampunks had any idea who James Blaylock was, let alone K. W. Jeter. Tim Powers was still well known, but not particularly for *The Anubis Gates*. But when I interviewed Blaylock at Steamcon II in 2010, there was only a handful of people in attendance. Panels and presentations on steampunk modding (be it mechanical or fashion) were far more popular and well attended.

None of this is to say that the maker takeover of steampunk was a bad thing. If anything, it was really good for steampunk's visibility. And I would be loath to lay the blame for this shift at Jake von Slatt's feet. Nevertheless, the co-opting of steampunk for DIY maker culture coincided with the co-opting of steampunk for a new generation of punk enthusiasts who rejected the earlier expressions of steampunk as somehow false and inferior to the new. Like the Italian Futurists of the early twentieth century, these steampunks had little interest in what had come before, though they regularly appealed to Michael Moorcock's politically-charged steampunk fiction as proof that steampunk had always been "punk."

Thomas Willeford, Brute Force Studios

There are always exceptions to rules, and the exception to the idea that Steampunk Makers were uniformly in the serious "punk" camp is a guy who looks like a steampunked Thor. And he is also an exception to the rule of steampunk personas being larger than the real person behind it (steampunks know who Jake von Slatt is, but what's his real name?). While his steampunk persona is Lord Archibald "Feathers" Featherstone, he's best known as Thomas Willeford, the man behind Brute Force Studios. He's one of the most recognizable faces in steampunk, perhaps thanks to his involvement as a judge on *Steampunk'd*; however, Willeford was a regular fixture of vendor rooms at steampunk cons back as far as I can remember. He stands out in every crowd of steampunk artisans, not only because he is physically taller than many of his peers in a striking military redcoat and that incredible mechanical arm, but because his work also stands taller than other steampunk makers'. Which is what makes the other exceptional thing about Willeford even more exceptional.

Unlike many steampunk makers, Willeford not only shared his designs for others to emulate but encouraged that emulation through the publication of several books devoted to steampunk making. Many times at steampunk conventions, I'd heard steampunk artists bemoaning the stealing of ideas, the way in which copycat versions of original ideas were being produced quick and cheap on Etsy to make a fast dollar, and the need for the preservation of an artist's intellectual property. The irony of much of the outrage was that it had quickly become almost impossible to do something that wasn't derivative of another steampunk artist's work without doing something ludicrous.

Despite these outcries, Willeford not only published tutorials of his designs, but did so in a popular press that made *Steampunk Gear, Gadgets, and Gizmos: A Maker's Guide to Creating Modern Artifacts* and the kid-friendly *The Steampunk Adventurer's Guide: Contraptions, Creations, and Curiosities Anyone Can Make* available to a public beyond maker culture. In many ways, Willeford acted as a bridge point between those who wanted to appropriate steampunk exclusively for makers and those who wanted to keep it exclusively as a narrative phenomenon. Willeford's books are filled with references to specific steampunk stories, literary and cinematic, but every chapter heading in *Steampunk Gear, Gadgets, and Gizmos* has its own epigraph from a fictional text in a steampunk history, like "*My Life in the Air* by Ms. Adelaide Grayson," a major in "Her Majesty's Aero-Forces."

Even the steampunk tutorials in *Steampunk Gear, Gadgets, and Gizmos* are storied. Willeford promises that the "anywhen" worlds of steampunk are filled with danger and adventure, and that the items his prospective student is about to build will keep the steampunk traveler safe: examples include Aetheric Ray Deflector Solid Brass Goggles (every steampunk needs them), the Tesla Chrono-Static Insulating Field Generator (a fancy-looking container for your smartphone), and the brass ring of steampunk making, Professor Grimmelore's Mark I Superior Replacement Arm with integrated Gatling Gun Attachment (the only project Willeford uses plastic for, out of practicality—a big metal arm is too heavy to wear all day at a convention or event).

But though Willeford is an exception to many of the stereotypes of steampunk makers, he shared a number of convictions about the essentials of steampunk making. His tutorial tool lists are serious business—for the neophyte, he recommends a variety of screwdrivers, saws, and hammers; a bench vise and metal shears; power tools including a dremel, power drill, and reciprocating power handsaw. For the more advanced maker, he recommends a CNC industrial milling machine, cutting laser and metal lathe, and the ultimate possession for a hyper-vintage workman, an *anvil*. According to Willeford and many other steampunk makers, steampunk making is serious business.

Consequently, the concept of "hot-gluing gears onto brown fabric," or as Willeford calls it "cog on a stick," has become a metaphor for any reductive expression of steampunk. I've heard the phrase applied to everything from actual maker objects to fashion to steampunk fiction where the steampunk feels like it was "slapped on." Among steampunk makers, there is mostly derision for shortcuts like using a glue gun and plastic. As Willeford says, "Metal is always preferable to plastic, and screwed is always better than glued." These axioms were evident repeatedly in Willeford's estimation of contestants' work on *Steampunk'd*; shortcuts didn't necessarily make for long delays, but in the eyes of Willeford and many steampunk makers, they are evidence of shoddy workmanship.

But whether one uses a hot-glue gun or a drill press, steampunk making reveals yet another aspect of steampunk hybridity that echoes its narrative roots: it is still the past blurring with the future. Willeford readily admits that it would be very cool to make his projects using period tools but doesn't go so far as to recommend it. Steampunk makers might idealize the past, but they do it with modern devices and techniques. Once again, we see that steampunk is not Victorian or nineteenth century, but a retrofuturistic gaze that looks back on a vintage past through a contemporary lens.

That contemporary perspective is seen through three guiding principles I heard in a number of workshops at conventions. Although Willeford never states these explicitly, his approach to steampunk making supports all three: whenever it can, steampunk design should be about reusing, recycling, and repurposing. Correspondingly, Willeford encourages makers to scavenge parts and materials from flea markets and antique shops, though he warns that antique shops will likely present a more expensive treasure hunting experience. He recommends flea markets, though the popularity of steampunk making created a cottage industry for sellers of cogs and interesting-looking junk. This desire to recycle and repurpose grew out of anticonsumer and eco-friendly intentions within the steampunk community, once again aligning makers with the punks. Which brings us to an oft-used reason for a frequently asked question, which is "why steampunk now?" Willeford provides that answer in *Steampunk Gear, Gadgets, and Gizmos*, but he quotes the late Richard Nagy to do so: "I see it as a reaction to the utter soullessness and disposability of modern tech. There are only so many garish space-eggs and tech bubbles you can look at before you just stop appreciating them."

Steampunk's Love-Hate Relationship with the Digital World

I am frequently asked, "Why steampunk now?" It remains a difficult question to answer. It's difficult because I have to explain that steampunk has already been happening, though in a far less visible way, for over twenty years. The question shouldn't be, "Why Steampunk now?" It should be, "Why and how is steampunk changing now?"

You see, when that question was first widely asked, the answers involved discussions about dissatisfaction with "magic box technology," such as smartphones and tablets. The idea that people used to be able to look under the hood of most technology and fix it was valorized. The irony of all of this was that, under the hood of von Slatt's steampunk-modded computers lurked that magic box technology. One of my favorite instances of this was a steampunk camera, which was an antique accordion-style camera with a digital camera inside. This irony was only amplified by the vehicle of steampunk's proliferation in those years: the internet, the magic box of all magic boxes. Nevertheless, whether rooted in any reality or not, one answer to that question is that steampunk is a rejection of the rise of the iPhone and technology like it, which is inscrutable to everyone save those who design and build it.

According to this response, steampunk is an attempt to get back to a time when anyone could tinker with machinery and fix it. Jake von Slatt said many times that steampunk was born out of a desire to return to a time when a high school diploma gave you all the necessary information about working with machines. I'm unconvinced there ever was such a time, but I'll certainly concede that, among makers, steampunk is attractive for this reason. And herein lies one of the ongoing challenges of defining steampunk, yet again. Which part of steampunk are you talking about?

I've also seen the "magic box technology" response to "why steampunk now?" in articles talking about the fashion or the literature. If I'm dubious about the response for makers, I'm downright opposed to it as a way of understanding steampunk as fashion or literature. And that's without considering that some of the best steampunk video games get played on those magic boxes. It's a reminder that what works for one expression of steampunk doesn't necessarily work for the rest.

In "How to Theorize with a Hammer; or, Making and Baking Things in Steampunk and the Digital Humanities," Roger Whitson, an Assistant Professor of English at Washington State University, laments the strong focus critical studies of steampunk have had on the literature and culture of steampunk while largely ignoring the material objects steampunk makers produce. Most popular treatments of steampunk making are either lookbooks or how-to manuals. Whitson's approach is a combination of these approaches, taking the critical theory of the university and applying it to how-to articles from *Make* magazine to better understand steampunk making.

Whitson is modeling an approach to steampunk objects whereby the viewer becomes a media archeologist, and he quotes Jussi Parikka's observation about steampunk fans combining the "punk-influenced spirit of tinkering" with their historical curiosity for "Mad science, experimental technologies and the curiosity cabinets that such worlds offer." It's an approach that treats steampunk making as a unique expression, not a real-world extension of steampunk fiction and film. In fact, quite often, steampunk making happens without a strong connection to steampunk narratives. However, the influence of steampunk making on steampunk fiction and film is far stronger than the reverse.

Consider the right arms of two characters in steampunk anime to see this influence. *Fullmetal Alchemist* was made prior to the widespread rise of steampunk making, while *Kabaneri of the Iron Fortress* was made after. Both series feature young men with steampunk technology on their right arm. In *Fullmetal Alchemist,* it's the automail of Edward Elric; in *Kabaneri*, it's the leather harness that steamsmith Ikoma wears to prevent his becoming a zombie. Edward Elric's automail is gunmetal grey and is sleek and streamlined; it bears no resemblance to second-wave steampunk. Ikoma's makeshift harness is an ugly array of bolts, brass, and leather, clearly influenced by steampunk objects like Thomas Willeford's steampunk arm as made famous on the television series *Castle*.

One Hundred Year Starship: Steampunking the Space Program

In 2014, I was invited to attend the *100 Year Starship Symposium* in Houston, Texas. The *100 Year Starship* project is planning and preparing ways for humans to travel beyond our solar system in the next century. Before you scoff, consider for a moment that a century ago, humans had just started flying. Now, you step onto an airplane that can travel across the oceans without a second thought. It has become an everyday event, devoid of any of the wonder previous generations had about traveling in the sky. The symposium is a gathering of space industry thinkers and producers, physicists, engineers, and astronauts; people who have either been in space or are making it easier for people to get there. I had no idea what such an event could want with an English professor who specialized in impossible technologies based in outdated theories. I thought maybe all I'd be doing is help people think outside the box.

When I arrived at *100 Year Starship*, Dr. Peter Swan, President of the International Space Elevator Consortium, was presenting on viable strategies for using space elevators to move resources and equipment from Earth to space, to the moon, and beyond. The basic premise of the space elevator is that a massive cable runs from a stationary point on the planet and extends out to a satellite in geostationary orbit. The earliest inception of the space elevator was in 1895 when Russian scientist Konstantin Tsiolkovsky imagined a tower that reached to space; that theory would be amended in 1959 by another Russian scientist, Yuri N. Artsutanov, who suggested the geostationary satellite and cable. But as Peter Swan told the group assembled at *100 Year Starship*, it's only recently that we've been able to manufacture the materials and parts necessary to make such a design viable.

I was stunned. I had come prepared to talk about a fictional space elevator in Kenneth Oppel's *Starclimber*, the third book in his *Airborn* trilogy. But I had been ready to ask the question, "How might this help us think about out-of-the box approaches?" Now, I was faced with the reality that the space elevator wasn't out-of-the-box thinking anymore. It was around-the-corner thinking. So, with great humility, I began my session with this admission and said, "Just let me know what other steampunk ideas aren't as crazy as I thought they'd be." It turned out you can add solar sails, real-world equivalents to the ones in *Treasure Planet*, to the list.

What was once considered impossible has become possible. We accept this as a reality of our wondrous technological age. The cell phone that resembled *Star Trek* communicators has come and gone. Between touchscreen devices and motion-capture technology, we're really not that far away from realizing the seemingly magical book that teaches the heroine of *The Diamond Age* how to achieve her full potential. But sometimes we overlook technologies that were dreamed up and abandoned because they weren't viable at the time. Charles Babbage's nineteenth-century difference and analytic engines weren't impossible machines—they simply didn't get built, and historians debate the reasons, from Babbage's prickly personality to erratic financing. Between 1985 and 2002, the Science Museum in London undertook the arduous task of building a realized difference engine based on Babbage's original drawings to discover if it would work and do what Babbage imagined it should. It turned out that it did precisely what Babbage imagined: at eleven feet long and weighing five tons, the difference engine no. 2 is a very large calculator. But it illustrates the possibility that old scientific theories that were abandoned might be realized more readily in our time. And in the case of the space elevator, those old, science fiction approaches might prove to be the key to scientific progress.

Joshua Tanenbaum, Karen Tanenbaum, and Ron Wakkary in a presentation at the 2012 Conference on Human Factors in Computing Systems describe steampunk as a "design fiction" in which objects "are created largely as an exercise in seeing what is possible." A naysayer might concede Dr. Peter Swan and his International Space Elevator Consortium might be on to something but that the average steampunk maker working in his garage is unlikely to produce anything to help us see what is actually possible. Nederlander Jos De Vink would prove that naysayer wrong. De Vink creates beautiful engines from scraps of brass and bronze that run on Stirling engines (for simplicity, just think steam engine without the steam) powered by the heat from tea light candles, a cup of hot water, or the warmth of a human hand. And he has done so in his retirement from a career in computer technology, without any specialized training in working with machines. Since Stirling machines can be found in submarines and can be heated by solar energy, I wonder about the conversation De Vink would have with those physicists and astronauts about wild steampunk possibilities to get us beyond the solar system.

Global Makers—from Oxford to Sweden and Beyond

The continued growth of maker art in steampunk demonstrates that this expression of steampunk was not just a passing fad. There was already steampunk art at the first steampunk convention I went to in 2008, where I met Jake von Slatt. In the fall of 2009 (which coincided with the release of many popular steampunk novels), the Museum of the History of Science at the University of Oxford launched the world's first museum exhibition of steampunk art. The exhibition was curated by Art Donovan,

The Anglo Parisian Barnstormer or Art Donovan piece.   *Rex*

a steampunk artist from New York. The participating artists were from around the world, and their contributions ran the gamut of steampunk making.

There were examples of steampunk jewelry: Amanda Scrivener's (UK) camera lens monocle along with necklaces adorned with pocket watches or antique syringes; Canada's Daniel Proulx's hybrids of insectile shapes built from mechanical industrial components. There were steampunk gadgets from well-known American makers Thomas Willeford and Richard Nagy, but also from more obscure creators such as Australia's Cliff Overton with his "Inspectacles," a pair of steampunk goggles inspired by Johnny Depp's Ichabod Crane in Tim Burton's *Sleepy Hollow*, comprised of magnifying lenses, tea strainers, old brass bits, and some shoelace. There were models such as Kris Kuksi's densely intricate mixed-media sculptures built from plastic model kits, dolls, and furniture parts. His "Anglo Parisian Barnstomer" looks like a collision of rocketship, prop airplane, oil derrick, schoolbus riding atop antique bike, and cart wheels. And there were clockworks, from the practical clocks of Vianney Halter (who is Swiss, of course!) to the stylish hand-machined brass and aged-paper-sculpture timepieces of Eric Freitas (United States), and in between those poles, the practical machinery of Japan's Haruo Suekichi, which track the phases of the moon, planets, or stars, or may simply feature the addition of a rubber-band gun. While those four categories of mechanical jewelry, functional gadgets, retrofuturistic models, and clockwork devices are not exhaustive of the breadth of steampunk making, they are certainly indicative of prevalent approaches. Of the seventeen artists who participated in the event, it's worth noting that only two were women, demonstrating how the maker side of steampunk creation is dominated by men, while the fashion side, as we'll see in the next chapter, remains dominated by women.

Four years after the close of the Oxford Museum of Science's steampunk exhibit, I attended a steampunk convention in Sweden, which had its own tiny exhibit of steampunk art from around Europe. Most notably, that event in Sweden featured what seemed to me to be the pinnacle of maker steampunk. Swecon is Sweden's annual science-fiction and fantasy convention, and in 2014, it was steampunk-themed. The organizers had partnered with the Sveriges Järnvägsmuseum, or Swedish Train Museum, in Gävle, where the event was held. This partnership presented a unique opportunity to Swedish steampunks: to steampunk one of the museum's steam trains. Swedish steampunks Erik Andersson, Kristin Thorrud, and a team of engineers, both old veterans and new apprentices, labored to steampunk-recondition an actual working steam engine, the E2 904, which was built in 1907. The project began in November 2012, with construction commencing August 2013, and a completion date of June 2014. The project involved welding, woodworking, milling, repainting, and brasswork to provide the E2 with retrofuturistic ornamentation. While the train itself remained unmodified, you might say it was decked out in steampunk finery of wood and metal.

The finished product was rechristened *Järnsaxa* after a female giant of Norse mythology, and its unveiling was made all the more spectacular by the unseasonably cold and rainy summer day; the steam from *Järnsaxa*'s funnel billowed out in a prodigious cloud. I've been to steampunk events

The Ætherkanon by Norwegian maker Thomas Nes.

with modded vehicles on hand: none, not even the infamous Neverwas Haul, were as breathtaking as *Järnsaxa*. Standing next to the massive engine, I understood why Walt Whitman wrote "To a Locomotive in Winter," a poem that praises the various components of the steam engine. I understood why the children's series *Thomas the Tank Engine* privileges "steamies" over "diesels." Steam technology isn't hidden; watching the "ponderous sidebars" of *Järnsaxa* engage its wheels to move the E2's 91 metric tons was awe-inspiring. Sadly, the engine returned to being E2 after a year as *Järnsaxa*, in a move that echoes the experience of many of the convention's attendees.

If you look closely at *Järnsaxa* or Jake von Slatt's infamous steampunk keyboard, you find that what you have is a veneer over what lies beneath. Von Slatt openly admitted that the first steampunk keyboard involved a glue gun, the dreaded shortcut tool that "real makers" look down their nose upon those who use. Ostensibly, "real makers" weld and mill, rivet and drill to pursue their craft. But not everyone is so skilled. Artisans who salvage techniques like handtooling leather and brass that are becoming forgotten in an age of mass production are certainly to be lauded, in the same way that great painters are to be praised for their work. But for those of us for whom craftsmanship is the making equivalent of a steampunk coloring book, the glue gun is our friend (when it's not giving us first-degree burns).

But the reality that a lot of steampunk objects are repurposed objects with a brass and wood veneer is instructive. I've heard conversations about authenticity in steampunk, and I think it's mostly a way to make steampunk more exclusive. Authenticity is a bit of a chimera. What makes an authentic steampunk object? Von Slatt's keyboard has the illusion of authenticity, and the aura of priority: it was one of the first steampunked objects. But it was really just a digital computer in new clothing. Arguably, *Järnsaxa* is the more authentic steampunk object; after all, it's an authentic train engine from the age of steam. But with its ornamentation removed, it goes back to being a working relic of the past, kept in a museum. It is not steampunk anymore.

I raise this issue of authenticity because it permeates the discussion around steampunk making. Those who create the "first" modded object are given greater merit than those who copy, though the sense of accomplishment may be greater in the person who hasn't done anything artistic since grade school who takes Thomas Willeford's how-to book *Steampunk: Gear, Gadgets, and Gizmos*, follows the steps therein, and makes their own steampunk goggles instead of buying them. Or what of the instances where the first is outshined by the copyist, where the originator had a great idea, but it took another artist to make it great?

Authenticity in steampunk is ephemeral, shifting and changing like the billowing column of steam from *Järnsaxa*'s funnel. What makes a computer keyboard, jewelry, or a train steampunk is a veneer, and one that we all have to agree on before we can recognize it as "steampunk or not." If *Järnsaxa* is authentic steampunk, so then too von Slatt's keyboard,

Steampunk steam train *Järnsaxa* from the press preview for Swecon 2014.   *Mikael Dunker*

and that hat on Etsy with all the cogs glued on. You might not like it, but that won't change its steampunk authenticity. And this discussion of authenticity is as important to the makers as it will be to the next chapter on fashion, wherein we find that the cog-laden hat as fashion accessory is the object that announces that a person has "become" steampunk. Short of tattooing steampunk art onto one's skin, we embody steampunk only once we adorn ourselves in the fashion of steampunk, which has become one of the most popular aspects of steampunk making.

12

Steampunk Fashion

When I went to my first steampunk convention, my wife cobbled an outfit together for me, so that I wouldn't feel ridiculously out of place at the first evening's steampunk ball. It consisted of a normal dress shirt with the collar turned up, a Mandarin-collar jacket with faux-metal buttons from a Canadian chain store called Le Chateau, standard lace-up dress shoes, a pair of black dress pants, and an ersatz cravat made from one of my wife's scarves, all topped off with a gold pocket watch that no longer worked. There wasn't anything authentically Victorian about what I was wearing (the zipper wasn't invented until 1917, for example). I did not have a modded Nerf gun (mostly because that craze had yet to happen), and I didn't have any goggles (though I did by the end of the weekend—they were given to me by members of a Vernian dramatic improv group). The closest I came to being "genuinely" steampunk was that Mandarin-collar jacket, which I had bought in the period when Le Chateau was experimenting with Goth designs in the 1990s.

Over the years, I've changed out every piece of clothing in that outfit except the goggles. I still wear the same ones, for largely sentimental reasons. But now it's the pants and a vest that are from Le Chateau, though the store has long abandoned catering to Goth fashion, while the jacket is a velvet blazer from Mark Ecko's now defunct Cut and Sew brand (which is apparently the spitting image of an Edwardian period smoking jacket). I still wear normal dress shoes and the same shirt I wear to work, though now I turn the collar down, because I'm not fooling anyone that I'm more steampunk with it flipped up. Oh, and I carry a beautiful leather book cover made by Thomas Willeford that holds all my papers for speaking engagements. It's the only item I "wear" that ever gets commented on.

Most importantly, I've learned to embrace my own steampunk style, you might say. I tried other looks: I added a hat, I tried something more adventurous looking, I wore costume boots (which is why I now just wear dress shoes with great soles: hours on your feet in costume footwear will cripple you). Perhaps more than any other steampunk expression, the fashion of vintage retrofuturism strains the boundaries of precise categorization.

Wander the vendor's room at a steampunk convention, or walk up to a steampunk vendor at a fan convention, and what do you find? A tumult of potpourri, bits and pieces of this and that, a posh haberdasher next to a junk seller with old clock pieces and odd antique geegaws next to a custom corset maker. One vendor looks like a homeless man transported from the nineteenth century while the next looks like a dandy who raced through the temporal rift, pulling along the woman in authentic-looking Victorian garb contrasting the girl wearing a Goth Lolita outfit capped by a tiny top hat strapped to her head with bright ribbon. Steampunk fashion is at once both unified and wildly diverse.

Some of you may be wondering why I'm devoting a solitary chapter to fashion when I've given multiple chapters over to books and film. It's largely because I can describe the plot of a film or a book with words. Describing fashion with anything approaching precision requires jargon that would require that both you *and* I be experts on fashion. I'm not a fashion expert, and I cannot guarantee that you are. Books on steampunk fashion are also usually filled with pictures and have very few words. This is a book filled with words with very few pictures. Consequently, you won't find advice on how to make a steampunk outfit, or an analysis of a particular item of steampunk couture. There are plenty of how-to books and online tutorials to that end. Instead, I hope to address some of steampunk fashion's broader movements and the fashion's relationship to other steampunk expressions. One of the most crucial movements in the history of steampunk fashion is its provenance in Goth fashion.

What Do People Mean When They Say That Steampunk Happened When "Goths Discovered Brown"?

There's no questioning the connection between Goth fashion and steampunk, as evidenced in the oft-quoted quip, "Steampunk is what happened when Goths discovered brown." The best jokes are always rooted in truth. And for the record, it was retro-literature scholar and writer Jess Nevins who came up with that clever definition of steampunk. However, Nevins admits it was steampunk writer Cherie Priest who made the joke popular. Priest and her fellow steampunk writer Gail Carriger, musicians Vernian Process, Abney Park, and Unwoman, and corset designer Autumn Adamme all participated in the Goth scene prior to getting involved with steampunk.

As with the "magic box" theory of "why steampunk now?", Nevins's witty definition largely applies to the fashion of steampunk. But because it's concise and clever, it gets a lot of cultural currency. Like so many other simple definitions for steampunk, it only addresses a facet, though in this case, it does so with a large degree of accuracy. But what did Nevins mean by that? Despite being oft-quoted, it's not often interrogated. We might admit our ignorance about steampunk, but how many of us could supply a decent definition or history of Goth fashion?

Consequently, a brief summary is likely in order: Goth fashion started in the 1970s and '80s in England as a branch of punk music and fashion. As Valerie Steele, co-author of *Gothic: Dark Glamour*, noted, in contrast to the classic punk style of the '70s, which emphasized masculinity, Goths might be said to have emphasized androgyny: while the masculine black leather of punk is sometimes used in Goth fashion, particularly in expressions that highlight overt and aggressive sexuality, more traditionally feminine materials such as velvet or lace abound. Goth fashion and culture was and is a mixture of archaic and traditional styles borrowed from the eighteenth and nineteenth century and wed to a fascination with horror, morbidity, melancholy, darkness, and the supernatural. The fashion grew out of emulation of Goth music by groups like Bauhaus, Sisters of Mercy, and Siouxsie and the Banshees. Goth music was dark, and the fashion was darker.

Around the same time, the New Romantics, a lighter parallel music and fashion scene, were likewise drawing inspiration from the Romantic past of the early nineteenth century, as seen in the early stage attire of Duran Duran. But New Romanticism didn't last like the Goth scene did. New Romanticism came in 1979 and was virtually gone by the late '80s. Goth remained and grew. And at some point in the late 1990s or the early 2000s, a branch of Goth fashion "discovered brown" and became steampunk fashion.

I've seen a number of articles and even a book or two mistakenly assume that steampunk emerged from punk and Goth at the same time that Jeter coined the term in the late 1980s. But there's no strong evidence to support this. There are many steampunks who claim that they were "steampunk before they knew there was a term for it," but that's neither helpful nor verifiable. Admittedly, the roots of iconic steampunk fashion go all the way back to the 1980s and the Goth club scene, making the foundations of steampunk fashion contemporaneous with the start of steampunk fiction. But I think it's a stretch to argue that those foundations were steampunk and not simply Goth.

"When did steampunk fashion begin?" is a tough question to answer, because there's a good chance that the first person to dress steampunk as fashion did so for fun, on a night out at a Goth club or at a comic convention or cosplay event. Maybe they didn't even know what they were doing was steampunk. They just mixed up some fashion elements they thought looked fantastic, and when they arrived at their destination, someone said, "Wow, that looks sort of steampunk!"

What we can prove for certain is that New York designer Kit Stølen, whose online handle was "Anachronaut," was among the first (if not *the* first) to combine fantastic elements with neo-Victorian couture on August 20, 2003, when he posted photos of his steampunk fashion on a LiveJournal steampunk group. Stølen claimed to have been dressing steampunk in the 1990s, but we don't have a record to demonstrate that. What we have a record for is the involvement of legendary fashion designer Jean-Paul Gaultier having an unspoken influence on steampunk in the designs he created in the late '80s and '90s. And the most influential of those designs involved a steampunk fashion icon.

Express Yourself

The corset alone would deserve an entire chapter in a book on steampunk fashion: a body-shaping undergarment used primarily for ladies to achieve a conventionally attractive silhouette (though men are reported to have worn them as trusses as well, and Dark Garden corsetry manufactures men's corsets in the guise of formal vests), steampunk corsets are worn largely *over* the clothing. This is only the most obvious of crimes against historical accuracy steampunk corsets commit. One of the complaints of the late-nineteenth-century New Woman movement was the Rational Dress campaign, which rejected the corset and other restrictive clothing of refined ladies. In short, real women of the late Victorian era were trying to get *out* of corsets; so there's something seemingly dissonant about so many early-twenty-first-century women looking to get *into* them.

Custom corsets by Dark Garden: a mix of old world fashion and new world couture. And corsets aren't just for women!

Largely abandoned in the early twentieth century, the corset made a number of comebacks before seeing a strong resurgence in the late 1980s. Though Wikipedia credits the popularity of *Moulin Rouge!* with the greatest revival of corsets, Autumn Adamme of Dark Garden Corsetry in San Francisco credits the greatest influence on the modern corset revival as the partnership of Jean-Paul Gaultier and Madonna on the *Blond Ambition* tour in 1990 (which featured the iconic cone-shaped corset). Madonna had already popularized wearing lingerie in public, anticipating the wearing of corsets as exterior pieces, not underwear. Adamme also mentions Christian Lacroix's use of corsets in his fashion in the '90s.

Gaultier's potential contribution to steampunk goes beyond just the revival of the corset: as the costume designer on *The City of Lost Children*, where he combined an array of retro styles without focusing on historical accuracy; and for his Frankenstein fashion, or rag-picking use of recycled materials and flea-market clothing, which anticipated the DIY and recycle and reuse approaches of steampunk fashion on a budget. Yet fascinatingly, Gaultier is rarely spoken of in relation to steampunk fashion. Perhaps it's the popularity of his Hot Topic lines that keep steampunks from admitting the connection to Gaultier; maybe it's the pop association with Madonna (not punk enough!).

Whatever the case, Gaultier's contribution is a largely unsung oversight. Instead, articles writing on steampunk fashion find it easier (or perhaps just catchier copy) to say that steampunk is a blend of Goth fashion mixed with the retro science fiction of Verne and Wells, though I've met few steampunk fashionistas who are big Verne and Wells fans. Instead, I find more Goths and ex-Goths who are fans of Tim Powers or Tim Burton. It's interesting to note that Powers's *The Stress of Her Regard*, a crossover novel that combines Romantic-era writers like Percy Shelley and Lord Byron with powerful vampiric creatures, was published in 1989, shortly after Jeter had coined steampunk. *The Stress of Her Regard* is clearly horror and is rarely included on any lists of steampunk books. Yet Autumn Adamme says it was one of her favorite books as a young Goth. Again, too much has been made of the cyberpunk roots of steampunk fiction; perhaps there should be more attention paid to its Gothic roots, not only in fashion, but in neo-Gothic horror. I can't help but wonder if the Goth fascination with horror elements and fashionably dark cinema of Tim Burton might account for the popularity of Gail Carriger's *Parasol Protectorate* books, with their polite vampires, sexy werewolves, and emo ghosts. As we'll see, Carriger's Goth influences are all over her books.

And that Goth influence isn't just in Carriger. Even if you think Tim Burton's *Sleepy Hollow* isn't steampunk, you can see the influence of that film (along with many other Burton films) on steampunk fashion. Likewise, I've heard the costume design of the *Harry Potter* films called "steampunk," but to be accurate, it's got a sort of neo-Victorian look, with most of the villainous Death Eaters clearly getting their wardrobe from the same place Goths get theirs.

I've asked a number of steampunk designers and people close to the steampunk fashion scene how it all got started, and I've received a disparate set of accounts. At Steam Powered, I was told by several people that the fashion emerged from people who had worked in costuming on steampunk movies like *Wild Wild West*. Others echoed the "when Goths discovered brown" quip. Some people talked about steampunk as a reaction to frustration with the hierarchical rules and regulations that accompanied participation in the Renaissance Faire community. As I walked around the convention, I could see evidence of all three: there were the steampunk Ghostbusters (two members of the then unnamed League of Steam), the sea of black dresses and corsets accessorized with goggles and gears, and the burly vendor in a puffy pirate shirt. It was a blurry blend of an unspecified vintage past, emerging from distinct costume- and performance-based subcultures.

In her travels as a regular guest at steampunk events, author Gail Carriger has observed that steampunk is expressed differently in different places, and has speculated how these differences are based on dominant styles that precede steampunk. She has seen more Goth influences in the Bay Area, which has a very strong Goth culture, while Seattle's steampunk appeared to have grown out of the grunge scene of the 1990s. In short, steampunk fashion is limited (and to some degree, dictated) by what is available to the designer or costumer.

To illustrate, I'll share an anecdote from 2010, when Autumn Adamme and her partner, Daniel Silveira, took my wife and me on a tour of vintage clothing shops in San Francisco. Both Adamme and Silveira attend a number of vintage costume events annually, their vintage wardrobes spanning eighteenth-century France to early-twentieth-century America. On that tour, I learned that many of the shops from other areas of the United States ship their Victorian- and Edwardian-styled acquisitions to the Bay Area because of the increased demand. The Bay Area has played host to many events that encourage attendees to dress in the attire of the past: One of the first I learned of was the Great Dickens Christmas Fair; since 1970, hundreds of costumed performers have inhabited the streets of a Dickensian London Town, "a city of winding lanes filled with colorful characters from both literature and history" that presently occupies 120,000 square feet of exhibition halls. The Art Deco Society of California puts on both the Gatsby Summer Afternoon, "A lively 1920s picnic held annually at the Dunsmuir Hellman Historic Estate featuring vintage fashions, dancing, music, and classic automobiles," and the Art Deco Preservation Ball, which encourages formal wear or costume inspired by that year's theme; in 1917, this was "Egyptian-inspired attire of the 1920s, 1930s, and 1940s."

I contrast this with where I live: we have no events of this kind, save those that the local steampunk association provides. Consequently, when I started trying to put together a steampunk outfit, my local thrift stores were a poor source compared to those I'd seen in California. A few shops in, and I concluded that I might be able to start a new movement called steamfunk, based on all the polyester bell bottoms I'd come across. We don't have much in the way of Victoriana in Alberta, but we have a lot of stampedes, so I've seen fewer dolly-mops and more saloon girls up here, fewer London dandies and more gunslinger cardsharps.

Consequently, steampunk fashion is often the least exclusive when determining the period the steampunk toolbox will draw on. I have seen everything from Regency era to World War I, from the Napoleonic Wars to Mad Max–inspired postapocalyptic steampunk fashion at conventions (and everything in between). To be sure, the nineteenth century dominates the toolbox, but I wonder if this is because people were told steampunk has to be Victorian, or because that is what people chose. At Steamcon, my wife wore an outfit that was American 1920s in style, to which Captain Robert Smith of Abney Park commented, "see, now *there's* someone doing something different with steampunk." And while such approaches were decried by costuming purists, costume designer Christopher Mueller observed that when "Steampunkers lack the resources to execute the style with a proper historical sensibility, [they] instead opt for Hot Topic-esque PVC bustiers in place of corsets, Dickies jeans in place of trousers, and similar 'close enough in look' replacements."

Of course, scavenging for costume elements is by no means the only way to create steampunk fashion. There are many steampunk makers whose tools are measuring tapes, scissors, and sewing machines. And for those makers, scavenging is unnecessary. What they want are patterns. Gretchen Jacobsen says that steampunk makers looking to sew their own dresses or frock coats should look no further than Truly Victorian patterns, and specifically, pattern 2172. As Gretchen puts it, "2172 catapulted steampunk in the sewing mainstream." She calls Truly Victorian the gold standard for historically accurate Victorian sewing.

Given the wide number of entry points for steampunk fans trying on the fashion, it's a wonder anyone was wearing anything similar at all. When I asked steampunks on social media for their story of how they got into steampunk fashion, the responses were incredibly varied: some mentioned steampunk books or comics, films or television, while others shared cosplaying as characters from their tabletop role-playing, or LARPing. Some mentioned seeing others dressed steampunk and rushed out to find their own. There was no dominant reason, and there was no dominant inspiration. So if there was such a diversity of motivations to get into steampunk, why did the result manifest as a sea of brass goggles, brown leather, black top hats and waistcoats, and corsets worn on the outside?

The answer is likely the internet. Bruce Sterling mused that "Steampunk is not inherently literary. It's native to network cyberculture. Steampunk direly needed broadband and social media in order to thrive. Steampunk was never about ink on paper." As steampunk fashion grew in popularity, the internet provided a medium to disseminate ideas about what steampunk fashion could look like, and many steampunk costumers found their inspiration in a Google image search. But this also led to the internet being the way in which ideas about what steampunk fashion *should* look like were disseminated, from an adherence to Anglocentric approaches to the sociopolitical ramifications of everyone dressing as the upper class.

Be Splendid!

Those who dress as high society have been criticized for reifying class issues from the Victorian era. The complaint is that there are "too many lords and ladies." But many of those lords and ladies are middle to lower class by modern standards. Talking with steampunk enthusiasts in the vendor room, you find people thrifting their costume, and augmenting with a few carefully purchased pieces. And even when you have someone spending hundreds or thousands of dollars on a magnificent steampunk costume, the intention is not necessarily a nostalgia for racism or sexism. I suspect it is, as Jeter says in his Angry Robot introduction to *Infernal Devices*, to allow "young women to attend science fiction conventions while laced into visibly complicated underwear, while their weedy boyfriends are bulked up the heavy armor of period tweeds and vests." In short, the goal is to look fabulous.

This is the rallying cry of the UK's longest-running steampunk event, *The Asylum*: "Be splendid." And I can't think of a better word to describe what most people are hoping to achieve when they buy or build or borrow a steampunk outfit, be it cosplay or couture. They want to look splendid, whatever that means to them. Because with steampunk, there are some loose guidelines, but no rules. And being splendid means more than just looking splendid; it means acting that way too. Rather than decrying someone's steampunk outfit because it isn't the right period, place, fabric, or material, being splendid might mean just saying, "You look great!" Or as we all know, if you can't say anything nice . . .

Besides, as I've argued repeatedly, the toolbox of steampunk is filled with elements from history, literature, and cinema. Consequently, while historical fidelity is admired in steampunk fashion circles for its research rigor and artistic achievement, it is by no means the benchmark of steampunk success. As Steamcon founder Diana Vick famously said, "Steampunk needs historical accuracy like a dirigible needs a goldfish."

Consequently, steampunk fashion is a hybrid of historical accuracy and complete lunacy, and lots in-between. Dresses and shirts showing any amount of leg; the absence of layers of undergarments like petticoats; miniature top hats in a riot of color; gears sewn or glued onto hats, boots, or canes; and those pesky goggles (I love them) hung about the neck or perched atop a top hat or bowler, all signal that steampunk fashion is about messing with the past, not aping it. One of the most stylish steampunk outfits I've seen was on a guy who had thrown the outfit together the day of the event, simply because he'd found out about it last minute. He was wearing ski goggles on top of the outfit, and it took me a moment to realize that. My first impression was just, "He looks splendid."

When Gail Carriger posted an image of herself sporting a short skirt from her attendance at the 2017 Steampunk World's Faire, Instagram user vulpix_rising commented, "I never think of steampunk with short dresses," even though Canadian cosplayer and media personality Liana K wore a short bustle skirt in her photoshoot for nerdgirlpinups.com in 2010 and featured a short dress in a steampunk Harley Quinn outfit in 2010. Jody Ellen, former vocalist for Abney Park (2009–2014), often wore shorter dresses onstage, going so far as to wear steampunk short shorts, which she attributed to the difficulty of dancing and performing under the heat of stage lighting in typical steampunk finery such as long skirts and corsets. As it happens, the shortening of skirts was not unheard of in the Victorian period: Natalie Rantanen of the improv group Legion Fantastique took inspiration for some of her steampunk fashion from photos of real Victorian women doing physically demanding activities, such as mountain climbing and exploring. These women often had shorter skirts to accommodate movement, and some were so short they barely met the top of mid-calf boots (to ensure there's still no actual leg showing!). Contrast that reticence to show leg with what Katherine Gleason calls the "retro-futuristic confidence" of the dip-hem, also called high-low, dresses of steampunk that are often far shorter in the front than in the back, sometimes displaying nothing but leg, or legs covered only in fishnet or boldly striped tights.

There are a number of possible reasons for the popularity of those short skirts in steampunk fashion, but one of the likely culprits are the Goths yet again, though this time from Japan.

Goth Loli

The anime of Miyazaki and others are only one of the avenues of influence Japan has had on steampunk. One of the other prevalent influences come from the Gothic Lolita fashion, popularized by its association with the 2004 film *Kamikaze Girls* and Tokyo's fashion-famous Harajuku district.

Characterized by a combination of frilly blouses, black pinafore dresses trimmed with white lace, black knee-length socks, and parasols, Gothic Lolita—or as it is often truncated, Goth Loli—emerged in Japan in the mid- to late 1990s. The elaborate Gothic-themed baby-doll costumes of Goth Loli fashion have led some to compare the look to a cross between a sexy French maid and children's fiction characters like Alice in Wonderland, but this assumes a North American understanding of Lolita, which was the nickname of the eponymous character in Vladimir Nabokov's controversial 1955 novel about a love affair between a literary professor in his late thirties and a twelve-year-old girl he sexually fixates on. In the West, "Lolita" is used popularly to denote any sexually precocious or promiscuous young woman. This is not the case in Japan, and the Goth Loli is arguably more about restoring a sense of traditional female beauty as resistance to mainstream fashion by women who wish to dress in a sweet and elegant manner. Goth Loli is therefore not about being sexually forward, but about making fashion choices for those who wish to project a sense of *kawaii*, of being young, small, fragile, or perhaps cute. Again, in the West, this has been misconstrued as infantilizing, but that is not the case in Japan, where the Goth Loli is an expression of female agency that expresses being neither ignorant child nor promiscuous woman.

It is also a resistance to traditional Goth fashion, rejecting Goth fashion's proclivities toward horror and morbidity with sweet and elegant or cute and bright choices, with the subset of Sweet Lolita choosing pastel colors to augment those frills and parasols. On display in the Harajuku district and the internet, Goth Loli grew to exert a transnational influence, creating a sort of feedback loop where Western Goth was appropriated by the Japanese to create Goth Loli, which was in turn appropriated by Western Goth again as some North American Goths were transitioning into steampunk: tiny fascinator top hats and the pinafore dresses found their way into steampunk fashion; after all, both were vague vintage expressions. But make no mistake, despite the European flavor of Goth Loli, the expression is Japanese. And it's an expression once again influenced by vintage anime: Ikeda Riyoko's *Rose of Versailles* (1979), another series that contributes to the Japanese "Paris of our dreams," had a huge influence on Goth Loli fashion, and by extension, steampunk.

Both Goth Loli and steampunk draw indiscriminately from history's toolbox, creating a fashion style that references history but no particular historical period. As Goth Loli drew from a romanticized version of eighteenth-and nineteenth century European nobility, so too did steampunk, mixing baroque and rococo styles alongside Victorian and Edwardian. Goth, Goth Loli, and steampunk alike are all fashion based in the past, but as we've seen throughout this book, a fantastic past that never existed.

Cherie Priest said that being Goth in her youth had an aspect of the theatrical to it, and surmises that this theatricality carried over to steampunk, especially for people who had the day job, the mortgage, and kids to take care of. There aren't many opportunities to dress up in masquerade and adopt a persona other than your own. But for people who love performance, steampunk offers an opportunity for theatricality that is formal and consequently, perhaps more socially acceptable.

Fashion as Performance: The Theatricality of Steampunk Fashion

One of the attractions for steampunk fashion fans is constructing the history of this fabulous fictional past through creative, narrative-based costuming. Many steampunk cosplayers have a story for the persona they've embodied in their fashion. I've had many conversations at steampunk conventions with enthusiastic costumers like Greg Medley, whose cosplay of Dr. Abner Perry from Edgar Rice Burroughs's *At the Earth's*

Core included a very involved backpack for journeying beneath the surface of the planet. Sometimes, the persona is the starting point, and the costume emerges from the story. In other cases, such as when the costumer is limited by available materials, the persona emerges from the costume. Edmonton-based steampunk stylist Virgo Vermeil assists steampunk fans in finding both, going to thrift stores and flea markets for people who lack the time and magpie finesse and locating pieces that match personas, or helping new fans to craft personas based on fashion items they're drawn to. David Drake and Katherine Morse imagined the adventures of their steampunk personas of Chief Inspector Erasmus L. Drake and Dr. "Sparky" McTrowell in a series of web fiction, alternating as authors from chapter to chapter. which culminated in their self-published hardcover collection *London, Where It All Began*.

In the spirit of research for this chapter, I attended a steampunk costuming workshop, to see what sort of advice I'd receive if I was new to steampunk. In addition to recommendations for local thrift and Goth fashion stores, the workshop focused primarily on constructing a steampunk persona (or "steamsona" as they are often called).

Katherine Morse and David Drake as their steampunk personas, Drake and McTrowell, in cosplay and comic art by Brian Kesinger.

At the costuming workshop, the presenter had synthesized several lists of steampunk archetypes, with Suzanne Lazear's list standing out. Lazear had originally compiled her list of archetypes for steampunk writers, but it also serves as an excellent inspiration for persona creation. The workshop list included a fairly comprehensive list of possible archetypes in clusters. The following is a list of those clusters along with my own examples from cinema and television, starting with the airship captain or pirate, embodied by the spirit of Harrison Ford as Han Solo or Johnny Depp as Captain Jack Sparrow, but with an airship instead of starship or sailing ship; the explorer or adventurer, usually sporting a pith helmet, but with a higher dose of *Tomb Raider*'s Lara Croft or Indiana Jones than Dr. Livingstone, I presume; the highborn lord or lady, seen often in films based on novels by Jane Austen or period cinema and television like *Downton Abbey*, or Anglophile royalist adaptations such as *The Crown*; the gambler or gypsy, which seemed an odd pairing to me but seemed to be intended as homage to gamblers of Wild West cinema and television such as Mel Gibson in *Maverick* or Val Kilmer in *Tombstone*; the philosopher or scholar, embodied youthfully in Milo Finch in Disney's *Atlantis*, or as older man in Peter Cushing's performance as Abner Perry in *At the Earth's Core,* and closely related to the next archetype: the inventor/ alchemist/ mad scientist/doctor, perhaps best exemplified by the real life Nikolai Tesla, or any cinematic version of Dr. Frankenstein, most notably Colin Clive, Gene Wilder, Peter Cushing, and James McAvoy; the dandy or femme fatale/saloon girl/chorus girl/burlesque dancer, which seems to simply suggest a steampunked sensuality or sex-positivity, as embodied by Salma Hayek in *Wild Wild West* or Nicole Kidman in *Moulin Rouge!*; and finally, scrappy survivor or street sparrow, which could be anything from Furiosa in *Mad Max Fury Road* to a steampunked Oliver Twist or Artful Dodger. I could add any number of additions to this list: the detective (Sherlock Holmes, obviously), the magician (the protagonists of *The Illusionist* and *The Prestige*), and the monster hunter (as with Dr. Frankenstein, a long line of performances as Van Helsing, notably Peter Cushing yet again, Anthony Hopkins, and Hugh Jackman).

Here again, though, steampunk's penchant for hybridity and diversity rears its head, since any of these archetypes could be readily mixed and matched. For starters, many of the cinematic inspirations I've listed are white and male. Any one of these archetypes could be gender bent or racially appropriated. Imagine a Latina monster hunter who is a scrappy survivor of a vampiric postapocalypse, a sort of steampunked Buffy the Vampire Slayer crossed with *Terminator*'s Sarah Connor. Steampunk fashion and cosplay is often a space for people exploring queer expressions, whereby the saloon girl is a male in drag, or the dandy is a female in a waistcoat with a pencil moustache.

But film and television are only one of the avenues of inspirations for steampunk personas. Many steampunk cosplays have emerged from steampunk comics as well: Autumn Adamme observed that steampunk fashion has often imitated the costume designs in Phil and Kaja Foglio's *Girl Genius*, while master cosplayers like Maurice Grunbaum take iconic heroes like DC's Batman and apply a steampunk treatment, deviating not only from canonical costume design, but in Grunbaum's Eurasian heritage. Others find inspiration in steampunk games, either adhering to

French cosplayer Maurice Grunbaum's steampunked Dark Knight.

the designs of video games like *Bioshock Infinite* or creating from scratch through tabletop role-playing games like *Space: 1889* or *Gurp's Steampunk*.

Diana Pho, an editor at Tor books, created the persona of Ay-leen the Peacemaker when she "joined the crew" of a group of friends who had realized characters from a role-playing game in cosplay. But because of her Vietnamese heritage, she didn't want to adopt a British heritage she didn't identify with. In accordance with the real-world history of Vietnam, Ay-leen fights French Imperialism. Diana's Ay-leen costume is a great instance of how steampunk plays with history: in this case, playful resistance to the effacing of cultural history. She combines an *ao dai*, a Vietnamese long-sleeved tunic with ankle-length panels at front and back, worn over trousers. The ao dai is a unisex garment but is worn primarily by women. Its evolution is one of the collision of cultures, between Vietnam and China, then Vietnam and France. As Diana writes, "The ao dai is not a frozen cultural artifact, existing untouched and idealized, but is a piece of clothing that had changed through the centuries, affected by war and imperialism as much as cultural influences and fads." It's also a great instance of why steampunk might have emerged from Victorian fantasies but has transcended them. In England, it would have been scandalous for women to wear attire that resembles men's trousers; in Vietnam, it would have been scandalous for women to wear a Victorian dress. Diana addresses this process of reimagining history:

> Steampunk clothes represent how our imagined histories are based on real history, and whatever steampunk fantasy we construct for ourselves can have a basis in who we are and where we fit in the world. When you see me, you can see a story, part fantasy, part reality. This is the story I give to you. When steampunks dress up, they engage in this performance of identity; when you see us, you see the stories we tell each other.

It is in this individual expression of identity, if we are brave enough to express ourselves and not simply replicate what others have done in steampunk fashion, that the archetypes are not archetypes at all, but simply starting points for the intersection of the real-world you with the splendid fiction of a steampunk you. The term "archetype" signifies recurrence and recognition, and steampunk fashion works within

Diana Pho as Ay-leen the Peacemaker.   *Rachael Shane*

those recognizable repetitions. But it also pushes at the boundaries of the archetypes, creating something new in each individual's creativity. To be sure, there are slavish imitations, but there are also splendid innovations. And with innovation comes change; the archetype shifts, and what was considered immutable changes. So it is that steampunk fashion breaks with its roots, often abandoning the overt narrative technofantasies of steampunk's roots for designs founded in burlesque and cabaret, not science fiction and fantasy.

Moulin Rouge!

I had wanted to include Baz Luhrman's *Moulin Rouge!* in the chapter on steampunk film, but felt that it fit better here, at the bridge point between fashion and music. I also thought it would be too much for technophile steampunks to accept. After all, there's no technofantasy at all. There's no overt interaction with science fiction, fantasy, or horror. But there *is* a sense of heightened reality from the beginning of the film, when a red curtain opens to reveal the proscenium arch of a theater stage. Director Luhrman said that this was to signal to the audience that the film was offering a "contract with the storytelling," one that would not lead to a storyworld of naturalism, but one that shared greater affinities with *Alice in Wonderland* or *The Wizard of Oz*. The camera moves through a model of *fin de siècle* Paris that simultaneously resembles a pop-up book and old silent films, utilizing black and white and desaturated sepia-toned digital color correcting.

Admittedly, I'm stretching my definition of fantasy here, implying that actual magic might be unnecessary for steampunk, that a stylistic magic might be all that's required. The visual style of *Moulin Rouge!* is steampunk in every way *but* overt fantasy, science fiction, or horror. But consider the wealth of retrofuturistic/vintage hybridity in this film: in the costuming, which is evocative of 1899 Paris, but is historically inaccurate; from the PG-13 nature of the Cancan dancers' undergarments to the inclusion of the iconic Tom Baker Doctor Who scarf; in the choreography, which is a blend of music hall and 1950s cabaret film musicals; in the music, which is the mother of all mash-ups, juxtaposing Nirvana's grunge hit "Smells Like Teen Spirit" with an R&B cover of disco classic "Lady Marmalade," or the title track from *The Sound of Music* with T. Rex's "Children of the Revolution," all recast with a vintage sound to evoke the decadence of the Moulin Rouge.

Anyone who dismisses *Moulin Rouge!* as part of the cinematic legacy of steampunk might be too focused on the industrial tech expressions of makers and mad scientists. Autumn Adamme credits it with the use of vertically striped stockings in cabaret, which in turn has influenced steampunk fashion, while Erica Mulkey says the visuals were definitely an influence on her work as Unwoman. Whether a direct inspiration or not, *Moulin Rouge!* certainly has many affinities with steampunk fashion and music.

By the time steampunk fashion was being utilized on the runway by Victoria's Secret in 2009, it was a facet of steampunk culture unto itself, largely unconcerned and unaware of steampunk's literary roots. In 2009, a person interested in steampunk fashion was far likelier to find inspiration in *Moulin Rouge!* than in a novel by Blaylock or Moorcock.

To admit *Moulin Rouge!* into the steampunk fold is also to admit that, once steampunk had become a maker and fashion phenomenon, no single work could encompass everything that it had come to represent. When Guy Ritchie's *Sherlock Holmes* movie came out, people asked, "Is it steampunk?" And the response was, "Aside from the doomsday device at the end of the film, no." But such a response ignores the steampunked costume design once again. Steampunks will readily say that steampunk fashion is so much more than the goggles. And we have to admit that steampunk is so much more than just technology. As I said at the outset of this book, technofantasy is only one aspect of steampunk.

And in fashion, that technofantasy is more than rivets and gears sewn on. I'd like to offer the argument that, as with the heightened reality of *Moulin Rouge!*, the technofantasy of steampunk fashion is the ability to combine the past with the future: to mix vintage fashions in a retrofuturistic way, in a way that combines modern fashion trends with Victorian ones; traditional Vietnamese with futuristic tech; that uses modern methods of textile manufacturing or materials that aren't historically accurate. This isn't to exclude those who seek to achieve that historical accuracy. But even when that accuracy is achieved, it's still worn by a twenty-first-century native who lives in a digital world.

That sort of technofantasy is also found in steampunk music. Nathaniel Johnstone is no stranger to steampunk music, having played one of his many instruments in Abney Park, the Nathaniel Johnstone Band, the Ghosts Project, and Dogwood & Johnson. Johnstone was influenced by the music used in *Moulin Rouge!* before it made its way onto the soundtrack, but also sees how the unprecedented mash-up of vintage and contemporary music anticipated steampunk music, yet another expression that jumped off the literary page and instead of the workshop or runway, onto the stage and the dance floor.

13

Steampunk Music

The Elusive Sound of Steam

I grew up in an evangelical Christian household, and as a child of the 1980s, I listened to "Christian rock," bands like Petra, who had a song called "God Gave Rock n' Roll to You." It was never one of my favorite songs, but it was catchy enough to remember when I picked up the soundtrack to *Bill and Ted's Bogus Journey*, which had a version of "God Gave Rock and Roll to You" by Kiss. Although artists like Alice Cooper and Dave Mustaine of *Megadeth* had conversion experiences, I was pretty sure none of the members of Kiss had found God. So I wondered what they were doing playing a Petra song (and doing a much better job of it).

Turns out it wasn't a Petra song at all. "God Gave Rock and Roll to You" was originally recorded by Brit prog-rock band Argent. Both Petra and Kiss's versions were covers. Both covers changed the lyrics, but all of the versions, including the original, claimed that God put rock 'n' roll in the "soul of everyone." The Petra lyrics contained, as most Christian rock in the '80s did, an invitation to get saved ("because it's never too late to change your mind"), neither the Argent nor Kiss version was particularly offensive from a religious standpoint.

So why I am I telling you this story at the outset of the chapter on steampunk music? Because the designation "Christian rock" was always an odd one. And not because I don't think religious music shouldn't be upbeat or downright loud; because it was a designation not of musical style but lyrical substance. However, "God Gave Rock and Roll to You" was, according to the rules of Christian rock, only Christian when Petra performed it. Why? Because of those altered lyrics? Argent's original lyrics encouraged listeners to "love your friend and love your neighbor," Or was it the fact that the members of Petra openly and proudly identified as born-again Christians, whereas the members of Kiss and Argent did not?

In many ways, steampunk music shares this identification of genre of lyric rather than genre of music. The first steampunk act I ever heard was Abney Park, and I assumed that their blend of '90s Goth music, rock music, and world sounds was the template for what steampunk music was. Then I discovered Professor Elemental and his "chaphop" sound. Here was another steampunk musician, but this one was a rapper. I had seen both acts live at steampunk conventions, indicating the steampunk community's approval. How can a style of music be both rock and rap?

The Steampunk Wikia lists five criteria for steampunk music, and argues that a band would need at least two or three of these criteria to be considered steampunk music:

- They call themselves steampunk.
- Old-fashioned dress or style (Victorian/Edwardian or '20s through '50s for dieselpunk).
- Classical instrumentation elements.
- Fictional (preferably alternate history) backstory.
- Steampunk (sci-fi/historical) lyrics.

You'll notice that of these five criteria, only *one* has anything to do with the musical sound of an act. In other words, similar to Christian music in the 1980s, steampunk music isn't about a particular *sound* but rather about an idea, expressed through the incorporation or appropriation of steampunk fashion and fiction. As a thought experiment to take us through a survey of steampunk music from the 1970s to today, I'm going to use Steampunk Wikia's criteria, as it reflects much of the discussion I've been privy to about steampunk music is.

Jeff Wayne's Musical Version of War of the Worlds

Almost a decade before there'd be a word for it, and twenty-five years before the first band would lay claim to that word, American composer Jeff Wayne went looking for rock 'n' roll fame in H. G. Wells's *War of the Worlds*. And against all odds, he found it.

Wayne had been writing commercial jingles and collaborating with British pop artists while aspiring to fulfill his father's unfulfilled dream of writing a great rock musical. Wayne found inspiration in the pages of Wells's seminal alien invasion story, and after procuring the rights, set to work writing the music, while his father, Jerry, and his father's second wife, Doreen, worked on the script. Since Wayne's concept album

Ricky Wilson singing "Brave New World" in *Jeff Wayne's War of The Worlds New Generation* at The O2 Arena in London, 2012. Wilson's costume and the stage dressing have strong steampunk influences.   *Rex*

is based on one of the great classics of early science fiction, it definitely fulfills Steampunk Wikia's last criterion for steampunk music, that it contain "steampunk (sci-fi/historical) lyrics." The album is very faithful to Wells's novel, with only a few departures. The double album structure even permitted Wayne to split the album's narrative at the same point as H. G. Wells did for his novel, at the point the Martians have conquered the Earth.

Three years later, in 1978, *Jeff Wayne's Musical Version of War of the Worlds* was released as a double album to critical and popular success. With popular British vocalists like Justin Hayward of the Moody Blues, Phil Lynott of Thin Lizzy, and Chris Thompson of Manfred Mann's Earth Band; legendary session players like Chris Spedding on guitar and Herbie Flowers on bass; and the unforgettable and chilling narration of famed actor Richard Burton, it was an unparalleled achievement in rock music. It won awards, climbed the record charts, and ended up on cassette in my uncle's car, where I heard it for the first time. I had read a *Classics Illustrated* version of *War of the Worlds*, so I was familiar with the story, but it was the music I was really floored by. I loved rock 'n' roll and I loved movie soundtracks, but I'd never heard music that seemed to combine them like Wayne's *War of the Worlds* did. The opening track, "The Eve of the War," mixed strings with a disco beat and rock guitars, scoring another point for the incorporation of classical instrumentation elements (unless you're listening to the dubstep remix of the album, and yes, there really is one).

Now obviously, Jeff Wayne couldn't have called what he was doing steampunk, because the term didn't exist yet, so the album fails the first of Steampunk Wikia's criteria. And while the original artists who recorded the album did not dress in Victorian fashion at the time of the recording, those original artists and their various successors have done so for the live stage show of the album which began in the UK and Ireland in 2006 and has since toured Australia, New Zealand, Germany, the Netherlands, and Belgium. Later stage designs and costuming for the live show were clearly taking design ideas from steampunk, with actors wearing goggles, top-hat fascinators, and sets covered in cogs and gears. So we might say that, better late than never, Jeff Wayne's album scores a point on the second criteria, for a grand total of 3/5. Steampunk Wikia declared that two to three of these criteria are needed for an act or in this case, a work to be considered steampunk music.

It's also notable that *Jeff Wayne's Musical Version of War of the Worlds* has sold over 15 million records worldwide, making it the most successful steampunk album of all time. And yet you won't find any mention of it in books on steampunk. Once again, articles on steampunk almost always invoke Verne and Wells, regardless of which facet of steampunk is the focus of the article. And yet one would think an album as commercially successful as this one, which later embraced the steampunk aesthetic for its live show, would garner some mention. And yet it hasn't. Until now, I suppose.

As we've seen in these last few chapters, steampunk makers and fashion had a different genesis point than the fiction and films did. And while we might expect *Jeff Wayne's Musical Version of War of the Worlds* to be an early influence on later steampunk musicians, it has never appeared on any steampunk musician's inspiration lists. Rather, steampunk music emerged from one of the same sources that steampunk fashion did: the Goth scene.

Abney Park: Airship Pirates

I know I've talked an awful lot about Steam Powered in this book. But I have to tell you one more story about it. On the last night of the event, attendees were bussed to a music-hall venue to see a performance by Abney Park, at the time the only steampunk band I'd ever heard of (and that's only because I googled them after learning they'd be at the convention).

I had played in a number of indie bands, so I sat down and got ready to critique the performance, which is what musicians do at shows. Fans dance and sing along. Musicians sit and experience envy or superiority. I was surprised to find myself on my feet and dancing, and for the songs I knew, singing along. Although they're often called the quintessential steampunk band, Abney Park is first and foremost great entertainers who understand what a live show needs to be.

Abney Park was formed in 1997 by Robert Brown, and for the first eight years, the band's sound was a mix of industrial, darkwave, and Goth before reinventing their look and, to a degree, their sound. In 2005, they became one of the first musical acts to appropriate steampunk to describe themselves (and since we're not counting Jeff Wayne

Abney Park's guitars on display in the vendor hall at Steam Powered in 2008.

and company, the first steampunk band was Vernian Process in 2003). So Abney Park fulfills Steampunk Wikia's first criterion: they not only call themselves steampunk, they are easily the most famous of the bands who have done so.

To complete their transformation from Goth to steampunk, the band created a backstory to explain their shift away from Goth, wherein their airplane crashed into a time-traveling airship, fulfilling the "fictional backstory" criterion, and perhaps trend-setting its inclusion as criterion. The result was steampunked versions of themselves and their instruments: the band adopted steampunk stage personas (Robert Brown became "Captain" Robert Brown of the airship *Ophelia*), donned steampunk fashion to match, and modded their instruments with steampunk embellishments, fulfilling the second criterion in style.

The core sound of the band remained initially very similar to their Goth sound. Keyboardist Kristina Erikson had always incorporated the sounds of classical instruments, but the addition of guitarist/violinist Nathaniel Johnstone brought an overtly vintage feel to their songs, fulfilling the classical elements criterion.

Further, the band has always retained one of their early signatures, namely that they do not use a live drummer. Instead, drum and electronic loops have been a layer of Abney Park's music since their earliest incarnation. So while the band's stage attire is unquestionably steampunk, and they have since incorporated more acoustic instruments (sometimes electronically modified, as in the case of Brown's bouzouki on tracks like "Your Escape"), their music retains noticeable ties to its industrial and Gothic roots.

Finally, Robert Brown is certainly a storyteller, with steampunk lyrical fiction in songs like "Airship Pirates," "The Secret Life of Dr. Calgori," and "Herr Drosselmyers Doll," while songs like "Steampunk Revolution" and "Building Steam" act like steampunk manifestos to march or dance to. The group's lyrical content has been unabashedly steampunk-related since the release of *Lost Horizons* in 2008, winning them a full 5/5 points by Steampunk Wikia's criteria. However, we have to ask the chicken-or-the-egg question when it comes to Abney Park and the definition of steampunk music. Given their status as one of the most prolific and enduring steampunk acts, it's likely that they inadvertently created those five criteria with their own, at the time, innovative creative choices.

Many steampunk bands followed Abney Park, seeking to achieve the same level of popularity by either emulation or unintentional similarity. But consciously or unconsciously, many steampunk acts relied too much on those five criteria without focusing on the one thing every good musical act needs: great songs. Numerous steampunk acts have amazing backstories and incredible stage attire but unmemorable songs. Others focus on having accurate vintage sounds, forgetting that steampunk music can be like steampunk fashion—a mix of forgotten styles with popular beats and melodies from today. Many steampunk artists were also heretoday, gone-tomorrow acts who are no longer performing, which is why I've focused on the stalwart Abney Park as the exemplar of self-declared steampunk band. There are notable exceptions, and though any list I create would be based in subjectivity, those exceptions include (but are in no way limited to) Professor Elemental's infectious chaphop The Cog Is Dead's combination of rock and ragtime, and just about any electro-swing that blends yesteryear's dance music with today's backbeats.

Take a look at Spotify's official steampunk playlist: it's a mélange of artists from self-declared steampunk artists to dark cabaret, neo-burlesque, country-folk artists you've likely never heard of, and song after song that appear to derive their inspiration from the soundtrack to *The Nightmare Before Christmas* or anything ever written by Danny Elfman.

One of steampunk's most prolific artists does not appear on that Spotify playlist, but is worthy of mention in a chapter on steampunk music. Erica Mulkey, better known by her stage name of Unwoman, has played with a host of steampunk artists at an array of steampunk events: she's performed with steampunk and Goth acts such as Abney Park, Amanda Palmer, Rasputina, Voltaire, HUMANWINE, The Ghosts Project, Nathaniel Johnstone Band, Dogwood, Eliza Rickman, Pam Shaffer, Eli August, Aaron J Shay, Psyche Corporation, and Monica Richards of Faith and the Muse. In short, if you listen to steampunk music, or have attended a steampunk concert, there's a good chance you've heard Unwoman, whether you knew it or not.

In addition to being an amazing songwriter whose catchy hooks and somber melodies beg the listener to sing along, Unwoman has covered a wide range of popular songs, from the theme to Joss Whedon's *Firefly* to *Careless Whisper* by Wham! And for $3 at her Patreon site, you can vote on which song she'll cover next. Unlike those steampunk artists who focus on the steampunk story over songs, Unwoman is about creating and covering great steampunk music.

Punch Drunk Cabaret: Outlaw Rockabilly and Steampunk Swing

On the flip side of bands that have actively promoted themselves as steampunk, there are groups like Punch Drunk Cabaret that have been embraced by steampunks and have subsequently incorporated steampunk elements into their look, as well as describing their sound as a mix of "outlaw rockabilly" and "steampunk swing."

Punch Drunk Cabaret was formed in 2011, and according to lead singer Randy Bailer, was a mixture of roots, rockabilly, swing, and old-time county. You'll notice the absence of steampunk as adjective for the band's style of swing. The steampunk addition came later, as a way of explaining the absence of a horn section in the band. As Randy Bailer explains, using the term steampunk was a way to indicate that Punch Drunk's swing was not big band swing; it was something new. But as a three-piece, Punch Drunk contains no classical elements—vintage music galore, but played on drums, semi-hollow-bodied guitars, and twelve-string basses.

Despite lacking those classical elements and only using steampunk as an adjective for an aspect of their sound (partial marks?), Punch Drunk Cabaret was booked to play the First Annual Steampunk Ball for the Edmonton Steampunk Society in 2013, and the performance led to an ongoing relationship between the band and Albertan steampunk fans. Unlike so many bands that include "steampunk" in their marketing, Punch Drunk Cabaret has built in more steampunk elements following their interaction with steampunk fans, rather than as a way to attract them in the first place.

This is significant.

Promotional photo of Punch Drunk Cabaret.

Remember, we've been told by many experts that steampunk is Victorian. If it's from some other era, then it's dieselpunk, or decopunk, or some other punk. Punch Drunk Cabaret is a band whose music combines rockabilly and swing. Swing is a type of big band music that contains off-beat rhythms that create a "swing feel," which was first made popular in the 1930s. Rockabilly is a portmanteau of rock 'n' roll and "hillbilly" or country, and denotes the earliest style of rock music made popular by artists like Elvis Presley, Buddy Holly, and Johnny Cash in the 1950s. Randy Bailer's vocal style has been described as a combination of Brian Setzer, one of the founding members of 1980s rockabilly band Stray Cats (who now performs swing music with the Brian Setzer Orchestra), and Tom Waits, who in addition to having a signature gravelly voice, combines blues, jazz, and vaudeville in his music.

Shouldn't someone be calling the atompunk fans to let them know their band is living on the western prairies of Canada? Or perhaps we ought to come to a different conclusion.

Perhaps the term steampunk is changing. Just as it was never intended to signify only Victorian works, nor to anticipate the DIY maker or fashion revolutions that appropriated the term, it was likewise never intended to be a label for a style of music. Abney Park appropriated a literary term and made it a musical one. Every steampunk act since then has done the same. But when the steampunk community appropriates a band and lays claim to it as their own, even if that band doesn't fit the criteria exactly, we see steampunk music undergoing a change.

From bassist Terry Grant's begoggled top hat, to Randy Bailer's waxed mustachio and impeccably fashionable vests, Punch Drunk Cabaret screams yesteryear. And their music screams it too. It's all hyper-vintage, but from that large umbrella of a "simpler time" before global communities and digital humanities. So despite only scoring 1.75/5 for steampunk attire and partial marks for a vintage style and some references to steampunk in their lyrics, steampunk fans have adopted a rockabilly-swing-revival band with open arms, without quibbling over its lack of accurate Victoriana or science-fiction storytelling.

And why?

Because, like Abney Park, Punch Drunk Cabaret is a hell of a lot of fun to dance to. And they have an old-timey sound and look. And when you want to party, that's plenty. While many steampunk acts rely on theatrical gimmicks, Punch Drunk Cabaret writes vintage-sounding songs that demand you dance to them. One of my criteria for a good live band at any event trying to be a party is whether they have to beg the audience to get up and dance. Punch Drunk Cabaret does not beg its audiences to dance. The audience begs Punch Drunk to come back so they'll play some more.

But not all artists who play near the steampunk backyard are as welcomed as Punch Drunk Cabaret has been, as witnessed by another Canadian back in 2011.

Steampop: Justin Bieber

In 2011, Justin Bieber released a steampunk video for his Christmas cover of "Santa Claus Is Coming to Town," much to the consternation of steampunk aficionados and gatekeepers who rejected Bieber's "appropriation" of steampunk style for mainstream marketing. Oddly, the prog rock legends of Rush not only steampunked their stage (and Neil Peart's drum kit) for their 2011 *Time Machine* tour, but the following year released a steampunk concept album and accompanying book without any backlash from the steampunk community. Given steampunk music's lack of a coherent sound, the divide between responses to Bieber and Rush's use of steampunk was indicative of an increasingly prescriptive subculture who wanted to keep steampunk underground, away from the mainstream.

'Twas the Night Before Christmas, and all through the house, not a creature was stirring, except all the steampunks who were still upset about Justin Bieber's so-called appropriation of their beloved underground subculture. In November 2011, the year after he had his first megahit with "Baby," Canadian pop idol Justin Bieber released two videos for his version of the popular Christmas carol "Santa Claus Is Coming to Town." The first video, the Animagic version, featured an animated puppet version of Bieber, in the style of the Rankin-Bass Christmas specials from the 1960s and '70s. Joining Bieber were the carrot-topped Kris Kringle originally voiced by Mickey Rooney and his penguin sidekick Topper from the 1970 Christmas special *Santa Claus Is Coming to Town*. In addition to the new footage of Bieber, Kringle, and Topper, scenes from the original special were edited in as well. The song includes samples from Jackson 5 hits "ABC" and "I Want You Back," and an arrangement that is unmistakably a tribute to the style of the Jacksons.

The second video was originally shown before the theatrical release of the animated feature *Arthur Christmas*. The music is slightly different from the original version and begins with the sounds of industrial machinery and steam whistles over images of Bieber working in a steampunk-looking version of Santa's workshop. Removing steampunk goggles, Bieber stands, fiddles with some dials, and then turns a windup key in the back of a clockwork girl, the object of his earlier mechanical attentions. Wound up, the clockwork girl begins to dance in a popping and locking style, emulating the movements of an automaton. The video continues with Bieber dancing about this steampunked workshop; all of the elves (the only diminutive one is a child) are dressed steampunk style,

A still from one of the two music videos for the Justin Bieber cover of "Santa Claus is Coming to Town" which was supposedly responsible for ruining steampunk.   *Alamy*

with goggles, bowler hats, vintage vests, and mechanical exoskeletons and prosthetics.

Using Steampunk Wikia's criteria, Bieber scores only a 1: he dressed steampunk. Nothing else about the song or Bieber's subsequent public persona would continue to be steampunk. So it wasn't surprising that steampunk fans were nonplussed about it.

I wouldn't say the internet exploded over the video, but high-profile geek website Boing Boing stated simply, "Cory, this is your fault," a reference to how often science-fiction writer and internet pundit Cory Doctorow had been talking about steampunk in the previous year. Website Gawker proclaimed that the video had ruined "entire nerd subculture" and advised steampunks to "get a new quirky aesthetic pastime before it blows it up among 14-year-old Beliebers." Both are indicative of the derision for Bieber's use of steampunk.

The comment thread at Gawker proclaimed it the "JC Penny version of steampunk," with "all the nifty details and gritty edges that make steampunk fun filed down." These comments about the mainstreaming of steampunk are artifacts of how steampunk subculture decried the popularizing of their niche: if it wasn't from the "true steampunk" community, then it wasn't actually steampunk. The problem was, it was *clearly* steampunk, JC Penny version or otherwise. As for the steampunk fun being filed down, the video is arguably lots of fun, though mindlessly so. And why not? As we noted all the way back with the work of Blaylock, Powers, and Jeter, steampunk doesn't have to be deep and meaningful. But there was a strong wave in the subculture who wanted it to be so.

The rise of steampunk into the popular eye that Christmas was evident in more than just Bieber's video. In 2011, Macy's famous storefront window display featured a gorgeous array of steampunk elements, which coincidentally used elements from both of Bieber's videos: steampunk gears and Victorian clothing mixed with marionette figures. Now I'm not suggesting that Macy's director of windows Paul Olszewski stole the ideas from Bieber's creative team. It's obvious that steampunk had reached a sort of cultural tipping point, and artists of various media and approaches were using it. But what's interesting is that Bieber's use was considered an abomination by many in the steampunk subculture, while the Macy's storefront was pronounced a wonderful work of art.

Arguably, both are about nostalgia, a feeling that runs high at Christmas time. What other time of the year do songs nearly a century old get regular rotation on radio stations? Christmas music is notoriously nostalgic; anecdotally, I prefer Christmas music that *sounds* old-timey. It's why an artist like Michael Bublé or Harry Connick Jr. will have hits with their Christmas albums: they're evoking a nostalgic sound. As cool as it might be to have this year's pop artists take their stab at a Christmas song, it's a rare event that any of those become seasonal classics. The ones that do have a sense of time gone by, be it in the lyrics or the style of the music. If you're a crooner like Bublé or Connick Jr., you evoke (or just cover) classic Christmas hits like "White Christmas" as sung by Bing Crosby or "It's Beginning to Look a Lot Like Christmas" by Perry Como. Whatever one thinks of the holiday, Christmas has a strong nostalgic element to it.

Bieber's cover of "Santa Claus Is Coming to Town" may not evoke nostalgia for its 1930s roots, but it does create a sense of nostalgia in its evocation of the Jackson 5. That music makes me think of Christmas when I was a kid, so was certainly "old-timey" for the average Belieber in 2011. Steampunk is likewise about nostalgia for a concept of the Victorian period; after all, historically speaking, Charles Dickens single-handedly rescued Christmas from the Puritan ghetto it had been forced into during the reign of King Cromwell. The celebration of Christmas in Dickens's *A Christmas Carol* popularized the holiday in a way that reflected the fiction, not the reality that preceded it. Consequently, Victoriana and Christmas go hand in hand. So one can't really blame either Bieber's or Macy's creative teams for using steampunk to create a sense of old-timey nostalgia. Nevertheless, many vocal steampunks did, and then conspicuously, in the case of my next example, did not.

Steamprog: Rush and *Clockwork Angels*

Oddly, although steampunks gave Bieber a hard time for appropriating steampunk (something every second-wave steampunk had already done, for the record, appropriating it from the first-wave writers and artists and then establishing a very narrow criteria for what would pass as steampunk), I saw no sign of invective for the Bieb's fellow Canadians, prog-rock giants Neil Peart, Alex Lifeson, and Geddy Lee of Rush. Rush's *Time Machine* tour (2010–2011) anticipated the forthcoming concept album, novel, tour, and finally comic book, *Clockwork Angels*.

Reviews for *Clockwork Angels* were positive, with a number calling the album one of the best in Rush's discography. It won Rock Album of the Year at the 2013 Juno Awards (the Canadian equivalent of the Grammys), and charted well.

For Rush fans, this is unsurprising. The trio have a solid reputation as virtuosos of their respective instruments, as well as songwriters of the highest caliber in hard rock. On *Clockwork Angels,* the band flexes its prodigious muscles in ways that always leave me a little awed, especially when I watch them perform the songs in live concert footage. But despite the stage dressing for the *Time Machine* tour, which looks like the stage Abney Park ought to have played on at least once, or the steampunk visuals on-screen for the *Clockwork Angels* tour, there is musically nothing that ties *Clockwork Angels* to steampunk. It does not sound like Abney Park, or Steampowered Giraffe, or Unwoman (unless you count the presence of strings on a few songs, but the use of orchestral instruments is not new to progressive rock, as evidenced by Jeff Wayne's *War of the Worlds* album).

The music is prog-rock. The music is Rush.

But the steampunk content of the album is all in the lyrics, and by extension, the story those lyrics tell. The tie-in novel was plotted by drummer Neil Peart, who has also been responsible for the cerebral lyrics of Rush since their inception. The plot is evident in the liner notes and art of the CD, which contained a narrative woven together with album's lyrics. The plot was further expanded upon in a novelization of the album, which was later turned into a comic book.

The plot is an oft-told tale: a young man finds his small-town life too constraining and dreams of going to the big city to seek his fortune. The book riffs on Voltaire's classic satire *Candide*, and shares in the denunciation of the idea that a loving God is in control of events and that all things work out for the best.

There was even a sequel to the novel called *Clockwork Lives*, an anthology of short fiction in the world of *Clockwork Angels*. It's a gorgeous literary object, designed to look like the leatherbound alchemical journal on which the short stories get written over the course of *Clockwork Lives*. Peart's lyrics are peppered throughout both books, and consequently, the anthology shares many of the same themes as the novel, and like its predecessor, is a steampunk reworking of another literary classic, this time *The Canterbury Tales*.

To create these books, Peart enlisted the aid of longtime Rush fan and friend Kevin J. Anderson, to expand upon his outline. Anderson is a prolific and best-selling science-fiction and fantasy writer, and while arguably no stranger to steampunk, is not particularly well known for it. Of the over 120 novels to his credit, only five could be considered steampunk: the novelizations of *The League of Extraordinary Gentlemen* film and *Sky Captain and the World of Tomorrow*, the brilliant pastiche of

Captain Nemo: The Fantastic History of a Dark Genius, and two books playing off of H. G. Wells's *War of the Worlds*. One might argue that, besides being a friend of Peart's, it was advantageous to tap into Anderson's existing fan base to ensure sales of the novel. But no one made this accusation. Bieber had appropriated steampunk. Rush was somehow doing it right, despite arguably doing the very same thing. And contrary to what you might think, they scored 1/5, the same as Bieber, according to *Steampunk Wiki*'s criteria, for steampunk-storytelling lyrics.

So why did Rush get a pass?

I heard arguments that Bieber's use of steampunk was more superficial, that it is the equivalent of just slapping gears onto something and calling it steampunk. There's no denying that the integration of steampunk into the visuals that accompanied *Clockwork Angels* demonstrates a greater sense of cohesion due to the marriage of Peart's concept-driven lyrics and retrofuturistic images.

Yet Bieber's awesome steampunk gauntlet was designed by Canadian steampunk maker Ian Finch-Field. Can it really be appropriation if "authentic" steampunk props are being used? Especially considering that the design teams from Sabian Cymbals, Drum Workshop, and Tandem Digital who built Peart's steampunked drum kit on the *Time Machine* tour contain no "authentic" steampunk makers. One could easily accuse every one of those artisans of appropriating the steampunk aesthetic to create Peart's drum kit. And they'd be right. Because they did.

It might sound like I'm quibbling, and I am. Intentionally. To make a point.

There is no quintessential sound that we can call steampunk music. Most artists who define themselves as steampunk musicians seem to be able to hold the name more because of the style of their stage attire and the content of their lyrics than any common musical thread. According to the criteria set by Steampunk Wikia, any musical artist from before 1914 should be considered steampunk: they dressed in Victorian or Edwardian clothing and played "classical" style instruments. The criteria are flawed. Rush got a pass because Rush is one of the greatest hard rock bands of all time. Bieber got thrown under the bus because he's considered a vapid bubblegum popstar. And there's the rub.

If Rush, prog-rock gods that they are, and Justin Bieber, pop uberstar that he is, decided to use steampunk, it's mostly an indication of when the aesthetic ceased to be a fringe concept, an underground movement, something you hadn't heard of. Arguably, if steampunk had never been appropriated by artists with the kind of cultural clout that Rush and Justin Bieber have, I wouldn't be writing this book.

But the appropriation of steampunk by mainstream artists like Bieber, Rush, Panic! at the Disco, and David Guetta was a strong indication of how much it had grown. Through makers, fashion, and music, steampunk was no longer confined to the pages of science-fiction and fantasy fiction and film. And it was looking for a place to get together and enjoy all these expressions under one roof. Starting in 2008, steampunk fans gathered to flaunt their fashion, display their art, celebrate their heroes, and dance to their music at steampunk events around the world.

14

Unconventional Conventions

Steampunk Gatherings

With increased popularity owing more to the visual media of cinema, fashion, and maker art than the written media of prose literature, steampunk transitioned from online fan culture to a visible subculture. While I've spent most of this book talking about steampunk literature, art, and film, one of the most visible expressions of steampunk continues to be those who would say they are part of steampunk culture. Culture is notoriously difficult to study—unlike a book where I can read it and it always has the same words, or a film where the same images flash across the screen, or even a video game where there are multiple options to interact with the game narrative, culture changes and diversifies. And while there have been voices that wanted to make steampunk culture unified under one umbrella expression, the very diversity of steampunk expressions I've already written about meant that people are drawn to steampunk for a variety of reasons: fashion, literature, politics, nostalgia, etc.

Maddeningly, though perhaps not surprisingly, steampunk fans often seek to make steampunk in their own image. I can't count the number of times someone said, "Well, how I interpret steampunk is . . . " as a preamble to explaining how they had decided to express this invented subculture. In my own experience, this has meant I am often disappointed at how many steampunks have no connection to the literature that the culture is supposedly rooted in. Others may be bothered that many people who identify as steampunks have no connection to politically charged "punk" cultures.

At the height of steampunk popularity in the United States around 2010, this resulted in heated online debates declaring some expressions to be "true" steampunk, while others were derided as inferior or false. While watching the television series of *Steampunk'd*, I still saw this sort of behavior, as the idea of "repurposing" used items or clothing was said to be "essential" to the steampunk aesthetic. To makers, perhaps. But to a writer or visual artist? Hardly essential.

Of course, someone might jump in here and say, "But all cultures are invented! We made them up." And that may be true. But unlike traditional cultures, the creation of the fan culture of steampunk is admittedly far more self-aware of its fictional nature than, say, Manitoba Mennonites. This is not to make less of steampunk culture. It is instead to highlight the unstable nature of this culture, to hopefully encourage a sense of self-awareness for steampunks. To say that anything related to steampunk is "essential" or "authentic" about steampunk is asinine. While there are clearly affinities between divergent expressions that get labeled steampunk, we've seen time and again that what is considered "essential" in steampunk in the second wave was not considered so by the seminal artists and writers of steampunk.

Now this isn't to say that steampunks are so diverse that they encompass all types of people. But there is certainly a diversity of expression hidden behind the umbrella term "steampunk culture." The quest to create a homogenized steampunk is doomed to failure. In 2010, in preparation for a steampunk gathering, I constructed a list of steampunk tribes. While a number of those tribes have either decreased, changed, or disappeared, the concept remains the same: steampunk culture is not expressed in a uniform fashion. But given that I prepared that diversity list for a steampunk gathering demonstrates there are times and places where steampunk culture comes together to give, if nothing else, the appearance of unity.

Prior to 2008, that visible unity was evident at fan conventions like the San Diego Comic Con and Dragon Con, where steampunk cosplay was attracting positive attention. In response to that attention, events like Convergence, an annual gathering of Goths associated with Usenet newsgroups, employed steampunk themes like "Dark Victorian Dreams" in 2007, while Saloncon, a neo-Victorian event that began in 2006, turned its attention to steampunk proper in October 2008, the same month that Steam Powered, the first North American steampunk convention, was

The conference program for the first Seattle Steamcon in 2009, featuring Boilerplate art by Paul Guinan.

held in Sunnyvale, California. The year 2009 saw the rise of Steamcon in Seattle, Washington, Teslacon in Madison, Wisconsin, and Asylum in the UK. Around the world, steampunk events ranging from small, daylong gatherings to weekends with thousands of attendees proliferated in the following years. While there was speculation following the end of Steamcon that a number of these events would die out, they continue to thrive around the world. In 2014, Sweden's national fan convention, Swecon, was steampunk themed, held at the country's national rail museum where local fans were permitted to steampunk an actual steam train. Even as I was writing this book, Camrose, a small city close to my home in Western Canada, gave their annual Jaywalker's festival a steampunk theme in 2017.

What's It Like to Go to a Steampunk Convention for the First Time?

It's a little bizarre for me to be writing this chapter so late in this book, as my first significant interaction with the steampunk scene was at a convention. In 2008, hoping to learn more about steampunk, I contacted the promoters of Steam Powered: The California Steampunk Convention, which claimed to be the first big steampunk fan convention in North America. I was hoping to experience the convention, but also wanted to be part of it, and thankfully, Steam Powered was still in need of presenters, and offered me not one but three opportunities.

I didn't know much about steampunk, but thankfully, at the time, neither did anyone else. There were people *doing* it, but hardly any in a professional, research-focused way. I spent the intervening weeks between that phone call and my flight to California learning everything I could about the various topics I'd been given to present and co-present on: Victorian Science, Steampunk writing, and my own presentation on Jules Verne's Captain Nemo as a sort of original or proto-steampunk. It was like cramming for an exam in under a month.

I'd never attended a fan convention of any kind, despite being a fan of science fiction and fantasy since I was a kid. I had no idea what to expect, though I knew there was a "Victorian Steampunk Ball" the first night, and that I ought to dress up for it. If I'd ever been thankful I'd played in an indie rock band for over a decade, it was in that moment. My wife raided my old band clothes and cobbled together something that ensured I wouldn't stick out like the proverbial sore thumb. As steampunk outfits go, it was terribly humble, but it was better than a t-shirt and jeans.

Arriving in Sunnyvale California, on October 31, 2008, I remember thinking how appropriate it was that I would be "dressing up steampunk" on Halloween. Through my taxi's windows, I watched little ghosts and goblins wandering the sidewalks, and figured none of the convention attendees would stick out much tonight.

When I arrived at the Domain Hotel, I was startled by that man in full explorer's outfit with a pith helmet emerging from the entrance I told you about back at the beginning of the book. He gave me a "pip pip!" in a faux English accent, starting the immersive experience that would last until Sunday evening.

Stepping into the Domain Hotel was a little like stepping into another world. In the hotel lobby, Gentlemen's Emporium, a steampunk fashion company, was set up behind a façade dressed like a Victorian storefront, while early attendees milled about in full steampunk attire. Though I'd see far greater costumes and fashions at future conventions, I was stunned at this first experience. Suddenly, my "costume" seemed not only modest but somewhat insufficient. Nevertheless, I was there to observe, not to win costume contests, so I started observing.

My contact for the event put me in the capable hands of two of the members from Legion Fantastique, a Bay Area theatre group that special-ized in Vernian improv. If ever there was proof that the Bay Area had a thing for steampunk in 2008, the existence of Legion Fantastique was it. Think about how small a niche is represented by live improv theater. Now reduce that niche significantly by making your improv group only do Verne-based characters. That's Legion.

One of the actors from Legion was Greg Medley, who was the actor responsibly for the group's Captain Nemo. We decided that we'd incor-porate Legion's improvisational skills into my talk on Nemo, address-ing Greg directly with questions about his doings in Verne's novel. This isn't the sort of thing that just anyone attending a steampunk convention might experience, but it's indicative of the kind of creative alchemy one finds in a million different ways at a steampunk convention. You'll see people with fantastic cosplay posing in the halls, not just mugging for the camera but posing in a frozen moment from the persona they've created through their costume.

Do I Have to Dress Steampunk to Attend?

So does one have to dress up for a steampunk event? Absolutely not. Will dressing up help you enjoy the event? Not necessarily. Take Christopher J. Garcia, computer historian and Hugo-award fanzine editor, for example. I first met Garcia at Steam Powered wearing a Fred Flintstone shirt to compliment his shaggy mane and wild beard. It's like a '70s Saturday morning cartoon mash-up of *Captain Caveman* and the *Flintstones*. I've never seen Garcia wear steampunk clothing. I've never seen him cosplay. It doesn't detract from his experience, but that's because Garcia is there to present on panels, and kibbutz with writers and thinkers—he doesn't dress steampunk, but he sure knows steampunk. Many attendees dress steampunk lite—semiformal clothing bedazzled by goggles or corset.

However, if you're the sort of person who enjoys the theatricality of steampunk, or who enjoys being the center of photographic attention, then yes, you should dress up. Contrast Garcia with someone like John F. Strangeway, aka Steampunk Boba Fett, who not only attends conventions dressed in his amazing retrofuturistic version of that bounty hunter with a reputation that exceeds his abilities, but gets asked to attend to improve other attendees' experience of the event. Steampunk events are often themed, and encourage attendees to match their attire to that theme. Sometimes, those themes produce wild and unexpected results, like some of the costumes at Steamcon III's *20,000 Leagues Under the Sea Theme*; several con attendees had inflatable fish attached to their costume, some filled with helium and floating above the cosplayer. The website for Teslacon in 2017 helped prospective attendees with galleries related to their theme of "Bucharest Bungle," to assist attendees in giving their steampunk attire some Romanian flavor. But don't let those themes keep you from dressing up; any steampunk is good steampunk at a con.

Display of Greg Broadmore's Ray Guns in the vendor room at Steamcon, 2008.

And if you're going to go all out with your steampunk outfit and you're sure you've done an outstanding job, be prepared to see the event very slowly. I've been in the company of some great steampunk fashion and cosplay at events like this, and my companions were stopped frequently for photo ops. So if you love to look fabulous, just know that many attendees are going to want a fabulous photo of your efforts.

On that note, make sure you bring a camera with lots of storage. Even the smallest steampunk event abounds with eye candy. But remember your manners and always ask if you can take a photo. Perhaps the best opportunity for great photos would be the nigh-traditional costume contest. Almost always for fun (I once entered one last-minute because my companions, bolstered by a few drinks, decided we looked fabulous enough to go on display), these contests are a chance for costume and fashion artists to get the attention their work deserves, and in some cases be judged and awarded for their effort and achievement.

Not interested in getting dressed up? There's a lot more to a steampunk convention than cosplay or fashion, though admittedly those are both big draws. Nevertheless, having fun at a steampunk convention isn't limited to fashion. There are panels on content steampunks are ostensibly interested in, ranging from fashion-related presentations like "how to thriftshop your steampunk attire," which was led by Gail Carriger at Steam Powered, to a history lesson on "19th Century Weapons" by period film consultant Gordon Frye at the first Steamcon. There are panels on books (both analysis of published works as well as advice on getting published), films, art, fashion, games, history, and demonstrations for how to tea duel or ballroom dance. There are photo booths, art exhibitions, and gaming rooms.

After all the presentations, panels, or performances are over, and after the vendor's hall is shut down, many steampunk gatherings are just winding up. There's almost always an opportunity to trip the light fantastic at a steampunk event. I've never been to a steampunk convention that didn't have a party that involved music and dancing. At some, it's a grand affair where you learn the proper steps for stately ballroom dances; at others, it's a rollicking concert where you might learn some swing dancing. At others, it's a mix: at one event, I wandered from a live show with Unwoman to a dance party with a DJ playing electro-swing.

Some events skip the presentations and panels entirely to focus more on entertainment and performance exclusively. At these steampunk events, you'll have more opportunities to watch bands and buskers perform live, see burlesque shows, participate in workshops, or see demonstrations of steampunk vehicles or gadgets. The infamous Neverwas Haul, a three-story Victorian house on wheels, has appeared at many steampunk events over the years.

Can I Shop at a Steampunk Event?

Is water wet? The vendor room at a steampunk event is inextricably tied to steampunk expression through fashion, maker gadgets, art, and books.

Often, the people presenting on how to steampunk your art, fashion, or writing are sellers in the vendor hall; the first time I spoke to Phil and Kaja Foglio of *Girl Genius* was at their booth in a vendor hall.

I'd actually argue that, if you're like me and don't have a sewing or leatherworking bone in your body, the vendor room at a steampunk event is the best place to buy costume elements. Unlike the risk of buying online, where you can't guarantee fit, you'll have the opportunity to try on that puffy-sleeved shirt, or be measured properly for a custom corset.

A good vendor hall at a steampunk convention could act as an archaeological site for studying steampunk culture. After all, the idea is to cater to all the things a steampunk could want, right? So what do you find in a steampunk vendor hall?

Firstly, you'll find steampunk clothing. From custom couture to steampunk off-the-rack, you can find something to augment your steampunk attire. In my own journeys, both my wife and I were measured for custom corsets (yes, there are corsets for men—some look like waistcoats, and they're fabulous!), tried on a top hat that was a prop on the television miniseries of the Western novel *Lonesome Dove*, and bought a *Dr. Grordbort* t-shirt. I'm confident in saying that, budget permitting, you could attend one of the larger steampunk conventions without *any* steampunk attire, walk into the vendor hall, and walk out with a complete outfit (or three). Frequently, I've asked people where they got one of their really great costume pieces, and instead of saying "I sewed it myself" or "I bought it online," they point me to a vendor booth only feet away.

You'll also find makers and their art. Thomas Willeford was a familiar face in the vendor hall at Steamcon every year I attended, and his booth is where my wife and some friends purchased the Brute Force Studios leather notebook cover I've carried to every event since. I've seen maker booths with steampunk armor, jewelry, carrying cases, luggage, and even a steampunk hand grenade. It's rare that you'll find larger pieces such as steampunk furniture in a vendor room, but odds are, a number of the vendors either have those pieces off-site, or can put you in contact with the people who build that sort of thing.

You'll find a range of visual art, from paintings to comic art. Many steampunk conventions host artist guests of honor, and their work is usually available for sale in the vendor room. Phil and Kaja Foglio were regulars in the vendor rooms at steampunk conventions with copies of their steampunk comic, *Girl Genius*, as well as original art from the series. I've purchased prints of steampunk art at conventions, though full-sized canvases with original art are sometimes available as well.

There are usually book vendors: although steampunks don't always like to read steampunk, many steampunks love to read. While steampunk titles are always available, book vendors at a steampunk convention usually sell an array of science-fiction and fantasy books as well as collector's items like first editions of books like Tim Powers's *Anubis Gates*. I've also seen entire tables devoted to nineteenth-century classics from authors like Austen, Dickens, Verne, and Wells. That table was filled with books that would look great as steampunk décor, even if the purchaser had no interest in reading them.

In short, you bet you can shop at a steampunk convention, though you can often find steampunk vendors at fan conventions devoted to wider fandom such as the San Diego Comic Con or Dragon Con.

Will I Meet Anyone Famous?

Firstly, it depends on your definition of famous. If you know steampunk bands, artists, or authors (and now that you've read this book, you know a few!) and consider them famous, then the answer is yes. If you're thinking you're going to see Will Smith at a steampunk event because he was in *Wild Wild West,* then the answer is no (but you never know!).

I've met all three of the California Trinity at various steampunk events, and acted as moderator for an interview with James Blaylock. If hobnobbing with the famous steampunks is your agenda, it's smart to volunteer as a guest handler or panel moderator. But you should know in advance, they're just people, and you aren't necessarily going to be best friends with Captain Robert of Abney Park just because you're in charge of the band's green room. Act natural, be yourself, and if you end up adding each other on social media, that's a new friend in your life.

Sometimes, you run into someone famous and don't even know it. I was ten minutes into a conversation with comic art legend Gary Gianni, the man responsible for the best comic book adaptation of *20,000 Leagues*

Under the Sea, before I realized who I was talking to. When I met Gordon and Nancy Frye, I had no idea they'd both worked on Kevin Costner's postapocalyptic film *The Postman*. When I met Autumn Adamme, it was through friends, and I was oblivious to the fact she'd made corsets for Christina Aguilera and Dita von Teese. But remember what I said: they're just people. And Autumn was as excited as I was to attend Tim Powers's Guest of Honor presentation at the first Steamcon.

The best way to approach a famous steampunk is the same way you would meet anyone else. Naturally. Just let it happen. The first time I was ever at an event where Blaylock and Powers were, we ended up dining at the same restaurant. Did I want to go over and introduce myself? I sure did. But I didn't, because I could tell these were old friends catching up. And it might be that you never get to meet that famous steampunk, or if you do, it's just that: a meeting, and nothing more. Which is pretty cool, all by itself. In other cases, by sheer repetition of run-ins, you find yourself invited out for food or drink, sometimes just to get away from all the hubbub and noise. If you do, just take a deep breath and remember—they're people too. They're hungry, thirsty, and their feet are sore. Don't go all fanboy or fangirl—just enjoy the meal and conversation.

Does that mean you shouldn't ask for an autograph? That depends on whether the event had special signing opportunities. Sometimes, one of the ways a celebrity guest makes money at a fan convention is by charging for autographs or photos. That might seem terribly mercenary, but consider what it would be like to be mobbed and asked to have your picture taken with a bunch of strangers. Or the chaos of trying to sign a book in a busy hallway. Then you'll see that standing in a line and paying a fee for that signature on a book or glossy photo isn't such a big deal.

But I like to think that everyone at a steampunk convention is a little bit famous. Take a look on social media after a steampunk event and you might be surprised at who you find there: people you were talking to at the bar, that woman who recommended which cravat to buy in the vendor hall, the steampunk with kids in tow who were so cute. And remember, the answer to this question is that it depends on what you define as famous. I've attended Guest of Honor panels that had a handful of people, while it was standing room only for the presentation for DIY approaches to creating steampunk art and fashion. Or people passing by the famous steampunk writer who is wearing street clothes while there's a group of photographers getting a shot of that unnamed steampunk in an amazing costume. Will you meet someone famous? Heck, maybe you're the famous one!

How Do I Get Involved with a Steampunk Event?

Fan conventions are almost entirely volunteer run, and they are often looking for helping hands to assist with their event. When I say that I speak at fan conventions, many people think it's a big deal. But the truth of the matter is, if you're a decent public speaker who knows something about steampunk, you're probably good to go. At the same time, you want to make sure to do a good job so you get invited to do it again!

But if you're the sort of person who doesn't enjoy public speaking or the spotlight, then you might volunteer to do less visible tasks: registration, badge monitors, guest liaisons, setup, teardown, gopher, green room, tech, social media, graphics/publications, artwork, publicity, hospitality . . . the list goes on. Depending on the size of the event, there's no end of helpful shoes to fill.

If you're an author, a steampunk event is a chance to promote your work, hear from fans about what they're looking for, and interface with other writers about the steampunk scene. For those just starting in steampunk, it's an opportunity to research what steampunk is.

Are Steampunk Conventions Still Being Held?

The peak of North American steampunk conventions arguably happened in 2012, the last year Steamcon was held. That year, you could hardly find a weekend in the calendar when a steampunk event wasn't taking place somewhere in the US or Canada. Jaymee Goh, author of the *Silver Goggles* blog, traveled around to a number of steampunk events that year on a sort of mini-tour, which she said was fun but exhausting. That she could do it all, even for a few weeks, is a testament to how many steampunk events were going on that year.

Steampunk author James Blaylock in an interview with Hugo-award winning fanzine editor Christopher Garcia at the Nova Albion Steampunk Exhibition in 2010.

Then Steamcon folded, and there were fewer and fewer events being promoted. The decline in conventions could be perceived as a decline in steampunk popularity, but that would deny too many realities of the difficulty putting on a fan convention entails. Anyone who has ever served on a committee will know that competing egos could have as much to do with the dissolution of a convention society as a lack of funds would. In the case of steampunk conventions, I suspect it was a matter of oversaturation, or flooding the market. There were so many cons that fans had to pick and choose which to attend—you simply couldn't attend them all. And when local groups were putting on an event, it drew attendance away from regional events and vice versa.

But the situation post-peak is anything but dismal. New events pop up all over the world, and there have been a few stalwart holdouts. While the majority of newer steampunk conventions are more modest endeavors than Steamcon was at its height, more like my first experience with Steam

Powered, there are big cons that have weathered the decline and either maintained or increased their numbers. Asylum in the United Kingdom kept calm, and has kept steampunking on, while in the United States, Teslacon has been going strong for eight years as of November 2017.

New events have stepped in to fill voids left by defunct ones, like Washington State's Steamposium picking up Steamcon's torch, or Gaslight Gathering in San Diego and Clockwork Alchemy in the San Francisco Bay area filling the gap left by Steam Powered and the Nova Albion Steampunk Exhibition.

How Do I Find a Steampunk Event?

Thankfully, it's nowhere near as difficult to locate a steampunk convention as when I first looked. I was really lucky to discover Steam Powered only weeks before it happened. Otherwise, I'd have been waiting a year to go to my first steampunk convention. Today, if you live in North America, you'd be waiting a month or two at the most.

I could have included a list of steampunk conventions and events that have been running annually for the past few years, but that list could be out of date within a month of this book's release. The best answer as to how to locate a steampunk event is the internet. A quick Google search will locate an event close to you, but there's an even faster and more reliable way: one of the best online resources for locating upcoming events is the Airship Ambassador website, run by Kevin Steil, who has been a well-known fixture of the steampunk scene since 2010. Steil's site is regularly updated with information about steampunk cons, from single-day events like the Watch City Festival in Waltham, Massachusetts, to multiday extravaganzas like the International Steampunk Symposium in Cincinnati, Ohio. At the time of writing, the Airship Ambassador listed over forty upcoming events for the 2017–2018 year, spanning the globe from Brazil to Germany, the UK to New Zealand, from Alaska to Iceland.

While big steampunk conventions are the gatherings where a person can take part in a wide range of steampunk experiences, single-day and event-specific gatherings are also very common. You might attend a steampunk band playing a show, go to a workshop on steampunk making or costuming, attend a steampunk tea or picnic. Steampunk associations often host photo events where they converge on a local vintage space, hire a professional photographer or two, and have a photo shoot where you can pose in your steampunk finery for posterity.

Speaking of steampunk associations, Airship Ambassador is also a great hub for finding local steampunk clubs, who are often the very people who have organized the event you're attending. Getting connected with a local or nearby steampunk group is a great way to stay informed about upcoming events.

So that's some of what it's like to go to a steampunk gathering for the first time. However, halfway into writing this section, I realized that, not only was it *my* first time at a steampunk convention, *everyone at* Steam Powered was having that experience for the first time. I had this perception of other people being the experts, knowing what was going on, being old hands at steampunk. And while it would be true that people like Christopher J. Garcia had been to many fan conventions before, he'd never attended a steampunk convention before. Jake von Slatt had been steampunk making for over a year, but it was his first time talking about making at an event like that. For everyone who was there, not just me, Steam Powered was the first of its kind.

So even if you're attending a long-running event like Teslacon for the first time, you're not alone. There are many other people in attendance who are there for their first time. Or maybe it's just their first time at that particular steampunk event. Don't let being the new steampunk on the block keep you from having a good time. Put on your best steampunk duds (or don't!), show up, and get to know some other fans of steampunk. Because like all other expressions of steampunk, a steampunk gathering is only as good as the steampunks who create it. Steampunk is no longer just about passively receiving what others say steampunk is. It's about rolling up your sleeves, getting involved, and helping to build the future of steampunk.

15

Steampunk Gaming

M any people prefer to watch, not read their stories. And an increasingly large number prefer to play their stories, choosing interactive narratives over passive ones. But long before the ubiquity of gaming on personal devices or high-definition gaming consoles, before video games outsold blockbuster films, before games like *Settlers of Catan* and *Carcassonne* made table games popular again in North America, before *Stranger Things* sparked nostalgia and first-time curiosity for *Dungeons and Dragons*, the worlds of steampunk were interactive. Beginning with the role-playing games of the 1980s, moving into the video games of the 1990s, and finally arriving at the complex and challenging board games of the 2000s and beyond, gaming has been part of steampunk since Jeter coined the term. And while you might assume that these games were a sidebar to everything we've talked about to this point, it's likely that these entertaining pastimes influenced the fashion and storybuilding of second-wave steampunk. I've left games until the end of our discussion because they form a distinctly different experience of steampunk than books or films due to games' interactivity. And the interactivity of gameplay is different from the interaction that costuming or making offers. For many, creating original works of art or fashion is beyond their abilities or resources, but games offer a way to interact with steampunk from your tabletop, home computer, or entertainment console.

Role-playing Games

The first steampunk games were tabletop role-playing games, riding the wide success of *Dungeons and Dragons* in the 1980s to allow dice-rolling gamers to travel to worlds other than those modeled on Tolkien's *Lord of the Rings*. Tabletop role-playing games were the offspring of complex wargames that simulated historical battles. Wargamers became interested in playing a single role, not directing entire armies or regiments. *Dungeons and Dragons* filled this niche by offering players the opportunity to imagine themselves as a creative agent in a fictional world. Initially, many role-playing games were set in high-fantasy worlds, but as the hobby increased in popularity, gaming companies rushed to meet the resulting diversity such popularity demanded. From epic fantasy, tabletop role-playing branched out to worlds of horror, science fiction, film tie-ins, and comic book superheroes.

Role-playing games vary in their mechanics, but almost all follow a standard configuration of participants. There is a game master who acts as a combination of rules referee and improvisational storyteller; the game master guides the players, who imagine themselves as the heroes of that improvised story. I've often explained it as "playing pretend with rules," or as "improv theater where the dice help determine the direction of improvisation."

Space 1889 (1989)

The first tabletop role-playing game to offer a steampunk alternative was *Space:1889*, created by Frank Chadwick and released by Game Designers Workshop in 1989, only two years after K. W. Jeter coined steampunk. Chadwick stated that he considered *Space: 1889* "Victorian science fiction," and was unaware of the term steampunk at the time of the game's release.

Space 1889 is one of the rare variant role-playing settings from the 1980s' role-playing fad to have remained popular and, following a decade-long hiatus in the 1990s, in print, changing hands from production company to production company over its nearly thirty-year history. The tagline for the original game read, "Everything Jules Verne *could* have written. Everything H. G. Wells *should* have written. Everything A. Conan Doyle *thought of* but never published—because it was too fantastic."

The premise of the current iteration of *Space 1889* under Clockwork Games retains much of the world building from the original 1989 game.

Most of the significant changes in the different versions of *Space: 1889* are rules-based. The idea is that the break in history came in 1870, when Thomas Edison and Professor Etienne Morea developed an Ether propeller capable of flying vessels beyond Earth. The colonial expansion of the nineteenth century shifts to outer space, with the world powers possessing holdings on Mars and Venus while scouring the solar system for more planets to plant their flag. Of course, the planets are inhabited: Venus has its lizardmen, and Mars has not one but three alien species, one of which lives in the Martian canals that in the nineteenth century were believed to exist on the Red Planet.

The different nations have different technologies, with the German ether ships based on zeppelin designs, while the British ships are built with Martian antigravity liftwood, a concept that David D. Levine employed in his 2016 novel *Arabella of Mars*. Players choose archetypes to play, such as Adventurers or Technicians. Those archetypes are broken down into more precise classifications such as Xeno-Archeologists or Inventors. Like most tabletop role-playing games, the world of *Space: 1889* is one of high adventure and daring combat. Typical adventures include voyages from the Earth to Mars or Venus, exploring those planets, uncovering dangerous cults or organizations, and engaging in battle with aliens or other nations' military.

Space: 1889 is not only the first steampunk role-playing game, but is also the first steampunk transmedia storyworld. Transmedia storytelling refers to the creation of a coordinated narrative or storyworld across multiple forms of media. While transmedia storytelling is relatively common today, as in the case of the *Hunger Games* books—which can be experienced as novel, film, video game, social media tie-ins, and even a website built to look like it exists in the world of the Hunger Games—it was rarer in the 1980s. While there were characters such as Superman or Batman that had been adapted for multiple media, the storyworld of those adaptations was fragmented: the Gotham City of Adam West's Batman in the 1960s does not match the Gotham City of Frank Miller's *Dark Knight Returns* comic book in the 1980s.

But *Space: 1889* was a world that fans could participate in as role-playing game, strategic board games, and as a video game (released in 1990). Later on, the franchise would include tie-in novels written by Chadwick and a host of other authors, audio dramas produced by Noise Monster productions, and very recently, a musical soundtrack for role-playing.

Chadwick credits many of the films identified in chapter five as inspirations for *Space: 1889*, demonstrating that the critical mass of 1980s steampunk creators was as much a cinematic phenomenon as a literary one. But just as cinema was crucial in inspiring first-wave steampunk, I'm confident that role-playing games like *Space: 1889* were crucial in inspiring the second wave. Role-playing games are immersive experiences. Players imagine themselves in the game's storyworld and have the option of co-creating both story and world. The interaction between a game master and players is a collaborative one, with gameplay generating improvised narratives. For devoted players of *Space: 1889*, the advent of second-wave steampunk with its realized fashion and gadgets was an opportunity to take their gameplay beyond the table and into the real world.

Castle Falkenstein (1994)

A decade before steampunk fashion became widespread, steampunk role-playing encouraged tabletop role-players to stand up and get dressed up to play Mike Pondsmith's *Castle Falkenstein*. Unlike its predecessor, *Castle Falkenstein* emphasized fantasy over science fiction, with the moment of the break involving the development of magic, which enabled the technological leaps into a fantastic version of the Industrial Revolution. It replaced the polyhedral dice common to tabletop role-playing with a deck of playing cards as its randomizing mechanic, and encouraged storytelling over strict adherence to rules. Players imagined themselves traveling, not to other planets, but other worlds within our own, such as the Faerie Court, which we'll see again later in this chapter when we look at the board game *On Her Majesty's Service*. Instead of aliens, players battled or allied themselves with magical and mythical creatures. And in the most significant departure of all, players were encouraged to stand up and not just play their character, but act and dress like them as well.

While live-action role-playing had been around since the 1970s, the 1990s saw the development of several games that were focused around theatrical, costumed role-play. Most tabletop role-playing games publish further resources for their games to ensure continued interest and sales. Expansions help players and game masters to flesh out the world, gain additional rules for more diverse circumstances, or provide insight into certain types of characters. When R. Talsorian Games published *Comme Il Faut* in 1995, they encouraged players to dress and act as their characters in a more theatrical style than most other role-playing games had previously—it was one of the first role-playing systems to commercially publish a guide to LARP within a preexisting universe. In addition to rules for live role-playing, the book is a guide to proper Victorian behavior and etiquette, from real-world historical examples of how to court a Lady, to how Mortals should politely interact with the Fey of Faerie. The chapter "Dressing Up (If You Don't Live in 1875)" is a guide to Victorian costuming on a budget, anticipating the thrifty costuming panels that abounded at steampunk conventions over a decade later.

But the game that preceded *Castle Falkenstein* in this live role-playing style of gaming was *Vampire: The Masquerade*, from White Wolf Publishing (the same people who published a hardcover omnibus of Michael Moorcock's *A Nomad of the Time Streams*). In *Vampire*, players imagine themselves as vampires from various clans, sects, and bloodlines. Although the game takes place in the modern world, the immortal nature and Gothic style of many of the vampires mirrored the Victorian costuming of *Falkenstein*. White Wolf published several books that were the first commercially published guides to LARP: *The Masquerade Players Kit* and *The Book of Props*. These books anticipate not only the growth of steampunk fashion, but also DIY making. And *Vampire: The Masquerade* was predictably very popular in Goth circles, the group that would give birth to steampunk fashion.

Anecdotally, I remember hosting a murder mystery night at Fort Edmonton, a historical park comprised of original and rebuilt historical structures representing the early history of the city of Edmonton. As our murder mystery was a Western, we had rented the fort's saloon, which was across the street from the Victorian teahouse. On our side of the street, people dressed in Western attire role-played as citizens of a town where a murder had occurred. Across the street, I was surprised to see people dressed in nineteenth-century formal wear. It wasn't until after our mystery was solved that I was able to venture across the street to ask what was going on.

It was a *Vampire: The Masquerade* Mind's Eye game in session. I'll never forget my last glimpse of that game as I packed up and headed back to my car: a couple dressed in Victorian finery, strolling arm in arm along the wooden boardwalk underneath a fake gaslamp as fog rolled in from the North Saskatchewan River, while I walked along, dressed as a saloon bartender, complete with fake handlebar moustache. It was as though I'd been shot back in time. It was an image that came readily back to me when I attended my first steampunk convention, years later.

Games like *Falkenstein* and *Vampire* did more than just encourage players to sit at a table imagining themselves in fantastic worlds based on the Victorian period; it encouraged them to assist their imaginations with period costuming and props that would help immerse them in the game's storyworld, arguably paving the way for attendees at steampunk conventions to dig into their old costume closets, converting LARP costumes into steampunk couture.

Iron Kingdoms: Fullmetal Fantasy (2004)

As was seen in chapter seven, 2004 was a watershed year for steampunk film. It was also the year several steampunk strains in traditional fantasy role-playing coalesced in Privateer Press's role-playing game *Iron Kingdoms* for the open-source d20 system, which enabled third-party publishers to create expansion materials for the third edition of *Dungeons and Dragons*.

Steampunk elements had been creeping into *Dungeons and Dragons* and other high-fantasy games for years, but the creation of the game-world of Eberron in 2002 made it official by blending steampunk elements with fantasy. The following year, Fantasy Flight Games' *Legends and Lairs* series released *Sorcery and Steam*, "A Resource for Steampunk Fantasy Adventure." The book offered character classes and variant rules for adding steampunk to a fantasy setting. But *Iron Kingdoms* was one of the first role-playing games to merge steampunk with fantasy in an overt way.

The *Iron Kingdoms* world was based on Privateer Press's table-top wargames *Warmachine* and *Hordes*. One of the core ideas of the *Warmachine/Iron Kingdoms* world are the warjacks, massive steampunk automatons and the warcasters, the magic users who control them. In a move that mirrored the birth of fantasy role-playing, *Iron Kingdoms* moved the world of *Warmachine* from strategic wargaming table to the role-playing one. The world of the *Iron Kingdoms* is a blending of dark, gritty fantasy with low technology, adding pistols, rifles, grenades, and goggles to a fantasy gamer's arsenal, and giving gamers the option to play as a gun mage (who channel wild magic through their black-powder-style pistols), an arcane mechanic (hybrids of magic users and engineers who build magical steampunk gadgets called mechanika), or a warcaster (who control the steam-driven warjack automatons).

Unlike *Space:1889* and *Castle Falkenstein*, *Iron Kingdoms* makes no attempt to set the action in a world derived from the Victorian era, though the design style shares affinities with the diffuse European "Paris of our dreams" in steampunk anime. This is a thoroughly high-fantasy world filled with elves (Iosans and Nyss), dwarves, and races that resemble orcs (Orgrun), trolls (Trollkin), and goblins (Gobbers). It is the world of Tolkien or *Dungeons and Dragons* after the coming of industrial technology, albeit powered more by magic than by steam.

Like *Space:1889*, fans of *Iron Kingdoms* can explore the storyworld further through fiction: at the time of writing, there are over twenty novels and several anthologies of short fiction set in the world of *Iron Kingdoms*. There is also a board game called *The Undercity*. In 2012, Privateer Press released a new version of *Iron Kingdoms* with new rules independent of the d20 open-gaming license which bear greater kinship to the company's wargaming rules.

These three games are by no means a comprehensive list of steampunk role-playing games. There are many more, such as the *Steampunk* sourcebook for the very popular GURPS role-playing system, which was uniquely situated to handle a hybrid aesthetic, given how the system was setting-agnostic, or *Airship Pirates*, a role-playing game set in a storyworld based on Abney Park's lyrics. But these three games are among the most popular from the past three decades; are still available either in newly published hard copies or as e-books; and finally, are indicative of the range of steampunk role-playing, which depending on the system focuses more on fantasy, science fiction, and possibly even horror.

Video Games

There are many video games that have a steampunk look to them but are generic puzzle-solving or side-scrolling points-based games. The steampunk is there as eye candy, but not as narrative function. These games are a testament to steampunk's popularity but offer little for videogamers looking for a steampunk adventure.

But even among video games where steampunk themes match mechanics, there are so many as to prove overwhelming to someone wondering where to start playing. As with any other area of steampunk, there's a lot to choose from, and hesitancy to choose poorly may result in someone just not choosing at all.

The following are widely recognized as some of the best steampunk video games ever created, both for theme and mechanics. These games are not only great looking, but they're a lot of fun to play. Despite steampunk gaming's propensity toward the role-playing genre, I've tried to include a range of role-playing variants as well as some non-role-play options, so that there's a little bit of steampunk adventure ahead no matter your favorite style of gameplay.

Final Fantasy VI (1994)

While the video game for *Space: 1889* has the distinction of being one of the first steampunk video games, *Final Fantasy VI* was the first great steampunk video game, and in many players' opinion, it retains that honor. And it isn't just considered one of the greatest steampunk video games, it's considered one of the greatest video games of all time. So while steampunk was largely underground in chapter six, *Final Fantasy VI* was very much above ground.

It isn't the only *Final Fantasy* game to include steampunk elements, but it was the first to do so, introducing gunpowder and steam engines to the game world, and integrated those elements seamlessly into gameplay. After all, how much more steampunk can a game be that features a boss fight with a steam train engine? There's also a striking scene in an opera house where, in the middle of the action-packed story of the game, the player stops to sing an aria (albeit one interrupted by a giant octopus attack, which is also pretty steampunk when you consider all those squid and octopi in steampunk cinema). The deliberate inclusion of a set-piece so firmly rooted in the nineteenth century attests to the intention of the Japanese game designers to place the action in that romanticized European storyworld, the "Paris of our dreams."

Second-wave steampunk purists might dismiss the simple graphics and design of *Final Fantasy VI* (after all, it's a giant *purple* octopus), or the use of Magitek to power the steampunk devices, but there's no questioning the game's story in the progression of steampunk. Beyond the obvious steampunk elements of airships, and magic technology, *Final Fantasy VI* is a role-playing game where the player is controlling a band of rebels seeking to overthrow an imperial dictatorship, and given the popular influence of this game, is likely part of the reason so many people conflate the punk in steampunk with rebellion. Unlike many older steampunk games, you can still join that rebellion, since the game was rereleased as an app for Android and iOS, as well as Steam.

Sakura Wars (1996)

Sakura Wars is an extremely successful transmedia franchise involving over twenty video games, a film, a number of anime videos, and a television series, along with many tie-in products from toys to costumes. A transmedia narrative is a story told across multiple platforms, which ultimately retains storyworld cohesion. Consequently, fans can experience the storyworld through a number of media, as interactive participants in games or passive recipients of film or television. The first *Sakura Wars* game was released in Japan in 1996, followed by a series of sequel and prequel games, as well as several OVA (original video animation) productions, which are akin to a television series, but were released direct-to-video rather than broadcast.

Although *Sakura Wars* rarely appears on steampunk video game lists, it appears on several steampunk anime lists. But since the popularity of *Sakura Wars* owes much to the games, I've included it here. As with other first-wave steampunk anime, it does not adhere to any prescribed aesthetic. Furthermore, unlike *Final Fantasy VI*, *Sakura Wars* does not share the setting of the "Paris of our dreams." Instead, it takes place in Japan, in the later years of an alternate Taisho period (1912–1926). While anime set in Japan (in the past, present, or future) are unremarkable, prior to 2000, *steampunk* anime set in Japan was noteworthy. Arguably, *Sakura Wars* paved the way for later steampunk anime such as *Samurai 7* and *Kabaneri of the Iron Fortress* to be set in versions of Japan's past instead of Europe's. In a sense, this move to imagine steampunk in one's own country is paralleled by American writer Cherie Priest rejecting the idea that steampunk had to be set in some version of the Victorian world when she chose to have the *Clockwork Century* stories take place in America.

Sakura Wars is also worth attention because of how different it is from other steampunk, anime or otherwise, insofar as its focus is on more traditionally feminine story lines, with emotional action as the focus rather than the political intrigues, mad science, or derring-do adventures that had dominated steampunk to this point. Over a decade before Gail Carriger's *Parasol Protectorate* would begin its slow climb to the top of steampunk publishing, *Sakura Wars* was steampunk with as many affinities with Jane Austen as Jules Verne. Both the 2000 anime series and the English-translated video game, *Sakura Wars: So Long, My Love* (2005), share the same plotline of a new recruit to a defense force (in the anime, a young woman; in the game, a young man) that uses steam-driven mech, but hides their existence behind a front as a theatre troupe. This odd narrative hybrid results in a mix of tactical role-playing game and sim-based story system. A player's relational skills with teammates is as important as his or her ability to control the steam-powered robot. Consequently, *Sakura Wars* is a kinder, gentler machine-gun hand on this list, mixing mech and romance with great results.

Arcanum of Steamworks and Magick Obscura (2001)

You couldn't walk into a computer store in 2001 and the following years without seeing a copy of *Arcanum of Steamworks and Magick Obscura* on the shelf. Yet another role-playing game, *Arcanum* is distinguished from *Final Fantasy VI* and *Sakura Wars* by its open game world, complex character creation, and real-time gameplay.

The game begins with the player as the sole survivor of a spectacular airship crash (in an opening cut-scene that initially looks like vintage film—you can even hear the ticking of the projector—before shifting to color, and arguably, the present). That survivor is entrusted with a mysterious silver ring by one of the dying passengers, which starts a quest that will reveal why the airship was shot down, the history of the game world, and an impending threat to that world.

As with *Final Fantasy VI*, *Arcanum*'s steampunk world is traditional fantasy colliding with an industrial future, and the conflict between science and magic that results. Both Tesla gun (technology) and lightning spell (magic) have the same result, but the way they get there is the heart of the conflict. That conflict is an essential part of the game's story, with science working with the natural order, and magic going around that order.

This struggle between science and magic is a common feature of steampunk video games, though it is often found in other steampunk expressions as well, begging the question why second-wave purists thought steampunk should only be science fiction, and that fantasy set in similar worlds should have a different designation.

Arcanum of Steamworks and Magick Obscura was initially released only for PCs. It was recently released on Steam, giving a new generation of gamers a chance to explore this fantastic open world caught between science and magic.

Valkyria Chronicles (2008)

Yet another tactical role-playing game, once again out of Japan (and developed by veterans of the *Sakura Wars* games), *Valkyria Chronicles* sets itself apart from its predecessors with a distinct design that looks like pencil drawings and watercolor in motion, with a manga style reinforced by the use of onomatopoeic comic sounds such as "blam!" It is also different from the other steampunk games in this chapter in that it is set in Europa, a slight variation on the "Paris of our dreams," wherein that dream has become a nightmare under the shadow of a conflict resembling World War II.

Players are Welkin Gunther, a young man thrust into commanding Squad 7, a militia unit attempting to repel an invasion. In addition to directing combat through a turn-based system in both overhead and isometric modes, Gunther's story echoes *Sakura Wars* as boy meets girl, and the two try to save the world.

There's nothing particularly Victorian or nineteenth century about that world, however. The tanks are not steam driven. The most overtly steampunk-looking tech in the game is the enemy's land dreadnought. Steampunk purists would consider *Valkyria Chronicles* a dieselpunk setting, yet this game appears repeatedly on Best Steampunk Video Game lists, once again demonstrating the elastic way steampunk is popularly perceived.

Perhaps it's the way in which *Valkyria's* developers sought to attract gamers who didn't like realistic war games by rendering the tanks and technology reminiscent of, but not accurate to, World War II. Perhaps it's that land dreadnought. Perhaps it's the fictional ragnite that fuels the economy and the war. Perhaps it's the inclusion of magic alongside technology once again.

Or perhaps it's that hyper-vintage element at work: the world of *Valkyria Chronicles* is a pre-atomic past, once that is increasingly difficult to imagine in a digital world. The more distant a past becomes, the easier it is to romanticize, and Europa, despite its violence, is certainly romanticized, though in a way that questions the nature of war and the way victors rewrite history.

Machinarium (2009)

For those uninterested in a turn-based strategy, or who haven't the quick hand-eye coordination for a first-person shooter (which every other game on this list is), *Machinarium* provides a breath of fresh, albeit dystopic-industrial-polluted, air. While it could still loosely be considered a role-playing game, the focus of *Machinarium's* gameplay is on puzzle-based point-and-click, making its availability on Android and iOS devices a good fit, though it's available for PC, Mac, and newer PlayStation consoles as well.

Machinarium is the story of a cute little robot named Josef who is trying to rescue his sweetheart and foil the nefarious plots of the villainous Black Cap Brotherhood, so there's still a core story. The game opens with Josef being dumped into a junkyard by an airship, making the first puzzle to put Josef back together, before heading to the city of *Machinarium* for the rest of the adventure.

Released in the same year as the pivotal fiction of Carriger, Priest, and Westerfeld, and well into the rise of second-wave steampunk, *Machinarium* is not only a triumph of puzzle-based gameplay, but is also noteworthy for its art, which parallels *Valkyria Chronicles* with a hand-drawn style, though a very different one. This is unsurprising given that the game was an indie effort, created by Czech developers who funded it with their own money. Consequently, the game bears no resemblance to the brown leather and burnished brass aesthetic of so much North American steampunk. Instead, the style of the game owes its inspirational debt to the cut-out stop-motion animation style of many Czech animators and, quite likely, Karel Zeman and his wondrous, Verne-inspired films.

Machinarium is also, in its own way, a moment of DIY punk; the reason the game isn't available for Xbox is that Microsoft required a publisher for it, and the indie team knew that would mean less money for them. In the end, they refused a middle-man solution, resolving their own puzzle by pointing and clicking over to Sony and PlayStation.

Guns of Icarus Online (2012)

I remember blue-skying a video game involving a B-52 bomber crew, where each player would function as a different crew member with the various roles of gunner or pilot. While it replaces that World War II heavier-than-air plane with a lighter-than-air airship covered in stylish industrial armor, and adds an engineer to that crew, *Guns of Icarus Online* is the multiplayer game I dreamed about way back when.

While the first half of this list was dominated by strategic fantasy role-playing, the last half is all about first-person shooters, with the player firmly in the driver's seat, or in the case of *Guns of Icarus Online*, the pilot's or gunner's seat (the engineer doesn't get a seat—they are running around fixing all the damage on the airship). The pilot's job is to either fly the ship out of danger or line up shots for the gunners, while the gunner's job is to obviously take those shots. The engineer runs madly around the ship with one of several tools (initially a wrench, a rubber mallet, and a fire extinguisher) for repairs.

A fast-paced and fun game of aerial combat, *Guns of Icarus Online* offers players a wide choice of airship types with a variety of speeds, strength, offensive and defensive capabilities, and maneuverability. In the sequel *Guns of Icarus Alliance* (2017), those airship choices are broadened, both through a greater interest in cultural diversity as well as the opportunity to build your airship from the literal ground up. As a multiplayer co-op game where players must act together as a unit, the *Guns of Icarus* games are unique on this list, but even a rarity in all steampunk videogaming, where players are usually encouraged to adventure alone, as we'll see in our next two games. It is also, strangely, one of the very few examples of airship combat in videogaming, which takes the gamer out of the usual urban cityscapes of steampunk games like the *Thief* franchise and *The Order: 1886* (2015), as well as several games on this list. The *Guns of Icarus* games are currently available only for gaming on home computers, though there are plans to release *Guns of Icarus Alliance* for the PS4 in 2018.

Dishonored (2012)

If *Final Fantasy VI* could be said to be the most popular first-wave steampunk game, then *Dishonored* is the most popular of the second wave. Boasting known celebrities for voice talent such as Susan Sarandon, Carrie Fisher, Michael Madsen, and Chloë Grace Moretz, this game is in the top three of just about every steampunk video game list in existence, with most choosing it for the number one slot.

Dishonored is a stealth-based first-person . . . sneaker . . . stabber? It's not just a shooter, that's for sure, given that players can employ pistols, crossbows, swords, and grenades to dispatch their opponents. But more than the diversity of death-dealing, a player can finish the game without ever killing a soul; so don't let that deadly knife on the cover or all the blood-splattered game trailers fool you. Despite the story focusing on Corvo Attano's quest for revenge against conspirators who framed him for the murder of the Empress of the Isles (for whom Corvo was the bodyguard), these reprisals do not need to be lethal. Sleeping darts, supernatural stealth, and subduing an opponent are viable, if not more challenging, options for players (one wrong move and you're discovered, at which point the choice of nonlethal solutions has left the building). *Dishonored* may be the first steampunk action adventure assassination game even a pacifist could play, if not enjoy.

That's not to say the world of *Dishonored* is rated E for Everyone. Regardless of whether or not players choose to kill their opponents with a weapon or eliminate them through political subversion, the brutality of the police force in the darkened streets and alleys of Dunwall, another dark dystopic reimagining of nineteenth-century London, would earn *Dishonored* its Mature rating. And as Harvey Smith, co-creative director for the game has said, he wanted to allow players to choose whether they would emulate that brutal world through violence or resist it by finding nonlethal solutions. Consequently, like *Sakura Wars*, *Dishonored* involves role-playing moments with moral and story implications that affect gameplay. As Dave Thier of *Forbes* put it, "Keep it nonlethal and the game rewards you with fewer rats, fewer soldiers, and a happy ending. Slice your way to the end and the world falls to pieces." This dynamic approach to the story results in high-replay value, unlike *The Order: 1886*, which only gave players the option to choose the gun they would shoot opponents with, and the order in which they'd shoot them.

The world of *Dishonored* is gloriously gloomy, its plague-infested and poverty-ridden streets filled with steampunk technology like energy-field barriers called Walls of Light that enforce plague quarantine, or my favorite, the stilt-walking Tallboys, elite units of the City Watch, who reminded me of the Martian tripods in *War of the Worlds*. And it's clear that a dark city that resembles London screams steampunk to most people, especially if those streets have whale-oil-powered rail cars driving through the cobbled streets. That whale oil is just one more example of how there doesn't need to be steam in steampunk, or at the very least, that videogamers don't care how the steampunk technology works, so long as it does. In the sequel, *Dishonored* 2, the coastal city of Karnaca relies on wind turbines for power, but permits a cityscape filled with as much treachery and intrigue as Dunwall. Whether the energy comes from whale oil, coal, or diesel fuel, the steampunk city's reliance on these power sources creates opportunity for the sort of industrial corruption these stories thrive on.

But just as there doesn't need to be steam power in steampunk, not every steampunk city should be dark and dystopian. Given the unbridled optimism of the late nineteenth century and early twentieth century, some of those cities should be filled with electric light, art deco architecture, or in the case of *Bioshock Infinite*, the unfiltered light of the sun in a city not beneath dark clouds, but above them.

Bioshock Infinite (2013)

Bioshock Infinite was the third game in the already hugely successful Bioshock game franchise, and one of the most highly anticipated games of 2013. While the earlier Bioshock games had contained enough retrofuturistic elements to provoke regular inquiry as to whether it was steampunk or not, *Bioshock Infinite* was unquestionably so.

Like its predecessors, *Bioshock Infinite* is a first-person shooter. The player's first-person perspective is as Booker DeWitt, a man whose past is lost to him. The game begins with a frame narrative in a rowboat off the coast of Maine in 1912. Booker is deposited beside a lighthouse in a rainstorm; upon investigating the lighthouse, he discovers that it is a relay between the ground and the floating city of Columbia. Booker is launched through the dark storm clouds into a light-filled cloud city. Art nouveau–style architecture abounding in religious iconography and nationalist propaganda blur together in crisp stained-glass windows and vintage-styled signage and banners. The design of Columbia is meant to evoke both heaven and an idealized American past. Columbia is founded on ideologies that mirror American exceptionalism, the idea that America is unique and superior to other nations insofar as liberty and democracy are concerned. These ideals and the paradise that cleaves to them hide a dark history: Columbia's prosperity is built on racial slavery.

It is this diabolical truth that Booker must uncover while locating and rescuing a girl, who aids him in his quest. Along the way, he gains the

The cover to *Bioshock Infinite*, the most explicitly steampunk title in the Bioshock franchise.

Skyhook, a very steampunk-looking device made of wood and brass that serves as both transportation and lethal weapon. In addition to the Skyhook, the game is filled with steampunk devices, from guns that are hybrids of different periods in firearm technology to ornate and impossible airships to mechanical steam-driven horses. Throughout Columbia, the player finds clues by watching Kinetoscopes or listening to Voxophones. Both devices are modeled on real-world equivalents; the Kinetoscope is a hyper-vintage version of actual kinetoscopes, single-person film viewers, and the Voxophone is a version of the early phonograph. Between the Voxophone's monochromatic, grainy footage to the scratches and pops on its recordings, the player is immersed in a sense of an indeterminate past.

The retrofuturistic technology of the game is explained by tears in space and time that can be manipulated. *Bioshock Infinite* shares this explanation of anachronistic technology (and songs: a barbershop quartet sings the Beach Boys' 1966 hit "God Only Knows" from an air-barge) with Chris Bachalo and Joe Kelly's *Steampunk* comic. In both cases, the borrowed technology halts around the late 1950 and 1960s, which seems to be the ultimate cutoff for steampunk borrowings; it's the last gasp of retro-nostalgia for Generation X and millennials.

Although the player controls a white male hero, *Bioshock Infinite* is notable for its female characters, particularly Daisy Fitzroy, a fierce black woman in the tradition of second-wave writers like Cherie Priest, who seek to give voice to people who were marginalized in the real-world history steampunk borrows from. Originally a "Negro convict" brought to Columbia to be an indentured servant, Fitzroy escaped being lobotomized and formed the Vox Populi, the underground resistance to Columbia's oppressive, racist xenophobia.

The conflation of racism and religious fervor is one of *Bioshock Infinite*'s most incendiary and intriguing aspects. Many players were offended by the blatant association of Christian motifs and beliefs with the game's villain, Father Comstock. But the use of religion in the game is somewhat ambivalent: early on, Booker is held underwater during a baptism; he passes out and has a vision of a darker, alternate dimension. When he wakes, he is in a different location, a spatial shift that seems intended more to emphasize the dream logic of the game than to demonize baptism. Nevertheless, some developers and players found the game's appropriation of American Christianity problematic.

I found it refreshing, given how steampunk storyworlds overwrite or sideline religion, rather than dealing with it. But a storyworld based on nineteenth-century America and ignoring the pervasiveness of evangelicalism in the wake of revivalism would be incomplete. To create a fictional religion out of whole cloth while adhering to so many other historical cues would have ruined Columbia's coherence.

Financially and critically, *Bioshock Infinite* is one of the most successful steampunk video games. But the key to its success wasn't simply that it was steampunk, though that aesthetic contributed a great deal to positive reviews. It was a combination of good gameplay, an engaging story, and a fully realized fictional world that captivated gamers. Steampunk on its own is never enough to guarantee a good game, as anyone who has ever shelled out close to one hundred dollars on a cool-looking game can tell you. And that's not just true of video games; it's true of any game, video or tabletop.

Board Games

There are many great-looking steampunk board games with gorgeous cover art and enticing-looking game components. I've picked up a number of new steampunk board games wondering if the heady price will be worth it. Will it be fun? There are a ton of great-looking steampunk board games, and if you know anything about steampunk by now, it's that steampunks like pretty things.

Thankfully, if you live in a big city, you likely have a board game café or two around and can go and try those games out. In the event you don't, this next section is a list of some of the best steampunk board games to help you sort out the difference between shiny and shallow and beautiful and rewarding.

There were steampunk board games that spun off from *Space:1889*, back in the late '80s and early '90s, but most of them are now out-of-print rarities. Instead of including those games, I thought it better to recommend steampunk board games that have been released in the wake of the board game renaissance that German games like *Settlers of Catan* cata-lyzed. These make up the majority of steampunk board games anyhow, and are easier to find.

Planet Steam (2009 and 2013)

Released in the year that steampunk was really gaining momentum, *Planet Steam* makes for an interesting study in how the look of second-wave steampunk can affect a single game. Like earlier instances such as the covers for Michael Moorcock's *Warlord of the Air* and Michael Swanwick's *The Iron Dragon's Daughter*, the original 2009 version of *Planet Steam* is a mash-up of steampunk elements with pulp-era space opera. The game pieces are likewise different in the original version: the 2013 rerelease of the game from Fantasy Flight Games is slicker and more heavily influenced by second-wave steampunk aesthetics. The original was difficult enough to find in North America in 2009, whereas the 2013 edition had a wide release, so I'll be referring to that edition.

I recall initial responses to the Fantasy Flight edition being somewhat lackluster, likely due to the dissonance between the game's visual theme and its gameplay. While the cover seems to promise a game involving driving airships around, *Planet Steam* is actually a really smart and fun (albeit initially complicated) economic speculation and resource manage-ment game. Rather than being the slickest airship pilot around, players are entrepreneurs on a planet being harvested for the resources of quartz, ore, water, and energy: the goal of the game is to build resource acquisi-tion equipment, attain resources, buy low and sell high, and finish with the most money (making it quite possibly the most un-steampunk game ever created if you were in the *Steampunk Magazine* camp of steampunk ideology).

The artwork for the game is gorgeous but is really only there to make the game beautiful. The steampunk theme could be thrown out entirely and the game mechanics would still work perfectly. For example, airships in the game are used to carry resources; these could just as easily be his-torical trains or steamships, or even modern semitrailer trucks. Nevertheless, if you love steampunk, that artwork makes the experience of gameplay more enjoyable as you imagine yourself as a resource baron on this newly discovered planet. That said, if you demand theme and mechanics mesh, you'll want to look elsewhere.

A word of warning or encouragement, depending on what you like from a board game experience: this is not an entry-level strategy game. The first round is deceptively easy—players have enough money and resources to do nearly everything they want, but scarcity can set in quickly. A few rounds later, players realize how hard it's going to be to keep extracting resources from the planet.

The extraction mechanic for *Planet Steam* is one of its most steampunk features: the Fantasy Flight version of the game comes with several plastic

The box art for Planet Steam promises high flying adventure, but delivers a game of economic speculation and resource management.

miniature pieces that will warm just about every steampunk fan's clock-work heart, beginning with extraction tanks, which look like steampunk boilers. These tanks can be fitted with one of three different converters that allow for versatility of resource acquisition. And finally, there are superchargers, which can be attached to the top of the extraction tanks to increase how many resources the tanks produce. No matter how many times I put those pieces on my extraction tanks, I always feel a little bit like a steampunk maker.

If you're looking for a fast and easy board game of high-flying adventure, stay clear of *Planet Steam*'s orbit. Steampunks looking for a game with strong strategic replay potential will want to get caught in its gravity well as soon as possible.

On Her Majesty's Service (2015)

On Her Majesty's Service is a fast-paced, slightly cutthroat game combining puzzle-based strategy with resource management. There's a greater amount of thematic integration with the game's mechanics than with *Planet Steam*. It certainly has one of the most steampunk gameboards I've seen, with cog-shaped location tiles that rotate throughout the game, ensuring a randomly challenging experience each time you play.

The setting of *On Her Majesty's Service* is the World of Smog, a transmedia storyworld created by artist Christophe Madura, set in an alternate 1886. The website for World of Smog has an introduction to the world, along with a great alternate history timeline filled with crossover fantasy elements: Phileas Fogg, Fu Manchu, Queen Victoria, Charles Babbage, and a race of aliens all inhabit the world of Smog. Like a lot of second-wave steampunk, it is a dark and sooty world, nature corrupted by tampering with both science and magic. The artwork is fanciful but grim, rooted more in the aesthetics of horror than fantasy.

This setting enriches the experience of *On Her Majesty's Service*, though it isn't essential for gameplay. A player could enjoy the game without knowing the backstory, though it's likely that, as with *Adventurers*, steampunk fans will enjoy the narrative elements in the rule book that flesh out the various Gentlemen (the characters each player chooses) and Agents (who thwart players' attempts to win). The rules are peppered with references to the World of Smog, hinting at a far richer experience than the game mechanics provide. For example, among the four Gentlemen players to choose from are Master Fox, a shapeshifting, fox-headed exile from the Faërie kingdom turned sleuth and Parvin Khan, survivor of a British massacre in Calcutta who has become a girl genius and suffragette.

As game, *On Her Majesty's Service* is a race to collect the four artifacts of keys made from adamant and Atlantean metal, a mithril padlock, and a magic change (four cards) and various amounts of the four ether types of blood, mana, titanium, and ectoplasm (four counters tracking resources). Players navigate through the legendary Shadow Market, a magical maze (an ever-changing game board of those cog-shaped rotating tiles), and the threat of the Shadow King, his Shadow Agents, and other players. There are some enjoyable cutthroat opportunities for the more competitive player, though the mechanic of the rotating tiles ensures that players must stay on their toes. The winner is the first player to collect the four artifacts and requisite ether and reach a Secret Gate to exit the Shadow Market and present your finds to Queen Victoria herself (who has a steampunked monocle in the game's cover art).

While there are plans for a comic book and a series of novels, the only other product set in the World of Smog was a second board game Kickstarter called *The Rise of Moloch,* which promises to be at the same level of component quality, if not gameplay. Perhaps *The Rise of Moloch* will enable fans of *On Her Majesty's Service* to further explore this mad world of machines and magic.

Steampunk Rally (2015)

Not all steampunk games are dark and serious, thankfully, and *Steampunk Rally* is one of the best of the brighter side of the steampunk game table. It's also one of the strongest integrations of steampunk theme and game mechanics on my list.

Steampunk Rally is a card-drafting racing game where players assume the role of one of the world's greatest inventors: many of the choices are steampunk favorites, including names like Nikolai Tesla, Thomas Edison, Marie Curie, and Ada Lovelace, all rendered in a lovely cartoon style.

The point of the game is to win a race by building a steampunk vehicle by placing cards together at cog connections, like a puzzle. Players begin with two cards, a cockpit and a main engine. Each round of gameplay, they have the opportunity to add to that vehicle using machine part cards, or activate a one-time effect using a boost card. But the race is through the Swiss Alps, and the terrain plays havoc with these steampunk vehicles. When a vehicle incurs damage, parts fall off, so players are constantly working to hold everything together while barreling along the racetrack (there's no stopping a steampunk vehicle once it gets started, apparently!). It's the only steampunk board game I've played that incorporates the maker culture of steampunk, making each player a mad steampunk race car inventor (and it's made me wonder about a board game that tries to incorporate the fashion side!).

The game relies on a great balance of spur-of-the-moment strategy and random dice pool results to keep the game interesting. This is a great party game, not only because it's a ton of fun to play, but because it can support up to eight players, a real rarity in board games.

Scythe (2016)

And then there's *Scythe*, a board game set in the 1920s that features retrofuturistic mechs at the core of gameplay. But don't let that fool you into thinking this is a combat-focused game. It's mostly about resource management and exclaiming frequently at the gorgeous artwork on the cards and various faction boards. It's like a mix of *Settlers of Catan* and *Risk* in a steampunk Eastern Europe reminiscent of the Clanker nations in Scott Westerfeld's *Leviathan*.

You play as the leader of one of five factions (although there are expansions that promise two more) who is trying to expand their holdings while simultaneously seeking to reach the center of the board, where an abandoned factory full of marvelous steampunk tech awaits. Even when I lose at *Scythe*, I've still had a great time. If you like strategy but want rich world building to inform your gameplay, then *Scythe* is for you: like *Planet Steam*, you could still play the game without all the steampunk veneer. Unlike *Planet Steam*, you'd lose out on one of the game's best features. Part of that enriched experience results from the encounter cards, which

Jakub Rozalski's art on the box for *Scythe*, depicting mech warfare alongside European farmers and peasants.

provide an evocative piece of art over top of three choices for you as a player to advance your position in the game. Every one of those choices is narratively based in the artwork. For example, one card features a mech and some soldiers standing with what appears to be someone's baba, a little old lady who is picking apples. The narrative choices on the card are as follows:

- Pick fruit for the lady and keep a few for yourself.
- Pay the lady to supply your empire with the apples.
- Banish the lady from your family lands.

Each of the choices has a strategic outcome. But because they're based in narrative, a player might choose to do something less strategic, simply because they can imagine themselves in this richly realized world. The game abounds with Jakub Rozalski's art, which envisions steampunk mechs alongside European peasants in his "1920" series of paintings.

Those paintings became an internet sensation in 2015 and lead to a Kickstarter campaign to build *Scythe* as a board game. In a month, that Kickstarter raised nearly $2 million. When the game was released in 2016, it was a huge critical success, and the buzz created a demand that Stonemaier Games was struggling to keep up with a year later, though they were able to properly manage their resources to produce more copies by spring 2017.

But anyone who says that steampunk is dead or in a creative cul de sac hasn't played *Scythe*. Rozalski's art and the game's focus away from individual achievement have created a socialist steampunk world, where high adventure matters less than taking care of your people. The encounter card that most exemplified this ethos to me pictured a mech using its flamethrower next to some soldiers; not to burn them to death, but to allow them to roast kielbasa on a stick. Steampunk fans love good art, and Rozalski's is some of the best I've seen, bar none. Combine art with story and most steampunks are hooked, which is not only why *Scythe* is such a great steampunk game, but also why comics have proven to be a steady expression of steampunk since its inception, and prove definitively in the next chapter that steampunk expression is incredibly diverse.

16

Steampunk Comics

Here at the end of the book, just like at the end of every semester I teach, I offer a review of everything we've learned so far. Okay, maybe not *everything*, but we'll be going all the way back to the beginning of steampunk in the 1980s with the first steampunk comic and coming right up to the present with new forms of steampunk that are challenging the boundaries of the term yet again. And I've saved this chapter for last, not only because I think comics deserve to be understood as their own form of art, but also because, unlike some of the other steampunk expressions in this book, several of these steampunk comic book series are still going, bringing steampunk to new audiences thirty years after its genesis.

The Adventures of Luther Arkwright (1978–1989)

Given the very visual nature of second-wave steampunk, it should be no surprise that the medium of comics would embrace steampunk style. What may be more surprising is that comic books have been a part of constructing the steampunk aesthetic as long as any other medium we've looked at.

As with prose fiction, steampunk comics got started in the UK years earlier than in the United States with Bryan Talbot's *The Adventures of Luther Arkwright*, which began in 1978 but was not competed until a decade later, in 1989. This is unsurprising, given that Talbot admits the strong influence of Michael Moorcock's *Nomad of the Time Streams, Dancers at the End of Time* (both arguably early steampunk works), and *The Cornelius Quartet* (this last the adventures of a literally gender-fluid secret agent) on his writing in general, but in particular with *Arkwright*. The influence is immediately apparent in the juxtaposition of the year *Arkwright* is set (1984) and in Luther Arkwright's retro-apparel, an ornate Royal Hussars uniform complete with ceremonial sabre; no Ocean Pacific or Polo shirts, common fashion trends of the 1980s, in sight. This anachronism echoes the late-twentieth-century setting of Moorcock's *Warlord of the Air*, as well as Bastable's initial position as an officer.

The story follows the adventures of a dimension-hopping albino who can travel between worlds through sheer force of will with the assistance of telepath Rose Wylde. Arkwright and Wylde are agents from a universe where stability and peace have been achieved, and who travel to other dimensions to stop "disruptors" (like Hitler) from creating instability and violence.

The comic's very structure conveys the complexity of the storyworld through abrupt crosscutting, a technique that comics share with filmmaking, both featuring oscillations between parallel scenes or action. Crosscutting requires close attention few comics in the '70s demanded, and is arguably the greater of *Arkwright*'s legacies (as opposed to being the first steampunk comic), since Talbot's temporal crosscutting was emulated by comic writers and artists in the 1980s (none of whom created steampunk comics at the time).

Talbot's crosscutting is a visual representation of the multiple realities Luther Arkwright travels through. Multiple versions of people, major world events, and actions in one reality impinge on one another. These are themes that steampunk would explore further in its second wave, primarily in the work of Mark Hodder, which plays with the idea of multiple worlds and the catastrophic effects of temporal disruption through the adventures of an alternate Richard Burton, the famed traveler-writer, and poet Algernon Swinburne, and the interference of a time traveler from a number of possible futures. Despite this affinity for the use of multiple worlds as plot device, it would be assuming too much to suggest an explicit connection leading from *Arkwright* to other steampunk fiction or comics.

Whatever the influence of *Arkwright* on later steampunk, Talbot visualized retrofuturistic technologies that have appeared in many other steampunk works. One of the most notable examples is the Imperial Prussian Command Ship *Siegfried*, a massive air-dreadnought held aloft by improbable propellers, which is described as "defying all the laws of aerodynamics," a design approach repeated many times in steampunk airship designs, both particularly and generally. Steampunk gatekeepers who suggest that the disregard for real-world physics was endemic to second-generation steampunk would do well to pay attention to Talbot's *Arkwright*. In addition to the dreadnoughts in the anime *Last Exile* and the *Wind Gambit* expansion for the board game *Scythe*, Talbot's *Siegfried* seems a likely connection to the steampunk dreadnoughts in Warren Ellis's "graphic novella" *Aetheric Mechanics*. Ellis openly admits his admiration for *The Adventures of Luther Arkwright*, claiming that it is an influence not only on him, but on the wider comic industry in general.

Bryan Talbot returned to steampunk in 2009 with a title better known in steampunk circles than *The Adventures of Luther Arkwright*. Talbot's *Grandville* takes place in a world where every species evolved as humans did in ours, so that nearly every character is an anthropomorphic animal, and humans are among the servile underclasses. *Grandville* and its sequels chronicle the adventures of a surly and burly badger who is a detective for the British government. But twenty years before that fictional Britain would need any sleuthing badgers, DC Comics started their *Elseworlds* line of comics by steampunking the superhero known as "the world's greatest detective."

Elseworlds: Steampunking the DC Universe (1989–1998)

When I bought *Gotham by Gaslight* in 1989, I had no idea who Mike Mignola was. His creator-owned project *Hellboy: Seed of Destruction* was still five years into the future, to say nothing of the fame the film's adaptation of that series would bring him. But in 1989, everyone was into *Batman*, and I was no exception. It was the year Tim Burton's cinematic adaptation of *Batman* was released, changing popular perception of Adam West's Caped Crusader to Frank Miller's Dark Knight the first time Michael Keaton stepped on screen. One might argue that Anton Furst's retrofuturistic version of Gotham City had a powerful impact on steampunk design, if only insofar as paving the way for audiences' reception of nostalgic fictional spaces, but *Gotham by Gaslight* is a clear foray into the same fictional spaces Blaylock, Jeter, and Powers were exploring at this time.

Gotham by Gaslight is less a "let's steampunk Batman" story than it is a "let's have Batman go up against Jack the Ripper" story. But in order to do so, the creative team of Bryan Augustyn and Mike Mignola had to set their story in another version of the DC Universe. The idea of alternate fictional universes was nothing new to DC: the company published *Crisis on Infinite Earths* in 1985–86, a miniseries that was meant to resolve continuity issues behind the multiple Earths the company's long tenure had produced. There had been many other instances of "What if?" moments in the DC Universe, such as "What if Lois Lane had Superman's powers?" But all those alternate realities were based in the ongoing twentieth-century "realities" of Superman, Batman, and Wonder Woman, whose first appearances were at least half a century in the past: 1933, 1939, and 1941, respectively. By contrast, *Gotham by Gaslight* was set *before* Batman's origin, effectively creating the same sort of alternate literary history I looked at in chapter four. But instead of a steam-powered anachronism, Augustyn and Mignola imagined a superpowered one.

The success of *Gotham by Gaslight* produced a solid decade of steampunk superhero stories from DC Comics; to keep continuity and canon out of the creative process, DC created *Elseworlds*, a publication imprint for these alternate literary histories. While the original edition of *Gotham by Gaslight* did not feature the *Elseworlds* designation and logo, subsequent reprintings have, making it the first of the *Elseworlds* line of books. All of the comics listed here are *Elseworlds* stories, beginning with another Batman story, *Master of the Future*, in 1991. Augustyn returned to write with a different illustrator to pit Batman against a villain inspired by Verne's Robur the Conqueror. The following year, Batman and Robin found themselves in the middle of the American Civil War in *Batman: The Blue, the Grey and the Bat* (1992), then in the world of Mary Shelley's *Frankenstein* in 1995's *Batman: Castle of the Bat*.

In 1996, several members of the Justice League were reimagined in the Old West in *Justice Riders*. In *Wonder Woman: Amazonia* (1997), the seminal female superhero was given a Victorian makeover as a circus performer. Of these forays into the past, Wonder Woman's is the most relevant with social commentary, arguably because Wonder Woman has always been an icon for feminism, and issues of women's rights are at the forefront of *Amazonia*. *Batman: Masque* (1997) imagined the caped crusader in the story of Gaston Leroux's *The Phantom of the Opera*, with the action shifted to Gotham City, where the scarred villain Two-Face takes up the murderous aspects of Leroux's Phantom, though it is Batman who is unmasked in his underground lair (the Bat Cave in place of the Phantom's hideaway beneath the Paris Opera House) by the story's paramour. In 1998, Batman would be synthesized with one of his most notorious enemies in another Victorian-era caper titled *Batman: Two Faces* that utilized Robert Louis Stevenson's *The Strange Case of Dr. Jekyll and Mr. Hyde* for inspiration.

That same year, Superman would receive the same Civil War treatment given Batman in *Superman: A Nation Divided*, which asks the question, "What if Superman had crash landed in Kanas a century earlier?": the answer involved Superman fighting for the Union as "a bulletproof soldier who can throw cannons." It's one of the best of these books, initially imagining a Superman who is more about the American Way than truth, since his alien heritage is hidden from him until the end of the book, when he learns that his Kryptonian father meant for him to be raised by Native Americans and fight on their behalf. Prior to this revelation, Atticus Kent/Superman bears the familiar diamond shield on his chest, but one that bears the stamp USA, with the S prominent. At the end of the book, as he rages over the epiphany regarding his intended destiny, that shield is obliterated by a lightning strike, which Superman takes to be a sign. He abandons his identity as the Union Superman and becomes a version of another hero of American Wild West mythology, one that was contemporary to the rise of the character of Superman on American radio: the Lone Ranger.

The lack of technological anachronisms in these comics would lead some to argue that there is nothing to mark *Gotham by Gaslight* and its *Elseworlds* successors as steampunk. But that's only by second-wave steampunk's standards. As we've seen, first-wave steampunk was an unintentional, uncoordinated exploration of speculative stories by creators working in the rise of the information age looking back at the industrial age—in a very broad way. And as I've already argued repeatedly, limiting the gonzo aspects of steampunk to technological anachronism is to see steampunk only through the lenses of second-wave steampunk. While technofantasy is prevalent in second-wave steampunk, largely due to gatekeepers who wanted steampunk to be science fiction, it is not as ubiquitous in first-wave works.

But even if I were to admit that most of these comics are not steampunk, I have to admit that, once again, there is a long line of potential inspirations for the self-aware second wave of steampunk. Just as the Vernian and Wellsian adaptations and pastiches of 1950–1970s cinema were likely antecedents to first-wave steampunk, we must at least consider that these superhero crossover fictions exerted some and, in the case of Mignola's *Gotham by Gaslight*, considerable influence on second-wave steampunk. If nothing else, they certainly prefigure one of the best steampunk comics yet written, the crossover fiction of crossover fictions: Alan Moore and Kevin O'Neill's *The League of Extraordinary Gentlemen*.

The League of Extraordinary Gentlemen (1999–2015)

As I said at the outset of this book, I wanted to focus on the works that were highly influential or just very popular. It's fair to say that Alan Moore and Kevin O'Neill's *League of Extraordinary Gentlemen* are both.

In 1999, Alan Moore was already a comics legend, having produced a mix of critically praised work. In some cases, he turned his considerable writing talents to long-running and well-known series or characters, such as Swamp Thing (1984–87), Superman (*Whatever Happened to the Man of Tomorrow?*), and Batman (*The Killing Joke*). In other cases, he created his own properties, such as the comic classics *The Watchmen*, *V for Vendetta*, and *From Hell*. He had just finished returning to mainstream comic book work with Image Comics' *Supreme* series when he was given his own comics imprint to publish under: America's Best Comics. The first book Moore published through ABC was *The League of Extraordinary Gentlemen*.

On the surface, the idea is simple, and one that has been repeated many times since *League* debuted: to create a superhero team in the nineteenth century. Most recently, IDW Comics did so with their line of heroes, bringing the steampunk aesthetic to characters as diverse as Red Sonja and the Six Million Dollar Man. But what Moore did was crossover fiction, by bringing together "heroes" from actual-nineteenth century sources. And simple as that concept may sound, it was Moore's writing coupled with Kevin O'Neill's art that made *League* special. So much so, that Jess Nevins called *The League of Extraordinary Gentlemen* "the ultimate crossover."

If most writers were tasked with putting together a group of superheroes from the nineteenth century, the obvious candidates would likely be Dracula or Sherlock Holmes, or both. But Moore passed over these obvious choices for less likely ones. He retained ties to both those titan figures, who I've seen listed as the most filmed literary characters in cinematic history. To ignore them in the *League*'s densely intertextual secondary world would have been conspicuous. Instead of Dracula, the *League* gets Mina Murray, the now-estranged wife of Jonathan Harker, the man who meets Dracula at the beginning of Stoker's novel. In *League,* Mina has survived a vampire's attack and a divorce from her husband: both are testaments to her resilience and grit. And instead of Holmes, the *League* gets Professor Moriarty for a villain. Holmes appears in a flashback to his demise at Reichenbach Falls. In an interview with Jess Nevins, Moore explained that he briefly entertained the idea of Irene Adler, Holmes's love interest, but felt that Mina-as-survivor would be a more interesting character. What is most striking about Moore's choice, as I identify in the chapter on steampunk film, is that he makes Mina not only the first member of the *League*, but also the leader. While 1999 wasn't all that long ago, it was still a time when comics were dominated by male heroes; Mina Murray's struggle to gain the respect of her male comrades mirrored the respect a female hero needed from most comic book readers. But in choosing a female who has survived a monstrous assault, Moore anticipated one of second-wave steampunk's defining features: it would largely be women who lead the charge in steampunk fashion, writing, and organizing the gatherings.

The first volume chronicles the League's origin, as Mina Murray seeks to recruit suitable compatriots to guard Britain against villainous forces. At the start of the series, Murray's only team member is Captain Nemo from Jules Verne's *20,000 Leagues Under the Sea*. Moore and O'Neill's rendering of Nemo is noteworthy, since it is one of the only high-profile versions of the character that are true to the Indian ethnicity Verne appointed for Nemo. While the Captain is a violent man (all of the League are deeply flawed, a hallmark of Moore's approach to character building), he is also a man of principle, and is at times one of the noblest members of the League. It is Nemo who takes Mina to India to retrieve Allan Quatermain of H. Rider Haggard's *King Solomon's Mines*. The once great white hunter is now a broken drug addict, and Mina retrieves her childhood hero from an opium den. While Quatermain agrees to be part of the League, like Nemo, he questions Mina's ability to lead the team because of her gender. Unlike Nemo, Quatermain not only will be won over, but will become Mina's lover in the second series. The League's next acquisition is Hawley Griffin, a character based on the one from H. G. Wells's *The Invisible Man* and arguably the most despicable member of the League: he is introduced to readers at a female boarding school where he rapes the students under the guise of a ghostly apparition. This is fully in line with Wells's imagining of an invisible man, which was an exploration of the depravity one might sink to given full anonymity. The final member of the team is Robert Louis Stevenson's Dr. Jekyll and his alter ego, Mr. Hyde. Unlike the small, ape-like creature of Stevenson's novel, Hyde is more a Victorian version of the Incredible Hulk without the sanitizing force of the comics code. Hyde is an animal brute, not only relishing violence, but engaging in gratuitous mutilation and cannibalism. If Moore has a genius for anything, it is in rendering such contemptible characters likable in any way.

The team assembled, the rest of the first series is about the League's mission to retrieve stolen Cavorite, a fictional antigravity mineral from H. G. Wells's *The First Men in the Moon*. Their investigation pits them against organized crime bosses Fu Manchu and Professor Moriarty. In *League*, Moriarty is a crime boss created and funded by the British government in a failed attempt to keep a closer eye on crime in England. Moriarty wants the stolen Cavorite and plans to bomb Manchu's holdings in Limehouse's China Town from an airship powered by the Cavorite. In the end, the League is able to foil Moriarty. The first series ends with the teaser of

Martian projectiles like the ones in H. G. Wells's *War of the Worlds* arriving on Earth.

The second book is the best of the series, in my opinion. It's a stunning pastiche of Wells's seminal alien invasion story and his *Island of Dr. Moreau*. Again, it's an instance of steampunk playing with alternate fictional history. Whereas the first volume of *League* involved characters from many nineteenth-century works of speculative fiction, the second volume asks, "What if Wells's aliens had met with resistance from the League of Extraordinary Gentlemen?" The comic stays true to Wells's assumption that such an invasion would bring out the worst in British citizenry, as the Invisible Man turns traitor to the League in the hope of saving his own skin. Hyde's retribution on Griffin for this betrayal and his assault on Mina is a disturbing combination of cathartic and horrifying. Moore redeems Hyde in one final, suicidal act of heroism that stalls the Martian invaders long enough for biological weapons to be used against them. Consequently, the comic ends as the novel does: with the aliens brought low by bacteria, a bacteria that will work as effectively on the collateral damage of the denizens of South London. This monstrous solution proves the last straw for Nemo, who leaves the League, never to return. Mina finds herself too overwhelmed by her complicity in the effective murder of innocent citizens and leaves Allan, effectively disbanding the League. The back matter of the second volume reveals that Mina and Quatermain are given eternal life, and go on to further adventures, which Moore and O'Neill chronicled in four subsequent volumes: *The Black Dossier*, which takes place in a post-Orwellian-dystopia 1958 and is therefore not steampunk, not even by my highly elastic definition of it. The next three volumes form a trilogy called *Century*, taking place in 1910, 1969, and 2009. Only the first of these can be considered steampunk, and it forms a bridge to a trilogy spin-off of the *League* comics focusing on Captain Nemo's daughter, Janni, who becomes his successor as Captain of the *Nautilus*.

Of the Nemo series, only *Heart of Ice* is clearly steampunk, and for my money, one of the finest of the *League* series. It's also far tamer than any of the *League* material. Exploring the monstrous in the human spirit isn't everyone's cup of tea, and many fans of steampunk like theirs with a dollop of sweet cream, not steeped so dark you can't see through it. *Heart of Ice* is a mash-up of a number of Antarctic stories: Edgar Allan Poe's *The Narrative of Arthur Gordon Pym of Nantucket,* Jules Verne's *The Sphinx of the Ice,* John W. Campbell's *Who Goes There* (the basis for John Carpenter's *The Thing,* which is more what Kevin O'Neill appears to be riffing from in this book), to name just a few. But the story *Heart of Ice* most closely follows is H. P. Lovecraft's *At the Mountains of Madness.* Once again, in addition to mixing multiple Victorian, Edwardian, and Pulp narratives, Moore and O'Neill draw together a motley cast from those stories. Janni and her crew are pitted against three of the most famous fictional boy inventors: Frank Reade Jr. and Jack Wright, both heroes of nineteenth-century American dime novels, and Tom Swift (rendered Swyfte in *Heart of Ice,* perhaps for copyright reasons), who was the hero of more than one hundred adventure novels targeted at young male readers in the early twentieth century.

Cliffhanger's *Steampunk* (2000–2002)

Do a web search for "Steampunk comics" and you're bound to get Chris Bachalo and Joe Kelly's *Steampunk* series, despite the fact that it only ran for twelve issues and ended without completing its story. I'm going to break my rule of focusing on influential and popular works, simply because *Steampunk* is an excellent example of how, in 2000, the term had yet to be uniformly conflated with Victoriana, leather, grit, and rust.

Although Paul Di Filippo had been the first to knowingly use the term steampunk in a title with his *Steampunk Trilogy* in 1995, the book's three novella-length stories were too bizarre and sophisticatedly inter-textual for a popular response. Bachalo and Kelly's *Steampunk,* on the other hand, was precisely the hybrid of steam-era tech and adventure and punk-driven visuals and attitude that many would expect of steampunk narratives in the decade to come. I have often wondered if the assumption that steampunk heroes are always revolutionaries was based on these comics, because there aren't many, if any, prior steampunk works where revolution is an explicit fixture of the heroes.

While there are certainly elements of that industrial garbage heap aesthetic in *Steampunk,* the character designs are colorful and madcap mix-ups that few second-wave steampunk works would play with until steampunk creators wanted to do something "new" and get beyond the sepia sea of browns inspired by vintage photography.

Bachalo and Kelly's story is as fractured as Talbot's *Arkwright*, with crosscutting turned to chaos, some might say, with one panel leading from a series of linear sequential art to an abrupt non sequitur, its meaning clarified only by the reader's careful attention, or in some cases, not at all. But page for page, *Steampunk* is as rich in its secondary world as Miéville's *Perdido Street Station*, with a number of similar fantastic imaginings in terms of hybrid humans, mixed either with animal or machine parts. In *Perdido*, this is either related to race, as in the insect/human hybrids of the khepri, or as punishment in the case of the "remade," criminals made hybrids of machine or other species. Kelly and Bachalo imagine similar hybrids, but for different reasons: some characters have chosen to become "remade" in "Sirloin Salons" to improve their social standing, while others, like the title's reluctant hero, were given no choice at all.

The creative notes in *Manimatron* and *Drama Obscura*, the collected editions of *Steampunk*, reveal just how untraveled the ground of steampunk was in comics at the time. Bachalo admits thinking Kelly's idea of a hero with "a pneumatic arm and a furnace for a chest" was "weird," and that he struggled through coming up with a suitable design. A decade later, steampunk artists would turn to the Web, asking google image search to reveal what a steampunk arm or a furnace for a chest might look like. But in 2000, there were few antecedents to turn to. Perhaps Kelly was appropriating the steampunk cyborgs from *Wild Wild West* the year before, but if he was, Bachalo took the visual realization far afield of that film.

Consequently, *Steampunk* is a wonderful visual artifact of the blending of hyper-vintage, retrofuturistic technofantasy before "Goths discovered brown." This is steampunk before the second-wave gatekeepers dictated the parameters of what steampunk was. Set *before* the Victorian period, in the enigmatic dating of 1838/89 (the first in Common Era dating, the second the Absinthian one, but I can't help but think it's also a reference to 1989 in terms of some of the design elements), but incorporating a wild array of vintage elements, from top hats to the back end of what appears to be a '50s-era Chevy, fins and all. It's certainly one of the few representations of steampunk where bona fide 1980s-era punks appear in the form of Rikk and Laslo, two members of a revolutionary uprising. Laslo is one of the rare instances of a person of color as part of the main cast in first-wave steampunk, and *Drama Obscura*'s vision of the Chasm Community where whites are called "ghosts" and treated dismissively for the way they have treated people of color in London and elsewhere anticipates the second-wave criticisms of racially conscious steampunks like Diana Pho.

Steampunk's villain seems more inspired by Marilyn Manson crossed with Prince and Batman's Joker, given Mortimer Absinthe's first appearance in a patchwork of purple cloth (including leopard print!), though one can also see links to the work Bachalo did with Neil Gaiman nearly a decade earlier. Bachalo and Kelly seemed to be combining as much rock 'n' roll with their hyper-vintage world as possible. It's an Absinthian age, with no Victoria on the throne. Instead, she's an assassin warrior-woman

Phil and Kaja Foglio, the respective artist and writer of long running steampunk comic *Girl Genius*, at Steam Powered in 2008.

in the skintight costume one expects from comic books, bearing a greater resemblance to Black Widow in *The Avengers* than to even the corseted heroines of second-wave steampunk.

Girl Genius (2001–present)

For many steampunks, there is only one steampunk comic, and that is the epic Gaslamp fantasy *Girl Genius* by Phil and Kaja Foglio. For the Foglios, *Girl Genius* isn't steampunk per se. When I met the Foglios at Steam Powered in 2008, Phil told me they didn't think their book was steampunk, but rather "gaslamp fantasy." I've since learned that Kaja apparently coined the term. The definition at the *Girl Genius* wiki says it's "a parallel universe of 19th-century-level technology corresponding to our world's Victorian age, but containing scientific and mechanical achievements in advance of Victoria's time." Which sounds an awful lot like steampunk. Kaja further explains her use of the term by saying that the series doesn't have much "punk" or "steam." Which, in 2008, could have described just about every available steampunk narrative. Looking at interviews with the Foglios, it seems that for them, steampunk was dark and dystopic. *Girl Genius* was lighthearted (and brightly colored!) and funny.

I would be remiss to deny the Foglios their right to define what they classify *Girl Genius* as. However, as I said at the outset, I am not interested in prescribing what steampunk should be, but rather what it is, as defined popularly by the people who produce *and* the people who consume it. Phil and Kaja Foglio were regular fixtures of the steampunk convention circuit, selling their books and associated swag in the vendor's rooms, acting out scenes from those books in the style of old-time radio dramas, and dressing in steampunk finery. Kaja Foglio might call *Girl Genius* gaslamp fantasy, but steampunk fans clearly think it is steampunk.

And given its tagline of "Adventure, Romance, MAD SCIENCE!" can you blame them? Call it gaslamp fantasy, call it steampunk, call it whatever you like, the pages of *Girl Genius* are crammed with gears, gadgets, and giant airships and clockwork automata. It's the story of Agatha Clay, a—wait for it—girl genius who turns out to be the last of the Heterodyne lineage. The Heterodynes were once the most feared Sparks in the world of Europa; Sparks are people with a knack for mad science or gadgeteering genius. Explaining the comic beyond that basic concept would take a book unto itself. In fact, there's a wiki devoted to the massive cast, madly intricate plotlines, and secondary world history of *Girl Genius*, and it's essential for doing a read-through of all seventeen volumes. At over two thousand pages, it's the longest-running steampunk comic series, with a loyal fan following as epic as its length.

The publication history of *Girl Genius* is nearly as convoluted as the comic's story line, starting out as a print comic, then becoming exclusively web-based, then becoming available in print again, but remaining free on the website. It's a testament to the Foglios' creativity that a web comic that costs nothing to read has had a consistent print run since its first volume. But the accolades for *Girl Genius* aren't just popular ones; the Foglios won the Hugo Award for Best Graphic Story from that category's inception in 2009, and then again in 2010 and 2011, when they announced they'd be withdrawing *Girl Genius* from nomination for the next year.

Girl Genius began in 2001 and is still being produced every Monday, Wednesday, and Friday. Consequently, it spans the time before the homogenization of steampunk, and has emerged on the other side. It is a perfect study for how a work can both influence and be influenced by the creative community it is a part of. With the Foglios in attendance at steampunk gatherings, they were not only selling *Girl Genius* but participating in those events. At the first Steamcon, Phil and the comic's colorist Cheyenne Wright gave on talk on steampunk art, while Phil and Kaja and friends performed "Girl Genius Radio Theater" several times over the weekend. I saw *Girl Genius* cosplay at some of the earliest steampunk events I attended. Agatha Clay and friends were leaving their mark on steampunk.

But looking through all seventeen volumes, you also see the influence steampunk was having on the Foglios' gaslamp fantasy world. Agatha's outfits change to resemble those you'd see at the conventions. Cheyenne Wright's hypersaturated color palette slowly desaturates, while that color palette shifts in favor of earth tones over the initial riot of hues. Perhaps that's just the growth of the artists, but I'd argue it's the feedback loop that artists involved in the steampunk scene are likely to experience.

That feedback loop is evident once again in a very different steampunk comic with another female lead: Joe Benitez's *Lady Mechanika*—when steampunk comics discovered brown.

Lady Mechanika (2010–present)

Joe Benitez's *Lady Mechanika* is more steampunk than steampunk. Usually, when someone makes a claim like that, it's as a pejorative; it's the idea that gears, goggles, cogs, and corsets are on every page, but without any narrative necessity or aesthetic plan. That is not the case for Benitez's comic series, which launched in October 2010 but didn't see completion of the promised six-issue story arc (numbering issues 0–5) until March 2015. The reason for the delay in completion was a combination of Benitez moving the series from Aspen Comics over to his own press, Benitez Productions, but it's also due to the care with which Benitez renders his art. Every page of *Lady Mechanika* contains gorgeous art.

Lady Mechanika is a fantastic example of a recurring pattern in second-wave steampunk: namely, that the fan culture's expressions helped shape the definition of steampunk in ways unprecedented in other literary genres. Again, it's why it's so difficult to talk about steampunk as a genre: what do we call what fashion designer Kato, originally of *Steam Couture* (now working through Draculaclothing.com) and creator of the steampunk erotica website Steamgirl.com does with clothing? We can't very well call it a genre of fashion; we'd likely call it a style. But Joe Benitez has listed Kato among the inspirations for the look of *Lady Mechanika*, and it really shows in the costuming of the series' eponymous character. Benitez pays particular attention to fashion, detailing costumes in a way that is both derivative and innovative. If you're familiar with Kato's fashion designs, you'll recognize a number of outfits she designed and modeled, such as Mechanika's action wear, which features a leather corset designed for flexible movement, as well as striped tights (from the steamgirl.com "Mahogany" shoot).

Fashion isn't the only inspiration from steampunk subculture to influence Benitez's art. Greg Broadmore's ray guns were clearly in Benitez's mind for his weapon designs throughout the series, particularly a

The cover to Joe Benitez's *Lady Mechanika* collected trade paperback, volume 1.

steampunk blunderbuss for the opening pages of the first issue of *Lady Mechanika*. And I can't help but wonder if Abney Park's occasional performances with the Wanderlust Circus were some of the inspiration behind the Cirque du Romani, a traveling gypsy circus Mechanika investigates and is later aided by.

But steampunk is not only open to borrowing and blending, it *encourages* it. The internet is filled with tutorials explaining how to steampunk your NERF gun or make your steampunk costume by shopping at thrift stores. Sure, there are still those prescriptionist gatekeepers making claims to proprietary licensing or copyright. There are makers who charge for those tutorials. But for every steampunk not interested in sharing, there are many ready to reveal how they did it. So *Lady Mechanika* isn't just steampunk because it has the requisite elements. It's also quintessentially steampunk because it looks to the culture that built second-wave steampunk and asks for help defining what steampunk is.

The rise of second-wave steampunk coincided with the massive swell of popularity for Stephenie Meyer's *Twilight* series, one of the first major publishing success stories to involve fans via social media. As the story goes, Meyer went a step further than the publisher's website for her books by engaging fans on social media sites like MySpace and reader forums. While science-fiction authors like Orson Scott Card had been using internet forums since the 1990s to poll readers about plot ideas, it had never been done with so many participants or with such immense success. The consequences of *Twilight* as the "first social networking bestseller" cannot be overstated. Arguably, this is one of the reasons for the success of Gail Carriger's steampunk paranormal romances: not that she has romances between vampires and werewolves and humans, but that she has engaged her fans in a transmedia experience that makes them feel like they are crucial parts of the narrative process. Transmedia is storytelling across multiple platforms; no one simply reads a book anymore. They can read the book in multiple formats, not just hardcover or paperback, but audiobook, e-book, or hard copy. There are book trailers and websites. And then, as noted in Meyer's and Carriger's successes, there are author's Twitter, Facebook, and Instagram accounts.

This is one of the answers to the question, "Why steampunk now?" Certainly, there are people whose nostalgia for a simpler time before inscrutable iThing technology has attracted them to the way in which steampunk reveals its inner workings. Undeniably, the rise of participatory internet cultures is another of steampunk's attractors. Unlike other media franchises, even one with the sort of participation *Twilight* encouraged, steampunk offered an opportunity to help construct, not a single story or even a chain of connected stories, but a sea of narratives and narrative elements.

This is, perhaps, why *Lady Mechanika* works in a way that *Legenderry* does not. The idea of steampunking a famous character like the Green Hornet or Red Sonja might have worked better in the 1990s, since it clearly worked for DC with Batman, Wonder Woman, and Superman. Or perhaps it cannot work past the point of novelty; the internet abounds with steampunked versions of just about every major media franchise, from the DC Universe to *Star Wars*. You can glue gears on C-3Po and make the droid a steampunk automaton. But it won't make for a good story, necessarily. A comic book called *Steam Wars* from Antarctic Press. That's just the same old *Star Wars* with some steampunk styling thrown on top. What Benitez did with *Lady Mechanika* was to create a new character based on a number of preexisting story elements: the female superhero, the lady detective, the bionic woman.

Likewise, second-wave steampunk was created from a sea of websites, from the *Brass Goggles* and *Steampunk Empire* forums to online zines like *Steampunk Magazine*. I helped moderate *The Great Steampunk Debate*, a laudatory but ultimately ill-fated attempt to define the term "steampunk" once and for all. My own blog was one among hundreds. At one point, there were steampunk conventions happening every other week somewhere in North America. Steampunk was not something dictated by a single facet of the fandom. It was a clockwork monstrosity like *Howl's Moving Castle*, an amalgam of ideas from artists, writers, craftsmen, costumers, fashion designers, architects, engineers, filmmakers, and musicians—and I've hardly exhausted the list of contributor categories there.

Consequently, one of the closest analogues to how second-wave steampunk operates is a media franchise. But unlike other media franchises that are centered on a single narrative world, usually controlled by a single corporate entity, steampunk is a transmedia franchise with endless permutations of worlds that no one owns the licensing rights to. And in the case of this next comic, steampunk creators were excited to share the creation of that transmedia franchise beyond the professional level.

Lantern City (2015–2016)

While *Lady Mechanika* builds from the steampunk creations of a single celebrity fan, *Lantern City* takes the approach of seeking direction from the fans to the wider steampunk community, from celebrities like steampunk maker Thomas Willeford, leather craftsman extraordinaire Tom Banwell, and curator of the Museum of the History of Sciences' Steampunk Exhibit in Oxford, Art Donovan, to steampunk fans who were encouraged to submit designs for props and costumes. The goal was to include the wider steampunk community in *Lantern City*'s design, an initiative that recognized how second-wave steampunk was an aesthetic being cobbled together by fans for fans.

The comic series began as an idea for a steampunk television series from Bruce Boxleitner, perhaps best known for playing the character of Tron in the 1980s hit film. While the television series has yet to be filmed and aired, the script and story found a new home at Archaia Comics and Boom! Studios, which released the story as a twelve-issue limited series.

The story of *Lantern City* is a mishmash of ideas found in other steampunk works, from the walled, layered city with the rich at the top and the poor at the bottom, to the rebellion of the poor rising up from below to overthrow those at the top. Both concepts are found in S. M. Peters's *Whitechapel Gods* and Jim Butcher's *The Aeronaut's Windlass*. Despite these conventional elements, *Lantern City* remains compelling for the journey of protagonist Sander Jorve, a working-class hero who is thrust into the machinations of an uprising in order to forge a better life for his family. When Sander inadvertently kills a member of the city guard during a political riot, his wife's brother suggests he take not only the dead man's full body uniform, but also his identity, to obtain close intelligence on the doings of the city's ostensible despot, Killian Grey. But things are not as they appear in *Lantern City*: Sander, separated from his own wife and child, becomes ersatz husband and father to the concubine of the dead guard and her child. Killian Grey turns out to not be the monster the uprising thinks he is, but is instead engaged in an attempt to make Lantern City a better place. His approaches are as flawed as those of the uprising, whose actions and motives Sander begins to question. It's the uncertainty of who is to blame that elevates the content of *Lantern City*. It rejects simple modalities of good and evil, taking Sander on a journey that reveals just how complicated creating a utopia really is. What begins as a story that seems to be leading toward a triumphant overthrow of a corrupt government becomes the story of a man who sees that redemptive violence cannot bring the necessary change to make his world a better place.

A perusal of the *Lantern City* website demonstrates how the series' creators continue to attempt to involve the larger steampunk community. The *Lantern City* Facebook page is regularly updated with news about steampunk creators and their achievements or appearances. Seeing a link for Thomas Willeford's Brute Force Studios booth at the 2016 San Diego Comic Con, I discovered images of leather outfits resembling those of the Lantern City Guard. Not only can I read the comic, I can wear it. But recently, there are steampunk creators looking to do something new, to break out of the leather-and-brass aesthetic of second-wave steampunk. And two of the best and brightest of those iconoclasts are writer Marjorie Liu and artist Sana Takeda with Image Comics' *Monstress*.

Monstress (2015–present)

Where both *Lady Mechanika* and *Lantern City* demonstrate how steampunk operates as a transmedia franchise heavily influenced by the participation of the steampunk community, Image Comics' *Monstress* by Marjorie Liu and Sana Takeda is a great example of how steampunk worlds can still break away from that influence, not so much as insult but as innovation resulting in steampunk evolving into what may be considered a third wave, where the gatekeepers who demanded steampunk be this or that are no longer relevant to the conversation of what steampunk can or should be. If one were to classify *Monstress* by genre, it would be

A new direction for steampunk comics from Marjorie Liu and Sana Takeda in Image comics'
Monstress.

dark epic fantasy. Takeda's visual style is a mix of anime and steampunk, but steampunk unlike anything I've seen before. While an evocation of a vintage past is present, it's difficult to determine which historical period or culture is being evoked in the costume designs and architecture.

A brief summary of the story of *Monstress* so far is difficult because of Liu's deep and non-expository world building. There are two races in a cold war: the half-divine arcanics and the pureblooded humans. Intelligent cats, capable of speech, form a third race, seemingly on the side of the arcanics; and the Ancient Gods and their defeated enemies, the Old Ones (clearly a Lovecraftian reference), form yet another faction. There are complicated political maneuverings within these factions throughout the series, but at its core, *Monstress* is about a mysterious young woman named Maika, an amputee missing the bottom half of her left arm. While escaping imprisonment, she steals an ancient artifact. Contact with that object results in Maika's being possessed by an ancient being that feeds on sentient life force. This monstrous entity manifests as a mass of tentacles and eyes that burst from her stump. Maika has limited control over the monster inside her, and so represents a terrible threat to her companions.

Interviews with Takeda prior to the book's release gave the impression that the story would be set in the 1920s, in a post-WWI Shanghai. What's clear from the finished work is that this alternate historical setting was rejected by Liu in favor or a fully secondary world called "The Known World." There is a massive Shield Wall that might be a reference to the Great Wall of China, but a cursory glance through pages of *Monstress* demonstrate that this is a fully realized fantasy world, not one slavishly built on our own.

So what is *Monstress*? It's more fantasy than science fiction, but can it be called gaslamp fantasy? It's so much darker than the world of *Girl Genius*, at times bordering on horror. What's clear is that once again, steampunk is straining at the confines of narrow definitions.

In addition to *Monstress*, several steampunk comics have emerged in the year I was writing this book: Aftershock Comics released and continue to publish *Rough Riders,* which chronicles the adventures of the young Theodore Roosevelt, soldier and patriot; Harry Houdini, magician and escape artist; Annie Oakley, legendary gunslinger; and Jack

Johnson, brawler and the son of ex-slaves. And inspired by steampunk anime, Humanoids Comics published *The Ring of Seven Worlds*. A survey of steampunk comics demonstrates the elasticity of the term steampunk; the fact that such a survey brings us right up to the present makes it abundantly clear that, at least in the funny pages, steampunk is far from dead.

Afterword

What Is Steampunk Today?

I started writing this book in the spring of 2016 and finished it a year later, and was very surprised to discover that a few years after steampunk was supposed to have died, it was very much alive and kicking, and not just in pockets of die-hard fans at conventions, but rather as I'd seen it in Sweden and at home in Edmonton, in new enclaves around the world. There are still people asking if it's dead; a new *Brass Goggles* forum thread began in May 2017 asking this very question. Others continue to declare that it most certainly has expired: see "A Requiem for Steampunk" on the Fedora Chronicles website. But in the first case, it's a question from a newcomer to steampunk, and in the second one, it's a matter of equating the loss of overt punk politics in the scene with the death of the scene as a whole, which has been a matter of debate since the first issue of *Steampunk Magazine* in 2007.

What is undebatable is that, after four years of relative quiet on the publishing front, steampunk is making a comeback as fiction. In 2015, urban fantasy superstar Jim Butcher, author of the extremely popular *Dresden Files* series, a sort of paranormal detective noir, released his first foray into steampunk with *The Aeronaut's Windlass*, the beginning of a series called *The Cinder Spires*. *The Aeronaut's Windlass* takes place in a fully secondary world where instead of airships, the sky is filled with what are essentially flying triple-masted ships. Despite second-wave steampunk gatekeepers' best efforts to reject these sky-ships, attempting to restrict steampunk to science fiction and not fantasy, with the success of *Aeronaut's Windlass*, it would seem that more fanciful approaches to the term "airship" are in store for steampunk. But more importantly, *Aeronaut's Windlass*'s classification as steampunk is another instance where the steampunk mode is no longer just about the nineteenth century, but about being "old-timey" in a way that's post-Renaissance, pre-atomic: hyper-vintage. Consequently, as narratively conventional as Butcher's writing is, some may see *The Aeronaut's Windlass* as unconventional for steampunk.

But using the word "unconventional" for a steampunk expression is just the remnants of second-wave steampunk's influence speaking. All analysis aside, Butcher's experimentation with steampunk is a ton of fun, with all the derring-do and high-flying adventure many readers want. In many ways, *The Aeronaut's Windlass* was what I was expecting to read when I first started looking into steampunk in 2008. But back then, too many writers were taking things too seriously. I can't help but wonder if the success of Gail Carriger's whimsical series didn't pave the way for Butcher's swashbuckling adventure.

Carriger continues to release steampunk; she finished her *Finishing School* series in 2015 with *Manners and Mutiny* (a title that embodies the extremes of steampunk), and in the same year embarked on a sequel to the *Parasol Protectorate* series with *Prudence*, a novel about Alexia Tarabotti/Maccon's daughter, whose metanatural ability allows her to steal the powers of immortals such as werewolves and vampires. She has also started self-publishing novellas set in the world of the *Parasol Protectorate* that are more risqué. While some fans have been disappointed with these new directions for the world Carriger introduced with *Soulless* in 2009, these fresh offerings have gathered a legion of new readers, and consequently, Alexia's offspring see Carriger continuing to dominate steampunk publishing.

There were other great steampunk reads in 2016, from Nisi Shawl's powerfully political and emotionally engaging *Everfair*, a steampunk alternate history of the Congo at the end of the nineteenth century and beginning of the twentieth. In nearly every way, *Everfair* was the answer for those who wanted steampunk to address the lack of persons of colors in most steampunk fiction. Another book that placed privileged white characters to the sidelines was A. J. Hartley's *Steeplejack*, a young adult mystery-adventure set in a steampunked South Africa, which was a steampunk read I wouldn't have put down, even if I wasn't writing this book. And this is just the tip of what appears to be another iceberg of steampunk writing, as there were many new steampunk books on shelves in 2017, of which I will mention a handful: Rajan Khanna's third steampunk offering, *Raining Fire*; Robyn Bennis's *The Guns Above*, a sequel to *20,000 Leagues Under the Sea* called *Nemo Rising*; and *Grim Expectations*, a brand-new steampunk book from K. W. Jeter himself, to celebrate forty years of steampunk!

On-screen, *Kabaneri of the Iron Fortress*, the most recent steampunk anime of note, aired on Japanese television and streamed online across the world in April 2016. While its production values are in line with steampunk anime like *Steamboy*, *Kabaneri*'s color palette is one of the most vibrant I've seen since *Howl's Moving Castle*. Steampunk is increasingly leaving the sepia-toned second wave behind and heading in new, less muted directions. *Kabaneri* also owes less kinship to steampunk anime set in European-inspired secondary worlds like *Fullmetal Alchemist* than it does to anime set in earlier periods of Japan, such as *Sakura Wars*. *Kabaneri*'s postapocalyptic world has abandoned nineteenth-century Europe entirely; it is set in a fictionalized version of what appears to be Meiji Restoration–era Japan, based on the costuming, traditional hierarchies between characters, and the presence of traditional, Bushido-bound samurai, all contrasted against the industrial hyper-vintage design of the *Kotetsujo* or "iron fortress," a super-train that carries the survivors of a zombie-apocalypse to freedom. Made by the same company that produced the brutally violent *Attack on Titan*, *Kabaneri* is a bloodsplattered, fast-paced steampunk adventure filled with cool gadgets and exciting escapes.

But steampunk wasn't only showing signs of life in the places you'd expect to find it. While it's neat to see steampunk making a comeback in the science-fiction and fantasy sections of the bookstore or in a popular new steampunk anime series, it's not particularly surprising. After all, that's where steampunk came from. It was far more notable to see it make an appearance on the miniseries *Gilmore Girls: A Year in the Life*. If you've never seen *Gilmore Girls*, original series or miniseries revival, all you need to know is that it is not set in the nineteenth century and has no elements of the fantastic to it. It's a dramedy about the relationship between Lorelei, a single mother, and her daughter, Rory. In the original series, Rory attended Yale, where she was part of a secret society called the Life and Death Brigade, which engage in dangerous and sometimes illegal activities, almost always dressed in some form of ostentatious costumes or formal wear. In the revival miniseries, Rory is reunited with a few dear members of the Brigade who arrive dressed in steampunk attire and provide Rory with some of her own. Rory and her Brigade friends and lover are pictured in a montage of night escapades, wherein the steampunk costuming serves to heighten the sequence's dreamlike tone. Here, steampunk acts as a signifier of the extravagantly madcap nature of Rory's friends, though I also joked to my wife that only someone as ridiculously wealthy as those characters could afford to buy those particular steampunk outfits on a lark. But beyond producing an amplification of the dreamlike nature of the scene, the use of steampunk on *Gilmore Girls* is a rarity for its comparable banality; even the use of steampunk on *Castle* was sensationalized by its conflation with a murder. On *Gilmore Girls*, steampunk is hyper-vintage fashion and nothing more.

Tanc Sade and Nick Holmes in steampunk attire from the *Gilmore Girls: A Year in the Life* TV miniseries (2016).   *Rex*

Whereas at one point in steampunk's history, it would have seemed essential to include a time machine or moment of adventure, *Gilmore Girls* appropriates but one facet of steampunk expression, and makes no attempt to encompass all others. This strikes me of indicative of steampunk's future. There are no steampunk gatekeepers of note anymore. Steampunk can just be fashion, can just be fiction, can just be fabrication.

More than ever, when someone asks, "What is steampunk?" the answer must be "which steampunk are you talking about?" The difficulty in answering the question, "What is steampunk?" should be clear by now. In short, there is no single creator responsible for it. It's only in hindsight that we can identify the most influential contributors. Jeter may have named it, but it was William Gibson and Bruce Sterling who made the term famous, and Gail Carriger who continues to do so. Vernian Process might have been the first steampunk band, but they were by no means the last, while it was mainstream musicians like Panic! at the Disco and Justin Bieber who gave the term even greater currency. For the punk in steampunk, we had Magpie Killjoy, who started the fire, but a host of steampunks who see it as a lifestyle keep it burning. Jake von Slatt was the first maker, but Steampunk Eddie was the "top maker" to nearly three hundred thousand television viewers. Steampunk fashion might have started as a branch of Goth culture, but it's transcended those neo-Victorian roots to incorporate other cultures, other times, and other styles.

As I hope to have demonstrated, there is no single unifying definition for steampunk, though now that I've taken you on a tour of steampunk's alternate worlds from inspiration to inception to the date of this book's publication, you'll know it when you see it. But then someone will do something a little new to it yet again, and we'll all be forced to ask, "Is *that* steampunk?" Steampunk is an idealized version of the past, whether that ideal is a positive, romanticized utopia or a negative, deglamorized dystopia. Both concepts contain extremes. Steampunk is filled with extremes: past and future, historical and fantastic, science and magic, colonial and colonized.

In my chapter on anime, I said that Howl's ambulatory castle in Miyazaki's *Howl's Moving Castle* was the embodiment of the changing nature of second-wave steampunk: a hybrid of disparate parts, tenuously constructed, held together only by magic, lurching forward toward inevitable collapse. Yet perhaps the best metaphor for where steampunk is headed next is the mobile London of Philip Reeve's *Predator Cities* series, which begins with *Mortal Engines*. Even as I write these words, principal photography on a cinematic adaptation has begun in New Zealand, with a projected release date of 2018.

Back in 2010, I was reading *Mortal Engines* for the first time and thinking it was definitely steampunk, and some of the best I'd read. In the same year, Philip Reeve published a blog post wherein he said he thought that steampunk "stinks." In that post, he enumerated what he thought was wrong with where steampunk was in 2010, but all the same, it seemed disingenuous to be decrying other writers for using airships and "rich villains hatching plots" when your book is filled with people flying in airships and "rich villains hatching plots." Every cover I've ever seen for *Mortal Engines* is being sold with the implicit promise that there's steampunk inside. The post is gone from Reeve's blog now, but as I found myself thinking about London on the move as a metaphor for steampunk, I found myself wondering how Peter Jackson and his film crew will represent the world of *Mortal Engines*, and what that will add to the beautiful mess steampunk has been creating for over forty years?

After all, Greg Broadmore, the man responsible for those amazing retrofuturist ray guns in the world of *Dr. Grordbort*, works at WETA Workshops, the people who realized *Lord of the Rings* for the screen, and have been responsible for visions of other fantastic cinematic worlds since. And though Greg assures me he's not working on the design, surely some of that vintage-SF goodness has rubbed off as he hobnobs with colleagues. It's going to be the steampunk film of 2018, whether it looks like what you think steampunk is or not.

Because steampunk is on the move, whether it's by Iron Fortress steam trains escaping zombie apocalypses or Traction Cities looking for salvage to consume.

Going back to my introduction, I've wondered if maybe steampunk *did* die once or twice. You might argue that it died sometime in the '90s and was brought back to life as a steam-powered spider-automaton when *Wild Wild West* was released. But I'd say that it dies and is reborn each time one steampunk artist finishes their work with it and a new one takes it up. Sometimes, this steampunk reincarnation looks very much like the ones before it, but unlike Reeve, I don't think that's necessarily a bad thing. There's something to be said for nostalgic comfort food. There's something to be said for things becoming conventional. Without conventions, we wouldn't be able to subvert them. You can't have the clever satire of the British Empire if British imperialism hadn't become a convention in so many adventure stories in print and film.

Likewise, *Mortal Engines* may break the mold on second-wave steampunk. And if it does, then it will join a host of works by artists great and small who have shaped this thing we continue to call steampunk.

Selected Bibliography

Bowser, Rachel, and Brian Croxall, eds. *Like Clockwork: Steampunk Pasts, Presents, and Futures*. Minneapolis: University of Minnesota Press, 2016.

Miller, Cynthia J., and Julie Anne Taddeo, eds. *Steampunk into a Victorian Future*. Lanham, MD: Scarecrow Press, 2013.

Renzi, Thomas C. *H. G. Wells: Six Scientific Romances Adapted for Film*. Metuchen, NJ: Scarecrow Press, 2004.

Renzi, Thomas C. *Jules Verne on Film: A Filmography of the Cinematic Adaptations of His Works, 1902 Through 1997*. Jefferson, NC: McFarland and Company, 1998.

Robb, Brian J. *Steampunk: An Illustrated History of Fantastical Fiction, Fanciful Film and Other Victorian Visions*. Minneapolis: Voyageur Press, 2012.

Taves, Brian. *Hollywood Presents Jules Verne: The Father of Science Fiction on Screen*. Lexington: University Press of Kentucky.

Index

THE FAQ SERIES

AC/DC FAQ
by Susan Masino
Backbeat Books
9781480394506...$24.99

Armageddon Films FAQ
by Dale Sherman
Applause Books
9781617131196.........$24.99

The Band FAQ
by Peter Aaron
Backbeat Books
9781617136139 ....$19.99

Baseball FAQ
by Tom DeMichael
Backbeat Books
9781617136061........$24.99

The Beach Boys FAQ
by Jon Stebbins
Backbeat Books
9780879309879..$22.99

The Beat Generation FAQ
by Rich Weidman
Backbeat Books
9781617136016 ....$19.99

Beer FAQ
by Jeff Cioletti
Backbeat Books
9781617136115 ....$24.99

Black Sabbath FAQ
by Martin Popoff
Backbeat Books
9780879309572...$19.99

Bob Dylan FAQ
by Bruce Pollock
Backbeat Books
9781617136078 ......$19.99

Britcoms FAQ
by Dave Thompson
Applause Books
9781495018992 ....$19.99

Bruce Springsteen FAQ
by John D. Luerssen
Backbeat Books
9781617130939.......$22.99

Buffy the Vampire Slayer FAQ
by David Bushman and Arthur Smith
Applause Books
9781495064722.....$19.99

Cabaret FAQ
by June Sawyers
Applause Books
9781495051449......$19.99

A Chorus Line FAQ
by Tom Rowan
Applause Books
9781480367548 ...$19.99

The Clash FAQ
by Gary J. Jucha
Backbeat Books
9781480364509 ..$19.99

Doctor Who Faq
by Dave Thompson
Applause Books
9781557838544....$22.99

The Doors FAQ
by Rich Weidman
Backbeat Books
9781617130175........$24.99

Dracula FAQ
by Bruce Scivally
Backbeat Books
9781617136009 .....$19.99

The Eagles FAQ
by Andrew Vaughan
Backbeat Books
9781480385412.....$24.99

Elvis Films FAQ
by Paul Simpson
Applause Books
9781557838582.....$24.99

Elvis Music FAQ
by Mike Eder
Backbeat Books
9781617130496......$22.99

Eric Clapton FAQ
by David Bowling
Backbeat Books
9781617134548 ......$22.99

Fab Four FAQ
by Stuart Shea and Robert Rodriguez
Hal Leonard Books
9781423421382.......$19.99

Fab Four FAQ 2.0
by Robert Rodriguez
Backbeat Books
9780879309688...$19.99

Film Noir FAQ
by David J. Hogan
Applause Books
9781557838551......$22.99

Football FAQ
by Dave Thompson
Backbeat Books
9781495007484...$24.99

Frank Zappa FAQ
by John Corcelli
Backbeat Books
9781617136030.......$19.99

Godzilla FAQ
by Brian Solomon
Applause Books
9781495045684 $19.99

The Grateful Dead FAQ
by Tony Sclafani
Backbeat Books
9781617130861........$24.99

Guns N' Roses FAQ
by Rich Weidman
Backbeat Books
9781495025884 ..$19.99

Haunted America FAQ
by Dave Thompson
Backbeat Books
9781480392625.....$19.99

Horror Films FAQ
by John Kenneth Muir
Applause Books
9781557839503 ....$22.99

Jack the Ripper FAQ
by Dave Thompson
Applause Books
9781495063084....$19.99

James Bond FAQ
by Tom DeMichael
Backbeat Books
9781557838568.....$22.99

Jimi Hendrix FAQ
by Gary J. Jucha
Backbeat Books
9781617130953.......$22.99

Johnny Cash FAQ
by C. Eric Banister
Backbeat Books
9781480385405.. $24.99

KISS FAQ
by Dale Sherman
Backbeat Books
9781617130915........$24.99

Led Zeppelin FAQ
by George Case
Backbeat Books
9781617130250 ......$22.99

Lucille Ball FAQ
by James Sheridan and Barry Monush
Applause Books
9781617740824.......$19.99

MASH FAQ
by Dale Sherman
Applause Books
9781480355897.....$19.99

Michael Jackson FAQ
by Kit O'Toole
Backbeat Books
9781480371064.....$19.99

Modern Sci-Fi Films FAQ
by Tom DeMichael
Applause Books
9781480350618....$24.99

Monty Python FAQ
by Chris Barsanti, Brian Cogan, and Jeff Massey
Applause Books
9781495049439 ..$19.99

Morrissey FAQ
by D. McKinney
Backbeat Books
9781480394483...$24.99

Neil Young FAQ
by Glen Boyd
Backbeat Books
9781617130373........$19.99

Nirvana FAQ
by John D. Luerssen
Backbeat Books
9781617134500......$24.99

Pearl Jam FAQ
by Bernard M. Corbett and Thomas Edward Harkins
Backbeat Books
9781617136122.........$19.99

Pink Floyd FAQ
by Stuart Shea
Backbeat Books
9780879309503...$19.99

Pro Wrestling FAQ
by Brian Solomon
Backbeat Books
9781617135996.......$29.99

Prog Rock FAQ
by Will Romano
Backbeat Books
9781617135873.......$24.99

Quentin Tarantino FAQ
by Dale Sherman
Applause Books
9781480355880...$24.99

Rent FAQ
by Tom Rowan
Applause Books
9781495051456......$19.99

Robin Hood FAQ
by Dave Thompson
Applause Books
9781495048227 ...$19.99

The Rocky Horror Picture Show FAQ
by Dave Thompson
Applause Books
9781495007477.....$19.99

Rush FAQ
by Max Mobley
Backbeat Books
9781617134517.........$19.99

Saturday Night Live FAQ
by Stephen Tropiano
Applause Books
9781557839510......$24.99

Seinfeld FAQ
by Nicholas Nigro
Applause Books
9781557838575.....$24.99

Sherlock Holmes FAQ
by Dave Thompson
Applause Books
9781480331495.....$24.99

The Smiths FAQ
by John D. Luerssen
Backbeat Books
9781480394490...$24.99

Soccer FAQ
by Dave Thompson
Backbeat Books
9781617135989.......$24.99

The Sound of Music FAQ
by Barry Monush
Applause Books
9781480360433...$27.99

South Park FAQ
by Dave Thompson
Applause Books
9781480350649...$24.99

Star Trek FAQ (Unofficial and Unauthorized)
by Mark Clark
Applause Books
9781557837929.....$22.99

Star Trek FAQ 2.0 (Unofficial and Unauthorized)
by Mark Clark
Applause Books
9781557837936.....$22.99

Star Wars FAQ
by Mark Clark
Applause Books
9781480360181......$24.99

Steely Dan FAQ
by Anthony Robustelli
Backbeat Books
9781495025129 ....$19.99

Stephen King Films FAQ
by Scott Von Doviak
Applause Books
9781480355514....$24.99

Three Stooges FAQ
by David J. Hogan
Applause Books
9781557837882.....$22.99

TV Finales FAQ
by Stephen Tropiano and Holly Van Buren
Applause Books
9781480391444.....$19.99

The Twilight Zone FAQ
by Dave Thompson
Applause Books
9781480396180.....$19.99

Twin Peaks FAQ
by David Bushman and Arthur Smith
Applause Books
9781495015861.......$19.99

U2 FAQ
by John D. Luerssen
Backbeat Books
9780879309978 ...$19.99

UFO FAQ
by David J. Hogan
Backbeat Books
9781480393851 ....$19.99

Video Games FAQ
by Mark J.P. Wolf
Backbeat Books
9781617136306 .....$19.99

The X-Files FAQ
by John Kenneth Muir
Applause Books
9781480369740....$24.99

The Who FAQ
by Mike Segretto
Backbeat Books
9781480361034 ....$24.99

The Wizard of Oz FAQ
by Dave Hogan
Applause Books
9781480350625 ...$24.99

HAL•LEONARD®
PERFORMING ARTS
PUBLISHING GROUP

FAQ.halleonardbooks.com

0218